By the same author

Backlash

Born in Wales, Rod Duncan now lives in Leicester with his wife and children. *Breakbeat* is his second novel.

visit www.rodduncan.co.uk

BREAKBEAT

Rod Duncan

POCKET
BOOKS

LONDON • SYDNEY • NEW YORK • TOKYO • TORONTO

First published in Great Britain by Simon & Schuster, 2004
This edition first published by Pocket Books, 2004
An imprint of Simon & Schuster UK
A Viacom company

1 3 5 7 9 10 8 6 4 2

Simon & Schuster UK Ltd
Africa House
64–78 Kingsway
London WC2B 6AH

www.simonsays.co.uk

Simon & Schuster Australia
Sydney

A CIP catalogue record for this book is available from the British Library

ISBN 0 7434 5020 5

Typeset by M Rules
Printed and bound in Great Britain by
Cox & Wyman Ltd, Reading, Berks

A riot is at bottom the language of the unheard.

MARTIN LUTHER KING

PART 1

Chapter 1

The dog arrives first, scraping its claws down the outside of the door. It isn't loud, but there's something in the sound that snags on Daz Croxley's mind. Even as he sleeps.

He turns over, stretches one arm. Then he opens his eyes and looks up at the cracks in the ceiling plaster.

The dog whines.

Daz rolls off his mattress-bed and starts crawling towards the place where he dumped his clothes last night. They sprawl across the thin carpet like the chalked outline of a murder victim. He scrambles his legs into the jeans – rip-kneed 501 copies – then pulls the T-shirt over his head.

It's Thursday. Damn. He's starting to remember.

The dog on the landing is sniffing under the door. And it's crying. Pleading. Daz would have let it in right away if he didn't know who the owner was.

He runs the tap and splashes cold water on his face and brushes a hand back through his hair, spiking it some more. Then he bends to pull a face into the small mirror above the splashback. The sleep is clearing from his head. But slowly.

He touches the cluster of safety pins dangling from his left ear. He must have forgotten to take them out before hitting the sack last night.

The dog gives a couple of staccato barks. Daz hears its paws touch down on one of the upper door panels. Another whine of canine frustration. But no footsteps. Not yet.

Daz has sharpened up enough now to know that there might still be time to escape. So he dives a hand under the mattress and pulls out what remains of his last giro payment. Twenty-something quid. The change goes into his pocket. The notes he stuffs into one of his mock-Doc Martens boots. His foot follows them in.

He's looking to the fire-escape window as he fumbles the laces into a knot. The dog has fallen silent. Daz is straining to hear as he ties the second boot. The barking starts again. Louder now. Expectant.

A creak from one of the loose floorboards on the landing. Then the voice Daz feared. Paul Raglan. Lilting, like he's speaking to a child: 'What's the matter, girl? Is he not playing the game?'

A knuckle raps twice on the door.

Daz lifts the sash window, but it comes up only six inches before the wooden frame squeaks to a stop, jammed in its runners. He increases the pressure, knowing from experience that it will move – given enough oomph. Noisily though.

Two more knocks, harder this time. The voice is still singsong: 'I know you're there. Don't piddle me around now.'

'Getting dressed,' Daz calls back.

'You don't want us to break it down. Really you don't.'

Daz is caught by indecision. He feels the pulse beat in his neck. Once. Twice.

'Just turn the key,' Raglan says.

There's no way to get through this without pain. Daz knows that. He just hopes he can find the least painful option. So he makes his choice, steps towards the door. But before he's halfway across the room an elbow cracks its way through the panel nearest the handle. Not Raglan's elbow. Direct violence isn't his style at all. It's a second man. The elbow pulls back and a hand is pushing in the broken plywood pieces. A broad hand, the fingers short. No rings. It gropes for the lock.

'Too late, Croxley,' sighs Raglan. 'Always too late.'

First inside is the owner of the hand. Smith is the only name Daz has ever heard for him. He's not huge or muscle-bound, but there's a quiet confidence to his manner, which is somehow threatening. Next in is the dog, Lady. A boxer. The stump of her tail motors with anticipated pleasure. And finally Raglan, a couple of inches taller and wider than Smith. He wears a grey suit to match his grizzled hair, and a salmon-pink tie.

Daz has shifted away from them. Another step back and his heels will hit the skirting board. 'Was coming to the door!'

'But too slowly.' Raglan looks around at the walls and ceiling. Then at Lady, already exploring the room, sniffing and slobbering over Daz's bed sheets. 'I did warn you,' he says. 'All this just expands the bill.'

Smith is still standing near the door, hands clasped in front of him. Only moving his eyes. Raglan has wandered across to the window. He's looking out through the iron fire escape to the paved yard and the alley that runs between the houses.

'You didn't answer my letters, did you. I could be playing golf right now. But no – you didn't respond.'

Daz tugs at one of the safety pins, feeling the stretch in his ear lobe. 'What letters?'

'Oh, come-come, now. You owe me money and . . .'

'The benefit pays you. I never . . .'

'Not rent money. The redecoration charge. It's in the contract. It's in the letter. Five hundred pounds, due today. Thursday.'

He pokes his finger into a corner of the windowsill, pulling away a large flake of paint with his nail. He examines it, tuts, brushes his palms against each other. 'If you wiped away the condensation every morning, this kind of damage just wouldn't happen. We wouldn't have to decorate then, eh?'

Lady has worked her way along Daz's bed, leaving strings of saliva splashed over the quilt. Now she's nosing the banana box next to the wall. Her tail is going faster. She starts chewing the cardboard at one of the corners. Daz bites his lip. Then he sees that his landlord is staring at him and he looks somewhere else.

Raglan smiles sadly. He turns and saunters along the edge of the room, running a hand over remnant Blu-Tack blobs and corners of peeled wallpaper. He's heading towards the old wardrobe now and showing every sign that he's about to look inside.

Daz says: 'Haven't got five hundred.'

'I suppose that shouldn't be a surprise to me.' Raglan's eyes travel down to the boots then up to the safety pins. 'Where *do* you spend it all?' He moves his hand towards the wardrobe door.

Daz knows he has to act quickly to minimize the damage. So he steps into the middle of the room, as if shielding the banana box with his body. That puts Lady behind him, but it's not her he's afraid of.

Raglan withdraws his hand and rests it on his hip. 'It seems we have a problem, Croxley, you and me. An arrangement is what we need.'

He gives a nod and points to the box. Smith steps forward. For a moment Daz holds his gaze. Then he looks at the carpet and steps away.

Lady barks as Smith rips off the cardboard lid. Then she jumps up on her hind legs. He upends the box, spilling the contents over the floor. The dog has her nose in the heap already. A cruddy old radio cassette player. Clean underwear. A penknife with tin-opener attachment. A shoebox of Social Security letters. Old cinema tickets. A spoon. Two large cans of Tesco Economy Dog Food. One open . . .

'Watch her!' Raglan shouts.

But Lady must have known what was coming, because she's already got her nose in the jagged mouth of the tin. Smith tries to grab her. Lady eels free.

Raglan is waving both arms. 'She'll cut herself! Quick!'

The dog growls and moves away, but Smith is ready for her this time. He catches her by the collar with one hand and with the other removes the can.

Raglan is next to her now. He shifts her head with his hand, inspecting the skin around her snout. 'Naughty girl!'

She licks her chops, her tail stump still wagging, an expression on her face that might be embarrassment. Then she sees the tin, which Smith is holding above his head. She jumps twice then starts barking. Raglan stands and brushes the hairs off his suit sleeves. Smith shakes out the remaining meat and jelly on to Daz's pillow. For a moment the only sound is the wet slop of Lady's mouth.

Then Raglan speaks: 'She might have needed stitches! If this happens again . . .'

Smith brings down his foot in the middle of Daz's spilled possessions. The cassette player smashes, sending out a shrapnel burst of black plastic fragments.

'We're going to have a payment plan,' Raglan says. 'With

an ascending scale of penalties if you default. Fifty pounds by eleven o'clock tonight. Then another fifty next week. We'll spread the payment over . . . let's say fifteen weeks.'

Daz knows the sums don't add up, but again he chooses silence.

Raglan takes the empty can from Smith. He reads the label, as if that might give him a clue. Then he puts it in Daz's hand. 'No pets allowed, Croxley. You know that.'

He turns and walks from the room. Smith follows close behind. Lady takes a final sniff in his sheets before running after her master. Daz closes the broken door, pausing before turning the key in the lock. He stands there for a moment, lost. Then he remembers something, and he sees a way that his problem might be answered. Temporarily at least.

Patty.

And then he thinks of his small victory and the morning doesn't seem quite so bleak. He opens the wardrobe and takes out a ghetto blaster. A monster, styled in matt black and cold chrome. Beautiful. He slips in a CD. Then he racks up the volume until a static hiss fills the room.

'You listening, Raggy?' he says, his own voice playful now. 'Should have looked in the pigging wardrobe!' But his words are lost in the ripping fury of a breakbeat bassline slicing through the air.

When people stare, which they do, Daz thinks it's because of his piercings, or his clothes, or the asymmetry of his expression. They're casting judgement – that's how he sees it. It would never occur to him that some might be attracted to his quick, grey eyes or the flash of his mercurial smile. Either way, he's hard not to look at.

He's keeping a tally of the people who stare this morning, as he walks across town towards Patty's house. He's caught the eyes of three so far. The first two were women, a little older than himself – mid-twenties, perhaps. Both turned away as soon as they saw him looking back. The third didn't flinch. But he was a policeman, so that doesn't really count. And, anyway, he seemed more interested in the ghetto blaster hanging from Daz's hand.

Daz has seen many uniforms on the street these last few days. Perhaps it's the weather. Hot streets. Trouble fermenting. The police making sure they're visible. None of which will have pleased Patty.

He first met Patty six years ago, but he still struggles to understand her. She likes rules. He knows that. She loves bridge and poker, enjoys chess, hates backgammon. There's a games club down at Humberstone Gate on Sunday afternoons. As far as he can figure it, this is her only social fixture. She regularly gives to charity – she's told him that several times – especially to the RSPCA and LOROS, the local hospice. Like most of the business people Daz knows, Patty keeps dogs. Hers are called Kodak and Dyson. Both are Dobermans.

She lives in an unimproved terraced house in a row of similarly unimproved houses, all of which front straight on to the litter-strewn pavement. The properties on either side have sale boards nailed to the front wall and newspaper in the windows. They've been like that for at least half a year to Daz's certain knowledge.

He steps to the door, pulls the letterbox flap and releases it so that it springs closed with a loud crack. He listens to the fraction of a second of silence that follows. Then the dogs impact against the inside of the door – a double thud that shudders the wood panels, followed by manic snarling and barking. Daz steps back and waits, trying to ignore the dogs. He prods at an empty crisp packet with first one toe then the other. He looks at the wall of mottled red brick receding towards the junction at the other end of the street.

Inside, the barking has grudgingly receded to a low snarl. Three bolts click and the door opens on its chain.

'Who's there?' Patty's voice comes through the crack, scratchy as an antique gramophone.

Daz steps forward again. 'Got something for ya.'

'Who are you, dammit?'

'Daz Croxley.'

'Pah!'

The door closes. There's a clatter of chain and it opens wide. She's standing there in a Crimplene dress, with a fag clutched between the thumb and first finger of her hand. There's a man's watch on her wrist. The dogs are one to each side, lips curled back, teeth showing.

'Why are you idling about out there?' she says. 'Come in off the street with that thing or people will talk.'

Daz steps over the threshold into the front room. She closes and bolts the door behind him. The window is draped in tired, yellowish curtains, through the threads of which a fair amount of daylight manages to seep. There's a dark wooden table in the middle of the room, on which rests a large cardboard box, factory wrapped, and a saucer of fag ends and ash. The room is stuffy with tobacco smoke and the smell of cooking gas.

Daz places his ghetto blaster on the table next to the box. She looks at it. Sniffs.

'How much?' he asks.

'Don't try this, Croxley.'

'Not gunna buy it?'

She makes a lemon scowl, puckering her lips. The skin around her mouth wrinkles into deep furrows. 'I thought you'd come for a cup of tea like you usually do.'

'Buy stuff from everyone else,' Daz says. 'Why not me?'

'Because!'

'Told me once, you treated everyone the same.'

She holds his gaze. 'Very well. I'll give you ten for it.'

'Winding me up, right?'

Up to this point Daz had thought his Raglan problem was solved. For one week at least. Not that Patty would give him an easy ride just because they know each other. That's why he's always felt at ease with the woman – she treats him just the same as all the others. Neither victimizing nor patronizing. And he knows he'll never have to feel in her debt. But he *did* think the ghetto blaster would be worth more. It's too beautiful to be that cheap.

'Well?' she prompts. 'Are you going to take it or leave it?'

'Paid seventy for it.'

Patty sucks another quarter-inch off the tip of her fag. 'It was new then.'

'It's mint! Not a scratch.'

'Fifteen, then. But that's my last offer.'

'How much you gunna sell it for?' Daz asks.

She taps her nose. 'Never tell one customer another customer's business. That's Auntie Patty's rule number three.'

Daz tugs the safety pins in his ear. 'Need fifty quid today though.'

'If I had a tenner for every time I'd heard that.' She crushes the remains of her cigarette into the rim of the saucer. 'Anyway, this is stolen property. You'll never get the full market value.'

'Not stolen!'

'Then show me the receipt.'

'You're the one sold it me!'

'Then it is stolen. Believe me.'

Daz bites his tongue inside his mouth, undecided. He's about to speak when Kodak and Dyson turn and leap from the room. A heartbeat later Daz hears the back door crash under their combined weight. They're going crazy, barking and snarling.

Patty spits out a breath of annoyance. She catches Daz's eye. 'Wait here. And don't touch anything.' Then she stomps out of the room, following the Dobermans.

Daz holds his breath and listens. She orders her dogs back then unbolts the door.

'You again!' Patty's voice.

'Got anything for me?' A man. Local accent.

'What are you doing with it all,' Patty says, 'eating it?'

'I could . . . could go somewhere else if . . .'

'Tsch.' Patty cuts him off. 'Try if you like.'

'But if you haven't got—'

'Who said I hadn't? What about a digital television? Samsung. To you, two hundred pounds.'

'That's . . . that's good.'

There's a pause, then Patty says: 'It's in the front. Follow me.'

He's a short man, the stranger who shuffles in from the back room. Stomach overhanging his belt, hair neat but long enough to cover ears and forehead. He wears a narrow tie and a tight-necked shirt that must be unbearable in the airless front room. Even in that dim light Daz can see the sweat-sheen on his upper lip.

The man doesn't look pleased to see Daz. He turns to Patty and shakes his head. 'This isn't . . . it isn't good!'

Patty snorts a laugh. 'Then make an appointment next time.'

Her scowl hasn't changed. So far as Daz knows, it's her

only expression. He watches her step over to the table and pat the cardboard box with a sandpapery hand.

'It's the new model,' she says. 'Not even on the shelves yet.'

The man wets his lips. 'How much?'

'I've told you already. Two hundred pounds.'

The stranger glances at Daz then back to Patty. He pulls out a fat wallet and counts ten crisp twenty-pound notes. Patty takes them to the window. She draws one curtain a few inches and holds the first note up to the light.

Daz watches her work through the bundle. He knows he shouldn't be seeing this transaction. She's always bustled him out of the door when customers have come calling. He wonders if it's supposed to be a lesson of some kind – teaching him the realities of the business. But he knows there's more going on here than is being spoken about.

At last she folds the bundle of notes in the middle and nods. 'Where are you parked?'

'Just down . . . down the street.'

'Then Daz can help you carry.'

It must be a white van, under the dirt. Someone has drawn a love heart on one of the back doors. A wonky arrow through it. And there's some writing that Daz can't read. He waits, holding the boxed TV, his fingers in agony. He's thinking that if he drops it, it'll be the stranger's own fault for not helping. He was parked much farther away than he said.

The man has found his keys at last and is opening up the van. He points inside. 'Put it up there. All the . . . all the way in.'

Daz hefts the box inside and then slides it forward, clambering up after it. There's nothing but a bundle of old newspapers here. And a smell. Alcohol turning to vinegar. Daz breathes it in. Not spirits. Stale beer and cider perhaps. Or some kind of fermented fruit. It's overpowering in the heat. He takes one more breath of it then clambers out into the sunshine and closes up.

The stranger is in the driver's seat already.

Daz steps around to the window. 'What about a tip?'

'I've paid already. Get your money from her.'

Daz finds Patty waiting for him, peering through a crack in the curtains. She lets him in then re-bolts the door. He knows better than to ask her for payment, and he's already decided not to sell the ghetto blaster for fifteen quid. He's hot and sweating and isn't any closer to finding the money he needs for Raglan.

Patty's looking at him. 'What's your problem?'

He shrugs. 'Just broke your rule three, didn't you. Showed me that bloke's business.'

She examines him for a moment, pursing her thin lips. 'You're an idiot, Daz Croxley. But we go back a long way, so I'll let you in on Auntie Patty's rule number two: never, never trust a customer who doesn't haggle.'

'So?'

'So I wanted you to see him, that's all. I feel safer that way.'

The man on the other side of the desk hasn't looked up yet. He's scrawling some notes in a rectangular box at the bottom of a Social Security form. Paperwork from the previous client. He looks hot in a jacket and tie.

'Name?' His voice sounds flat and distant.

'Daz,' says Daz.

'*Sur*name.'

'Croxley.'

Daz places the ghetto blaster on the floor and grips it between his ankles. There's a computer monitor on the desk, angled so Daz can't see the screen. The claims adviser clicks his mouse a couple of times and then types something on the keyboard.

'David Croxley?'

Daz nods. 'Need some cash. Just fifty quid.'

'Severn Street?' Eyes flick to Daz's ear jewellery then back to the screen.

Daz has never had a proper job, but he's seen enough to know how things work on the other side of the counter. It's a matter of putting ticks in enough boxes. Matching yourself to a set of predetermined categories. If he were married, with children, with a physical disability. He's not. So he tries with what he has.

'Gunna be *unintentionally homeless*,' he says. 'Got to give the landlord fifty quid tomorrow. Skint though. Need an *emergency payment* – just to get me through.'

'Were you supposed to come for an interview last week?'

Daz shakes his head.

'Only I'm getting an alert on your file. If you could just . . . I need to check something.' Then he gets out of his chair and hurries away.

Daz looks back at the queue. It's grown already, reaching halfway to the door. The guy in the front has a roll-up between his lips. He blows a stream of smoke towards the no-smoking sign. Behind him is a man with a plaster cast and crutches. There's a child crying somewhere further back. Over the years Daz has learned how to switch off in this kind of place. He does that now. Letting himself drift.

'Mr Croxley?'

He turns and sees her looking at him across the desk.

'My colleague called me to speak to you,' she says. 'Are you all right?'

It's her eyes that have thrown him – pale green and witchy. Unexpectedly vivacious. It takes him a moment to answer: 'Sure.'

She's got short-cropped hair. Very blonde. He doesn't think he's seen her working here before – though there's something about her that seems familiar.

'What happened last week, then?' she asks.

He raises his eyebrows in a gesture that he hopes will convey a degree of innocence that he doesn't feel. 'Last week?'

'You had an appointment.'

'Didn't get a letter.'

'You've had three missed appointments before this, so—'

'Bloke downstairs nicks my post.'

'—and so . . . you've been assigned to me. And luckily for you, I can see you straight away.'

Someone painted the interview room yellow – that must have been a good few years ago. It was probably a cheery shade back then. Buttermilk or ripening corn. But layers of smoke and despair have insinuated their way into the surfaces, dulling them to the colour of an old bruise.

Daz crosses his ankles under the table. One hand rests on the top of his ghetto blaster, the other picks at the edge of the plastic seat. Green Eyes is sorting through her papers. At first he'd thought she was about thirty. But that was just the smart blouse and name badge. The barrier of authority. Having had a few more minutes to check her out, he's decided she can't be much older than he is. Twenty-three, perhaps. He can see now that her eyebrows are much darker than her hair. There's an edginess about her that seems strange in the context of her job. The outsider look. For a moment he wonders about her. Then he reminds himself which side of the desk she's on.

'Chucking me off the benefit?' he asks.

'That depends.'

'On what?'

She looks up. 'You've heard of the New Deal for Young People?'

He shrugs. 'Did it already.'

'Well, this is the Fresh Horizons Project. It's different. It's designed to give younger jobseekers a genuine opportunity to develop their potential, acquire skills and experience work.'

She's saying all the right phrases. It's as if she's reading them from a hymn sheet. But something in the voice tells him that she doesn't really believe it.

'It's specially for people like you who are having ... difficulties with the old system. That's why your name has been selected. This is a client-centred scheme, so the emphasis is on listening to you.'

Daz would like to tell her what he really thinks about training schemes – that they're just a way of getting people off the jobless list for a few weeks, so that when they sign on again they're no longer classed as 'long-term' unemployed. But he doesn't think that'll get him closer to solving the cash-flow problem.

So instead he asks: 'When does it start?'

'It's started already. I'm your personal adviser.'

'If I don't want to do it?'

'That's fine.' She sits back and folds her arms.

This wrong-foots him. She's off the script. He sits up a little in his chair. She slides down in hers. He waits for the catch, but she doesn't volunteer any information.

'But . . .?'

A flicker of a smile touches her mouth. She sits forward again. 'If it wasn't for this project, you'd be needing to reapply for Jobseeker's Allowance – having failed to turn up for so many appointments.'

She's intoning the old stuff again. He feels a twinge of disappointment – something lost. He's been in this situation before, so he can guess most of what she's going to say. Either he accepts a place on the scheme or they stop his Jobseeker's Allowance – which means losing Housing Benefit – which means being kicked out of the bedsit.

He watches her mouth as she delivers the speech. Then other parts of her face. She'd never fit in a glossy magazine. He sees a tiny mark on the side of her nose – a healed-over piercing, perhaps. It's strange to see something like that on the other side of the desk.

'Do you understand?'

Daz wasn't listening to what she was saying – her face distracted him. He nods anyway. He decides that she's too quirky to work in the Jobcentre. She narrows her eyes slightly and he gets a sudden fear that he might have spoken his thoughts out loud.

The moment passes.

'This is a pilot project,' she says. 'It's only being trialled here in Leicester, so it's your good fortune to be able to take part. As your personal employment and training adviser, I'll set up sessions for you over the coming weeks, in which—'

'Got no choice, right?'

He expects her to brush off his cynicism. Instead she says: 'Not really.'

She marks a cross at the bottom of one of the papers and slides it across the desk. He picks a Biro from the table and holds it over the page. If he doesn't sign, he'll end up sleeping rough. If he does sign, they'll have him pretending to be trained – which usually means pulling shopping trolleys out of the canal.

'*Client centred?*' he asks.

'Sure.' A nod and an encouraging smile.

'Can ask questions if I want?'

'Or you can tell me things in confidence. It's all confidential.'

'Can ask anything?'

'Anything. Though I don't promise to answer.'

'OK. What's your favourite film?'

She opens her mouth and closes it again. Then she says: '*Amélie.*' And just for a moment a real light flashes behind her green eyes.

That's enough for Daz – though he's never seen the film. It was enough that she turned into a real person. He scrawls something illegible on the paper and passes it back across the desk. 'Do I get any cash now?'

'Nothing changes for two weeks. You sign on as usual. We'll have a series of counselling sessions in the days after that – to get you ready. Then you can sign off properly and the programme will begin.'

'What about an emergency payment?'

She shakes her head. 'I'm sorry.'

And with those words she goes back to being an official from the Jobcentre. Except that Daz can't un-know the flash of individual he's seen behind the eyes.

Chapter 2

The riot begins at nine in the evening. A bungled stop and search – this is how many of the papers will present it tomorrow. Others will talk about yob culture and drug crime. But all will agree that this particular event could not have been predicted – a statement that isn't strictly true.

At two-thirty that afternoon, Daz already knows that something is going to happen. He can't put it into words, though. It's like a trace of a smell in the stifling air as he walks through the city. Or a flicker in the intense sunlight on the periphery of his vision. He feels it radiating from the brick and asphalt.

He hasn't eaten anything since breakfast. He's sweating, and the weight of the ghetto blaster is cramping his finger muscles. The anticipation builds until it feels like a pressure across the front of his skull. He tries to concentrate on the immediate problem – of how to get hold of thirty pounds in the next few hours. Time is slipping past him.

He trudges back across the Sparkenhoe Street Bridge and up St Peter's Road. There's a group of men leaning on the railings outside the Conduit Street Mosque. Some white, some black. He passes another group on the corner of Saxby Street. A police car prowls past at kerb-crawler speed.

By the time he reaches the place where he lives, there's sweat standing on his skin. He feels a drop run between his shoulder blades, down his back all the way to the top of his jeans.

It's a large nineteenth-century house. The kind of place with two staircases and servants' bells on the wall of what used to be the kitchen. If it wasn't on the edge of the red-light district it would be worth a fortune – and Raglan might be prepared to fix the gutter, the doorbell, the leaky taps and the toilet flush.

Inside is cooler, and dark after the glare of the sun. He toggles the light-switch a couple of times but no one has changed the bulb yet. There are letters on the table in the hall. He picks them up and takes them over to the small pane of orange glass in the door. He walks his fingers through the pile, squinting with concentration.

Carrying the ghetto blaster and two letters, he climbs the stairs, passing his own landing and heading on up to the flat at the top of the house.

It's a woman's voice that answers his knock. A Newcastle accent. 'Who's there?'

'Me,' says Daz.

A bolt scrapes and the door opens.

She's about five feet ten and wearing a dressing gown in turquoise silk. Her coppery hair is tied back in a ponytail. She's trying to rub a grain of sleep from the corner of one eye – a gesture that would appear everyday in someone who didn't have that kind of grace. Then she smiles at him.

Daz looks down to the carpet and sees that her toenails are the same colour as her gown. 'Sorry, Freddy,' he says, 'getting you up.'

'Are you all right?' she asks.

He risks another glance at Freddy's face, then he holds out the ghetto blaster. 'Need someone to look after it.'

She takes it from him. 'What's wrong with your place?'

'Door's buggered.'

'You're not telling me that banging this morning . . .'

He nods. 'Raglan.'

'Shit!' she says. 'There are laws, you know. He's not allowed. Not like that.'

Her eyes have found his. He breaks contact again.

'What about you?'

Freddy swings her hair. 'He did send us a letter – about redecoration charges. But we phoned the Citizens Advice Bureau. They told us we didn't have to pay. We could take him to court if he tried anything. So could you, you know.'

Daz shakes his head. 'Judge is gunna believe *me* over Raggy?'

'He's just a man. And it would be a magistrate, not a judge.'

'It'd be a suit.'

'We could dress you up a bit.' An impish smile dances in her face for a moment. She lowers her voice. 'You'd look good in pinstripes.'

A floorboard creaks somewhere in the apartment and a man comes into view. He's tall, shaven-headed, black. And he's wearing a sheet as a makeshift sarong. He sees Daz and breaks into a grin. 'Hey,' he says.

'Hey, Ginger,' says Daz.

Ginger drapes a bare arm over Freddy's shoulder. 'What's the trouble?'

'He needs us to look after his sound box,' says Freddy.

Daz still has the letters in his hand from downstairs. Freddy reaches out and takes them from him, her fingers touching his. 'You better come in.'

Freddy and Ginger's flat is the biggest in the house. It's got a tiny kitchenette, a boxroom with an entrance into the raw attic space, and a huge open area, which serves as bedroom, lounge and dance-floor. But it's not the size that attracts Daz. It's the way the sloping walls and ceiling match the shape of the roof outside.

Daz follows them down the short corridor. Inside he sees a scattering of rattan chairs, spider plants and spilled cushions. On the wall opposite the double bed are five racks of CDs, an expensive-looking music centre and two serious groups of speakers. Regular to super-woofer.

Ginger steps away into the boxroom, dragging his sheet. Freddy parks herself on the corner of the bed, legs crossed at the knee. She slits open the first of Daz's letters.

'It's from Raglan,' she says. 'Dear Mr Croxley. Further to our conversation this morning.' She looks up, wrinkling the skin above her nose. 'God, he makes it sound so reasonable when he wants to. Is this the same man that broke your door?'

Daz nods towards the letter. 'What's he say?'

Freddy scans the page. 'Blah, blah. Letter of the twenty-seventh. Blah, blah. Here it is. Weekly payments of fifty pounds. Starting today.' She's shaking her head. 'He can't do this, Daz. You know he can't.'

'Just did, didn't he.'

'But this is fifteen weeks. Seven hundred and fifty quid. That's half again what he was asking before!'

Daz stares at his boots and shakes his head. 'And the other letter?'

Freddy opens it. 'It's from the Social Security people. Saying you've missed another interview.' Her eyes flick up to his. 'You need a calendar, Daz. And a watch. You'll get in real trouble one of these days.'

He holds out his hand for the letters, but she reads on.

'They've rescheduled you for . . . God, you've missed it already! You know they can cut your benefits, don't you?'

'Just come from there,' Daz says. 'It's sorted.'

Ginger steps back into the room, dressed now. T-shirt and jeans. He's carrying a black leather jacket, shop labels still attached. He puts it on, does a catwalk turn.

'What do you reckon?'

Daz grins at his friend, relieved at the change of subject. 'Deadly!' He raises a hand, which Ginger catches in a high-five.

Freddy folds her arms but doesn't say anything.

'Yeah!' Ginger slips off the jacket and walks to the boxroom, removing the labels as he goes. He comes back clicking his fingers, as if to a tune in his head.

'I'm doing pancakes, Dazzo. Are you up for it?'

Daz stands. 'Gotta go earn fifty quid for Raggy.'

'Shit. I could lend it you tomorrow night. After I get paid.'

'It's today or I'm out.'

Ginger gets out his wallet and extracts some crumpled fivers. He holds them towards Daz. 'I've got twenty you can have now. Pay us back when your giro comes in, OK?'

Daz backs off. He's had to accept many kinds of hand-out in his life, but never from someone he thinks of as a friend. 'Don't need your money!'

'Don't be stupid. I can use plastic till tomorrow night.' He's making a move to stuff the cash into Daz's trouser pocket. A flicker of concern crosses Freddy's face. She jumps up from the bed and catches Ginger's arm.

He wrests himself free. 'Hey!'

'Leave him be, hun,' she says. Then she dips into Ginger's wallet. 'Here.' She puts a name card on top of Daz's letters and holds it all towards him. 'Ring the Club if anything goes wrong, OK?'

Daz looks at the bundle.

Ginger turns towards the kitchenette, shaking his head. 'Fuck it! Why's everyone so strung out today?'

At last Daz nods and takes the letters and the card from her hand. He walks away, still feeling the momentary touch of her fingers on his, telling himself that accepting a phone number hasn't put him in their debt. Then telling himself again.

'Get yourself a calendar,' she calls from the doorway. 'Please. And a watch. Do it for me.'

In the days when Daz wore a watch, he always turned up for appointments hideously early. Then he'd have to walk around the block, feeling stupid, repeatedly looking back to his wrist to see how many seconds had passed since he last looked. The more uncertain he was, the more often he'd check. The more often he checked, the more anxious and uncertain he became.

He's forgotten what the trigger was, but he remembers the moment he finally broke. He was standing on the platform of Leicester railway station. He threw his watch to the concrete, kept stamping on it until the display stopped blinking. Then he stamped some more, twisting his heel, grinding the glass to white powder.

It took a couple of weeks from that day before he stopped checking his bare wrist. Longer before he could let go of his time anxiety altogether. He's never been on time for anything since. And he's been happy with that.

But today he's uncomfortably aware that the hours and seconds are flowing past him. Some of the shops are closing. There's rush-hour traffic choking the roads. It must be six-ish, he reckons.

He's been trudging the streets looking for inspiration all afternoon. He's raided the coin return slots of all the payphones from the railway station to the clock tower, and netted one pound ten for his trouble. He's picked up a twenty-pence piece and a fallen apple from the pavement next to the covered market on Cheapside. He's asked around the usual places, but no one was looking for a cash-in-hand labourer. There have been too many people, too much heat and not enough goodwill to go round.

The street is completely in shadow now, but the paving stones are still hot. He's been feeling the tension build all afternoon. Logically, he knows the situation is hopeless. Raglan will throw him out tomorrow. He'll have to crash on a friend's floor. That or a bed in the homeless shelter. He doesn't like either option. But he's never been one to follow logic at the expense of intuition. He feels that something is about to happen. He's sensed things like this before and been proved wrong.

But not today.

It's the sound of the first explosion that brings him running. He catches a lamppost with one hand and slingshots himself around the corner of the street. Between him and the burning police car are a crowd of silhouettes. Thirty perhaps. Forty if you count the kids.

The car is on its roof, flames making bright-yellow circles of the wheels. Behind it, the wall of the Waterfields Youth Club glows smoky-orange. Above, the sky is black. The riot is about to start.

Daz's first feeling is elation. He releases himself towards the centre of the action. Accelerating. Five long paces before he realizes that everyone else is backing away.

The blast of the second explosion hits him like a slap on

the chest. There's a ball of flame rising into the night sky and everyone is scattering. Running crouched, as if a few extra feet will lessen the scorching heat.

Daz skids to a stop. His heart is pounding. He wants to be part of the excitement. He wants to get his own back on the world for what it's done to him today.

But in the crowd he's seen Vince the Prince and his gang. Dangerous men. Daz has known some of them since school. Bullies then and now. He wavers, undecided. But Vince has seen him already and there's no way back.

More people are running in now. Blacks, whites, Asians and every mix in between. A siren wails above the shouting and smashing glass. Not the police this time. They're gone for now. This is the sound of a fire engine; horn blaring as it crosses a junction against the red lights. Getting closer.

One of the gang is using a length of pipe to lever up paving stones. Vince grabs Daz's wrist and pulls him in. His eyes are wide and there's a lump of concrete in his hand. He jabs it towards Daz's face, then pulls back. He laughs and tosses the concrete. Daz catches it.

'You'll need that!' Vince shouts.

His lips are curled back in a grin. Wired on speed, perhaps. He snatches an empty vodka bottle from the ground. 'We're gunna have some fun!'

Daz feels the angles of the cold concrete in his hand. He's trying to work out what Vince is doing so far from his usual territory. Why someone he knows to be a racist should be getting his kicks in the middle of Waterfields – the most racially mixed part of the city.

The fire engine is close now, motoring down the narrow road, pulling up short of the blazing wreck. Daz is breathing hard, sweating. Firemen are scrambling from the cab, unreeling a hose. The crowd hasn't stepped towards the truck yet. It's as if there is an invisible shell holding it back. A brittle shell.

Then Vince flings his bottle. It smashes on the wall of the Youth Club, sending out a burst of glass. Sharp fragments scatter on to the firemen below and the crowd heaves forwards.

Daz is moving with them. He's one of them and he's going to do it. But then one of the firemen turns his head, and for a moment Daz sees the expression on his face, side-lit by the flames. Fear. And suddenly Daz isn't one of the crowd any more.

He stops, turns and hurls the concrete blindly into the distance where there are no people to be afraid. Then he runs from the fire, from Vince. Only when the darkness has swallowed him does he stop. He'd been so close to doing it. His hands are shaking.

The riot is spreading now. New fires burning. A power cable must have been cut somewhere because the streetlights have just blinked out. Daz can see a wall of headlights across the road down by the Youth Club. Police vans. He gets up from his place in the shadows and starts to put some distance between himself and them.

He's gone about a hundred yards when he comes to the ruined front of an electronics shop, alarm light flashing blue-white under the eaves. There are two men and a woman scrambling over the jagged glass that once made up the window. They're pulling out TVs and computers, loading them into a dented van, parked with its rear wheels on the pavement.

There are only two sources of illumination here – the van's rear lights and a yellow flickering from inside the shop. One more fire that's going to spread. It doesn't look like there's going to be any evidence left for the police by the time it gets hold. And the insurance company will pay out either way. This is what Daz thinks. Besides, his need is greater than theirs. So he clambers in through the window and pulls a boxed computer off a shelf. It's a small one, to judge by the picture. Flat screen and mini-tower. But it's awkward to carry and he has to pick his way over the shattered window.

'Put it fucking back!'

It's one of the ram-raiders shouting at him. A bulldog of a man who has rolls of fat where his neck should be. He's carrying a top-of-the-range microwave oven like it was an empty shoebox.

'It's my raid!' he bellows. 'You can sodding piss off!'

There's a moment in which Daz wavers. But only a moment. His mind flashes to the van he loaded earlier in the day. 'Just helping you,' he says. 'Where you want me to put it?'

The man blinks a couple of times, then turns. 'In there with the other stuff.'

But by the time he looks back again, Daz has moved sideways into the deeper shadow behind a wheelie bin. He's standing motionless. Invisible.

The man drops the microwave on the pavement and casts about him, searching. If he only stepped out of the window, away from the light, he'd be able to see Daz easily. But there are other people scrambling into the shop now. The looting frenzy is catching hold. He roars at them. No words, just rage. He may as well shout at the fire to stop burning.

Daz steps backwards into the alley that runs down the side of the shop. Then back again and away.

Chapter 3

It's a journey of about half a mile from the burning electronics shop to Patty's house. Daz hasn't been in this particular side-alley before, but he knows there's a bricked-in stream somewhere behind the buildings up ahead, so he starts to heft his load in that direction. By the sound of it the riot is gaining strength, though he's moving steadily away from it now.

Five minutes of careful walking brings him to an easily climbable fence behind which he can just make out a concrete culvert. He can hear the water trickling. The tricky bit is going to be taking the computer with him. He can't take it over or around the fence. The answer comes in the form of some loose planks further along. He pulls the box through after him and scrambles down to stand on the sloping concrete to one side of the channel. There's a smell of moisture here. And decay. It looks like one of the factories that backs on to the river channel is still open for business. Its lights catch a curl of steam, rising from the black water. But there's no sound of machinery.

The river isn't covered over, but it lies a good ten feet below the level of the pavements. People don't bother looking down into these places unless the gutters get blocked and filthy water backs up onto the streets. Daz relaxes as he walks, thinking of how much the computer would have cost off the shelf and how much he might get for it. A smaller amount, he's sure, but enough to keep Raglan off his back for a month or so. Perhaps enough so he can splash out on himself as well.

After a quarter of a mile he finds a landmark he knows – a section of tumbled-down wall. He clambers out of the culvert and picks his way over the broken bricks. He's at the end of a walkway now, with back yards to the left and right. It would be just wide enough for two people to pass, brushing shoulders. But there's no one here.

This is the red-brick no man's land between lines of terraced houses. A world of fly-tipped garbage and silent cats.

Daz hears the dogs snarling as soon as he steps through the gate from the alley into Patty's back yard. Their claws scrape on the inside of the kitchen door. The light comes on.

'Who's there?'

Daz carries his box closer. 'Got something for ya.'

'Croxley?'

He hears her turn the key and slide the bolts, above and below. The door opens and yellow house light spills out into the yard. Patty has a fag in her mouth. The dogs are just behind her, snarling. They seem healthy enough. Perhaps Dobermans don't suffer from passive smoking.

She looks at the box, then at Daz's face. 'Well?'

'Found it,' he offers.

'Don't insult my intelligence, boy.'

'Gunna let me in?'

'There are rules in this game. And I don't mean the law.'

'So?'

'It's your own risk, boy. If you come here with that.'

'Really need the cash.'

'You're not on drugs, are you?'

Patty's question strikes Daz as curious. Half of her clients must be feeding habits of one kind or another. Her sudden concern for him seems almost parental. Then again, his role probably seems strange to her. He's bought stuff from her in the past, but never sold anything.

'No way,' he says. 'Never done drugs.'

She steps back, making room for him to enter. The dogs retreat with her. Daz lifts the computer and steps over the threshold. She leads him through to the front room and clicks on the dim light. It takes Daz a couple of heartbeats before he adjusts to the image. The place was almost empty when he came in earlier. Now it's stacked to the ceiling with boxes. Vacuum cleaners, game consoles, microwave ovens.

'It's been a busy night,' she says.

Daz slides his own box on to a coffee table. 'How much?'

She runs her finger over the sealed top of the box, tracing the edge of the factory tape. 'A hundred.'

Daz scratches at the back of his neck.

Her expression doesn't change. 'It's a buyer's market.'

'Worth ten times that!'

She flicks ash from the cigarette on to the floor then takes a long drag. 'Then slip out the back,' she says, speaking smoke. 'Take your box with you.'

'Two hundred?'

She hesitates. Her eyes narrow. 'One forty, last offer.'

He nods.

She shuffles out of the room. 'Wait!'

Daz does as he's told. So do Kodak and Dyson, who sit watching him as if in eager anticipation of some wrong move.

There's a scraping of furniture from the back room, then another scraping. She returns and hands him a bundle of twenties. They feel new, as if they've come straight from the bank. He walks his fingers through them, counting slowly. Then he splits the money into two piles, folds each one and secretes them in his clothes in the usual way.

'Thanks.'

'*Don't* thank me.' It's an instruction.

'Is it eleven o'clock yet?' he asks.

'You don't know if you're coming or going,' she says. 'It's twenty-past nine.'

Daz feels a prickle of excitement run from his scalp down to the back of his neck. There's plenty of time to get across town to Raglan's. But he still wants to get out of Patty's place quickly. He glances towards the back of the house, then to the front door.

'Your choice,' she says.

He takes the front way, opening the door then stepping out on to the pavement.

'Don't say I didn't warn you,' Patty says as she closes the door.

But he isn't listening. He's breathing the fresh night air. His heart is thumping double time. Excitement. Relief. Exaltation.

He's about to turn away from Patty's door when an iron bar cracks down on his shoulder.

He finds himself on hands and knees, looking at the kerbstone, knowing that there is a lot of pain somewhere around and that logically it must belong to him. A booted foot swings in from the left, knocking the breath from his lungs. He collapses on to his side.

'Couldn't keep your sodding hands out of my sodding business!'

Daz can see the man with no neck standing next to him. The man from the electronics shop.

'Was my raid,' the man bellows. 'The computer was mine.' Then he emphasizes the point with a kick to the head. 'That's the rule!'

Daz sees flashbulbs exploding.

The next thing he's aware of is a hand shoving him over. He's looking upwards, he thinks, at the black sky. Someone is frisking him. Then he's being rolled again and his face is on the ground, one cheek pressed into the cold concrete. There is a hand pulling the wad of cash out of his back pocket. There's a voice, very close, and breath on his upturned cheek.

'And don't fucking mess with me again.'

Then footsteps, walking away.

After that there's a blank time without feeling or colour. Then there are sirens, pulling him back to the world of pain. There's a blue-white double flash, pulsing so brightly that Daz feels as if he's being beaten again. He tries to close his eyes and finds that they're already closed. There are hands on him. A stretcher. He lets them carry him into the ambulance. The engine starts, but not the sirens this time, so he allows himself to relax into the ride, feeling his body shift one way then the other as they move through the lanes of traffic.

How Ginger finds him, Daz doesn't know. But he's there in the hospital corridor next to the trolley when Daz next opens his eyes. There are worry lines all over his friend's dark face.

'Hell, Daz, but you blew it this time.'

'Thanks, Ginger.'

'Do you know who it was?'

Daz circles his right foot. 'What's the time?'

'Shit, man, I dunno. Ten something.'

Daz moves his right foot again. 'Take my boot off.'

'What?'

'Do it.'

So Ginger undoes the knot and starts to ease the Doc Marten away from the foot. Daz yelps with the movement. As it comes free, a small bundle of notes falls to the floor.

'I thought you were robbed,' says Ginger.

'I was, but . . .'

'You don't keep all your eggs in one basket?'

Daz watches Ginger examine the money. There are the two tenners that Daz stuffed in there when Raglan came visiting, and eighty pounds in twenties from Patty's place, still crisp in spite of everything. There's a blotchy red stain on the uppermost note. Ginger frowns and counts the money a second time, scanning the serial numbers.

'Did you rob a bank or what?'

'Just get fifty to Raglan,' Daz says. 'Before eleven or I'm cooked.'

There's a space, then. Not sleep, exactly, but a moment that blurs into five minutes, ten. He doesn't know how long. But when he finds himself, it is with the image of ceiling tiles and recessed strip lighting blinking past. He closes his eyes and opens them again. The image resolves itself. He's on the hospital trolley-bed, being wheeled down a corridor in the A and E department.

He'd been thinking about Patty. How their friendship of years has just crumbled into nothing. That hurts more than any of the physical damage. He'd always thought there was something special between them. Unspoken. But neither of them would have been comfortable to talk about it. It wasn't a friendship, exactly. Loyalty, perhaps. Or something else that he can't put a name to.

Until today.

Daz tries to sit up, but a man wearing hospital-green overalls reaches out and presses him back down. He feels a stab of pain in his right shoulder.

'Almost there.'

'Where?' Daz asks.

Then he sees that Ginger is walking alongside, keeping pace with the trolley.

'Hi, Dazzo,' says Ginger. 'They're gunna do an X-ray.'

Daz is trying to sit up again. Panicking. 'You're supposed to be going to Raggy's place!'

Ginger looks sheepish. 'I've been there and back, man. They gave you a painkiller or something. You've been out of it.'

'You give him the fifty quid for me?'

'Take a chill pill, Dazzo. It's done. You're sorted.'

Daz sighs and lets himself back on to the bed.

The porter manoeuvres Daz around a corner. 'Mind your backs!' he calls. Then the foot of the trolley nudges open a pair of double doors and Daz finds himself being parked at the edge of a brightly lit room. The porter whisks himself away, leaving Daz and Ginger alone.

'You gave us a scare this time, you know.'

Daz doesn't answer. He's thinking about Ginger. Feeling just a little guilty. The man must have travelled clear across the city to reach the Royal Infirmary. At least he's finding out who his real friends are.

Ginger runs a finger along the steel railing at the edge of the trolley. 'That money,' he says. 'The twenties you gave me to take to Raglan – where did you get them?'

Daz looks at him. 'You know,' he says. 'Places 'n' stuff.'

'What's that supposed to mean?'

'Means it's a question you don't ask.'

Ginger shrugs his eyebrows. 'Sure. It's just that . . . you know . . . you were skint this morning.'

A man in a perfect white coat strides into the room. Indian, perhaps. He steps over to the trolley side and flashes a work smile down at Daz.

'We need a picture of the right shoulder, yes? That means the shirt coming off.'

Daz shakes his head. 'Can't lift the arm.'

The man nods. 'I could get some scissors or—'

Daz clutches his left hand to his chest. 'Not cutting my shirt!'

'—or it's the gas and air.' He pulls a gas bottle across to the trolley side and hands Daz the anaesthetic mask. 'Deep inhalations, please.'

Daz holds the mask over his nose and mouth and breathes. Three lungfuls before he feels the world start to soften and dissolve. The pain is still there; it just doesn't seem so important. Then he's forgotten about it altogether. A couple more breaths and he stops counting. Instead he thinks about money. He asks himself why people who have none of the stuff spend all their time thinking about it. There's no answer to the question. Money is one of the few things in life that Daz has never understood. Ginger must understand, though. He earns and spends but never seems to worry in between.

Daz is dimly aware that he is being pulled into a sitting position. His right arm is lifted and his shirt slips over his head.

Ginger wouldn't know about poverty. He wouldn't know about Patty the Fence. It's only people like Daz who have that kind of connection. Desperate people.

Sunday in Humberstone Gate, waiting for them to play some music on the radio. Daz sits back and absorbs the sun's heat. His arm is in a sling. A can of Coke and the ghetto blaster sit next to him on the bench.

There's a fountain here, set into a shallow bowl in the wide plaza. There's no pool, just a series of jets in the rim of the circle. They send out arcs of water, rising to the height of a man before they tumble together in the centre. There's a drain hole right in the middle from where the water splashes its way down into some underground cistern.

Daz watches the kids take turns to run the gauntlet, ducking as they dash under the arcs of water. They scream and laugh. Some come through with only a few drops darkening their clothes. Mostly they just enjoy the soaking.

He's thinking back over the last few days. Raglan breaking his door. The riot. The beating. His shoulder still aches when he tries to lift his arm. Bruising around the joint, the doctor said. Not a fractured collarbone. Anti-inflammatory drugs and a week off work. Daz had laughed at that.

And then there's the Jobcentre. He's been chewing over an idea to get himself out of the training scheme. He could make it look as if he's got himself a job. That would get his name off the list of long-term unemployed. A couple of days later he could sign back on as unemployed and seeking work. He'd probably earn himself six more months of hassle-free signing. There would be a heap of forms, of course. And he'd have to get the cash together to last out the days he was off benefits – including the rent money. It might just be possible because the scheme doesn't get under way for two weeks.

But there's another thought in his mind, which seems to jar with this plan. The green-eyed woman from the Jobcentre – he doesn't want to be part of her training scheme, but he does want to see her again. It's his curiosity, he thinks. Always getting him into trouble. He wants to know what makes her so different from the others.

On the radio, the announcer is working her way through the main story of the day – ten million in damage after two days of rioting. Some community leaders blaming the other communities. Some blaming the police.

Daz takes a drink from the can. He knows it's never that simple. What, for example, was Vince the Prince doing there, stirring up trouble? A man like that always has a reason for everything.

'Now the rest of the news,' says the announcer. 'Police are appealing for information regarding the disappearance of pensioner Agnes Wattling some time last night. Signs of a break-in were found this morning at her house in Waterfields. According to a neighbour, there were signs of violence at the scene, including blood on a wall and floor but the police haven't made any statement on this.'

Daz rests the can against his left cheek, enjoying the shock of the cold.

'The missing woman has past convictions for receiving stolen goods,' the announcer says. 'In some circles she is known by the alias Patricia or sometimes Patty.'

Chapter 4

Patty's house with police tape around it. There's something profoundly wrong about that image. Daz feels his stomach clench up. One end of the tape is tied to a downpipe. It's looped around a lamppost and a telegraph pole. The other end is secured to a wheelie bin. The entire pavement lies within the cordon along the narrow frontage of the house.

He wonders how much of her stolen property remains inside. Perhaps the police have already dusted it all for fingerprints and carted it off for whatever other forensic tests they do these days. And the computer he sold her – he assumes that was still in the room when they arrived.

There's no sign of life at the front of the building. Door and curtains are closed. He walks to the other side of the street, crouches down, undoes his shoelace then starts to retie the knot. It's a slow operation with one arm all but useless. But slow is fine today. He scans the road up and down as he works. There are no police cars here. No people either – though he's pretty sure there will be watchers behind some of the net curtains on the street.

He gets up, makes his way around Patty's block and finds the entrance to the walkway that leads along the back of the terrace. He picks his way between the brick walls, stepping over an old bicycle frame, counting off the houses on his left. There's no incident tape here. Not even when he gets to her back yard. Someone must have forgotten. He pushes open the gate and steps inside.

It's quiet. That is the first thing he notices. No dogs flinging themselves at the back door. There hasn't been any mention of Kodak or Dyson in the news reports that he's heard so far. He wonders if they've been dragged off to the pound, if they are right now whining behind locked gates. It makes his skin crawl to think of it. He stands there for a moment, playing with the possibilities. But none of them seems to work. He can't imagine Patty without her dogs or the dogs without Patty.

He edges along the left side of the yard, so that the wall of the outside toilet building keeps him hidden from the house. Then he sidesteps to the corner and peers around. The curtains are open in the back rooms, upstairs and downstairs. Patty always kept them closed.

Now he's thinking about it, there's a lot he doesn't know about her. Like the name thing. *Agnes.* The news report was the first he'd heard of that. He has heard of a *Wattling* somewhere before – though that was a different person, an ancestor of his mother from way back.

Patty has always been Patty the Fence to Daz – ever since the first time he showed up at her back door. He was a fifteen-year-old truant, tagging along behind some kids who'd just ripped a CD player out of a parked car. She gave them a couple of pounds for their trouble and that was the end of it. Except that she asked for help shifting some boxes. The others must have known she wouldn't give them a tip for the work. They ran off, leaving him. That was the beginning of their relationship.

On the day of the riot, when he sold her the computer, he didn't expect to be treated differently from any other customer. Being mean in business was just her way. But he still trusted her to a degree, and trusting people isn't something he's had a lot of experience of.

He gets a flashback now. He's on his hands and knees outside Patty's front door. A boot catches him in the stomach, sending him onto his side. There's no physical sensation in the memory, no vision. Just the shock of the movement and his awareness of Patty's presence behind her front door.

Daz knocks his forehead against the rough brick of the outhouse wall – hard enough to provide physical pain to go with the memory, and to push back the creeping feeling that he was a fool to believe there was any friendship between them. He's not even sure why he's here today. Curiosity, perhaps. And a masochistic urge to prick himself with memories of his own gullible stupidity.

He edges sideways along the wall until his head is around the corner. He still can't see much, so he steps out further to give himself a full view of the main building. The first thing he sees is a line of police incident tape across the back door. Then he registers that the door itself is open. His next movement is instinctive. He jags his body back behind the outhouse wall. But he's too slow. Too late.

'Stop there!' A commanding shout.

The after-image fades from his mind. A uniformed policeman framed in the doorway. Daz has to decide whether to run or stand. The damaged shoulder will slow him. But he knows the alleys and culverts well. Better, he thinks, than any police officer. He takes half a step backwards, towards the gate.

The policeman is already striding around the corner. 'Don't even think it!' He looks young and fit.

Daz stops his retreat and tries a grin. 'Officer?'

'What's your name?'

Another moment of choice. But Daz is on the bluff-it-out run now. That means playing innocent. Keeping the lies to a minimum.

'Daz Croxley,' he says.

'And what are you doing here – visiting?'

Daz casts around the yard. 'Seen my tennis ball?'

The policeman frowns. 'What happened to your arm?'

'What's it to you?'

'Look, I can ask you these questions down at the station if you want it that way.'

Daz scrunches his face up. 'Had an accident,' he says.

The constable may be young, with no stripes on his arms, but he seems to have a fully developed sense of scepticism. He's looking at Daz's shoulder sling, eyes narrowed. 'And what's this you were saying about a ball?'

'Was in the road. Chucked it too hard. Went over the roof.'

'I don't see it here.'

Daz raises his eyebrows. 'Gunna give us a hand looking in the other yards?'

The constable gets out his notebook and starts writing something. He walks as he writes, subtly putting his body between Daz and the gate.

'Do you live nearby?'

Daz points over his shoulder with a thumb. 'Over that way a bit.'

'Road name?'

'Severn Street.'

'A long way from home, aren't you?'

'Look,' Daz says. 'Lost my ball. Not a crime, is it?'

'Not necessarily.'

'Guess I'll go then,' Daz says – though he doesn't try to leave.

'Do you play ball here often?'

'Nah.'

'Occasionally?'

Daz shrugs with one shoulder.

'What about Saturday – were you here at all?'

Daz knows there is danger in this situation. But there are possibilities as well. Questions can work both ways.

'What time Saturday?'

The constable hasn't looked up from his notebook, but there's a hint of tension in the way he's standing. 'You tell me.'

Daz curses himself for underestimating the man. He pats his sling with his good hand. 'Laid up all day Saturday.'

'You seem to have recovered quickly.'

'Suppose.'

'I guess it's not your throwing arm.' He writes some more. 'Did you know the lady who lived here?'

That catches Daz off-balance. The past tense. 'No,' he says – though the word feels like betrayal.

'What about the dog?'

Dog. Singular. Daz scratches at his nose, trying to cover the surge of ideas that he's sure must be washing across his face. 'Don't live round here,' he says.

'Ah, yes,' the policeman muses. He taps his notepad. 'Severn Street. You did say. But you might have noticed in passing.'

'What kind?'

The policeman shakes his head. 'I thought perhaps you could tell us that.'

It was *The Dirtchamber Sessions* that changed things for Daz – an album of remixed music, some of it decades old, spliced together and given a fresh fizz by the Prodigy. A disparate collection. Chemical Brothers. Bomb the Bass. LL Cool J. And somewhere in the middle of it was a track that jumped right out of the speakers and grabbed him by the ears. It was the first time he'd heard the Sex Pistols.

After that, he started keeping an ear open for punk rock from the late 1970s and early 1980s. The Pistols, the Clash, the Stranglers. And though he latched on to most music with energy and attitude, especially if the rhythms were complex, it was early punk that really did it for him. Anti-fashion, before it was boxed and branded. Before anyone knew what to call it or what it was going to become. He sometimes wonders what would have happened to him if he'd been born a quarter of a century earlier. He's thinking about music now as he walks – the Clash, the Manics, Cold Cut. He plays the music in his mind.

Ahead he can see his destination – the Club. *The* club. The last of the sunlight is on the building, tingeing one pale wall a rich marmalade. In the early evening it looks just like any other warehouse unit on the industrial estate. Windowless. Silent.

He breathes in the chemical-sweet smell from the Bostic factory chimney in the distance. But that's the only sign of business. There are no people here at this time of day. No cars moving. He's making his way down the road, tumbling an idea in his head, crossing and recrossing the centre line as he scuffs along. Then he gets far enough around the corner to see the front side of the building. His gaze jags over the signboard above the entrance, cutting across the grey outline of letters and words.

He climbs the kerb, walks up to the doors and puts his eyes close to the glass, hands cupped as a shield against the low sunlight. He hammers on the metal doorframe.

'Open up.'

There's no answer and no sign of movement in the entrance lobby. He can hear music playing somewhere inside. Techno. Trance, probably. Only just audible. He hammers again, waits for a moment, then makes his way around the side of the building to one of the fire exits.

It's been years since Daz found this place. That first time he followed a poster trail from the clock tower. There weren't any words on the posters – just a picture of a crooked smile. He'd liked that. And there wasn't any entrance fee on the door. No entertainment licence. No organizer to throw him out for being underage. No fire exits either. They added the safety features later. And a licensed bar. The rave venue became a legitimate club. *The* Club.

Daz raps a knuckle on the door. No answer. He pulls it and finds it unlocked. The boss would go spare if she knew. He steps inside and closes the door behind him. A short corridor leads him into the one huge room that takes up ninety per cent of the building. *The* Room in *the* Club. Black walls. Black floor. And, high above, a black ceiling.

There's a platform in the middle – raised a yard from the dance-floor, lit by stage lights suspended from a high gantry. Standing under the light, two dancers, Freddy and Ginger. They've got a portable CD player on the stage next to them. Daz recognizes the track they're playing. 'Trance Experience' by the Cynic Project. One-sixty BPM. It's a favourite of Ginger's. Freddy counts them in and they start to dance.

Daz watches. It's not often he gets to see them together without them knowing he's there. Ginger is dressed in grey trousers – loose-fit but really well cut – and a white sleeveless shirt that shows off the muscles in his torso. Freddy is wearing a body-hugger in sparkling, green Lycra patterned with cutaways.

Skin, hair, figure – everything about each of them is different from the other. It's impossible not to look at them. They move like two parts of the same body, as if there is one mind driving them. They separate then recombine like the bass and melody of the music.

And it's sexual. Stylized, perhaps, but the two bodies are moving together, glowing in health, growing in physical intensity. Watching is almost uncomfortable. He doesn't want to see these performers as the Freddy and Ginger who share a house with him on Severn Street.

She's standing in front of Ginger now, crouched low, snaking herself up his body. His hands grip her waist. She bends to the left and then to the right, her movement riding a slow wave in the melody line, while he body-pops his arms and shoulders to the fast tick of the techno beat.

Suddenly Ginger breaks away from the dance and from her. He crouches to the CD player and jabs the music off. 'No! No! No!'

Freddy is shaking her head. 'I forgot! I'm sorry, OK?'

'You're supposed to re-sync on the last phrase!'

'Look! I'll get it next time round.'

Daz feels himself tensing. He knows they won't be able to see him from where they're standing under the lights. Logically. But he feels as if he might somehow become visible to them. He wants to step back into the corridor, but the movement would give him away.

'How many times do we have to go through this?'

Freddy has displaced him at the CD player. She's pressing buttons. 'I'll get it right. I promise. This time.'

The music starts. They go back to their positions, he still

scowling, her sulky. He counts them in and the dance restarts. Their faces switch expression to the longing half-smiles they'd worn when they were dancing before. Daz backs from the stage, moving slowly at first. Then he turns and strides away towards the other end of the building, the office, the chill-out rooms and the bar.

There's a white man with dreadlocks here, unpacking piles of plastic skiffs from a cardboard box, stashing them under the bar. He waves Daz over.

'You come to see Ginger and Frederica?' the man asks. He has an Italian accent.

Daz shakes his head. 'The boss around?'

'Not today. You got business, then?'

'Maybe. Looking for a couple of days' work, that's all.'

The man leans forward, elbows on the bar. 'Ginger and Frederica want to have a theme night, you know? Breakbeat special. All pumped-up music. Ginger said you could be a consultant for it.'

Daz nods and parks himself on one of the bar stools. 'Think the boss will pay me?'

'You ask the boss. Maybe pay you. Maybe just a free ticket. Who knows? But you have a special friendship with the boss, yes?'

'Years ago maybe. Not now.'

The man takes one of the plastic skiffs and holds it up. 'I give you a free drink, OK? What you want?'

Daz looks at the glass-fronted chillers. Cans of beer and soft drinks. It looks like the only bottles are plastic.

'Coke.'

The man swings his dreadlocks like a horse's tail. 'You're driving today?'

Daz shrugs. 'Cheers.' He takes a mouthful straight from the can and feels the bubbles biting into his tongue. Then he pours the rest into the skiff. The man gets back to work, stacking the shelves.

Daz takes another swallow of coke and looks about him. The place is kept pretty clean, but there's still a smell to it. Stale beer. Fermenting fruit juice. He sniffs the air. He feels the floor with his foot – but there isn't any stickiness there. He runs a hand over the bar surface. All irritatingly smooth.

The Italian has finished stacking skiffs. He throws the box out through a doorway and starts tidying up. He takes Daz's empty can and drops it on top of a pile of others in a plastic dustbin.

'Why no glass?' Daz asks.

The Italian raises his hands in a you-know-how-it-is gesture. 'It's what the boss say. Safety, eh?'

Daz points to the bin. 'The smell – it's from there?'

'It's just for the recycling we keep them. You stand here another five minutes, you don't notice it any more. You don't like the smell?'

Daz scratches his ear. 'Just reminds me of something. That's all.'

'It reminds me to clean the bar!' the man says with a quick smile.

'What you do with them?' Daz asks, pointing to the dustbin. 'When it's full.'

There's a squeal of delight and both men turn to look. Freddy is skipping across the room towards them. She leans across the bar and kisses the Italian on his cheek, then she grabs Daz's wrist and pulls him in for the same. He moves his head left. She goes in the same direction and the kiss ends up lip to lip. Just a touch before he pulls away. Her eyes flash something at him that he can't read.

He looks down to the floor. But Freddy has already

turned away. She's speaking to the Italian. 'Water, please. It's so hot today! Can't you turn on the fans?'

He fills a pint skiff for her from the tap. She takes a long drink. Daz looks at the profile of her throat as she swallows. He can still feel her sweat on his face where they touched.

'Dazzo!' It's Ginger, walking into the room, the dance beat still animating his movement. 'I didn't see you come in, man!'

He raises his palm. Daz catches it in a high-five hard enough to leave his skin with a hot after-tingle. Then Ginger stands back and does a three-sixty twirl. 'Trousers,' he says. 'What do you reckon?'

'Looking good.'

'There's this new place on Silver Street. They knocked twenty per cent off everything on the opening day. Saved me a pile!'

The Italian has put another pint of water on the bar. Ginger drains half of it in one. He wipes his mouth on the back of his arm.

Freddy comes up to Ginger's side and wraps her arms over his shoulder. 'You're *so* hot, hun.'

'You bet I am!'

They share a smile.

Daz slips himself off the bar stool. 'Gotta go.'

The front doors of the Club are unlocked now. There's a cooler edge in the air outside. He stops to look back at the building. The name sign is illuminated. Red, blue and gold lights flashing into the darkening sky. There's a vapour trail high above the building, still touched pink with the sunset. The aeroplane catches a glint of light on its wing, then it ducks under the earth's shadow and turns dark.

The industrial estate is still quiet. It'll be another hour before the first punters start turning up for the Club. Daz can hear the faint buzz of the neon tubes above him. He starts walking away, towards the waste ground. There's a cut-through ahead, leading to Humberstone Road.

Daz's eyes catch on a single parked car on a side-street. It's a stupid place to leave a vehicle, unless you want the wheels stolen. There could be people inside it, of course. They might be waiting for the RAC to come and rescue them. He considers going across to make sure they're not in trouble. But it's more likely to be a drug dealer or a prostitute with an early client.

He's looking at it without turning his head, trying not to make his interest too obvious. He draws level with the side-road, then he's past it and he can't look any more. Only when he's halfway to the waste ground does he hear the car engine fire up behind him. He quickens his pace, listening to the growl of the car approaching.

Then he runs, as fast as his bruised shoulder will allow. The car roars with sudden acceleration. If he could only vault the fence he'd be in the thistle ground and they'd have to follow him on foot. But he hasn't got the mobility for that with his arm still in its sling.

He pushes his stride longer but the car has passed him already. It brakes hard, scattering gravel, skidding in towards the fence. The front wheels mount the pavement just in front of him. The bonnet is blocking his way, cutting him off from his escape.

He could U-turn. Run back to the Club.

The driver and passenger doors open. Daz sees the men scrambling out and knows he's not going to be able to get away. He stands facing them, panting hard.

'David Croxley?'

He doesn't answer, but takes a half-step backwards. Not enough to match their advance.

'You're cops?'

'Bright lad. Now how about you accompanying us to the station?'

'That a question?' Daz asks.

'Not really.'

Chapter 5

Daz hates walls. Not walls with windows: they're fine. And even if they're blank, he doesn't mind – so long as he knows what's on the other side. He's had this problem as long as he can remember.

He's sitting in a windowless room right now. His feet are spread under the table, his arms crossed in front of his chest. One of the walls is easy to cope with – the one with the door. He came in that way. He doesn't know how long ago that was, but he can remember the corridor on the other side. He can still sense it there, just a few inches behind the nicotine-cream paintwork.

It's the other surfaces of the room that are eating at him. Three walls, floor, ceiling. All impenetrable. Behind them could be anything. Another interview room, perhaps. For a moment he has a nightmare impression of other windowless spaces above, below and around. Room after room stretching away towards infinity.

In his mind he grasps a sledgehammer, lifts the weight of it to his shoulder. There's a moment of stillness as he centres his balance. Then he hefts it forwards into a descending arc, gravity and muscle power accelerating it right up to the moment of impact. Plaster falls away from the wall in flat chunks. He lifts the hammer again, holding the shaft just behind the metal head. No pause this time. It's swinging through the same bit of air. It hits the newly exposed brick. The impact shudders back through the wood to his hands.

The first layer of wall is crumbling. Sharp fragments are scattered around the floor. They scrunch under his shoes. He launches more blows, wildly now. A shard hisses past his left ear. He drops the hammer, gets on to his knees, picks crumbling lumps of brick out of the hole, his fingers scrabbling, trying to reach through to the other side.

It's now that the door opens. Daz is still in the chair where they left him. The wall he's been staring at is untouched. It takes a moment for his eyes to focus. There's the sound of a scraping chair just behind him. A uniformed officer gets to his feet and leaves. Daz *had* known he was there, though that awareness must have slipped away somehow. Two detectives come into the room and sit themselves on the other side of the table. One of them, a woman, checks the tape recorder then clicks it on and recites the formalities.

The other, a man, places a sheet of paper on the table, blank side up.

'David Croxley,' he says, rolling the 'r'.

Being pulled back suddenly into the real world has left Daz agitated. He blinks a couple of times. He bites the inside of his mouth.

The man, Detective Sergeant Leech, introduced himself before. That was at the beginning of the first interview some time ago. The thought of a boneless parasite has kept the name in Daz's mind. He would have forgotten otherwise. The man has an oval face, flabby-looking lips and the complexion of a night-shift worker. The woman, a detective constable, hasn't taken part in the questioning.

'You've been informed of your rights,' he says. 'They're still the same as when we started.'

'Wanna go now,' Daz says.

The DS slides his gaze down to the table then back. 'I'm not quite finished yet.'

'Said I could go when I want.'

'Of course. But there's still the matter of your relationship with Mrs Wattling to clear up.'

'Don't know her.'

'So you've said. And I'm also curious about your injury.'

'Got beat up.'

'Yes. But you don't know who it was. You've told us you were robbed of some money and that you didn't report it.'

'So?'

'So we did some checking. Apparently the ambulance crew found you on the street right in front of Agnes Wattling's house.'

Daz's ear lobe is itching. He keeps his hands below the table.

'What were you doing in front of her house?'

'Walking.'

'A coincidence, then. Perhaps.' He nods. 'But then we get to the really curious bit. I've had this transcript made up especially for you to see. It's the emergency call that brought the ambulance to you that night.'

The detective turns over his sheet of paper and slides it across the table to Daz.

'Read it.'

Daz looks at the page. The lines of words. The letters. He can feel a pressure behind his forehead. He clenches his teeth but the pressure won't go away.

'Why don't you read it out loud. For the tape.'

That pushes Daz over the edge. He slams both fists down on the table and stands, ramming his chair back, sending it crashing on to the floor.

The detectives are on their feet a fraction of a second after him. Leech holds his hand out, palm downwards. 'Whoa there. Pick your chair up and sit back down.' There's no aggression in the man's voice, but it carries authority.

Daz unclenches his fists. 'Gunna go now.'

'That would be a stupid move. No good to you or me. Take a deep breath. Let it out slowly.'

Leech glances at the DC. She nods, steps around the table, rights the chair. 'Please,' she says, inviting him to sit.

Daz closes his eyes for a moment and feels the limits of the room pressing in on him again. He longs to run. To crash himself against a wall. To find release through the pain of impact, through the violence of the act itself. But he sits.

DS Leech pulls the paper back across the table, rotates it. 'We'll make it easy. I'll read.' He clears his throat. 'The section at the beginning doesn't matter to us now. The operator asking for a name and location. The caller not saying. The interesting part starts about here.' He taps a finger halfway down the page.

'Caller: "There's a boy down. Daz Croxley."'

'Operator: "Is he breathing?"'

'Caller: "He's bleeding, dammit."'

'Operator: "We need your location or we can't dispatch the ambulance."'

Daz digs his thumbnail into the palm of his hand. He looks across to the door, stares at it.

Leech sits back. 'You know, of course, that the caller eventually gave Mrs Wattling's address.'

'So?'

'So it's someone who knows your name. Any idea who it might be?'

Daz feels the pressure building in his head again. He

keeps his arms tight across his chest. 'Said she didn't give her name, didn't you!'

'Interesting that you think the caller was female. I didn't say so.'

Daz clamps his mouth closed so hard that his teeth start to ache. A trap. Stupidly simple. Suddenly he sees why they showed him a transcript rather than playing him the tape.

Leech lets the moment hang before continuing. 'As it happens, you are right. It was a she. And the call was made from a mobile phone that'd been stolen earlier in the day.'

'You don't know who, then?'

'It's hard to be certain. But we did find the phone – which does go some way to help. Especially since it was in Agnes Wattling's house. Together, I should say, with a considerable quantity of other stolen property.'

Dawn is still a couple of hours away. Daz Croxley is sitting on the fire-escape platform just outside his bedsit window, dangling his bare feet in the cool air. There's an open tin of dog food next to him, with a spoon in it. He's wearing a pair of lime-green jeans and a black T-shirt. His arm is still in the sling. The only light in the yard below comes from a downstairs window. He's peering into the gloom, waiting.

There's muffled techno music in the air. Very faint. A window slides open above, and for a moment the music is clearer. Then the window closes again. Daz hears the light ringing of footsteps descending the metal fire escape. He doesn't need to look around to know who it is. The rhythm of the movement tells him. And now she's standing close, he can smell the scent she uses. It reminds him of something from years ago. Family holidays – when he still had a family. Gorse flowers by the seaside.

'What are you doing, Dazzo?' she says.

He answers in a whisper. 'Hi, Freddy.'

She crouches down next to him and gets her head close enough to look along his arm as he points into the darkness. 'I can't see anything,' she says, dropping her voice to match his. 'You must have eyes like a cat.'

Daz picks up the tin and excavates a dollop of meat and jelly with the spoon. Then he flicks it in the direction he'd been pointing. There's a faint splatter as it hits the paving stones.

Slowly then, with its head low as if smelling its way, a fox steps into the glimmer. They watch it eat. It looks up, licking the sides of its mouth. Daz flicks more dog food, this time on to the lowest step of the fire escape. The fox moves forward and eats again. Freddy is crouching so close to Daz now that he's aware of the warmth radiating from the skin of her bare arm. She's holding the railing with one hand. He can't hear her breathing.

Daz waits until the fox is looking around for more. He spoons out the last dollop right next to where he's sitting. The fox's paws are silent on the metal steps. It's eating again. Daz reaches out his left hand in one invisibly slow movement until his fingers are stroking the back of the animal's neck.

'Hiya, foxy,' he whispers.

The fox looks up, sniffs at his wrist. Daz feels the cold touch of its nose against his skin. Then it turns and pads away down the steps and into the darkness.

They're alone again. Neither of them speaks. Daz eases himself back, till he's lying on the metal. The movement makes his bruised shoulder joint ache – though the pain isn't as bad as it was the day before. He looks up at the dark sky, tinged with dull orange from the city's lights. He listens to the distant traffic noise.

When Freddy speaks it's still in a whisper. 'That was *so* beautiful.'

Daz looks across to her. 'Been a shitty day till now, though.'

She shifts herself back, so she can sit on the step above. She's changed from her outfit at the Club. Now she's wearing dark leggings and a long T-shirt – it looks like one of Ginger's. Her hair is tied back. A few strands of her fringe are stuck to the sweat on her forehead. There's a fat spliff resting behind her ear, a disposable lighter in her hand.

'How shitty?'

He rolls his eyes.

'Tell me,' she says.

So he does. He tells her about the police. The questioning in Charles Street nick. The way Leech allowed him to lie his way into a corner – then produced the phone transcript. And Daz tells her the story he told Leech. That he does know Patty – did know her. That he'd been afraid to admit it. That he was worried about what had happened when she went missing. This is all true, as far as it goes.

He leaves out the fat man who was buying up Patty's stock of bent electronics. That still feels like someone else's business. And at the moment he might be the only other person who knows about it.

'Leech kept asking the same questions,' he says. 'Over and over.'

'Ouch,' Freddy says.

'Ouch,' Daz agrees.

'But they did let you go.'

'Not a crime, is it – lying.'

'No . . . but I still don't see what Patty has to do with the man who beat you up.'

'Knew he was there, didn't she?'

Freddy looks sceptical. 'I still don't get it.'

He can understand why she isn't going along with this. He hasn't told her enough for the story to make sense. He's said nothing about his looting of the electronics shop. Nothing about his money dealings with Patty. He isn't exactly ashamed of it. But he doesn't think her reaction would be good if he did let it out.

'Only thing that matters,' he says, 'is they want to find a missing person. *One way or the other*.'

He watches these words hit Freddy.

'No!'

'Was blood all over the place. That's what they said on the radio.'

'You think she's dead?'

Daz shakes his head. 'Kinda hoped she was – at first. Set me up for a beating, didn't she? Must've done. But now . . . Just dunno. Known her for years. She's always been straight with me – in her kind of way. Trusted her. Next thing I know, there's a bloke trying to finish me off with an iron bar.'

Daz feels a sudden self-conscious anxiety pressing down on him. As if he's exposed too much. Or lied too much. Or both. He levers himself back into a sitting position.

'But,' Freddy says, 'if she's the one who called the ambulance . . .?'

He looks away, out into the night. 'I know. Kinda doesn't help me feel so great.'

'And, Daz, there's something else. How do you think we found out you were in the hospital? I got a phone call at the Club. An old woman who wouldn't leave her name – that's got to be her, right?'

'Shit,' says Daz. 'How come she knew your number?'

'I gave it to you, remember? She could have found the name card in your pocket.'

'I guess.'

'Anyway,' Freddy says. 'You'd better leave it. There's no point digging yourself in any deeper.'

He nods. She's right and he knows it. There's just one more thing he has to check and then he's going to put it all behind him.

Freddy takes the roll-up from behind her ear and lights it. Her face glows yellow for a moment in the flame. Her eyes are closed. She draws the smoke in, holds it for a beat, and then breathes out, long and slow. She smiles and puts the joint in Daz's mouth. He takes it out again and offers it back.

'Don't do that stuff.'

'Go on,' she says, nodding towards his shoulder. 'It'll kill the pain.' She takes his hand, pushes it back towards him. 'They use it for medicine nowadays. It'll help your shoulder.'

She guides it to his mouth.

'Now draw it right in,' she says. 'Just like a ciggie.'

He watches her face as she moves herself to sit next to him. Her hips and shoulders are touching his. He can feel the warmth of her. She takes the joint from him, drags on it, then puts it back in his mouth.

'You see? Nice and deep.'

He's not sure if he should be using cannabis on top of the prescription painkillers. But he takes another drag anyway, and lets his shoulder press back into hers.

It's much later. Daz is drifting, dawn seeping in through his closed eyelids. For a time he thought he was out on the fire escape still. But he can feel the edge of the mattress-bed with his hand.

He can remember talking to Freddy – about Patty perhaps. Or about Ginger. He's not quite sure what was said. They laughed. Uncontrollable. Tears ran from his eyes. She put her arm around him. Somehow their faces came to be pressed together, mouth to mouth. It was more like a dream than being awake. At that moment she wasn't Freddy any more. He was kissing a different woman – whoever she was – with complete desire. He reached up expecting to find short-cropped hair and it had been all wrong. He was confused, but he carried on anyway. He doesn't even know which of them it was that broke the contact and pulled away. He buries his head in the pillow, hoping to his guts that it was him.

Chapter 6

Monday morning near Western Park. The Eco-House is here – an environmentally friendly show-home. Next door stand the offices of Environ, a charity that runs a recycling centre among other things. There's something that looks like a large garage next to the car park. That's where Daz is standing. Right arm hanging in the sling, left arm propped against the doorframe.

Inside the building he sees old computers stacked on the floor and racks of used timber down the length of one wall. But it is a machine that has caught Daz's attention, right at the back of the building. It has a conveyor belt rising at an angle out of a large blue hopper. It crashes and clanks as a stream of aluminium cans cascades into a bin. Everything about the machine is noisy and angular.

'Can I help you?'

Daz turns to see a man clomping across the car park in green Wellington boots.

'Just looking.'

'It's not disturbing you, I hope?'

Daz shakes his head. 'Love it.'

'You do?' The man offers his hand and beams a smile. Daz gives him a left-handed shake.

'I'm Mark,' the man says. 'Are you one of our New Deal trainees?'

'Nah.' Daz lets go of Mark's hand and nods towards the conveyor noise. 'Good for the earth, is it?'

Mark laughs. 'You could say that.'

He leads Daz into the building. 'There's a powerful electromagnet in there, separating the aluminium cans from the steel ones. Every can recycled saves energy. That means less stress on the world's environment. But we get complaints all the same. The noise mostly. And the smell.'

Daz takes a deep breath through his nose. Beer running to vinegar. Fermenting fruit juice. 'It's the smell that got me here.'

Mark gives the edge of the hopper an affectionate pat. 'I guess if there's nothing else, I'd better be getting back . . .'

'One thing.' Daz points to the heap of cans. 'Where d'they come from?'

'People collect them. Businesses. Individuals. Charities.'

The words carry a joyful enthusiasm and Daz can't help warming to him.

'We pay for the aluminium, you see. Forty pence a kilo. Forty-five pence at Christmas.'

'Not bad.'

Mark shrugs. 'You couldn't make a living picking cans out of litterbins. Not unless you lived in a tepee or something. But still . . .'

'A tepee?'

'If you're looking for one of those I know some people.'

Daz shakes his head. He's thinking about the money he's got to find for Raglan. He's got three days before the next payment. 'How many cans get you fifty quid?'

'That would be . . . a hundred and twenty-five kilos.'

It sounds like a lot. More than Daz could collect in three

days. He sighs. But he should get a cheque from the DSS on Wednesday. That thought jogs his memory. He's got to sign on in a couple of hours.

'How d'people get the cans here?' he asks.

'Bike is the best way – for the environment.'

Daz pulls a sceptical frown.

'Most use cars, though,' Mark admits.

'Vans?'

'Sure. A few.'

'Transits?'

'Perhaps.'

'A white Transit?'

Mark cocks his head and looks at Daz for a moment before answering. 'I'd want to know a bit of what's behind your question before answering.'

Daz tugs one of his safety pins. It would have been easy for the man to say 'no'. And it would have been easy to say there were loads of white Transits.

'There is one, then?'

'Who are you, and why do you want to know?'

'Daz,' says Daz. 'Just need to find him – the guy with the van.'

'I can't give out names. You understand that.'

Daz puts his hand on the sorting machine. The vibration makes his fingers tingle. He stares at the cans juddering up the belt. 'Could tell me when the van comes here, couldn't you?'

Mark seems caught between following the rules and helping. He picks a can off the floor, crushes it in his hand and drops it into the hopper. 'Wednesday. I could do with some help on Wednesday. If you want to come back then, you could give me a hand.'

Daz pats the sorting machine. 'Work on this?'

Mark nods. 'And you never know, you might meet some of our customers as well.'

Daz makes his way across the car park and out on to the Hinckley Road. If he can just clear this anxiety about Patty from his mind, he'll be able to concentrate on getting his next payment for Raglan. Wednesday's benefit cheque is supposed to pay for food and clothes.

He's past the bus stop now, having decided to save the sixty-pence fare. A half-hour walk back to town. Some chips from the Granby Fisheries and a bit of dropped fruit from the market will do for lunch. Then he can go to the Jobcentre and sign on as unemployed and seeking work. He crosses the road and strides down the hill, thinking about aluminium cans – where he could find enough of them to make any kind of serious money.

There's a battered silver Ford illegally parked just ahead of him. He's almost level with it when the driver opens the door, barring his way.

'—king idiot!'

The driver climbs out, the smile on his face a saccharine apology. He's a few years older than Daz, perhaps thirty. He's got a sinuous figure, and his thin face has a slightly worn, leathery appearance. His fingers gleam with silver rings of different shapes and sizes.

'Sorry, mate,' he says. 'Accident.'

He's holding out his hand. Daz moves automatically to take it. But the driver shifts an inch to the side and his hand strikes forward, his fingers locking around Daz's wrist. In the same movement the man is throwing his weight forward, twisting Daz's arm around as far as it will go without pain, then further. And then a little further again.

Daz holds his cry back behind clenched teeth. The man's head is close to his. He smells of liquorice.

'Time to go for a little ride.'

Daz sees a blink of steel in the space between his stomach and the driver's. A blade catching the light.

'Get in the car.'

There are people driving past. They must see what is happening, but none of them stop. Daz finds himself being shoved in through the driver's door. Then the knifepoint is encouraging him sideways to the passenger seat.

They're heading out of Leicester, past the outer ring road already. Daz is trying to work out who he might have annoyed enough to get this kind of treatment. The whole abduction thing feels too subtle for someone like Vince the Prince or any of his gang. They'd sooner shove a bottle in his face. This is more like Raglan's style. Other than that he's got no ideas. What he does have is a brooding fear of what lies at the end of the journey. Pain, he guesses.

He sits quiet, waiting for some chance. The driver pulls up at a traffic light junction. Daz takes a breath and tries to let it out steadily. He counts to two in his head, then grabs the door handle. Pulling. But the door is child-locked.

The driver turns to look. Then he draws the knife from his pocket, moving slowly, and presses the tip into Daz's leg. There's a point of sharp pain, then the lights change.

The knife is gone and there's a new rip in Daz's jeans. The driver eases his foot off the clutch. They accelerate gently. Keeping within the speed limit. Leaving the city behind them. The driver doesn't turn his head to look again. And Daz doesn't try to escape.

*

Low, concrete buildings in the distance. A perimeter fence surrounded by open farmland. A roadside checkpoint. It's all got a military feel to it, but without the guns. The driver hands some papers through the window. The security guard checks them against his clipboard then peers at Daz.

'That's David Croxley?'

The driver nods. 'Yup.'

The guard straightens himself and waves them through.

Daz keeps quiet at first, though he's got questions boiling up inside him. When the pressure gets too much he says: 'How come?'

The driver gives a crocodile grin by way of answer. He eases the car into a slot between a green Land Rover and the wall of what has to be the reception building.

'Place feels like a prison,' Daz says.

'You're not so dumb after all,' says the driver. 'Welcome to the inside.'

These are the things that Daz manages to work out as he's led through the corridors: it's a low-security prison. Not open, exactly, but you wouldn't have to be Harry Houdini to break out. Secondly, his visit has been arranged in advance. There's paperwork with his photograph stuck to it – how they got hold of that he hasn't any idea. Thirdly, the guards are calling the driver 'Guy' – which could be surname or first name, Daz isn't sure. But it leads to the final bit of knowledge. The driver, Guy, has been here often enough for them to remember his name.

A man in uniform ushers them through to a small interview room.

'If you don't mind . . .'

He gives Guy a quick pad down. Pockets and sides. Then he turns to Daz. 'Now you.'

This time it's a thorough frisking. Daz empties the contents of his pockets on to a tray. Some change. A bus ticket. House keys. The uniform still isn't satisfied.

'Boots off.'

There's no chair so Daz crouches down and unlaces his mock Docs. He hands over the left one first. It's as the guard is examining this that Daz pulls off the right boot. His remaining twenty-pound notes slip out. He palms them and stands.

The uniform finishes his inspection 'No offence,' he says.

But there is offence meant, and Daz knows it. He's had lots of experience in recognizing hidden insults. They don't get to him, though – not while he can win his own small victories. The uniform leads them out of the room and Daz slips the twenty-pound notes into his back pocket.

Then it's down another corridor, past a large room set out for table tennis and darts. More like a youth club than a prison. They turn in at the next door, a visiting room. The guard slips away, leaving them alone. Nine identical tables laid out three-by-three. Strip lights hanging above. A faint smell of bleach.

Guy, the driver, walks to a window and gazes out. Daz drags a chair and drops himself into it. The adrenaline rush has ebbed now. There's not a lot of violence they can do to him while he's inside the prison.

He's thinking about that glimpse of his picture on the pass documents. A mug-shot that looked as if it had been cut from a group photo. It must have been a couple of years old, because his hair was bright red. There was a girl's shoulder next to his in the picture, her arm draped across him. It's Freddy's arm. He knows that. But he can't remember the event or having seen the photograph before.

Then the guard returns, swinging the door wide, letting through a man in prison-grey. Guy stands to attention. Daz knows what is expected of him – to show some kind of respect. He instinctively does the opposite, letting his back slump another couple of inches down the chair.

The prisoner moves to the opposite side of the table and sits.

He is a slab of a man. His face a wall. Cropped black hair with a touch of silver on the sides. Eyes like wet slate.

'Mr Croxley.'

'They call me Daz.'

'Thank you.' He nods towards the others, both of whom move away – the guard to the door, Guy to the window.

Daz folds his arms across his chest and waits.

'Very good. Daz it is. And I am Bishop.'

Slumped halfway down the chair, Daz now feels uncomfortable. He wants to sit tall, eye to eye, but doesn't want it to seem as if he is extending some kind of courtesy to the man who's had him brought here under threat of violence. He inches himself a little higher.

Bishop has got a packet of cigarettes out of his shirt pocket. He lights up and sits back, looking at Daz through the smoke. 'You have something I want,' he says at last. 'I don't blame you. You didn't know it was mine. Not till now.'

Daz chews on the inside of his cheek.

'This is my first question,' says Bishop. 'How did you get it?'

'Get what?'

Bishop looks disappointed. 'I have plenty of other things to be doing, even in here.'

'Straight up! Dunno what you mean.'

Bishop leans across the table. 'The money you used to pay off Paul Raglan. Where did you find it?'

Two things hit Daz at this moment. First, that this indistinct but ominous trouble has suddenly merged with his money worries. Secondly, Bishop's question is tugging at something in the back of his mind. An echo of a memory.

'Sold something,' he says.

'You sold what?'

Daz shrugs. 'Stuff. You know.'

'H'm. Sold to whom?'

This is the clinch question. Daz tightens his fists under the table. He still doesn't know what he should be feeling about Patty. She might be dead or alive. She might have set him up for a beating. She definitely rescued him by calling for the emergency services. And even if he could solve those puzzles, he's now starting to question the nature of their relationship. Though he's bought stuff from her once or twice over the years, it's not been business that has kept him going back to her house. And more puzzling still is the question of why Patty, the ultimate businesswoman, always opened the door to let him in.

'Well?' Bishop prompts.

Daz glances at the guard over on the other side of the room. No help from that direction.

'Bloke in the pub,' he says at last. 'He's the one I sold it to.'

'Which pub?'

'The Charlotte.'

'What was the man's name?'

'Dunno.'

Bishop takes a slow breath and narrows his grey eyes. 'What did this man look like?'

'Kind of normal.'

'Hair?'

The speed of the question trips Daz for a moment.

'Was . . . he was bald.' He pats his own head. 'Shaved, I reckon.'

Bishop runs the tip of his tongue over his lower lip. 'And how much did he give you?'

This time Daz doesn't hesitate. 'Hundred and forty.'

'How much have you got left?'

Daz looks at the rim of the table. 'Forty.'

Bishop gets to his feet, shaking his head when Daz makes a move to follow. He stands looking down, hands in his pockets. 'I have a big problem with man-in-pub stories,' he says.

He walks around the table until he's standing just behind Daz. He leans forward and whispers. 'There's no way to check, is there? I'm supposed to believe that some bald man in a pub has my money?'

Then he presses his hand down on to Daz's bruised shoulder.

Daz tenses against the pain. 'But it's true.' He hisses the words through his clenched teeth.

Bishop's fingers dig into Daz's deltoid. 'Then why,' he breathes, 'do you tell different stories on different days? Why did you tell me it was a man in a pub, when the other day you said it was the fence, Agnes Wattling?'

It's as he releases the pressure that Daz cries out. The guard looks around, but Bishop is already making his way across to the window. He says something into the driver's ear and then walks to the doorway.

'Goodbye, Mr Croxley,' he says. 'I'll be seeing you again.'

Daz sits forward and rests his head on the Formica tabletop. His ears are buzzing from the pain. And he's feeling the shock of what he's just heard. Because he's damned sure he hasn't told anyone that the money came from Patty.

Chapter 7

The green eyes are just as bright as he's been remembering over the last couple of days. But there's a suggestion of shadow on the skin beneath them. Tiredness, perhaps. She seems to be waiting for him to begin. He's finding it hard to look right back into her stare, so he drops his gaze to her hands, resting on the interview room desk. Her fingernails are bitten hard back.

'Why?' she says at last.

He wants to shrug or say 'why not?' or just chew on his lip. But she's more than just an official. She's a real person with a favourite film. And more than that – there are things under the surface of her that he can't yet name but which he wants to uncover.

So he says: 'Wasn't my fault this time.'

'All you had to do,' she tells him, 'was come into the Jobcentre, queue up for five minutes then sign at the bottom of the page. It's not asking much.'

'I was kidnapped.'

'Excuse me?'

'Was going to sign on. But he forced me into his car and . . .'

He looks up to her face, expecting scorn, and sees her mouth hanging open.

'I can't write that!' she says.

'But it's true.'

She leans forward as if the conversation might somehow be overheard. 'Is there a . . . a police involvement?'

'No.'

'In which case, I—'

'He let me go – after he'd done. Why bother the police?'

'After he'd done what?'

This conversation started off feeling like a confession. But the further he gets into it, the more it is turning into something enjoyable. He's hooked her curiosity. The energy is back in her face – like it was a few days ago when they first met.

'He took me to see this guy in prison.'

'And?'

'Threatened me. Then let me go.'

She's biting her thumbnail now. She stops and folds her arms. 'OK. I will write it that way – if that's what you really want. But—'

'But?'

'But no one's going to believe some gangster story. Guns and kidnapping.'

'Was a knife, not a gun.'

'Knife?'

Daz nods.

'Do you want your benefit cheque or not?'

'Want me to lie?'

She leans even further forward this time. He mirrors her action so his face comes close to hers. She doesn't pull away. 'I'm not telling you to *do* anything.'

'But . . .?'

'But if you tell me you went for a job interview yesterday, or something like that, then I might have a chance to get this straight. That way they'll send you a giro.' There's a flicker of enjoyed wickedness in her eyes. 'You might tell me the prospect of work was so intoxicating that you forgot to inform us.'

Then she sits back. He does the same.

He refolds his arms and clears his throat. 'Went for a job.'

She nods encouragement. 'And?'

'Forgot.'

She flashes him a smile and writes something on a form. Then she slides it across the desk with a Biro. 'Read and sign, please.'

Daz goes through the motions, flicking his eyes backwards and forwards across her writing. Then he scrawls a mark on the dotted line. 'Doing anything after work?'

There's no indication from her expression that she's even heard the question. She says: 'This will take a couple of days to work through the system. You might get a cheque by Saturday. Monday, perhaps.'

'But . . . should be Thursday!'

'Of course. But you were late signing. *Again*. There are procedures.'

'Gotta pay Raggy tomorrow!'

'Raggy?'

'He'll kill me.'

He looks right into her eyes and just for a second sees a flash of something that might be uncertainty. But she's shaking her head.

'I'm sorry,' she says. 'But there's nothing I can do.'

Daz gets to his feet and hits the heel of his hand against his forehead. 'Shit!'

'But if you *do* survive, perhaps I'll see you at the next appointment.' And then she winks.

*

It's two in the morning and as quiet as it gets in the inner city. There's the sound of individual cars on the main road up at the end of the street. A drunk is shouting somewhere in the far distance.

Daz steps into the walkway that leads behind the houses. He stands for a moment, letting his eyes adjust to the dark. The dull orange streetlighting reaches one of the enclosing walls, but an angled shadow leaves the paving and the other wall invisible. He's aware of the sound of his own breath, of the moisture in the air.

Daz edges forward, stepping over the bicycle carcass that blocks his way. He places his feet carefully, but fragments of broken glass still crackle as he walks. In the distance a car with a boom box drives past. The hip-hop bassline recedes towards silence.

There are no lights at the back of Patty's house. And no lights in the empty buildings on either side. Daz crouches in the rear yard, keeping himself in the deepest shadow. Everything seems empty, but the skin on the back of his neck is prickled tight – as if Patty might at any moment jump out from some hiding place and bark an insult at him.

In his mind there are two versions of the events that have led to this point. In one version Patty is alive, hiding out somewhere. In the other she is dead, buried in a shallow grave. These scenarios are hazy, ghost-like, but he knows he will have to live with both of them for the rest of his life if he can't uncover the truth.

Not that this trip is about playing detective.

From where he's crouching Daz can see that the back door is no longer blocked by incident tape – though a ripped end is still tied around the handle. The whole Agnes Wattling thing has dropped out of the news now, replaced by the murder of some Asian factory owner. The police have moved on.

For all his problems, Daz has never got into housebreaking. When he was a teenager he got dragged along a couple of times with other kids from the remedial class. He saw how it was done. He even went inside the houses. But he never felt easy with it. And he never got anything more than street cred out of those adventures. Somehow the others always ended up with the cash.

The way they used to do it was to kick in the lowest panel of the back door – thin plywood, usually. Then they'd crawl through the hole, put the front door on the chain, to avoid being surprised by the owners, then run through the house looking for small things, easy to sell. Jewellery. Games consoles. Cash would have been ideal – but people didn't usually leave that kind of thing lying around where Daz grew up.

He's standing next to her back door now, feeling the outline of the lowest panel with the fingers of his good hand. He straightens himself, draws back his foot and kicks. Boom. The impact leaves a hiss in his ears. His heart is pounding out a breakbeat rhythm on the inside of his ribcage. He kicks again, harder this time. Boom. The panel shudders slightly. Boom. Boom. More kicks. A dog starts barking in another house somewhere.

He thinks about all the locks and bolts Patty used to use. Her back door isn't going to be a pushover. Then he remembers another trick someone taught him all those years ago. Kids carrying crowbars could be arrested by the police. So the coolest operators always went in empty-handed and searched for tools in the gardens of the houses they were about to burgle. A hammer, perhaps, or a spade. It's amazing what people left lying around.

Daz steps across the yard and opens the first of the outhouse doors. Inside it smells of rotten wood. He pulls a disposable lighter from his pocket and flicks the flame into life. There's a pile of old paint tins here, a five-litre paraffin can, a brush stuck in a lump of gunge in the bottom of a jam jar. Lots of dust. He moves to the second outhouse. The door is stuck on this one, and he has to heave it upwards as he pulls. This is the outside toilet. An old-style pull-chain. A tiled floor. Nothing else. On the off chance, he reaches up and feels along the top of the high cistern.

The better you lock up your house, the more stuck you are if you lose the keys. In the end you can't risk it and you do something stupid. Like this. Daz has to stop himself laughing out loud. From its high hiding place, he retrieves a set of house keys, lightly greased and covered in brick dust.

He walks towards the back door, wiping the keys with his fingers. But each step he takes is shorter than the last. Slower. Up to this point he hasn't done anything that they could lock him away for. They don't put people like him in cushy open prisons. That kind of place is reserved for the men who take a few million from a pension fund, not the ones who lift a couple of hundred from a handbag.

He's still moving towards the door. He puts the key in the lock. This is the result of the injustice done to him today. Not by the woman down at the Jobcentre. It's the system that's screwed him. What he's doing now is the inevitable result. He takes a breath, turns the key and steps inside Patty's house.

This is the moment that her disappearance really hits him. It's the smell that does it. Dog and stale tobacco smoke, things he's always associated with her. It's as if her presence and her absence are both here, each reinforcing the other. He closes the door behind him, then locks it to be sure.

He can't risk turning on the light, so he holds his hand above his head and flicks a flame. It's when he looks across to the kitchen wall that he sees it – no more than two paces away. He recoils, dropping the lighter on to the floor. It's suddenly dark, but he knows what's here.

'Pigging hell!'

His breath is coming too fast. He slows it down, gropes for the lighter. 'Get a grip.'

He lights a flame again. This time he's ready for the image. A dark stain at knee height. Blood. A dark patch, the size of a dinner plate. Lines running down where drips must have run. And smears across the vinyl, as if the body had been dragged towards the back door.

'Oh, pig!'

The idea of Patty the corpse has suddenly grown more tangible, and Patty the fugitive is fading in Daz's mind. But he knows he can't stand staring. Every minute here is a risk. He forces himself to move through to the front room. The streetlight is flooding through the open curtain here. He doesn't need the lighter to confirm that Patty's haul of stolen goods is gone.

Now to the back room – the real objective of his visit. He didn't dare try this before – the police were still crawling everywhere. A fingerprint left in the night could, he figured, be found the next day by a scene-of-crime officer. He didn't want to end up being charged with murder. He'd die in prison. He's sure of that.

He knows that Patty kept her money here. Being who she was, she must have hidden it well – which means the police might not have found it. There are two ways of thinking about this. Daz runs through them again. Patty could still be alive – the blood might not be hers. If so, she will have taken the money with her. Or she is dead – and no longer in need of the cash. Either way, he can take what he finds.

He holds the lighter above his head and looks around the room. It measures roughly three paces by four. A short passage leads to the front room. There are two open doors, one giving access to the kitchen, the other to the foot of the stairs. He's seen this layout in many other terraced houses. The stairs themselves are sandwiched between the front and back rooms.

He thinks back to the night he sold her the computer. She came in here, told him not to follow. He heard her moving something heavy – a bit of furniture, by the sound of it. It scraped across the floor. There's an armchair here and a coffee table. There's a fireplace with fitted cupboards to one side of it. A small desk and chair are tucked away in the alcove.

Daz gets down on his knees, looks at the carpet in the light of the flame. There are definite marks where the desk legs have compressed the pile. And scraping marks where they have been dragged. He pulls it out far enough so that he can get in behind. The carpet comes up easily at the edge of the room. He tries the floorboards. The second one from the end is loose. He pulls it up, peers inside. Nothing but a nest of dust-covered electric cabling. It doesn't look as if anyone has been in this cavity for a long time. He lies down so that his good arm can get into the hole. He feels along under the boards to the next wooden joist.

Nothing.

Then he hears it – the click of a key turning in the back door lock.

He's up before the door is open. There's no time to replace the floorboard, so he just kicks the carpet back roughly into place. He uses both hands to lift the desk over the hole. His bruised shoulder feels as if it's on fire, but he doesn't cry out.

The back door closes. The lock clicks. There are footsteps just outside the room. Daz steps lightly through the open door to the foot of the stairs. He eases himself backwards, climbing out of what little light there is. He can still peer into the room from here but he doesn't think he'll be seen.

A figure enters the room. It steps across and pulls out the desk, dragging it across to the fitted cupboards.

All Daz can see is an outline. But that's enough to tell him this is a woman. It could even be a girl – she's small enough. His physical fear is ebbing. He could overpower her if he needed to. He feels an urge to step out and confront her. But her confidence is unsettling. It's as if she has a right to be here and he doesn't.

She's moved the chair across now, and Daz is sure that the floorboard he's moved is about to be discovered. But instead of getting down on her hands and knees and pulling back the carpet, she steps up on to the chair, then on to the desktop. There's a lightness in her movements which suggests youth.

She's opened the highest cupboard now. And she's standing on tiptoe to reach inside. He hears the sound of brick scraping on brick. Then she's pulled something out. For a moment he sees a thick wad of notes silhouetted against the faint light from the window.

Again, he wants to step out – this time to demand his own cut of the money. Again he holds back.

Brick scrapes on brick again. She closes up, jumps down, replaces the furniture. Then she's out of the room. Daz waits till he hears the back door close before following. As he crosses the room he catches the tang of her scent. Some kind of soap or perfume. Cheap, sharp and sexy.

The girl has already reached the end of the walkway by the time Daz peers out from Patty's back yard. She's revealed in the streetlight for a blink, then she's turned the corner and gone. He runs to catch up, making more noise than he wants, knowing that he'll lose her if he doesn't. He gets to the end and scans the street but she's already gone. It's at the next corner he has his first proper view of her. She's got long, raven-black hair. She's wearing some kind of loose top and stretch jeans. She must have slowed down her walking because she's only just passed the first lamppost. He ducks back and catches his breath.

This is going to be the difficult part. Following her down the street without being seen. But he has to try. This girl has the money. And, perhaps more important, she must have some knowledge of Patty. Daz looks around the corner again and sees her stepping inside one of the houses. The door closes and she's gone.

The house is number 24. He puts his hand on to the letterbox, thinks of tapping it to bring her out. But he's still unsure. So he steps away, walks back to the corner of the street and waits.

Most of the houses on the street are dark. The people asleep. He looks from window to window down the line of the terrace. He's on the outside again, looking in. It's always been like that for him – at the Jobcentre, at the school, with the foster parents. All the way back to when he was still living with his father. It's as if he's excluded from a secret that everyone else has always known. Something to do with the written word and money and time. Everyone else knew he was an outsider – even before he accepted the fact himself.

He gives up waiting, walks back to the house. There's no rear alleyway here. Access to the back garden is via a side passage between the two adjacent terraced houses. There's a bolted door at the mouth of the passage, but the wood is rotten. Soft as wet cardboard. It only takes a push for the screws to pull free.

Daz props the door in a closed position behind him, squeezes between the brick wall and a stinking wheelie bin and creeps into the garden at the rear of the house. There are lights on upstairs and down. The curtains are partly drawn, but he can see through a gap into the downstairs room. There's a bed next to the window.

The girl is lying on her back. Daz pulls away suddenly.

Then he thinks about what he's seen and he knows he can move forward again without fear of being discovered. Her eyes are open, the pupils dilated wide. There's a man's belt around her arm. If she's been mainlining on heroin, the syringe must have fallen on to the floor. He can't think of anything else that would have got her so far out of it quite so quickly.

Now he can take his time looking, he sees that she's more like a waxwork than a living person. Eyeliner. Lipstick. An impression of life painted on to the skin. For a moment he thinks she's not breathing, then he sees the slightest movement of her chest. There's a feeling of disgust welling up inside him. Towards the girl for giving herself up to the drug. And towards himself for looking at her.

Then the door into the room opens. Daz holds his breath. A man with a pierced eyebrow looks inside. He sees the girl, cocks his head.

'She's done,' he says. 'What did you sell her?'

There's an answering voice from deeper in the house. Too faint for Daz to make out.

The man shakes his head. 'It must be good shit. She's totally fucking slammed back.'

Then another man steps into the room. This one has his hair tied in a ponytail. He walks across to the bed, holds his hand just above her mouth for a moment. 'We'd better get her out of here.'

They take one arm each and pull her upright. She clings on to the ponytail man and says something into his shirt. The words are a meaningless blur.

'Come on, Vicky.' He gives her face one wake-up slap, then another. 'Time you were going home.'

Daz stands next to the stinking wheelie bin. He hears the front door slam, then listens to the men moving Vicky away from their house. Dragging and cajoling. When he can't hear their voices any more he steps out on to the street. They're already up the far end of the road, leaning her against the corner of the furthest building. He walks towards them. Quietly at first, then starting to scuff his feet as he gets closer. He wants them to see him, to assume he's heading home from a party.

They're on their way back now, about to pass him. They're not talking any more. He eyeballs them for a moment, and then looks down. A moment later and their conversation has started up again behind him.

Daz waits by the corner, judging time by the passing of cars on the main road. After the tenth vehicle, he walks back to the girl, Vicky.

'You all right?'

She gives him an empty stare. 'I'm shit tired.'

She pushes off from the wall and staggers forward along the road. Daz catches her arm to stop her falling. She tries to push him off. He keeps his grip tight.

'Where you live?' he asks.

She points into the vague distance ahead.

Daz is thinking as he walks. Trying to figure out what he should do. Vicky must have the money on her somewhere – whatever she didn't spend on junk. It's not in her pockets, that's for sure. Her jeans are so tight that he can see the outline of her keys. The money has to be in her shoes or under her loose-fitting shirt.

The other question that's nagging him is the coincidence of it all. Himself and Vicky. They both turned up at Patty's house at the same time, looking for the same thing. Coincidences demand answers. But perhaps this one isn't so difficult to explain. Vicky would have had to follow the same logic as him – holding back until the night after the police vacated Patty's house.

Whoever Vicky really is, she had a set of Patty's keys. And there was no searching for the money. She knew exactly where it was hidden.

The girl isn't moving forward any more. She leans one hand against the front door of the house they've stopped in front of, then fumbles her key into the lock. She shakes herself free of his grip, steps inside, then turns. Her eyes are looking right through his head and into a distance that only she can see.

'Bye.'

The door slams closed with Daz still on the outside.

Daz wakes at dawn shivering, feeling stiff in his elbows and knees. He's lying on the ground, weeds crushed under his body. He looks up and sees tall thistle plants on either side of him.

He remembers then, how he waited and watched at the back of Vicky's house. The upstairs light went on, then off. After a long time it turned on again. He must have fallen asleep then.

He stretches his arms, pushes himself into a kneeling position. It was too dark last night to make out any detail, so this is his first proper view of the garden. The whole thing is knee-high in thistles. Then he turns and sees that there is one patch clear of weeds. A couple of feet wide and twice as long again. And though it's got cut greenery laid over the top, he can still make out a gentle mound of freshly dug earth.

Chapter 8

It's hard to sleep in the daylight. Daz is lying on his mattress, wishing the thin curtains would do more to stop the sunlight. He doesn't know what time it is, but it must be early to judge by the hush on the streets.

He tries to forget his many questions. Patty. Her money. The girl, Vicky. The fresh grave. The thoughts cascade like clothes in a launderette tumble dryer. And he knows he'll never get to sleep.

He's woken by a soft knocking. He rolls over to see Freddy's face looking at him through the broken door panel.

'Are you awake?' she says.

She must be crouching to get down that low. He doesn't answer.

'I just got home,' she says. 'From the Club. Could we talk . . . about the other day . . . maybe later?'

He tries to speak, but his mind is still half in a dream and his mouth doesn't come up with anything more than a grunt. He closes his eyes.

'Come up to the flat this afternoon,' she says. 'You look tired. I'd better let you . . . you know.'

Then she's gone.

He can't remember all the things that happened the other night on the fire escape with Freddy. But the things he does remember he'd rather forget. Guilt is the dominant emotion here. And he's never given guilt much room in his life before. There were always other people to blame for the things that happened.

It isn't the kiss that's gnawing away at him. A kiss doesn't mean anything. It's like shaking someone's hand. The trouble is the way he'd wanted her – or whoever the woman was in his mind. Perhaps it was the cannabis, but it had seemed as if he could feel himself through her senses – his touch on her skin. He was so turned on he'd have done it all with her. He'd wanted to. He'd have betrayed Ginger, his friend.

He buries his head under the pillow. And as he starts to drift off into sleep again he gets an unexpected memory of a woman with short-cropped hair and green eyes. A woman on the wrong side of the Jobcentre counter.

It's knocking that wakes him a second time. Not loud, but firmer than Freddy's had been. There's traffic noise outside now. A constant rumble that sounds like the morning rush hour.

The knock comes again, louder this time. Daz can't see much through the hole in his door.

'Croxley?'

He sits up, his mind racing to work out what day it is. That was his landlord's voice. Raglan. There's money owing. He casts around the room for anything of value that needs to be hidden.

'Wakey-wakey.'

Daz is out of bed and pulling on his ripped 501s. There's something different about Raglan's voice today. It's quieter. But there's more than that. It's almost jovial.

'I won't bite, you know. You're quite safe.'

This is definitely strange. Daz struggles his head and arms into his T-shirt. 'Coming,' he says.

Raglan is waiting on the landing in his grey suit. Today's tie is floral. He has a lidded Styrofoam cup in each hand. He passes one of them to Daz.

'From Brucciani's.'

Daz sniffs the cup. 'Chocolate?' He doesn't know what else to say.

'They make the best cup in the East Midlands. Italians, you know.' Raglan steps past him into the room. He goes to the curtain and pulls it back, letting a bar of sunlight shine across the floor and up one wall. Then he turns and looks at Daz. He seems to be waiting for something. Daz pulls the top off his cup and sips. The liquid scalds the roof of his mouth. It's far too hot to be able to taste anything.

'Well?'

'Good,' says Daz.

Raglan nods in appreciation. He places his own cup on the windowsill. 'I need to let mine cool a bit. But you go ahead.'

Daz pretends to sip again. He's trying to figure out whether this is a new, subtle approach to torture or if his landlord really is trying to be pleasant. Neither option seems to fit with what he knows of the man's character.

'Where's Lady?' he asks.

'In the car.' Raglan actually seems pleased by Daz's concern. He looks out of the window, hands clasped behind him. 'I'll be taking her for a run later,' he says. Then, after a pause: 'The trouble we've been having between ourselves. The unpleasantness. It needn't be like that.' He turns his back to the window. 'You know?'

Daz busies himself with another pretend sip.

'A lot of people work for me. Perhaps you weren't aware of that. And not just the ones with tax reference numbers.'

The landlord steps forwards. Somehow Daz finds the new friendly Raglan more disturbing than the old bullying one. This is a different game and he doesn't know the rules.

'You could work for me.'

'The fifty quid a week?' Daz asks.

Raglan shakes his head. 'You move out.' He gestures towards the hole in the door panel. 'The place is falling to pieces, for God's sake. You don't want to live here. I'll find you another apartment. One without a redecoration charge.'

'Deposit?'

'We'll transfer it from here. Intact. How about that? And in exchange . . .'

Daz is tensed up so hard that the biceps of his good arm is starting to cramp.

'. . . in exchange . . .' Raglan moves back towards the window. He picks up his cup, peels off the top and inhales the steam. 'You get around the city,' he says. 'You see things in your wanderings that would be valuable for me to know about. That's all I ask – information. And I can pay.'

When Daz doesn't respond, Raglan adds: 'Don't worry about the Social Security. This is just between you and me. No one else will know.'

'What information?'

'Different things on different days. Nothing too difficult. And for that, a beautiful new apartment.'

'I like living here,' Daz says.

Raglan shakes his head. 'You *need* to move.'

Daz thinks about this. He wants to attack that idea. To ask questions. But he doesn't know how thick Raglan's new shell of politeness might be. He has a sense that much more pushing and cracks will start to appear. So instead he says: 'What you want to know?'

Raglan says: 'Good boy!'

And Daz is suddenly aware that he's passed through some kind of barrier. A doorway that was invisible from the other side.

Raglan puts a friendly hand on his bruised shoulder and leans closer. Daz tries not to flinch from the pain. 'The money you paid me with. You got it from Patty the Fence, right?'

This hits Daz harder than any of Raglan's hired muscle could have done. He hasn't told anyone where the money came from, but everyone seems to know. It feels like layers of his skin are being stripped away and Raglan is examining the flesh underneath.

'You don't have to hide it, boy. You're on my team now. The trouble we've got is this Patty business, right? She's gone and got herself killed or something.' Raglan gets closer still. His breath smells of mouthwash. 'I don't care what you sold her. I don't even need to know if you were the one who did for her. You just find out for me where the money came from that she paid you.'

Raglan's grip tenses on Daz's shoulder as he speaks, though whether he's doing it by design – like Bishop did – or accident, Daz isn't sure. Either way, he's not going to let Raglan see a reaction. The pain sharpens to a fierce point of heat. Like a soldering iron probing the muscle.

'You understand?' Raglan says.

'Money—' Daz's voice sounds ragged in his own ears '—or cash?'

'You're a bright lad. I knew you'd be best playing on my side. The cash, Croxley.' Raglan rubs a finger and thumb together. 'The folding purple. Find out where she got those twenties. And while we're about it – do you have any of those notes left?'

Raglan gives Daz's shoulder a final squeeze, then lets go.

The shock of release is so great that Daz inhales, involuntarily sucking air in over his clenched teeth.

'Yes.' The word escapes with the out-breath.

'You'd better let me look after them, then, Croxley. Yes?' He holds out his hand. 'A token of our new relationship.'

Daz crouches at his mattress, cursing silently as he reaches underneath. He gathers the two remaining twenties in his hand. The cash is important. He knows that now. The physical rectangles of paper with the queen's head smiling out. Unique serial numbers. He should have copied them out. If he loses them, his last connection to Patty will be gone.

There's no time to weigh up the decision. So in the middle of his movement, halfway between crouching and standing, with his hand still on the blind side from Raglan, he drops one note to the floor. And with the first placing of his foot, he covers it from view.

The landlord snatches the other note and pockets it without looking. Then he steps towards the door, taking a swallow from his Styrofoam cup as he goes. 'The dash of black coffee – that's what makes Brucciani's hot chocolate so good.'

'This house,' Daz calls after him. 'Why you want me out?'

Raglan turns in the doorway. He casts a look around the room and shakes his head. 'You can't stay here. That's all.'

'Why not?'

Raglan lances Daz with a stare. 'I'll be round tomorrow. Make sure you have something to tell me.'

Daz leaves his bedsit and bounds up the stairs towards the studio flat. Two steps at a time. Then one. He reaches the top landing and stops, one hand on the door. And he feels a contraction of his stomach muscles. An uneasy emptiness just below his ribs. A week ago he'd have woken them – told them everything. Today he turns and walks down the stairs, all the way to the street.

Daz went to a funeral once in a country church. The Jobcentre has always reminded him of that – lines of people waiting, no one speaking above a mutter, a tangible sense of shame. He sits at the back now, as he did then, in a chair set up against the back wall. From here he can see the entire room. The only differences are these – at the funeral he'd been the only one dressed in jeans, and there'd been the expectation that he'd sit on the front row with his father.

He watches and waits.

There's a queue away over on the right side of the room. The regular signing-on crowd, shuffling forward, hands in pockets. But not at the desks directly opposite. The men who go up to confess their sins there seem to know their order without queuing. He watches three men go up in turn. From their body language it looks as if they are answering questions. The first two take a long time to complete their business. The last one is over quickly. But each ends in the same way – with a sheet of paper being slipped across the desk, signed and returned.

Then the last one leaves. The woman who has been dealing with them leaves too. Daz gets up and advances across the waiting room.

He raps his good hand against the desk. No one comes. He knocks again, louder. Then he sees a button with some printed words next to it, black letters on white plastic, stuck down to the surface. He presses the button and hears a buzzer ring. Still no one comes. He presses again, but this time doesn't take his finger off. The buzzer note wavers, long and angry like a trapped wasp.

It's an Asian woman who comes at last. There's a scattering of crumbs on her creaseless blouse. She doesn't look happy.

'Yes?'

'Wanna talk to someone.'

'You have a letter of appointment?'

'She works here,' Daz says.

'You need a letter. If you don't have a letter you go over there,' she points. 'Line C or D. After two-thirty.'

'Then I get to see her?'

'Who?'

'She's got green eyes.'

The woman seems to notice the crumbs for the first time. She brushes them off with the back of her hand. 'Line C or D,' she says. Then she leaves.

Daz jams his thumb down on to the button and waits. The buzzer sings its uncomfortable, high-pitched note. Daz absorbs the sound, forming it into an emotion inside him. Insistent. Aggressive. He presses harder, soaking the feeling in.

There are voices somewhere in the back. He can't make out any words. An argument, perhaps. He considers tapping out a beat on the buzzer. Giving them some angry Morse signals. But the continuous note is better for his purpose. Unrelenting.

'I'll call security!'

It's the Asian woman again. No crumbs this time. She's got one fist on her hip. The other dangles, fingers working against the thumb. Daz releases the pressure from the button. The abrupt lack of buzzer is even more solid than its presence was.

'Is she here?' he asks.

'Line C or D.' She's emphasizing every word, as if talking to a particularly slow child. Daz feels good about that.

Emboldened by the prejudice in her judgement of what he is.

'Is she here?'

'What part of "Come back after two-thirty" don't you understand?'

'It's all right.' Green Eyes has come up silently. 'I'll deal with it.'

Something passes between the two women. Unspoken. The Asian woman leaves. Green Eyes looks down for a moment, then sits in her place. She's wearing a blouse like the other woman – pale blue. And a grey skirt. But she doesn't look comfortable in them. It's as if they were borrowed for an interview and never returned.

She looks up and fires a laser-beam stare at Daz.

'What the fuck do you think you're doing?'

That catches him off-balance. He's never before heard any of the Jobcentre staff swear. It wouldn't have occurred to him that they'd be capable of it.

'Wanted to see you.'

'You know how much trouble this is going to get me into? It's not as if I'm flavour of the month here anyway.' She shakes her head. 'You've got no idea!'

Daz tugs at the safety pins in his ear. 'I'll go.'

'No.' She bites the nail on her little finger for a moment. 'Now you've dropped me in the shit from a great height, I may as well know the reason.'

He sits down and looks at his hands. He's made a career out of winding up Jobcentre staff. But this one is different and he feels sorry.

'Go on,' she says. The playful warmth that he'd seen in her last time is all gone. 'I could do with a good tall story. They kidnapped you again?'

He looks up and catches her eye. 'Bit of a cow, isn't she?'

The woman purses her lips. She frowns. She puts her hand up to her mouth, and for a moment Daz thinks that she's starting to cry. Then a splutter escapes from her mouth, and the hardness of her face dissolves. Her laughter sounds fresh and clear to Daz. Beautiful as breaking glass. And as unexpected in the mausoleum of the Jobcentre.

She turns her hand so she can bite the skin between her thumb and fingers. The convulsions subside. She straightens her face and leans forward to speak. 'A major cow,' she whispers. 'Queen of all cows.' Then she sits back. There are teeth marks in the skin of her hand, changing from white to red as Daz watches.

'You look rough today,' she says.

'Thanks.'

'You're *most* welcome.'

He feels her gaze on him, over-aware of it. There are hints of shadow under her eyes again. The moment stretches.

Daz says: 'Didn't come to make trouble. Got enough of that already.'

'Then why?'

Now he's about to say it, his reason for coming to see her feels pathetic. He says it anyway. 'Needed someone to talk to.'

'Haven't you got any friends?'

He winces.

'I didn't mean it like that,' she says quickly, as if scolding herself.

'First time I came here, you said I could ask anything.'

'That's right.'

'Or tell anything.' He can feel the humour draining from the moment.

She nods.

'You have to report it – the stuff I tell you?'

'If you come to see me in office hours, and you tell me you've been working and signing – then, yes, I'll report it.' She looks at her watch. 'But it's my lunch break. Right now I'm just me. You've got twenty minutes before I change back into a monster.'

Daz leans forward. 'What's your name?'

She touches her name badge, as if checking that it's still there. He looks at it, then meets her eyes again and shakes his head. It's a tiny movement, a tremor. But it's enough. He sees understanding wash over her face.

She doesn't say she's sorry. She doesn't blurt it out or look away or do any of the things that people do. She just nods.

'I'm Katrina.'

'Kat,' he says.

'OK. Kat.'

He came here, intending to talk about hypothetical situations rather than the real thing. To hint. To bounce his own ideas against her and see how she reacted. That's what he was going to do right up to a few moments ago. But he's aware that something has just changed between them. Another barrier has been crossed.

He takes a deep breath and starts the story that he hasn't felt ready to tell anyone else. The whole thing. Getting money for Raglan. Patty the Fence. The man with his white Transit. When he gets to the riot, he keeps looking up to her face to check for expected disapproval. There isn't any, so he tells her about the looting as well and about getting beaten up.

Kat is sitting further forward as the story progresses. Daz describes his night visit to Patty's house, Vicky the junkie and the mound of freshly dug earth. Then Raglan's strange appearance at his bedsit a few hours ago.

'Then I came here,' he says.

Kat glances at her watch. 'Hell, but they should make a movie about you. I'm still not sure why you're telling me all this, though.'

'Want me to go?'

'No.'

She chews on her thumbnail for a moment. 'You can tell the landlord about the white Transit. That'll get him off your back. He'll give you a new flat. Then you can phone the police anonymously – from a call box. Tell them about Patty being buried in Vicky's back garden. Even if she isn't, they'll have to go and look.'

Daz shakes his head. 'That's what you'd do?'

'It's what a normal person would do.'

Daz holds her gaze.

'OK,' she says, holding up her hands in surrender. 'OK. OK. I'd want to know why everyone was asking where your cash came from.' She smacks her lips. 'But I never claimed to be normal.'

Which is exactly why he is so attracted to her.

He bends down, undoes his left boot and pulls a folded twenty-pound note out from next to his ankle. Then he flattens it on the desk.

'This is it?'

'Yup.'

'I thought Raglan took the last one from you.'

'So does he.'

Daz pushes it forward.

'Here's a turn-up for the books,' Kat says. 'Money doesn't usually cross the counter in this direction.'

'Need it back,' Daz says, alarmed.

She winks. Then she smoothes the note with the fingers of both hands. Narrow fingers. He sees that her nails are bitten shorter on one hand than the other.

'The other notes,' she says. 'Were they sequential?'

He shrugs. 'How d'you mean?'

She taps a finger on the paper. 'Serial numbers. If it's new money – straight from the bank – the numbers are in order.'

'Didn't see.'

Kat lifts the note to the light, pulling it taut. 'Looks genuine. Not that I'd know.' Then she puts it back on the counter, the other way up. There's a picture of a church on this side. And a man with a big moustache.

'What's this?' Kat says, pointing.

Daz looks. It's a splattering of bright-red spots next to the picture of the church. Small as pinheads but vivid. 'Dunno. Other notes had 'em too. More than this, even.'

Kat looks up at him, her green eyes alive with excitement. She gets close to the stick microphone and whispers. 'You know they've got security devices to mark cash if someone tries to steal it? Jets that spray out brightly coloured dye.'

She takes a Biro and copies the serial number on to the palm of her hand. Then she slips the note back across the desk. 'What's that slogan the police use?' she says. '*If it's stained it's stolen.*'

Daz walks out of the building, his mind jumping between Kat's words and the look she'd given him after he stood to leave. The Queen of Cows had been standing behind her, so there'd been no chance to follow it up. He'd have asked what she was doing after work and if she'd see him. She'd have held back, he guesses. But he'd have worked on her until she'd given him something. A hope, perhaps.

If it's stained it's stolen.

There's an empty Coke can on the Jobcentre steps. He

crushes it under his heel, absorbing the sound of crumpling metal.

The notes being stolen means nothing. A hundred and sixty pounds. Raglan wouldn't be bringing him hot chocolate for that. Daz jumps back in his mind to the day of the riot. He remembers Ginger taking the cash for him. Stained notes. Raglan would have seen that. But stolen money wouldn't have meant anything. How else did Raglan think Daz could get hold of fifty pounds by the end of the day?

Daz is walking down the road when he notices that a car is crawling level with him. And his first thought is that Bishop must have sent for him again. But then he looks properly and sees a man he doesn't recognize. A man with a strong jaw and bags of tired skin under his eyes. White.

'David Croxley?' says the man.

Daz sees past the car to the other side of the road. There's an alley he could skip down. His shoulder is feeling stronger today, even after Raglan's attention. And this man doesn't look fit. 'Shakespeare,' says the man. 'Superintendent Shakespeare. This might be a good time for you and me to go for a little ride.'

Daz has ridden in unmarked police cars before, but always in the back. And never with an officer as senior as this. He chews on his lower lip, waiting to be told what it is he's done wrong, looking for clues. But Shakespeare doesn't speak, and the only objects that he can see in the car are bits of paper with writing on them in the shelf under the glove compartment.

At first Daz thinks the superintendent is going to drive him to the police station, or perhaps back to the bedsit on Severn Street. But instead they take the turn for Waterfields.

Daz watches the people on the street without moving his head. Muslim men on their way to the mosque. Hindu women in bright saris. A tall black man with dreadlocks down to the small of his back. Some white and mixed youths carrying a football, heading up Dean Street past the mosque.

Then into the silence the superintendent says: 'The trouble with a riot – when you get down to questioning people afterwards – is that no one was ever there.'

On the edge of his vision, Daz sees the policeman glance at him. They're at the top of the road now, overlooking the park. Shakespeare pulls the car up outside the Majestic Hotel. 'Let's walk,' he says.

They take the path along the top. Below them the grass sweeps down towards a line of poplar trees. There are people around, but not many – a huddle of drunks off down the slope, a jogger making her way around the edge of the park.

'You know how many people we've managed to definitely identify as being in the riot?'

Daz doesn't answer.

'Twelve.' Shakespeare shakes his head and huffs a kind of half-laugh. 'Twelve! There must have been five hundred on the street – absolute minimum. I've seen reports from the Royal. The A and E had five people in with serious petrol burns that night. They all have to have been involved, right?'

Daz shrugs. 'I guess.'

'Wrong. Three claim to have hurt themselves fuelling up a lawnmower. At night!'

'Other two?' Daz asks.

'They were policemen.'

They've strolled halfway across the top of the park now, Daz keeping pace with the superintendent. The jogger is approaching. Her mousy hair is tied back. It swishes to left and right as she runs. Then she's past, leaving a waft of perfume in her wake. He listens to her footfalls getting fainter behind him.

'Twelve people at the riot,' Shakespeare says. 'And wouldn't you know it, they were all innocent bystanders, caught up in the crush.' He pauses for a moment, then says: 'But I know a thirteenth. That's you, David Croxley. And the reason I know you were there is because of the investigation into the disappearance of Agnes Wattling. I've read your statement.'

'Disappearance?'

'Do you have a problem with that?'

Daz wants to ask if there is any way for a missing person case to be upgraded to a murder investigation without a body being discovered. He could tell them about the mound of freshly dug earth in Vicky's back garden, but he'd have a big problem explaining how he knew about it. Especially if his fingerprints have turned up on the stolen computer.

'Who did you see at the riot, Croxley?'

Daz keeps his mouth closed.

'It's OK,' Shakespeare says. 'This is off the record. And I haven't told you your rights, so you're safe anyway. I couldn't use this conversation as evidence.'

They walk on another few paces before Daz speaks. 'Everyone else – they say they weren't there, right? Why you think I'm gunna squeal?'

'Because they were all going to be safe if they didn't speak. For you it's the other way around. You're linked in already via Agnes Wattling. What I'm offering is to keep your name out of the riot investigation – in exchange for a bit of cooperation.'

Daz stops walking. The superintendent turns and looks back at him. 'I'll make it easy for you. There was someone there out of place. Does that jog your memory at all?'

Daz nods. There's no question of loyalty here. 'Vince,' he says. 'Vince the Prince. Shouldn't have been in Waterfields. Isn't his run.'

Shakespeare steps back towards him. 'What did you see?'

Now Daz has said the name, he feels good about it. If the man gets put away it will only be for the best. The more information he gives, the more likely that is to happen. So he says: 'Vince and his gang. It's like they were getting the riot going. Dragging everyone in. Wouldn't have been big like that if it wasn't for them. At least, not so quick.'

The superintendent is standing close now, too close for Daz's comfort. He speaks quietly, though there isn't anyone within hailing distance. 'Good. You've told me now. And I'll do my part – keep the riot investigation off your back. But if someone does come and question you . . . another policeman—' He holds Daz's gaze '—if anyone asks about it, you keep your mouth shut. Understand? No mention of Vince or his gang. He wasn't there.'

Chapter 9

Daz has seen enough modern crime movies to know something about forensic science – or what it is supposed to be able to achieve. Latent fingerprints. Fibres matched with clothes. DNA from a drop of blood or a single hair. That's why he's brought lighter fluid with him.

The clothes he's wearing are new. Black T-shirt and tracksuit trousers. Navy-blue socks and plastic sandals. Everything smells of the shop. Everything as cheap and dark as he could find. He likes none of it. The good stuff – his boots, the lime-green jeans and an original Sex Pistols T-shirt – is all bundled inside a Sainsbury's bag, together with the can of butane and his disposable lighter.

It's all an investment. Fourteen pounds and change spent in the hope that he'll be able to clear his mind and find some balance in his feelings. Fear of the police cells on the one hand and on the other a residual loyalty for Patty that he hasn't yet been able to wipe away or explain.

It's well past two in the morning now. The traffic on the main road has ebbed to a trickle of cars heading out to the suburbs. No one is going into town. Except the police, of course. Patrol cars doing low-speed drive-bys. The occasional van with its windscreen grille up.

It didn't matter them seeing him back on St Peter's Road, but the closer he gets to his destination the more he finds himself wanting to look away as they approach. That's bad. It's always safer to look the police in the eye. So he cuts back through a side-alley to an area of derelict factories just behind the front row of shops. It's darker here, the streetlamps spaced far enough apart to leave voids between.

There are patches of scrub where Victorian mills once stood. The landscape is a chessboard of dead buildings and vacant lots overgrown with buddleia and thistle. Daz looks up at the first of the factories. Its brickwork carries the imprint of floors and chimneys from the buildings that must have been torn down to either side. It looks too narrow for its height. And the front and sides meet at an odd angle, not quite ninety degrees. He catches himself drinking in its beauty.

It feels strange to be enjoying this. But his senses have sharpened as he's walked further into the post-industrial wasteland. Perhaps it's the danger. The fear of the police. The fear of other people he might come across.

He breathes in through his nose. There's been a change in the air. A crossing of the dew point. The skin on his arms tightens. The hairs stand. A sparse gravel of broken brick crunches between his soles and the cracked pavement.

He's reached the halfway point between two streetlamps when he hears an engine change gear far away behind him, a car turning off the main road. He doesn't need to look back. There's no one he wants to meet at this time and in this place. So he drops himself to the pavement and rolls sideways to the wall of the building, covering the white plastic bag with his body, keeping his bare arms underneath him and his face pressed down to the ground.

The car engine growls closer. He can feel the headlights through his eyelids. Then the lights swing away and the car

starts to recede. Daz lifts his head to look, but it's gone –
though not far; he can still hear the engine somewhere
behind the factory. He scrambles to his feet, then steals
forward, brushing sharp gravel from his skin as he runs
under the dark brick of the railway bridge.

He's coming to the far edge of the old factories now.
There are the backs of terraced houses ahead of him across
another rectangle of thistles and fly-tipped rubbish. He stops
halfway, crouching low next to the silhouette of an old sofa.

He can't hear the prowling car now. He closes his eyes
and can just make out an anonymous rumble of engines far
away. A faint smell of mildew. A fox barks in a nearby street.
Daz has no sense of being followed.

He opens his eyes and looks at the brick wall ahead.
Seven feet tall. It marks the limit of the back gardens in the
row of houses where Vicky the heroin addict lives.

It's not just crime movies Daz watches. He's seen the full
range of horror flicks, including vampires, zombies and
every other kind of living dead. And he knows that people
who go digging up graves in the middle of the night are in
for trouble. He doesn't consciously believe that Patty's
fleshless hands are going to burst out of the earth and grab
him by the throat. His unease is less formed than that. It's
the combined fear of everything he is about to get into. The
possibility of his precautions not working – of being charged
with murder. Of being locked away. The creeping horror of
burial in one form or another. Different sources of dread
blurring and merging to form an amorphous disquiet.

Daz moves forward in a crouching run. Then he skirts the
wall, looking for a way to cross. He finds it in the form of a
broken milk crate, already propped against the brick. He
steps up on to it and, in spite of his shoulder, manages to
throw first a leg then his entire body over the top. He lands

with a jolt of pain and his hand sunk wrist-deep in soft earth.

His first reaction is instinctive. Driven by revulsion. He snatches his hand free, tries to shake off the clammy touch of the soil. Only when he's rolled away, skin needled with thistle spines, does the strangeness hit him – that he's landed in Vicky's garden out of the thirty-odd he might have chosen in the row. He's not superstitious, but the proximity of death is gnawing at the back of his mind.

He stands now, finds the patch of flattened weeds that mark the place where he slept the night before. He pulls out the disposable lighter, drops the rest of the things in his bag and turns to look at the mound of earth. But he's over-aware of the space behind him and can't focus his thoughts until he repositions himself with the cold brick of the wall pressing against his back.

Now he looks and sees, as before, the cut weeds laid over the mound. He's got the lighter set on maximum and the tall flame gutters. In that strobe-like light the greenery appears alive.

Everything focuses down on to this moment.

He's manoeuvred himself to the brink without letting himself think about the act itself. It's a trick he's played on himself before. He wouldn't have been able to take the first step otherwise. And if he bottles out at this point, it will all have been wasted. He drops himself to his knees, touches the earth again.

He imagines Patty, trying to think what she might say. *Don't mess with my grave, idiot!* He can hear her voice in his head, barking home-baked wisdom. *Remember rule ninety-nine: never disturb the dead after midnight.*

No. For all her irritability, Patty had a mind like a razor. There was no place in her life for sentiment. *What are you waiting for, boy? Afraid to get your hands dirty?* That was more like it.

Daz pushes his fingers through the surface and shovels a handful of soil to one side. The surface is dry. Lumps of soil hard, like small stones. But below a fingernail's depth it's moist and crumbly. He sits back on his heels, rubs earth between his fingers and thumb. It seems strange that it should be this way after so many days of baking sunshine.

You don't know what real work is, that's your problem!

'Shut up, Patty.'

He leans forward and sets to work, scooping with his hands. He had thought to search the outhouses for a spade, but the earth is so loosely packed that he doesn't need one yet. He's digging steadily, heaping the earth to one side. His end of the mound has become a hollow already.

He catches himself tensing as he plunges his hand in. His heart is beating hard. Breath coming too fast. He knows he's being stupid. There's no way he's going to touch a body. There would be a smell first. He'd know. He bends forward so his nose is just above the earth. Inhales dampness. Earth. And something else. He has a flash of awareness of his heart pounding high in his chest. His pulse throbbing in his neck.

'Oh, hell!'

A vaguely sweet odour hangs over the soil. The decay of flesh.

'Oh, shit!'

This is what you came for, idiot! What did you expect?

He reaches his hand down to the hole, inches his fingers into the yielding earth, every muscle in his body tensed. His hand is in as far as the second finger joint. He pushes deeper again. The cold rises to engulf his palm. Now he feels it. Not hard, but a different texture. He scoops the earth away. Some of it tumbles back down into the slope. He pulls out another handful of earth. And another. Racing to get it done. The crinkle of plastic sheet in the bottom as he grabs the soil clear.

He holds the lighter above the hole and between flickers of shadow catches the black reflective surface of a bin-liner. Shockingly clean between crumbs of earth.

He scrambles around to the opposite side of the hole. His back is to the house now, but he's past the stage of creeping fear. This is the horror of something that can be touched. The smell isn't any stronger than before, but he's aware of it now, focused on it. It is everywhere. In the pit, on his hands, coating the inside of his mouth. And there is a pressure in his bladder now. A need to piss. He clenches his stomach muscles, holding it back.

He reaches into the hole and presses his fingers down on to the plastic, fearing the slippery softness of decaying flesh. But needing to feel it anyway to transform his doubt. The plastic crinkles again. The lump underneath does not give. He presses harder on to the firm surface. He knocks his hand against it. Not as firm as wood. A bundle of newspaper, perhaps. A stack of magazines.

Daz shakes his head, trying to clear the tumble of thoughts. He rubs a soil-covered hand back through his hair. His mind is in the hole. Senses tunnelled towards the few inches of exposed smoothness. He holds the void in his head, oblivious now to the world around him.

Then he reaches forward with his good hand, digs his fingers into the plastic and rips them sideways. The object breaks free of its tomb, and though he can't see he knows that it's not body-sized. It's a roundish bundle no bigger than a head of lettuce. His fingers have torn through the wrapping. He can feel a loose flap of plastic. He fumbles for the lighter, holds it up and flicks the flame into life.

There in the pit he sees the bundle with a triangle of black plastic hanging limp to one side. And exposed in the rip he sees a face. The queen's face smiling from a twenty-pound note.

He reaches down to pull some of the money out of the bundle. But halfway through the movement he hears a crack and his body stops working for him. He pitches forward into the ground, blood running from a new wound in the back of his head, streaming across his cheek and dripping into the soil.

And the last thing he is aware of as he slips into unconsciousness is a scratchy voice close to his ear.

'Croxley, you idiot boy! Why did it have to be you?'

PART 2

*D*az had a strategy for dealing with his teachers in the days when he still went to school. He'd sit right at the back, pretend that everything was working. He'd get his head low to the desk, curve his left arm around the top of his writing book and make himself look busy. With thirty other kids to deal with, most teachers were happy to play along with the pretence.

It was a skill he started developing right back at the beginning. And he was bright enough to become an expert. It was like being a magician, misdirecting an audience. When they asked why he hadn't done his homework, he'd give them the answer they wanted to believe – that he was just bad beyond any redemption they could provide.

He didn't say it in those words, of course. He'd tell them that he'd lost his book, or that his father had made him do some other work, or that he'd forgotten. That way they'd have the satisfaction of thinking they'd seen through his lies. It was all a matter of keeping them happy.

He would probably have managed to keep it up all the way through school. But then came a teacher who was bright enough to pierce the deception.

It was the public humiliation that hurt him most of all. The standing out in front of the class, being told to read a photocopied text that everyone else had in front of them. Something really simple – perhaps Janet and John. He still doesn't know what it *was. She made sure there were no clues. No pictures. No way of guessing it from cold.*

Everyone in the class knew that he wasn't much good at reading and writing. No one but this teacher had sussed he was completely illiterate. Not till then.

In the weeks after that he started to get into real trouble. Truancy. Vandalism. Four months later they threw him out.

Chapter 10

'Roll him, dammit. Right over on his back.'

'I'm *trying*. Jesus!'

'Well, try harder, girl.'

'You should call a doctor or something.'

'No!'

There are nails pricking into the flesh of Daz's arm. The sensation of being dragged. Wetness on his face.

'Hold the torch still, dammit! He's coming round.'

Daz feels the light on him rather than sees it. He tries to open his eyes and finds that they're open already. There's a buzzing in his ears, a cramped-up sensation below his stomach – which feels familiar, though he can't quite name it.

'Who is he?' That's the younger voice. Vicky, he thinks.

'None of your business! Just get him up.'

Daz finds himself being lifted and folded into a kneeling position. There are hands under his armpits on either side. Then he's standing. The feeling in his stomach is stronger now. 'Need to piss,' he says.

'Trying to run before you can walk!' That's the older voice. She breathes a scratchy laugh.

'Patty?'

'Prop him against the wall,' she says. 'He can do it in the corner.'

'He won't manage,' says Vicky.

'Hold it for him if you want. That shouldn't bother someone like you!'

She doesn't. Daz finds himself leaning with his back against one wall and his shoulder against another. He fumbles with his zip, gets himself out, then relaxes, letting the pressure release. He's got questions pinging around inside his head. He can't even guess their number yet. They won't stay still enough to count.

Patty says: 'What are you doing, girl?'

Vicky says: 'Just looking.'

'Well, you can make yourself useful. Go inside. Get the kettle on.'

Daz tucks himself away and watches Vicky walk back into the house. He breathes deep, hoping the cool night air will sharpen him up. The kitchen light turns on, projecting a dull yellow bar across the yard and up the side wall.

He puts a hand to his face and feels the blood. Still wet. He can't have been out for long. He traces the path of it with his fingers, sideways along his cheek to a sticky mass in his hair, then to the back of his head. His fingers find the wound. It's not a big one, but it stings. 'Aow! Pig!'

'Keep your voice down!' Patty hisses.

'Who was it hit me?'

She tuts. 'How was I supposed to know that it was you?'

Then she steps across to the mound of earth and levers herself to a kneeling position. Daz hears her knees crack with the movement. She reaches into the hole and pulls out the wrapped bundle. Getting back to her feet is harder. She tries twice before turning her head towards him. 'What are you waiting for? Get over here!'

Daz steps over. She doesn't take the hand he offers, but grips his belt instead and pulls herself until her legs straighten.

'Bloody useless doctors.'

She's standing now, folding the flap of loose bin-liner plastic back over the rip Daz made in the bundle. He watches her for a moment.

'Thought you were dead,' he says.

'You're not getting rid of me that easily!' She purses her lips and looks daggers at him.

'What happened?' he asks.

'Questions, questions. It's always the same with you, Daz Croxley.'

'The money?'

'*My* money. Remember that. And what were you doing trying to steal it?'

Daz doesn't answer. He's still searching for a pattern in the jumble of new knowledge. A load of questions have vanished but another load have come into focus. And he's swimming in a new emotion. Though he's been confused about his feelings since the attack, seeing her alive has flooded him with relief.

'Why put it in the ground?' he asks.

'You don't know Vicky.'

'Hid it from *her*?'

'From my own niece, yes. Or from the junk she puts into herself.'

'Your niece?'

'My great-niece, if you must know.'

'She fetched the money, didn't she? Brought it here.'

Patty's eyebrows hunch forward. 'You've been spying on me, Croxley?'

He gives her a one-shoulder shrug.

She huffs. 'I sent her out for it. Only some of it came back here, though. Never, never trust an addict.'

'That one of your rules?'

'Perhaps it should be.' She laughs again. But her wheezy exhalation turns into a cough, which cascades into more coughs. She arches forward in their grip. Daz steps up to help but she waves him off. Slowly the convulsion subsides.

'You all right?'

'Of course I'm bloody all right!'

Daz stares at the earth mound.

Patty steps across and starts pushing the loose soil back into the hole with her foot. 'This was the one place she wasn't going to look. And Croxley comes and ruins it.' She pokes him with a glance. 'It's only been down there a few hours.'

'Thought it was a grave,' Daz says.

'It is a grave. My dog is under there. They killed him, the bastards.'

It's Kodak who's dead. The dog Dyson lies by the door to the back room, blocking the way. It manages to look up when Daz enters. But only for a moment. Then it rests its head back on its paws and closes its eyes. It doesn't growl. Not even when Daz steps over it.

The house layout is the same as Patty's. The standard unimproved terrace. But the furnishings here look like a cheap trawl through the charity shops. Nothing matches anything else – except in the respect that none of it is contemporary. There's a high-backed wicker chair from the early 1970s – in which Patty is sitting, nursing her tea. There's a dark sideboard from some time before the Second World War, far too bulky for the room. And a 1950s kitchen table with a yellow Formica top and three non-matching chairs. A Take That poster has partly escaped from the wall above the gas fire, and now hangs from three Blu-Tack corners.

Daz takes his mug from the table. It's cold. The shark's fin of a teabag circles slowly but doesn't do anything to colour the milky water. He drinks anyway. Three long, gulping draughts to clear the taint of soil and decay from his mouth. It doesn't work.

He's finding bits of the puzzle that fit together now. Blood in Patty's house. That was what started the police off on a murder hunt. But it couldn't have taken long for the forensic scientists to come back with the information that it was a dog that had been killed. After that, what did they have? A missing person and a stack of stolen consumer electronics. Investigation downgraded. All a bit embarrassing for the police.

Then there's the bundle that Patty buried in Vicky's garden. Money. And other things, he thinks. It wasn't the right shape to be just notes, and it looks more bulky than the wad that Vicky rescued from Patty's house. Some jewellery as well, perhaps. Or anything else that Vicky might be able to flog. He doesn't know where the package is now. Patty didn't have it when she came into the house.

'How did you find me?' she asks, breaking into his thoughts.

'Followed her back from your place.' He nods to where Vicky stands, pouting under the poster. She's dressed as if she's just been out. High-heeled boots. Matching skirt and halter-top. Wet-look fabric with a touch of glitter. Her skin is as white as his tea. But there is something familiar in her face. It is almost as if he's seeing an aspect of himself. He looks away.

'I didn't see him,' Vicky says.

'Idiot child!'

She flinches. 'It's not my fault!'

Patty makes a spitting sound, as if she's trying to remove a hair from the tip of her tongue. 'It's never her fault.'

'Well, it's not!'

'Typical addict!'

Daz looks down at the thin carpet. He hears Vicky's footsteps rushing from the room. The front door opens and slams. There's a long space after that, which begs to be filled with words. Daz scrunches his toes inside his boots. He watches Patty take a slurp of her tea. She makes a noise of general disgust then puts it to one side. It sloshes a crescent of milky water on to the tabletop. She levers herself to her feet.

'You're thinking I'm too hard on her,' she says.

Daz doesn't answer.

'She stole from me.'

'The money she took,' Daz says. 'It's the same lot as what you paid me from?'

Patty narrows her eyes. 'What if it was?'

'Dunno,' he says. 'Just thinking.'

'Are you being straight with me, boy?'

He's not being straight. But he still hasn't decided how much to tell her about the money. *If it's stained it's stolen.* Raglan. Bishop. The recycling centre.

He rolls his bruised shoulder, feeling the pain, dull now after so many days, but still strong enough to help him remember the beating outside her old house. It's been a week now. He raises a hand to touch the new wound on the back of his head. The blood is dry already. Cleaning it up is going to be hell. But he's had worse.

'I didn't know it was you,' she says suddenly. 'I'm—'

He thinks she's going to say she's sorry. He waits to hear the word but it doesn't come.

'You looked different,' she says. 'That's all. It's your clothes. Why do you want to creep around dressed like that, eh?'

He'd forgotten the clothes. His bag of belongings must still be out in the garden where he dropped it.

'That bloke,' he says. 'Knew he was gunna beat me up, didn't you?'

'That?' she asks. 'You're still sore about that?'

'Could have killed me.'

She shakes her head. 'You're a fool if you think I'd let him kill you. Not outside my own front door. I'd have had the police all over me. Asking questions.'

'Knew he was waiting for me, right?'

She pushes on the arms of the wicker chair, levering herself into a standing position. Then she turns to look at her mug on the table.

'I knew, yes. He'd come looking for you a few minutes earlier. But he said he was just going to get things straight. He said you'd taken the computer from him. He was going to talk, not fight – that's what he said. It wasn't my business anyway.'

'Not your business . . .'

Patty clasps her hands. 'At least I called the ambulance.'

'Thanks a million.'

'Then what did you do?' She wheels at him. 'You went and told someone I'd given you the money!'

The anger in her voice hits him. 'Did not!'

'Tell that to Kodak.'

Daz pulls at the safety pins in his ear.

Patty steps towards him. 'Twenty-four hours after I paid you, a man called, saying you'd sent him. I was a fool to take the door off the chain. But it was your name. I thought . . .' She shakes her head. 'He had a big hunting knife inside his jacket. He wanted the rest of the money I'd paid you from.'

'How did you get away?'

'Kodak.' Patty turns and looks away. She pulls a tissue from her sleeve and blows her nose. Then she looks back at him. 'Just tell me why you let someone else know about our business. You broke our Rule Two.'

'Never did!'

Patty holds his gaze. She steps forward. 'If I found you were lying to me . . . I'd kill you, Daz Croxley.'

He doesn't let go of her stare. 'Stolen, isn't it, the money you gave me.'

'What if it is?'

'Weird shit's been happening since I paid off Raglan with it.'

Patty narrows her eyes. 'Go on . . .'

'Been threatened. Been kidnapped. They all want to know about the money. But I never told no one.'

'Then perhaps we've both got an axe to grind.' She pauses, scowls in thought for a moment, then says: 'If there's a pot of stolen money somewhere out there, we may as well be the ones to find it. You'll have to tell me everything you know.'

'Gunna tell me everything *you* know?'

She shakes her head. 'I know more than you ever will, boy. But I'll tell you what you need. It'll be a fair trade.'

Dawn still isn't showing over the jagged line of factory roofs that forms the horizon. Daz finds his bag of clothes in the back garden. Something else as well – a short length of timber propped against the brick. It's too convenient to be random. He steps up on to it and swings his other leg over the top of the wall. The broken milk crate matches it on the other side. A back entrance on to the wasteland. Vicky thinking ahead, he guesses. An escape route in case any unwelcome guests come calling. Booze-heads can be amateurs. But not junkies. You have to be resourceful to keep a smack habit going.

Daz picks his way through the thistle ground. Halfway across he stops and strips from the new trousers and T-shirt, dropping them in a heap. His old clothes feel good. His own smell.

There's no need to dispose of the new stuff now. No forensic team is going to crawl over Vicky's garden. But he'd promised himself this moment – a reward for all he's gone through tonight. So he takes the can of butane and squirts it on to the pile until the fabric glistens. The sharp smell of solvent is in his nose. He flicks the lighter, watches the yellow-orange flame catch and grow. He feels the heat on his skin. And his heart speeds with the exhilaration of the sacrifice.

Chapter 11

The clock tower. A carved sandstone arrow pointing to the blue sky. A five-ways crossroads at the centre of the city, all but paved in by creeping pedestrianization. Daz scans the area. Doesn't find the face he is looking for. So he sits on a bench, out of the flow of people.

Watching the crowds is like staring into a river. First you look at the movement of it. That's all you can see. Then it starts to blur, and you notice the little islands of stillness. Like the woman with braided pink hair, selling the *Big Issue* next to the shoe shop. Or the huddle of men in leather jackets – Turkish, perhaps, or Albanian – heads close together, breathing secrets and cigarette smoke. Over by the clock tower itself, he sees a white man with a flip-chart and a microphone talking about Jesus. And in a diffuse semicircle around him, other white men and women standing listening. Unfaded jeans. Smart casuals. Sheep from the same flock.

'Dazzo, my man!'

Ginger comes around the bench, catches Daz's raised hand and hauls him to his feet.

'Hey.'

'We're gunna hit the shops, right?'

Daz shrugs. 'You buy. I'll watch.'

They press through the jostle, bumping shoulders. Along the High Street, squeezing past the bus queues, past Irish

Menswear. This is the bit of the city centre that Daz likes best. Small shops. Individual. The prim and the wicked cheek by jowl. If there was a reason for money, beyond just getting by, then it would be to spend it in places like this.

Ginger is examining the display in the window of Tin Fish. Absorbed. Daz looks at the back of his friend's head. Watching other people spend money isn't so much fun. He wouldn't usually have come on one of Ginger's famous shopping odysseys. But he's not felt comfortable with the man for the last couple of days. Not since his clinch with Freddy on the fire escape. The taste of her is still splashed over the back of his consciousness somewhere. Daz knows he needs time with his friend to clear it away. Time away from her.

'You see them?'

Ginger is pointing to a pair of shoes in the display. Black leather. Beautiful.

Daz pulls a face, scrunching the top of his nose. 'Nah.'

'You *know* I've got to try them.'

So he does. They go inside. Ginger gets the assistant to fetch a pair in his size. They are Italian leather brogues, she tells him. He laces them, oozing satisfaction. Daz watches as he steps down the length of the shop, more dance than walk. The other customers stop looking at their own shoes and watch his instead.

Ginger pulls a credit card from his wallet. 'This is a must-have buy.'

Next stop is Another World. Daz has never bought anything here, but he loves the counterculture feel of the place. Martial arts hardware, *Star Trek* models, magazines on fetish clothing. Upstairs, a whole floor devoted to computer games. He takes a magazine from the shelf. Tattoos and body art. A five-quid glossy. The cover, a shaven-headed woman with black eyeliner and three spikes jutting out from the skin under her lower lip. She's stunning. Ginger takes it from his hand and carries it to the counter, along with a DVD he's picked up for himself. The man on the till swipes his card.

'Didn't need to do that,' Daz says, as they step out on to Silver Street again.

'You like it, don't you?'

'Sure, but—'

'But nothing.' Ginger puts the shop bag into Daz's hand. 'It's yours.'

Daz doesn't say what he thinks – that it was enough just to look.

At the back of his mind he's got the idea that he should perhaps tell Ginger about the other night. Explain that it was just the cannabis. The painkillers. He hadn't planned it. He just found himself kissing her. Dream-like. Just warmth and touching and excitement. Recognizing the smell of her – on one level of his mind. But at the same time thinking that she was someone else. Then it was over. He knew what had happened, and he was dying with the guilt of it.

He thinks that perhaps if he says it, then the guilt will go. And once it's out in the open, he feels sure it won't happen again. Freddy will keep more distance between them. And Ginger won't offer gifts like this.

A debt of guilt and a debt of goods, multiplying each other.

They've reached St Martin's Square now. There's an open-air music stall here. Ginger is walking his fingers through the lines of CDs on the barrow. Daz is trying to work out what words he's going to use to confess to his friend. How to make it seem not as bad as it was.

Ginger looks up at the stallholder. 'You take credit cards?'

The man taps a handwritten sign on the till. 'Sorry, mate.'

Ginger slots back the discs he'd selected.

Daz knows he can't say how good the kiss felt. But he's going to say all the rest. Say it straight. He takes a series of quick breaths.

Ginger turns suddenly, his face serious. 'You know how Freddy is,' he says.

Daz feels his neck and cheeks warming. But Ginger doesn't appear to notice. He drops his gaze to the pavement between them.

'She's special, you know. Different. I've never met another one like her, Daz. And I don't know what I'd do . . .' He shakes his head, then looks up.

Daz feels his sweat cooling.

'*You* know her,' Ginger says. 'She lights everything up. If she's in a party, everyone . . . it's just different with her in the room.'

'Don't need to tell me,' Daz says. His resolve has frozen over. All he wants to do now is change the subject, to move on to some other shop. 'Come on. Let's—'

Ginger grabs Daz's wrist, pulling him back. 'I need to tell you this – so you don't think I'm losing it.'

'Never thought that!'

'She's got problems,' Ginger says. 'It's a kind of insecurity thing right down inside her. From stuff that happened when she was a kid. That's why she shines so bright – so people will shine back at her. We both work on stage. But it's different for me. If I give a good performance, I'm happy. It's enough. But for her – if the audience is flat she gets this real black mood after.'

'Likes people,' Daz says. 'That's all. Extrovert, yeah?' He prises his wrist free, takes a backward step, trying to draw his friend away from the music stall to some other shop. Anything to distract him from this conversation.

'Let's go get a coffee or something.'

Ginger isn't following. 'She flirts, you know? Sometimes. When she's in a flat mood. It's so she can feel loved. But it's not real. It's just that she's different.'

'Why you telling me?' Daz asks.

'So you know why I have to spend on her. That's all.'

Then Ginger smiles. Relieved, Daz thinks – as if he's just unloaded some baggage that was weighing him down. Daz feels his own load increase.

'Come on,' Ginger says. 'Let's go look round Voodoo.'

They've gone ten paces when he glances across at Daz again. 'Shit. I've been yakking on about me. Haven't even asked about all the police stuff. Anyone figured where the old woman went yet?'

'Patty?' Daz looks away. 'Nah. Dead or something, most like.'

And that feels like another betrayal.

Patty is alive, but her skin looks grey. She's sitting on a kitchen chair in Vicky's rear yard, under the angled shadow of the back wall. The last of the cigarette in her mouth is burned up in a thirsty inhalation. She flicks the filter tip on to the soil.

Daz counts three stubbed-out butt ends near her feet. 'You OK?' he says.

She coughs a cloud of tobacco smoke through her clenched fist. A cough that seems to come from somewhere in her stomach. It takes a moment for her to catch her breath.

'Stop fussing, boy!'

'Just asking.'

She waves away his protest, then pulls out a handkerchief from her sleeve and dabs at the corner of her eye. 'We both know something about where that money came from,' she says. 'And I suppose it's your business to know the rest, seeing as you've got yourself tangled up in all this trouble. So we'd better settle on a split, before we start.'

'Split?'

Patty refolds her handkerchief and prods it back into her sleeve. 'Thirty–seventy,' she says. 'That's fair, seeing as you haven't got my experience.'

Daz can't get to grips with the idea of dividing money that he doesn't believe they will ever get to see. He doesn't even know if he wants to go searching for it. His only concern is to get Raglan and Bishop off his back.

But still, the idea of his worth being less than hers seems wrong.

'Well?' she says.

'No way!'

'Sixty-five–thirty-five, then.'

Daz twists the safety pins in his ear, feeling the metal tug on his skin.

Patty spits on the ground. 'Sixty–forty. Last offer. Any lower and I'd be insulting myself.' She holds out a withered hand. Then she coughs again. And this cough racks her whole body, leaving her panting. Daz looks at her for a moment. Then he holds out his own hand. The skin on her fingers is as rough as dry brick. She nods, a faint gleam of satisfaction in her eyes. And suddenly he wonders if the cough was put on. A ploy to soften him up in the negotiation. He tries to put the idea out of his mind.

'That man,' she says. 'You carried the Samsung wide-screen to his van. He's been a customer of mine for a few years now. Don't know his name, of course. He used to bring things to me. First it was old VCR machines, then he got into computers. They were all scabby things, really. Looked like they'd come out of a skip. But two months ago it changed. He started buying up all the consumer electronics I had. Vanloads of expensive stuff. Carting it off. He always had cash and he never used to bargain. I didn't trust him as far as I could spit.'

'Why deal with him, then?'

Patty looks at Daz and shakes her head. 'Idiot boy.' Then she reaches for the box of cigarettes on the ground next to her chair. She shakes one out, lights up with a match.

'It was like taking sweets,' she says. 'He was too green to be in this game. I could see that his money must have been stolen, but why should that have stopped me? It's easier to handle dirty money than dirty goods. I should know. And, anyway, it would only have ended up filling someone else's pocket if I hadn't taken it.'

Daz thinks about this. There's so much about money that he doesn't understand. He sits himself on the soil with his back to the side wall of the garden, his legs and feet in sunshine. He picks up a stone and turns it in his hand. 'Buys that much gear, he's gotta be selling it, right?'

'Of course he's selling it. He doesn't want twenty wide-screen televisions for himself! But if it was just trading, then why didn't he press me for a better price? I'll tell you why – he's devised some scheme to launder the cash. An electronics shop somewhere. In another city – I'd know if it was in Leicester. Turning dirty money into dirty goods. And turning dirty goods into clean cash from the punters.'

She rattles another tubercular-sounding cough into her fist.

Daz waits for her to finish. He tosses the stone on to the ground. It skips to one side, coming to rest at the edge of Kodak's grave. Then he says: 'Gotta be going somewhere else, hasn't he? Now you're disappeared.'

'Perhaps.' She doesn't look convinced.

'Perhaps?'

Patty sighs smoke. 'Perhaps.' This time Daz is sure she doesn't believe it.

'What, then?'

'How am I supposed to know that, boy? Anyway, the important thing is this. There was enough money for him to set up a laundering scheme. You just think about that.'

He stares at the ground between his knees, trying to work out how Patty always manages to end up on top. Perhaps, he thinks, it's because she always tries harder than the people she deals with. But that doesn't seem to be the whole reason. So he asks: 'What's your rule number one?'

'I'll tell you,' she says. 'Seeing as we're partners now. The first rule is this – everything has a price. And everyone. Now you tell me what you've discovered.'

The taxi pulls up at the entrance to Western Park. Patty seems to need help getting out. Daz offers his arm, but she bats it away with an exhalation of disgust. It takes three tries, but she eventually manages to rock herself up into a standing position, one hand clinging to the top of the door. Daz pays the driver out of Patty's purse. She doesn't blink until he hands it back. Then they move on up a short path to the recycling centre.

Mark is working there like before. He waves when he sees them. 'You came.'

Daz casts around the place. 'Course.'

'It's late. I thought you'd given up on me.'

The sorting machine isn't on, so the place is soaking in a peaceful silence and a heady smell of fermentation.

'Introduce me, boy!'

Daz hunches his shoulders and looks between the two. 'Mark. Patty.'

Mark grins towards the old woman. 'Are you after that bloke as well – the one with the white Transit?'

'What if I am?'

'If you were, you'd be in luck, that's all.' Mark shoots Daz a quizzical look, as if to ask what a punk and a Crimplene-wearing pensioner could possibly be doing together.

'My great-aunt,' Daz says.

Mark's eyes jump from Daz to Patty and back, as if searching for a family resemblance. He nods, apparently satisfied.

Patty prods his arm with a finger, pulling his attention. 'Why am I in luck?'

'It's past four,' Mark says. 'We'll be closing soon but he's still not been. It'll be in the next few minutes – if he's coming at all. I don't suppose there's any point in asking why you two would be wanting to track him down?'

Daz looks to Patty.

Patty purses her lips to form a generally unfriendly and uncooperative expression.

After a couple of very long seconds, Mark shrugs. 'Just asking. But it's hard to help if I don't know what's going on. Like—' He leans back against the wall '—like I don't even know if it's the van or the man you're interested in.'

'One leads to the other,' Patty says.

'So the driver has something you want. But does he know

you're looking for him? I'm only asking because . . . if he's going to run off the moment he sees you, I won't be having to write out a cheque for him.'

Patty looks at Daz.

'Money for the cans,' Daz explains.

'A month's worth of cans,' Mark says. 'Plus whatever he brings today. He's a very keen recycler.'

Daz wants to ask if there is a place where they could watch unseen. He glances into the recycling shed, casting around the back for a place to hide. He sees a fire-exit door in the side wall.

'What's his name?' Patty says. 'Who will you make the cheque out to?'

Mark laughs. 'You don't give up so easily, do you?'

Daz hears the chug of a diesel engine entering the car park behind him.

Mark is looking over his shoulder. 'Talk of the devil. Now you can ask him yourself.'

Daz doesn't turn. He takes Patty's hand and pulls her, protesting, towards the back of the recycling shed.

'Will you let go of me!'

They're at the fire exit now, partly shielded from view by a rack of reclaimed timber. Daz risks turning to look. The white Transit is reversing towards the open front of the building. It stops a few paces short. The engine cuts and the driver climbs out.

Daz recognizes the figure from the time at Patty's house before the riot. Too wide in the stomach for his height. A short-sleeved shirt. A narrow tie. There are sweat stains under his arms today. He opens up the back of the van, revealing a heap of stuffed bin-bags. Mark shakes his hand. The two men are talking together.

Daz tries the door. It opens. He takes Patty's hand again.

She shakes free of his grip, then leads him out to the sunshine at the side of the building.

'Now what?' he says.

But Patty has already started to pick her way around the outside of the building.

'Now what?' he says again, then follows her along the wall towards the front of the building. He can see the Transit from here. He can hear the clank of cans being loaded into the sorting machine. Patty is standing as far forward as possible without actually stepping out and revealing herself.

Daz moves up close, ignoring her hand, which is waving him back. He hears the sacks of cans being ferried into the shed. Suddenly, Patty grabs his wrist and pulls him forward.

'Move!' She hisses the word.

Daz resists.

'Into the van! Before he comes back.'

'But—'

Daz stumbles out into the open. Events are happening too fast for him to think them through. Mark and the man have finished unloading. Daz glances back at Patty. She stabs her finger towards the open back of the Transit and mouths 'get in'. He starts to do as he's told, still not sure why. He can see Mark and the man inside the shed, bending over some paperwork. And Patty's face by the corner of the building. He eases one of the rear doors closed to give himself some cover. Mark must have caught the movement, because he glances up, an expression of alarm on his face.

Daz squeezes himself into the shelter of the door, knowing he's been seen. There are footsteps approaching. Then Mark's voice, an urgent whisper.

'What the hell are you doing?'

'Close the door,' Daz hisses back.

'And where's your aunt?'

'Close the door.'

'This is not happening!'

'And tell me his name,' Daz whispers.

But there isn't time for Mark to reply. More footsteps approach. Mark swings the second door closed. Daz sees the catch mechanism extend into the lock position.

'That's it for another week,' says a voice outside.

Then comes Mark's reply. 'It certainly is, Mr Salt. Take care.'

Daz repeats the name under his breath. 'Salt.'

It's hot inside Salt's van. The floor is sticky and the smell of fermenting sugar is strong enough to make him feel short of breath. There doesn't seem to be any ventilation back here. The cab is sealed off with a Perspex screen, fogged with scratches. Daz scrambles forward until he is directly behind the driver's seat. He hears a door open, then slam. The engine starts and the Transit lurches forward.

The first turn is easy to follow. The van swings left out of the car park, down the hill towards the city centre. There's a stop for traffic lights, then a climb and another descent. If he could look out of the window, he knows he'd be able to see the city centre from here. The spire of St Mary de Castro. The Lego-like block of the city council offices. As it is, he has to track the journey through the way his body is thrown left and right.

He's got himself wedged in now, feet on the sliding side door, one hand on the opposite wall. It's a good position, but tiring, because he has to brace himself for turns that might take place at any moment.

More traffic light stops. Then on to King Richards Road, he thinks. Two turns follow, a long right and a shorter, sharper left. That puts him on the clockwise lane of the inner ring road.

He's feeling pleased with himself. But doubt has started to grow in the back of his mind. What if Salt parks the Transit somewhere and locks all the doors? It might be days before he came back to fetch it. Daz could starve. Or suffocate.

And now they're on the inner ring, he's started to lose track of their position. There's no way to guess the distance they've travelled. He tries to get some clues from the rear windows, but there's so much grime coating the outside of the van that all he can see are patches of light and shadow.

Suddenly the van is veering left. The movement catches Daz unprepared. His arm buckles and he slides across the metal floor. His head crashes into the wall. He rolls himself back behind the driver's seat. But Salt must have heard the noise. Daz feels the van slowing. Changing down through the gears. The creak of the handbrake. He can see the shadow of Salt's head against the plastic screen above him. The man is peering into the back. Daz holds his breath.

The moment stretches. Then they're moving again.

There's something new in the air now, strong enough to be smelled over the stink of fermenting sugar in the van. A spice of some kind. It takes him a moment to work out that it is cinnamon. This brings two thoughts. First, that there's a spice-milling plant somewhere off the Belgrave Road. And second that he's not going to suffocate because some outside air is definitely getting to his nose.

The turns are coming rapidly now. And the van isn't getting above third gear. Another sharp corner. Slowing down. First gear. The engine is suddenly loud, as if they've driven into an enclosed space. Then it stops. The door slams and Daz is left with his ears ringing in the silence.

When he can't bear the waiting any more, Daz gets up on his knees and peers out through the front window. All he can see through the fog of scratches is a brick wall. The back window shows him nothing. He tries the door mechanism. It clunks open.

The van is parked in a narrow passage linking the road outside to a yard. Daz can feel the uneven cobbles under his boots. He looks up at an arched roof of blackened brick. Victorian. Industrial.

He crouches low and skirts the van so he can look into the yard without being seen. Three of the enclosing walls seem to be the backs of factories or houses. Only the fourth wall has a door and windows at ground level. It looks like a small factory or workshop. The glass is all papered over with sheets of tabloid newspapers, topless women and jumbles of words.

Daz moves forward till he's level with the driver's door. There's no sign or sound of activity.

He's not sure what he expected to see in the workshop, but it wasn't this. Apart from a workbench at the far end, the floor space is entirely taken up with broken concrete pieces, some with protruding metal rods.

Daz's first reaction is to look up at the roof, to see if there has been some kind of collapse. But these are the smashed-up remains of a reinforced concrete structure, not a Victorian factory. He picks his way across the room towards the workbench.

There's a pillar drill here, plugged in to an electric wall socket, a selection of hammers, cold chisels. Daz runs his finger over the bench near the drill. Everything is covered in fine concrete dust.

Daz knows the direction that time moves in, but he can never work out the speed. He sometimes sees himself as a man wandering through a huge sandy desert. He knows he's going forward, but there are no landmarks, no means of gauging how fast or slowly he is travelling.

It's like that for him now. In a room with a puzzle. He knows the afternoon is moving forward, and that Salt could return at any time. But it's easier not to worry. So he disengages his time-anxiety and thinks instead about the blocks of concrete.

He starts with the biggest piece. A two-yard-long chunk, perfectly flat to one side and on the top. The regular surfaces meet at an angle greater than ninety degrees – as if the block was once part of a polygonal column that now rests on its side. Iron reinforcing bars poking out of broken surfaces to left and right. The cut ends of the bars don't look rough. Daz feels the texture of the surface with one finger. The cut of a welding torch, perhaps.

He runs his hand over the end section of the block. There's another large chunk away to his left. A quarter-ton, perhaps. In his mind, he lifts it, brings it close to the first chunk so he can feel for a fit. He turns it by ninety degrees, flips it end over end, then tries again. This time it's a match. The two blocks form a section of a hexagonal prism. An irregular hexagon. He hasn't seen anything like this before. Some kind of modern architecture. More style than function.

He jumps on top of the larger block, looks down on the rubble around him, searching. He finds what he's looking for in what appears to be another section of the same column. This one ends in a smooth, concave fracture – distinctive enough to work with. He jumps down and starts prowling around the room, looking for the convex shape that will make the block whole again. It takes him longer to find this because the surface is jammed up against the wall of the room, hidden from view. He reaches his hand into a gap, feels the shape and he knows it's a match.

He picks his way back across the room, stepping block to block. There's a cut on his forearm. He probably caught it on the sharp end of a metal rod, or a corner of concrete – though he didn't notice it happening. He licks the blood as he looks for his next target.

In Daz's mind a shape is starting to form. He knows he won't be able to fit every lump into it – a significant quantity of the concrete seems to have been reduced to sand, which is piled up on the floor in drifts. But he's already gleaned enough from the major blocks to start working out the form.

He's looking at demolition remains from a modern building. Enough to fill a couple of large skips, now inexplicably spread over the floor of a large workshop. One puzzle is how the blocks were brought into the building. But then he sees a set of tyre tracks in the dust and figures that a forklift truck could have been used. The doorway looks wide enough.

But the more he thinks about this puzzle, the more the scene feels wrong. The amount of dust and sand is too great compared with the volume of large blocks. The floor is inches deep in sand. But there's nothing of intermediate size. No rubble. No fist-sized lumps. Nothing, in fact, between sand and monolith.

There's a rusty six-inch nail lying on the workbench. Daz takes it, crouches next to a block the size of a wheelie bin and starts to scratch. At first he prods at it, loosening a few grains. The smooth surface crumbles easily and he starts to gouge hard, sending out showers of sand with each stab of the nail.

He's scratched patterns on concrete before – on the walls of multi-storey car parks, at the back of the school bike sheds. But he's never before seen concrete as easy to crumble as this.

Chapter 12

Damp, night-time smells. The air cool enough to taste. Daz feels the can with his fingers – lifts its satisfying weight. Tesco Economy Dog Food. He fits the rotary tin-opener in place, squeezes its arms together. The blade punctures the metal with a sigh.

He's sitting in his bedsit window, bare feet resting on the metal fire escape. He takes a spoon from his pocket, digs it into the meat and jelly. Smells. He's often thought about eating the stuff himself. The fox loves it – and that's an animal that he respects. It's cheap, too, compared with the tinned stew – which he guesses is the nearest human equivalent. Thirty-something pence instead of a couple of pounds.

Daz excavates a spoonful. He's hungry tonight. Salivating. But the closer he moves the jellied meat to his mouth, the more the idea turns his stomach. He's heard stories about the kind of stuff they put in dog food.

He puts the spoon back in the tin, peers out into the back yard, trying to penetrate the shadows. And he waits. He's sure the fox will come again tonight. He's been feeding it regularly. Each time it comes more easily, tolerates his touch for longer. In the contact, Daz finds the kind of peace that's been missing in his life since Raglan started menacing him for money.

Foxes don't worry.

Daz turns the spoon in the can, idly mixing its contents. There's so much on his mind that he needs to get straight. Knowledge, wild guesses, premonitions. He feels as if he has become snarled in the threads of several different stories. He is aware of loops and tangles and loose ends, but he isn't sure which belongs to which or how to untie them in his mind.

Somewhere in the middle of the tangle is a vague sense of unease at the state of his friendship with Ginger. He's known the dancers upstairs for a couple of years. He first met them through the Club. Them moving into the same house as him was a coincidence. A good coincidence because they were always friendly. And they never asked too many questions. It was comfortable.

First his relationship was with the two of them. But after a time he started hanging around with Ginger. That was different. Two blokes together. Sharing a laugh and a love of wild clothing. Things changed so slowly that he didn't notice it happening. He'd go up to the attic room and find Ginger was out shopping. But he'd stay to talk to Freddy anyway. They got closer. Like brother and sister, almost – that's how he'd seen it. He was comfortable with that.

But there comes a moment when you see something and you get given a bit of knowledge that you'd rather not have had. You can never un-know it. Freddy's need to be the centre of attention. Ginger spoke the words, and Daz listened. But as soon as he heard it, it was like he'd known it all along. The dancing on stage. The flirting off it. Daz looks into the shadows and wonders.

Perhaps, if he wishes hard enough, she'll just go away. Ginger will come and knock on his door and tell him that she's left. Perhaps everyone would be happier that way. In the end. So he scoops a spoonful of mushed dog food from the can and flicks it into the night. And as it flies he makes a wish that Freddy will get out of his life. He hears it splat on the slabs below. Then he hears a knock at his door.

'It's open.'

He figures that it has to be one of them. And the way his luck is running, it's probably her. But he doesn't turn to see. The door opens, then closes. He counts the pulse beats in his chest, feeling the shape of the two possibilities. Then he smells the perfume, a heady-sweet scent – like almond or coconut flesh or something else he can't quite identify except to say that it is entirely *her*. He inhales deeply, unable to tell her to go.

She slips herself through the gap and sits beside him on the windowsill. Her shoulder is touching his. She looks into the darkness, following his gaze. He listens to her breathing.

'Is it there?' she whispers.

It takes a moment for her words to make sense in Daz's mind. 'The fox?' He shakes his head.

She takes the can from Daz's hand, smells it tentatively, and passes it back. The silence builds.

Then she says: 'I wanted to talk.'

'Me too.'

'You and Ginger are good mates,' she says.

Daz hears her swallowing. He knows what she's about to say – that the other night was a mistake. But she doesn't.

'You understand him, right? You're both blokes.'

Daz doesn't turn to look at her, but all his focus is directed towards the place where she sits on the periphery of his vision.

'Everyone's got problems,' she says. 'Right? Everyone. And he's a really good man. The best.'

'What problems?'

'It's just . . . we're all made differently.'

'What problems?'

Freddy sighs. Daz feels her head shifting to rest on his shoulder. The alarm bells are clanging in his mind. He knows he shouldn't have let her get so physically close without other people around. And he certainly shouldn't be tempted to respond.

'I don't know what I'd do without you, Daz,' she says. 'I don't deserve a friend like you.'

There's silence then. Daz is tensed up, mouth clamped closed, cursing himself. His hand is still gripping the tin of dog food. He wants to put it down. But at the same time he doesn't want to let his hand be free. He knows she's waiting for him to say something. To tell her she's wonderful, that he loves to be near her. That he wants to have her, now.

But he can't forget the things that Ginger told him. Freddy needs flattery. It's her drug. It's so obvious that he can't understand why he never saw it before. And he hates himself for seeing it so clearly now. Because he can't see the woman any more without seeing the flaw.

'Do you think,' she says, 'if things had been different, that you and me . . .' Her voice is smaller now.

Daz pulls himself away from her. 'Yes,' he says. 'If things had been different. But they're not, are they?'

'But if they had been, would you—'

'What problems?' he says, breaking in.

'Oh,' she shakes her head. 'He just needs a few weeks, you know . . . to sort himself out. If they'd give him that—'

She's tilted her head over on to his shoulder again. He can smell the cannabis smoke in her hair.

'—but they're so unreasonable, you know?'

'Who?'

'Oh, Daz, let's not talk about it . . . please . . .' She snakes an arm around his waist.

He closes his eyes. 'Said you wanted to talk.'

'Couldn't we just cuddle up for a bit? Wouldn't you like that?'

Her other arm is sliding around him now, easing across his chest. Encircling him. He doesn't pull away. Her face is pressed up to his neck. She places one kiss, then another just above it. He can feel the touch of warm breath moistening his skin. She nuzzles his ear.

'Do you like this?'

'Yes.'

'And this?'

'Yes.'

He wants the physical pleasure of her so much that holding back is making his head swim. He feels the metal tin start to buckle in his grip. His other hand holds on to the flaking wood of the windowsill. A splinter pricks into his palm. He presses down on it, feels it penetrating.

She whispers into his ear. 'And do you like me?'

He's being torn. Ginger's voice replays in his mind. *It's a kind of insecurity thing.* He feels sick. Then, unbidden, a thought of Kat comes into his mind. He focuses on that instead, on his appointment with her tomorrow. He shifts the force of his desire in Kat's direction instead of Freddy's.

Then summoning up all his willpower, he says: 'What's the trouble Ginger's in?'

Freddy moves back from him, releasing her grip. 'Daz! I thought—' Then she steps back through the window into the bedsit, flees across the room and out through the broken door.

He slips off the windowsill to kneel on the fire escape. He puts the can down next to him then lies out full length. He knocks his forehead on the cold iron, again and again. Until the pain is strong enough.

Daz wakes, cold, to a scrape of movement. There's a tongue licking between his fingers. The click of claws on metal. Then the clatter of a can being overturned. He opens his eyes, but the animal has gone already. All that remains is the smell of fox and the wetness on his hand.

He clambers back through the window, crawls to his mattress and drifts into a sleep that he never properly left.

When Daz next becomes aware, he finds himself sitting up in bed with his heart pounding out a heavy beat in his throat and chest. It's light outside. He must have been asleep a long time.

He struggles to his feet, knowing he's heard something to pull him across from dreams into consciousness, not remembering what. He's looking for his Docs when he hears a crash somewhere upstairs. A woman's scream. Freddy. And Ginger's voice shouting. He runs for the door, but catches his toe in a pile of dirty clothes and topples, slamming on to the floor.

'Shit!'

He's scrambling forward. But there is movement outside. Heavy footsteps coming down the stairs to the landing. The door opens in one abrupt movement.

'Wakey-wakey. Time I paid you a visit, eh?'

Raglan steps inside, smoothing his hair back with the flat of one hand. Smith remains outside, holding Lady's lead. The dog is straining to get in, tail stump working like a souped-up metronome. Front paws in the air. Smith hauls her back again, then closes the door. It's suddenly just Daz and Raglan and the muffled sound of sobbing coming through the ceiling.

'Good morning, Croxley.'

Daz bites his teeth together.

'Lady thinks you've still got dog food in here.' Raglan scans the room. 'It's no pets allowed. I'd take measures to get rid of it – if you had a dog. You understand?'

Daz understands perfectly well. He wonders what his landlord would use. Poison probably.

'Anyway,' Raglan says. 'You'll be out of this place within the week. The new flat's being decorated even as I speak.'

'Don't want to move,' Daz says.

It looks for a moment as if Raglan is going to respond, then he saunters across to the open window and bends to rest his hands on the sill. 'I've already given you longer than I said. That's my generosity. It's your turn now. Tell me what you've uncovered about the cash. That's your part of the deal.'

Daz is still foggy from sleep. In part of his mind he's wondering if that is why Raglan always seems to call early in the morning, to catch him off-balance. But mostly he's trying to figure out if he can get away without telling the man anything at all. Or, if he does have to let something out, which bits of information would be the least damaging to himself and to Patty.

He points up through the ceiling. 'What happened?'

Raglan is still looking out of the window. 'It was just business.'

Daz listens but can't hear Freddy sobbing any more.

'Kind of business?'

'Money. The only business. You should know that – of all people. Now—' He straightens himself and steps back towards Daz '—now. Where did Agnes Wattling get hers from?'

Daz sidesteps and walks across to the window where Raglan was standing a moment before. 'Found something,' he says, though he hasn't decided what to say yet.

'Good boy.'

'Gotta know something, though.'

Raglan wets his lips.

'How'd you know I got it from Patty?'

Raglan laughs, as if relieved at the question. 'You're the one who's supposed to be giving information. But I might tell you – if you come up with what I'm looking for.'

Daz has been worrying about this moment for two days, ever since Raglan bought him the hot chocolate. He's been trying to work out a way of not ending up with a broken arm. But now he comes to it, he starts speaking without knowing what he's going to say.

'Money came from this guy – been dealing with Patty for a couple of years. Bought right before I sold. Cash came from him.'

'A name, Croxley?'

Daz shakes his head. 'Not got one yet,' he lies.

'Do you have an address, then? A description?'

'Tomorrow,' Daz says. 'Might find more tomorrow.'

Raglan steps closer. He puts a hand on the side of Daz's head, fingers reaching around to the back of the neck. For a moment he doesn't do anything. Daz is tensed, ready to throw himself back. But Raglan just smiles.

'That's not really good enough, is it, eh?' He releases Daz's head and walks towards the door. 'I'll come back tomorrow for my answers.'

'How did you know?' Daz blurts.

Raglan is turning the door handle. 'You think I'll tell you

that – when you haven't even found a name yet?' There's a mocking edge in his words. It catches Daz off-balance for a moment. He feels as if he's missing something obvious.

'The twenty quid,' he says. 'Gunna give it me back?'

Raglan turns, the amusement still glinting in his eyes. He reaches into an inner jacket pocket and pulls out the banknote. It is sealed in a clear plastic bag, not much bigger than the note itself. He holds it for Daz to see, makes as if to pass it over, then pulls it away as Daz reaches out.

'I'll see you tomorrow, Croxley.'

He laughs openly this time, showing his teeth. On the landing, Lady barks her excitement, trying to jump up. Smith holds her back and Raglan's suit is saved.

Daz listens to them walking away down the stairs. The front door slams. He closes his eyes and takes a deep breath. He's missed something obvious and Raglan's mockery has fired the anger inside him. Part of him wants to go upstairs to comfort Freddy. But he knows Ginger will be there to do that, and right now he has another impulse to follow.

So he starts to move, grabbing his boots, jamming his feet into them. There's no time to fumble with knots, so he stuffs the laces inside the ankles. And there's no security to the bedsit – not that he's got anything left to steal – so he just slams the door behind him and vaults down the stairs four and five at a time.

There's a bike leaning on the wall of the downstairs corridor, chained to a radiator. An old-style drop-handlebar racer. More rust than paint. Daz thumbs in the combination and springs the lock. Then he's out of the back door, manoeuvring the machine across the yard and through to the walkway.

There's a space reserved for doctors just up the road. That's where Raglan usually parks. But when Daz reaches the front door he sees the slot is empty. He scans the road in time to see Raglan's car at the junction with Saxby Street, indicating left. Disappearing around the corner.

Daz jumps into the saddle from a running start. It's downhill and he's pumped up inside. He gives the brakes a token squeeze, then leans into the turn. There's a car between Daz and Raglan's Jaguar, but Daz is moving as fast as they are. The wind is whipping across his forehead, rippling the sleeves of his T-shirt. Raglan has reached the London Road junction now. Daz is thinking that with any luck the traffic should give him time to catch up. But the Jaguar finds a gap and slips into the stream of cars.

Daz turns just before reaching the junction, jumping the front wheel to mount the kerb, riding the pavement next to the road. He's standing off the saddle, pumping the pedals for the climb up to the top of the hill, throwing his weight to left and right. The traffic lights are against Raglan, and Daz is catching up. He's going so fast that the moment has arrived before he has time to think about it. He's level with the Jaguar, then he's leaving it behind.

There are side-roads that Raglan might turn down when the lights change, but it seems unlikely, so Daz keeps going, all the way up to the corner of Victoria Park. Then he puts down a foot and waits, panting. He feels the skin on his arms prickle as sweat droplets start to well. There's a line of stationary cars all the way to Raglan, fifty, a hundred yards back.

Daz knows that his problems will really begin if Raglan carries on heading out of town. He's always reckoned that, given a straight race across the city, his rusting bicycle will beat a hundred-thousand-pound Ferrari nine times out of ten. And he's always happy to remember that he picked up his Raleigh for twenty-five quid. But on open roads he doesn't stand a chance.

And then there is the second question. At first it was enough to be following unseen. There was the fantasy of riding alongside the Jaguar and kicking dents in the door panels as he passed. Or running a bit of sharp gravel over the paintwork. But that was self-gratification, not a real possibility. The angry fire in Daz's gut is starting to cool now. If he does manage to tail Raglan all the way to his destination, what does he hope to achieve? There's no answer to that question.

There is something else nagging his mind. The sight of his twenty-pound note. It reminded him of police dramas on TV. Evidence bags. Fingerprints.

The lights have changed. The traffic is growling forward. The pavement is wide enough here, and Daz is far enough off to the side, so he has no fear that Raglan will spot him as he passes. He looks back, trying to figure out which lane of traffic the Jaguar is in, where it will go at the junction. Too late, he sees that Raglan is turning right. To follow, he is going to have to cross the stream of traffic. He dismounts, pushes his bike towards the roadside. Jabs at the button on the pelican crossing.

Raglan is level with him now, just two lanes of traffic away. Then he's past, turning down Granville Road towards the university. Daz stabs the button some more.

Now the lights have changed, and traffic is streaming across the junction the other way. Daz runs out into the road. He's still barred by three lanes of moving cars. The Jaguar is just a flash of maroon paint in the distance. Daz knows he is going to lose. So he steps out into the stream, pushing his bike ahead of him. A horn blares. Engines rev their anger. Daz walks into the second lane, causing a van to come to a skidding wheel-lock halt. Daz is running now, across a gap in the third lane and on to the far pavement. He vaults himself into the saddle and he's off, leaving the angry snarl behind him. He's racing, head down, along the slalom of the pavement. Pedestrians stare like rabbits. He looks over their heads, squinting to the place, two hundred yards ahead, where the road veers around to the right. He hasn't seen the Jaguar make that turn yet and there isn't another road – just an entrance to the grounds of De Montfort Hall, a rock concert venue that Daz knows well.

Daz slows, waiting for the flash of colour as the car turns. A hundred yards to go. The Jaguar hasn't made the turn. Daz's eyes are watering, but he won't let himself blink and miss the moment. He freewheels to a stop.

'Bloody cyclists,' growls a man in a suit who has to walk around Daz's bike.

With the cooling airflow stopped, Daz's sweat starts to bead again. Still scanning the road, he wipes his palm back across his forehead into his stiffly spiked hair. And then he sees it. Parked in the Victoria Park pay-and-display under the shade of the trees.

An hour later and Daz is wondering why he bothered. There wasn't going to be any chance for him to leave his mark on the immaculate maroon paintwork because Smith stayed with the car, reading a glossy magazine with a picture of a half-dressed woman on the cover. Raglan is doing what he's been doing since he arrived – strolling the tree-lined paths of the park with Lady's lead looped in one hand. The dog has raced in zigzags between the trees, covering miles but keeping within earshot of her master. A kind of freedom, perhaps.

Daz started off tailing Raglan close – using his wits and speed of reaction to keep out of sight and to disengage from Lady when she came back to sniff at his heels. But as time has dragged past, he's gradually relaxed, letting the distance increase until Raglan is just another figure in the distance, anonymous but for the fact that he is the only person in the park wearing a suit.

Daz finds a comfortable-looking tree and sits with his back against it, legs bent at the knee, the soles of his boots on the floor. He watches Raglan for a moment and then closes his eyes. When he opens them, Raglan has hardly moved, so he rests them again.

In his mind he's got a kind of map. He can't see it exactly – he's never been able to see pictures in his mind – but he knows where all the different parts are. Instead of showing buildings and landscape, this map marks the positions of things that are worrying him. Freddy is right at the centre today. Then there is Raglan with his demand for information – that is over to one side. Instead of streets, this map has connections and relationships. It's the line joining Raglan to Freddy that is concerning him now. There was always a join between the two – Raglan is her landlord. But when she screamed this morning the line got upgraded from a B-road to a dual carriageway.

Daz feels a shadow flick across him. He opens his eyes to see that a man has just walked past and is marching away down the path. In the second it takes him to register that the man is wearing a suit, he also registers that he's had his eyes closed too long, because Raglan is out of view.

Daz is on his feet and running. Not down the path, but out across the grass away from the trees, widening his view. This is high risk, he knows. Because he's also putting himself centre stage. Halfway out to the middle of the field, he catches sight of Lady. From this distance she's just a nut-brown speck racing across the park. Daz slows, drops himself to the ground. The dog's run curves, turning back on itself. Daz's eyes skip ahead, projecting Lady's path back to the place under the trees where Raglan stands waiting. But Raglan isn't looking at his dog. He's moving towards the only other person in the park who is wearing a suit. Hand outstretched.

It doesn't look as if Daz's run and abrupt stop have attracted their attention. He lies down on the grass, resting his chin on his hands. In the distance, the two men stand facing each other. The newcomer hasn't shaken Raglan's hand. Instead he looks back the way he's come, scanning the area of the park around them. Daz drops his head and makes an impression of just another sleeping waster, but with one eye taking in the man finishing his three-hundred-and-sixty-degree security sweep.

It's hard to be sure of much from this distance, but the body language suggests that it's the newcomer doing the talking. Raglan nods from time to time, perhaps answering questions. Then there's a final, decisive nod and Raglan reaches inside his jacket. He pulls out something small and hands it across. The other man pockets it without a look. The operation takes perhaps half a second. Then both men turn and walk away in opposite directions.

Daz lies still, thinking. He's wasting time here when he should be talking to Patty or going back to see if Freddy is all right, or even following Salt around on Raglan's behalf. But he feels uncomfortable with the first two, and the last is something he's not managed to work up any enthusiasm about. He doesn't really believe in this secret hoard that the man is supposed to have stashed away.

The thing that is really intriguing Daz right now is the possibility that he might have just witnessed Raglan in an illicit meeting. Daz's weakness has always been curiosity, rather than avarice. Information rather than cash. And there is the enticing thought that the right kind of information, the incriminating kind, might be enough to get Raglan off his back.

So instead of tracking his landlord and Lady, Daz watches the other man. He's already passed the tree that Daz was sitting against. Now he is striding away, towards De Montfort Hall. Daz gets to his feet and sets off in pursuit.

Chapter 13

Patty reaches to the table and grinds out the stub of her cigarette on the inside of an empty mug. 'It's about bloody time you showed up, Croxley!'

'What?'

She's sitting by the window in Vicky's back room, staring out over the weed patch to Kodak's grave. Dyson, much more himself today, is lying by her side, growling through his side teeth.

'Don't play all innocent on me,' Patty says. 'We had a deal. You and me working togeth—'

Her shoulders shudder forward in a heaving cough. Daz curls his toes inside his boots and waits for her to catch her breath. She dabs at the side of her mouth with a handkerchief.

'Been busy,' he says at last.

'Busy? Pah! I've been cooped up in here. Vicky's no good for anything. Out day and night. And all you've been doing is lying around in the sun.'

'Have not!'

Patty points to the knees of his jeans. Green-stained. And then to his T-shirt. Daz picks off a loose strand of grass and drops it to the floor. He feels as if he should justify himself. But he's already decided that he's not going to tell her about Raglan leaning on him for information about her customers. As for the meeting in the park – *that* he's still pondering.

Raglan definitely passed something to the other suited man. It was the act that marked the end of their meeting. And then, when they'd split up, and Daz had followed, what had he expected to find? That the man was a small-time criminal, perhaps. Or a businessman. A local politician, even. From the back, Daz had been able to see that he was used to wearing a suit. He had that comfortable air. Confident, too. And with no reason not to be, given the precautions they'd taken in their meeting.

Daz allowed himself to get closer than when he was following Raglan earlier. This man wouldn't know his face. There was no great risk in being seen. They approached the line of trees at the edge of the park, with Daz barely fifty paces behind. Then across the small access road and through the entrance of the De Montfort Hall grounds. There was a police car parked in front of them. Daz stopped walking and watched the man get out his keys and climb into the driver's seat. This was all wrong. Raglan couldn't be a police informer. But things were about to get worse.

Daz stood back and pretended to look at the concert hall. But as the car turned towards him, he kept his eyes locked on the windscreen, hoping to catch a glimpse of the man's face through the reflection of trees. The car moved up level with him and stopped. The window slid down and Superintendent Shakespeare looked out.

'Well, what have we here?' he said. 'David Croxley. The boy who's never where he's supposed to be.'

Vince the Prince, Superintendent Shakespeare, Raglan. The connections in Daz's map are getting more tangled the more he discovers. That's another reason that he's decided not to tell this story to Patty.

She's still looking out of the window. Her skin as grey as net curtain.

'Where's Vicky?' Daz asks.

Patty pulls another filter tip. 'How do you expect me to know?' She jabs an accusing look in his direction. 'Idiot boy! I told you she's never here. You're the one who gets out. You tell *me* where she is. I could starve to death here and no one would know. For weeks probably.'

This thought hits Daz hard. He knows about being hungry. 'Need food?'

'That's not the point. You abandoned me up at Western Park.'

'You—'

She waves the cigarette at him, cutting off his protest. 'How was I supposed to get back home on my own?'

'—told me to get in the van. How—'

'You were supposed to come back and tell me where he went.' She puts the fag in her mouth and lights it, closing her eyes for the first hit of nicotine, then blowing smoke towards the back yard. 'Never think of other people, the young!'

Daz isn't sure why he's taking this from her. He doesn't need to be here at all. He remembers his own long walk back from Salt's workshop. There was no money in his pockets for the bus fare. Nor for food. The feeling of injustice prickles. If a friend tried to lay this kind of thing on him, he'd just walk away and leave them to stew. But his relationship with Patty isn't like that. There's no way he could call her a friend. She's more like family. He imagines a mother or an elder sister would have treated him like she does.

'What have you been doing since I put you in the back of Mr Salt's van?'

'Stuff.'

'Stuff? Hell's teeth, boy! Salt has his hands on a fortune in stolen banknotes, and you've been doing *stuff*?'

Daz looks at the old woman. 'Want to know what I found?' he says.

Patty doesn't answer.

'Drove to a workshop,' Daz tells her.

'TVs? DVDs?'

'None.'

Patty's scowl softens into a frown. 'Then what?'

'Rotten concrete.'

He tells her about the three-dimensional jigsaw of broken blocks. The pillar drill. Gouging a hole with a rusty nail.

'Where exactly?' she says.

'Back behind Belgrave Road.'

Patty stubs out her second cigarette, then rocks herself to her feet. 'Very well, Croxley,' she says. 'You'd better take me there.'

Vicky hasn't paid the phone bill, so Patty has to call for a taxi on one of her mobiles. They say it'll come in five minutes, but it takes a lot longer than that. Strangely, Patty's mood seems to lighten as she waits.

'Feed the dog,' she tells him.

Daz goes to the kitchen and rummages in the cupboards, where he discovers a hoard of canned food. Beans, tomatoes, mushy peas, stew, instant mashed potato. So much for her starving to death. He eventually finds the dog food under the sink.

Daz finds Patty stuffing her bundle of savings into a voluminous black handbag. This is followed by a fresh packet of Marlboros, a disposable lighter and something that looks like a narrow leather wallet.

'What's that?' he asks.

She dismisses the question with a wave of her hand.

'And why take all that cash?'

For just a moment, Patty lets a half-smile slip across her face. 'You think I'd leave it here when Vicky might come back any time?'

Then there's the beep of a car horn from the road outside. 'Taxi's here,' she says.

Daz doesn't know the name of the street where Salt has his workshop, so he gets the driver to take them up along Belgrave Road while he looks for landmarks. They call this part of town the Golden Mile, on account of the quantity of jewellery sold over the counter. Daz has seen the gold worn by Asian ladies. Not the pale, nine-carat stuff he sees in the windows of the high-street chains. This is a darker, more sultry metal. Thousands of pounds' worth on a wrist or around a neck. He finds that easier to understand than credit cards and bank accounts. But it is still strange.

He's looking out of the side window, registering the sari shops and Indian sweet shops. There are famous curry houses here. Sayonara and Bobbies. He's trying to figure out which turning they need to take. By the time he sees it, they're already past, so they have to detour and cut back. The driver doesn't mind. Even Patty only grumbles a little.

The streets are one-way here. Lines of parked cars on either side and just enough room for the taxi to slip through in the middle. The red-brick terraces are uniform. The only individuality is in the detail. Pictures of different Hindu gods in windows. Rangoli patterns chalked on some doorsteps, not others. One house has a line of leaves strung on a thread over the doorway.

Then he sees the entrance he's looking for. Tall wooden doors, faded blue. The paint peeling. 'It's here,' he says.

Patty waits until the taxi has driven off before turning to look at the doors. Padlocked. A big hunk of metal and a length of heavy chain. 'Chinese,' she says, holding the lock.

'Could go look round the back,' Daz suggests.

Patty is rummaging in her handbag. She extracts the slim wallet. As she unfolds it, Daz sees a row of silvery tools like a watchmaker's screwdrivers.

'Can't do that!'

But she is doing it already. The lock in one hand, the picking tool in the other. Daz looks up and down the street.

'Make yourself useful and stand closer, Croxley,' she says, her voice quiet. 'My hands aren't what they used to be. This might take longer than—' The padlock springs open with a bright click. 'Cheap Chinese locks.'

Daz threads the chain out of its run and opens the door wide enough for himself to slip through. Patty shuffles after him, talking to herself. 'Not bad, eh?'

He pushes the door closed. There's no way to replace the chain from the inside. 'Could've been seen.'

'So?'

'Might call the cops!'

Patty takes a cigarette out of her bag and lights up. 'We're white. Salt's white. This street is ninety-eight per cent Asian. Everyone will think we're something to do with him. For all they know, he gave us the key. Now if I'd taken a long time over it . . . that might have been different.'

He sees the suggestion of a smile on her face, then it's gone and she's turning, stepping away along the passage

towards the courtyard. He pulls a face at her back, then
follows.

'Where does he keep the consumer electronics?'

Daz has already told her that the only thing he found
here was broken concrete, so he doesn't bother answering.

'He must be storing them somewhere.'

Daz walks across the courtyard to the workshop. The
door is unlocked. He looks inside. At first he thinks that
nothing has changed. Then he sees that one of the bigger
lumps has gone. He clambers across to where it was before.
The pulverized concrete looks deeper on the floor here than
it was before.

Patty steps into the doorway, blocking out some of the
light. Daz turns and looks at her. 'It's different,' he says.

She blows smoke. 'Come out here, boy. Time you started
to earn your cut.'

In the corner of the yard are two cylindrical waste bins.
It's these that Patty is pointing to. Each is as tall as Daz. And
wide, like a section of sewer main standing on its end. There
are small wheels underneath, like the casters on a chest of
drawers.

'I want to know what's inside.'

'Could tip 'em over,' Daz suggests.

Patty shakes her head. 'He'd know something had
happened if he came back to find all that filth spread over
the courtyard.' She pokes her fag at the first of the two bins.
'You'd better climb inside instead.'

Daz looks at it. He can't see any footholds on the battered
metal sides. So he grabs the rim with two hands, puts one
foot on the wall and jumps. He's half up, the edge of the bin
under the top of his chest. He scrabbles with his feet, trying
to find purchase on something, working himself further
over the lip. He can see some cardboard boxes in the bottom

now. It doesn't smell too bad, so he swings his feet over the lip and drops himself inside.

His feet come down on a yielding surface of cardboard. There's a screech of protesting polystyrene as he sinks down six inches into the contents of the bin. It smells vaguely of mildew in here. He bends down, pulls a crushed box to one side and pokes around in the junk underneath it.

'Well?'

Patty's voice sounds faint outside. He ignores it and continues to excavate. It certainly looks as if someone has been unpacking consumer electronics. He can see plastic bags, some kind of granular packing material, bubble wrap and a printed booklet that looks like it might be instructions for a microwave oven.

'Well, boy?'

Daz steps into the space he's excavated and starts moving the rest of the contents around. After a minute of turning over more of the same, he gives up.

'Boxes 'n' stuff,' he shouts.

'Stuff? What does that mean? Hurry up, we haven't got all day!'

'This.' Daz throws the booklet out over the side of the bin.

There's a pause. He hears the double crack of Patty's knees bending.

'It's one of mine,' she says. 'The instruction booklet for that Daewoo combi oven I sold him.'

'Why so sure?'

'It's the latest model. Not even on the shelves until next month. He can't have got it from anyone else.'

'How come you got it, then?'

The booklet flies back over the side of the bin and hits Daz on the head.

'What else can you find, boy?'

Daz raps his knuckles against his forehead to stop himself shouting something obscene. Then he takes a breath and crouches down to search again.

'Come on. We haven't got all day!'

Daz pulls a slip of paper from underneath his foot. A receipt, perhaps. Now that he's down among the bits of trash he finds more similar slips. He bundles them into his fist, scrunching them small, then throws the ball of paper over the top.

Getting into the bin was easy. It's only when he tries to get out that he realizes the reverse journey isn't going to be as simple. First he tries clinging to the lip of the bin and using his arm strength to hoist himself up. That would have worked if his shoulder hadn't been injured so recently. All it brings him now is pain.

So he wedges himself across the width of the circular bin and starts to work his way up towards the top, walking his feet on one side, sliding his back up the other. After a lot of scratches and a rip in his shirt, he manages to get almost to the top. But here he finds himself stuck. As soon as any part of him gets over the lip, he's going to lose his grip. He struggles his arms around behind him and tries to hoist himself the last few inches. But his shoulder stops him again. He lands back in the bottom of the bin, with the hard corner of a cardboard box jabbing into his kidney. There's sweat running down the sides of his face.

He stands, starting to worry now. He doesn't want to call out to Patty for help. He imagines the scorn she'd pour on him. She's probably smoking a cigarette out there, waiting.

He slows his breathing. Closes his eyes for a moment. Then he starts to search the bottom of the bin again, collecting all the blocks of expanded polystyrene packing material. He places the first few on top of each other, flat near the wall. The last one – which looks as if it once cushioned the side of a television – he puts on top of the platform he's created, standing on its end. That will give him a two-foot boost if it will take his weight. He puts his foot on top and pushes down.

It works. His arms are over the lip. His head follows. He's looking out into the yard, breathing the fresher air. And standing out in the middle, with his back to Daz, is the man himself. Salt.

Hanging on the edge of the bin, Daz searches the yard for a sign of Patty.

Salt also appears to be looking for someone. 'Hello?' he shouts. 'I know . . . I know you're there.'

Daz can see something looped through Salt's hand. Then he realizes that it is the chain from the outside doors.

Salt walks towards the workshop door. He's swinging the chain in his hand now. It might be a bit slow to use as a weapon. But if it hit, the weight of it would be devastating. Salt opens the door and steps inside. If Patty is hiding in there she'll be caught for sure. He holds his breath.

It's a whispering rustle that makes Daz swing his gaze downwards. His first reaction is to think that there must be a rat somewhere behind the bin. But then he hears it again. Fabric brushing against brick. Patty emerges. She glances back at him once, puts a finger to her lips and then hobbles across the yard towards the gate. She's under the brick arch when Salt comes out of the workshop. If he turns his head a couple of degrees in her direction, it's all going to be over.

Daz drops himself back into the bin, knocking his boot against the metal side, making it boom like a gong. Then he waits for Salt's attack.

It's moments like this that shape Daz's future. That's what he's thinking as he stands in the bottom of the bin. Not the times when he can think things through. They almost always lead to inaction. The moments where his future changes are the ones where he has time only for instinct.

He looks up at the sky and the line of a red-brick factory chimney. Deep blue and terracotta. Then the chain crashes against the outside of the bin, a sound so loud that it feels as if the noise is being generated inside his head.

'Get out!' Salt's voice is higher than Daz remembers it. Nerves, perhaps.

Daz covers his ears with his hands. The chain crashes again. It's still unbearably loud. Crash!

'Out!'

Crash!

'OK!' Daz shouts quickly, trying to avoid another impact. 'Stuck, though.'

A pause.

'St . . . stuck?'

'Sides are too high. Can't get out.'

'Then how did . . . how did you get in there?'

'Used the wall. Levered myself up.'

The bin starts to move, tilting over. Daz shifts his weight across to the side that Salt must be lifting from. The floor bumps back down flat. There's a longer pause after that.

Then Salt calls: 'Who are you?'

'Vince,' says Daz.

'Vince who?'

'Vince the Prince.'

'And what are you doing in . . . in my yard?'

'Just looking.'

The chain crashes on the outside of the bin again. Three times. Daz works a finger into each ear, deadening the intensity, but not shutting out the violence of the noise completely. Then there is a crash that isn't followed by another one. Daz's ears are ringing too loud for him to be able to hear any departing footsteps. He waits, listening for some real sound through the tinnitus hum, trying to decide if Salt has gone, if it is safe to clamber out.

Then it starts to rain. Daz looks up at the clear sky and sees an arc of water splashing down on him. A hose jet fired from outside.

Then Salt's voice: 'If you can't climb, we'll have to float you out.'

Daz looks down at his shoes, droplets standing proud from the black leather. His trouser legs are dark with the splashing. There's a childlike simplicity to what Salt is doing. The image of himself bobbing along with the other flotsam is somehow appealing. Ridiculous as well, of course. It would take hours to fill a container of this size. A day, perhaps. Daz isn't sure if Salt seriously believes this is going to work, or if it's intended to get him so fed up that he'll come out of his own accord.

There's a sudden thought that perhaps Salt isn't the brightest of men.

So Daz says: 'I can't swim.'

There's a pause. 'Better . . . better start learning.'

'Get out of my depth and drown.'

Daz steps back, avoiding the worst of the splashing. He folds his arms and leans back against the side of the bin.

'Everyone . . . everyone floats.'

'Be a murderer, won't you, if I drown?'

The water stops.

'Bring a ladder,' Daz calls. 'I can get out, then.'

'R . . . right. You wait there.'

Daz doesn't wait. But as he climbs out of the bin, he feels a sudden pang. The chain made Salt look like just another bully, but he was so easy to manipulate that Daz finds himself almost worrying on his behalf. It's not that the man acted stupidly. The idea of floating Daz out of the bin did have a certain logical beauty to it. But it implies a kind of detachment from reality. An innocence that feels wrong in a grubby adult. Daz isn't sure how Salt got his hands on a haul of stolen money, but the whole thing looks too big and too serious for a man like that to handle.

Daz jogs across the empty courtyard and out on to the street, cooling as his clothes begin to dry. He feels strangely guilty.

Chapter 14

He's sitting on a plastic chair in the crowded waiting area, legs crossed, foot jiggling. He's been studying the clock on the wall, but it's not digital so he's having trouble figuring it out. He observes the second hand clicking forwards. He flips the clock face around in his mind, mirroring it left to right, then top to bottom. It doesn't help. However he works it, he always comes up with the same answer. For the first time since he smashed his wristwatch all those years ago he's turned up for an appointment early.

'David Croxley.'

He looks up. Kat is at the far end of the room, scanning the rows of people. He stands, waves a hand. She gives a curt nod. Nothing more.

It's a different interview room from the one they met in before, but it has the same shape and smell. She's laid out a barricade of papers on the desk between them. She folds her arms and looks up at him for the first time.

'Right. Let's get underway then. Today I'd like to go over some of your previous experiences with employment training, and what your expectations are for the Fresh Horizons Project.'

Daz's mind is struggling to interpret the things that have just happened. When he was last with Kat, he'd felt something. High voltage. Ozone in the air between them. It's as if this is a completely different woman in front of him.

'Kat?'

She swallows. 'It's best if you call me Katrina.'

'You got hammered, right? By the Cow Queen?'

'This is a pilot project – as I said before. There is the possibility that we'll be joined by an observer later in the meeting. All part of the evaluation process. We have to restrict our discussions to the subject in hand.'

He catches her eyes. 'Doing anything after work?'

For a moment he thinks she's going to answer. Then she says: 'Can you tell me about any specific problems you have when it comes to work and training?'

He folds his arms to match hers. 'No.'

'Nothing you find difficult?'

'It's all difficult.'

'I had one client who couldn't stand heights. There was no point in getting him to work on a building site. Another one couldn't drive. You see what I'm getting at . . .?'

'Fuck this!' Daz gets up and paces over to the wall.

'Mr Croxley . . .'

'And fuck that! I'm Daz.'

'Daz. Please . . .' There's panic in her voice. It's the first non-corporate emotion she's let slip today.

'Don't want to talk about it,' he says.

'Then we'll change the subject. But please sit down.'

He forces himself back to the chair. It's just three paces, but it feels like a long walk. 'Ask something else.'

'Tell me the things you *can* do, then. What are you good at?'

'Can dance.'

'And?'

'Guess the end of movies before they come. What *are* you doing after work?'

'Please, Daz. While you're on this scheme I can't—'

'After then – when I'm off it?'

'I . . . I don't know. We need to talk about *you*. If my supervisor comes in and we're not on the script, I'm going to be in the shit.'

'Say you'll see me tonight and I'll be good.'

'I'm not giving in to blackmail.' But there's a smile on her face now. She says: 'Tell me about the last training scheme you took part in.'

'What music are you into?'

'The training scheme, Daz?'

'Ever been to the Club?'

She's looking down at her papers. 'It says here that you took part in a job-creation scheme as a warehouse operative.'

'It'd be safe there for you. Cow Queen doesn't hang out at the Club.'

'You're being so difficult!' She's speaking and laughing at the same time. 'The warehouse! Tell me about it. Please.'

'Say you'll come out and I'll be good.'

'Daz!'

'Say it.'

A brisk knock and the interview room door opens. The Cow Queen walks in and takes a seat slightly back from the table. 'Did you discuss this with the client?' she asks.

Kat nods. Daz sees the sudden tension in the set of her mouth.

'Please continue.'

What Daz wants to do is tell the woman to her face what he thinks, and that he won't discuss his private business in front of her.

'The warehouse?' Kat asks, her eyes pleading.

'Was huge,' he says, giving in. 'Like Wembley Stadium, but with shelves.'

'What did they teach you?'

'Gave me a brush and a hard hat. Told me to sweep the floor.'

'And?'

'That's it. Two weeks with nothing to do. Just sweeping and thinking. Figured something out for them, though. There's a way they could get more shelves in. Just had to switch things round. Told the boss. Drew it out for him.'

'That does show initiative.'

Daz shakes his head. 'Gave me the boot. Said he didn't like smartarses.'

The Cow Queen coughs towards Kat. 'Once you've covered the background details, you can move on to the next subject.'

Kat looks flustered. Or angry – Daz isn't sure which. She continues anyway, back on the script: 'Before we get underway arranging things for you, do you have any ideas? Jobs you might like to try? Companies you might like to work for?'

Daz has already started shaking his head when an idea starts to form. 'No. Maybe. Yes.'

'Which?'

'There's this place might take me on. You can talk to them for me?'

'Sure. If you can give me their number and a contact name.'

'Thing is, you need to go see them. They're no good on the phone.'

The Cow Queen looks dubious.

'What's *client centred* mean?' Daz asks her. He can see Kat stifling a smile.

'It means,' says the Cow Queen, 'that we impose few predetermined patterns on the training process.' Her eyes narrow, as if she suspects that she's just been led into a trap. 'I suppose we could allow a visit,' she says. 'But it will mean more work for you, Katrina.'

Kat shrugs, sweetly. 'That's all right.'

'And what kind of business is this, Mr Croxley?'

'It's a nightclub.'

'What took you so long?'

'Had to go down the Jobcentre.'

'Scrounger.'

There's no sting in Patty's rebuke. Daz catches a flicker of a half-smile between her scowls. Even so, he's decided not to tell her about Kat. It would be like discussing a new girlfriend with his parents.

'Get yourself a cup of tea,' she says. 'If you want.'

He has to step over Dyson in the corridor. The dog is back to its lethargic mode – lying flat out. It manages a sniff as he passes, but doesn't move.

Daz fills the kettle. 'Where's Vicky?' he calls.

'She was here when I got back. Went out pretty quick, though.' Patty's voice from the back room sounds flat.

'Everything OK?'

'Of course it's not! She's a junkie.'

'Your niece, though, isn't she?'

'My great-niece.'

'She got any other family?'

Patty snaps back at him: 'Why do you have to ask so many stupid questions? Vicky may as well be dead already!'

Stung, Daz takes his time making the tea. But by the time he returns, Patty's waspish mood seems to have passed. She has the papers he threw from the dumpster spread out on the table. She's flattening them out with the wrinkled palm of one hand. He sits and watches.

'This is why you need me,' she says. 'My brain. Look at these. What do you see?'

'Receipts?'

She seems pleased. 'Any fool could have told me that.'

He folds his arms, hugging his narrow chest.

'Look again,' she says, touching the receipt nearest to her. 'This one. What does it tell you?'

He looks away for a moment, then he picks up his mug and takes a noisy slurp.

'Are you waiting for something, boy? Go on, read it!'

He gets up and paces away from her across the room.

'What's the matter?' she heckles. 'Are you illiterate or something?'

Patty's insults don't usually hurt. But this one feels like a stab wound. He finds himself gripping the mug too hard. The heat of it is burning into his skin. He imagines himself throwing it at the wall, feels the movement, the crack of splintering ceramic.

'You should have told me,' she says, speaking into the long silence. 'It's nothing to be ashamed of. It's not even that unusual. Half the men in my family never learned to read – my brother and my father and Vicky's dad. I'm not saying they weren't sharp-witted. It's just that not everyone's cut out from the same pattern. And what is it they read these days anyway? Horoscopes and lottery scratch cards.'

Daz doesn't respond.

'Anyway,' she grumbles, 'the way they run education, it's a miracle anyone learns anything. All this nonsense with the schools going back so early this year! Why do they have to change things around all the time?' She pauses for breath, then adds: 'I could teach you if—'

'No.'

'It's not so difficult, you know.'

'No!'

He walks away from her into the front room. He puts his mug on the table and finds his hand shaking. There's a deep-red patch on his palm where the heat has soaked into his skin. He puts his hands over his face. There's a splashing from the back of the house. The clatter of crockery in the sink. The squeak of the kitchen tap.

Then Patty shuffles into the room. 'All the receipts are from shops in the East Midlands,' she says. 'He's buying his petrol in Leicester – from Sainsbury's on Belgrave Road. He gets food there as well. Microwave meals for one. And a few cleaning products.'

Daz drops his hands from his face. He feels exhausted but Patty's eyes are bright. She's looking right at him.

'Cleaning products,' he echoes.

'Bleach and detergent. Nothing special. But almost everything else he's been buying in Nottingham. We've got receipts for paper, pens, a receipt book, stamps, all kinds of junk food. You know what this means?'

Daz shakes his head.

'If he's been selling it all on – all the goods he's bought from me – then he must have been doing it in Nottingham.'

'So?'

'That,' she says, 'is where we're going to next.'

Chapter 15

The arrangement is that they meet in Burger King. Neutral territory. Then they'll go on to the Club and talk about the Fresh Horizons Project with the boss. And then he hopes she'll loosen up a bit – being away from the Cow Queen and the Jobcentre. That's all assuming she turns up at all.

When he gets to the Humberstone roundabout he finds he's early. This is the second time in a couple of days. He's not got enough money to hang around inside the fast-food restaurant, so he goes for a walk – up towards the chip shop and the taxi company. He walks slowly, trying to spin out the time, kicking fragments of gravel so they skip and jump along the pavement ahead of him. Trying not to think about Kat.

There's a bus stop here, with an elderly Caribbean man waiting and, standing a little apart, a Muslim woman in a veil. Daz tries a grin, but both just stare back. It's not the kind of place where people feel comfortable being approached by strangers.

He pushes his hands further down in his pockets and carries on walking. He turns the corner at the end of the block and carries on around the buildings, doubling back. It's very quiet here, away from the main road. The edge of the industrial area. There's a white woman at the junction ahead of him, looking the other way. Handbag on one shoulder. Black miniskirt. It seems too early in the evening for prostitutes to be out. He carries on walking towards her, scuffing his feet deliberately so she hears him. When he's about fifteen feet away, she turns and smiles through him.

'Hi, darling. You looking for business?'

'Vicky?'

'Have I been with you before?'

'Vicky . . .'

'How about it, gorgeous?'

Daz shakes his head. 'Not looking.'

'Why not?'

He doesn't answer.

She glances over her shoulder, then back to Daz. 'Look – you couldn't lend me twenty pence for the phone, could you? I'd be really grateful.'

'Skint,' Daz says, though he knows he's got the money in his pocket.

She steps closer to him. 'I'd be *really* grateful.'

He moves away to the side. 'Skint. Sorry. Gotta—'

'Please.'

But Daz is already past her, walking away, quickening his step, feeling nauseous. He hurries on to the end of the street, turns the corner. When he's sure he's out of sight, he pulls the change out of his pocket, looks at it in the palm of his hand. There are no twenty-pence pieces – which somehow feels like a relief.

He makes his way back to Burger King. There are only a couple of customers inside. Both men, sitting drinking at a window table. Daz goes to the counter and offers a pound coin to the girl at the till.

'Change it for me?'

She looks over her shoulder, then back to Daz. 'I guess.'

Daz retraces his walk, cutting into the back-street where Vicky is still standing. He sees her bending forward from the waist, talking through the window of a maroon car. And for a moment he thinks it might be Raglan's. But it's a different make. Not the old-style Jag. A four-door saloon. A family model. Then Vicky stands straight and the car pulls away. Daz walks towards her, scuffing his feet again. She turns to look, and her mouth breaks into a wide smile.

Daz opens his own mouth to speak.

'Hi, darling. You looking for business?' The same words, delivered in exactly the same tone as before.

'You wanted twenty pence,' Daz says.

Her smile stays the same. 'Sorry, darling?'

'Just now. Said you needed it for the phone.'

'Oh,' she says. 'Yeah. I—'

Daz holds out twenty pence. 'Here.'

Her smile drops. Then flashes on again, and just for a moment it seems like it's real. 'That man,' she points in the direction that the car just drove off in. 'He gave it me. But thanks.' Then she says, 'You're Daz, aren't you.'

'Yeah.'

'Thanks Daz.'

'It's all right.'

He turns to go.

'You don't want business, do you?' she calls.

'No,' he says. 'Sorry.'

He hurries out on to the main street, back towards Burger King. His disquiet isn't from her offer. It's from her vacancy. It's as if he is seeing a bit of himself in her. If he'd started on drugs, he'd be no different. He's sure of that. There's a similarity between them. He can sense it, even from the shell that she's become.

He thinks of the way music takes him over, wonders if

that is the same. But in his heart he knows it isn't. The music stops and he is himself again. If his player got smashed, he wouldn't go into withdrawal. Not like Vicky and drugs. Not like booze.

'Hi, Daz.'

Kat's voice. He turns, feeling a wash of relief. She did turn up for the meeting. Then he sees her. He hadn't really thought about what she'd wear. Blouse and skirt is all he's ever seen her in.

'You look . . .' He can't find the right words to say what he wants to express.

She puts her head slightly on one side. 'Thanks – *I guess.*'

Daz is still looking at her clothes. Stretch leggings, green and blue. And a sequined emerald top, short enough for him to admire her pierced navel. There's a faint finger stripe of glittering, green war paint on her left cheek. He feels his heart force in an extra beat.

'I thought that, as we're going to a nightclub, I should wear something so I don't stand out.'

Daz is suddenly unsure about what she is expecting. 'Gunna talk to the boss?'

'That's what you said you wanted.'

'And after?'

'We'll see.'

Kat is more at ease with this world than he could have imagined. He's expecting her to complain when he takes her around the side of the building to the fire-escape door instead of bringing her in through the front entrance. But she allows him to take her hand and lead her through.

He risks another look at her, though he doesn't turn his head. She's used some kind of styling gel to spike her short-cropped hair up at the front. If anything, she looks more the part than he does. Not that he's ever tried to follow any particular style.

'Great place,' she says, looking from the empty floor to the lighting gantry in the ceiling. 'How come you're so in with them here?'

'Kinda help them out sometimes,' he says.

'Do they pay you?'

He glances at her. 'You on duty, or what?'

She stops. 'You asked me to come here to help you get work.'

'But—'

'Was there another reason?'

'Really, really wanted to see you.'

'And if I hadn't wanted to come, I would have found an excuse.' Then she steps close, touches her lips to his cheek and steps away again. 'You smell good,' she says.

'You, too.'

'But I think I'd better see the boss as well. Don't you? Just so I've got something to say to the Cow Queen. And she *will* ask.'

Daz's mind is spinning. He can still feel the touch of her lips on his face. There's a queasy, roller-coaster thrill in the pit of his stomach. He starts leading her through the cavernous dance hall towards the chill-out rooms and the bar. He doesn't know if her kiss is just a sign that she wants to be his friend – or if it means something more. They're at the back of the hall now. He takes her hand and gives it a gentle squeeze. Then he leads her up the steel stairs that lead to the mezzanine floor. And as they climb he feels her fingers squeeze his in return.

The boss's name is Liz. She wears loose cotton clothes and keeps her hair tied back in a long ponytail. She tells Daz and anyone else who will listen that she's been to all the really important rock festivals and raves of the last twenty years. She has an MBA, though that is not so widely known – as the certificate hangs on the wall of her bedroom.

The thing that always hits Daz about her office is the sudden change in sound quality as he steps inside. There are egg boxes stuck over all four walls. When the music is racked up high in the main hall, she can still work here almost undisturbed. But when the music is off downstairs, like now, Daz finds the place claustrophobically quiet. It's as if every slight echo or breath is sucked away before it can reach his ears.

Liz examines him as he closes the door behind them. 'Daz,' she says. 'It's been a while. Who's the new friend?'

He realizes he's still holding Kat's hand. He lets go, just a shade too suddenly.

'I'm Katrina,' says Kat.

The two women nod their greetings. From behind the desk, Liz looks the other woman over, head to feet and then back. Kat narrows her eyes. It's only then that Daz starts to see that he might have made a mistake getting into this situation. There's a certain amount of history between Liz and himself.

'I've fixed a new theme event,' Liz announces. 'We're calling it Breakbeat Night. Next Saturday.'

Daz nods.

'That's in eight days' time.' Then to Kat she says: 'He can't do dates. Have you found that yet? And times. Always late.'

Kat gives a stiff smile. 'He's always been early with me.'

'So far,' Liz says.

'Eight days,' Daz says. 'Eight days' time.'

Liz sits back from the desk and crosses her legs. 'There's a big government conference on that weekend. Multiculturalism – or something like that. It'll bring a heap of people into town. Young people, too, by the sound of it. Talk to the Doctor. Give him some advice – what's in, what's out. Breakbeat isn't really his scene.'

'Should get someone else,' Daz says. 'Specialist MC.'

Liz nods. 'You never did understand money, did you, Daz. Money and time. We're a stack-'em-high, sell-'em-cheap operation – in the entertainment sense. This is the nearest thing to the old free-rave scene. I get rid of the Doctor for a night and bring in a name. You have to pay for it on the door.' She looks at Kat. 'Not that he ever pays. That's another thing you should know from the start.'

Kat steps closer to Daz and links her arm through his. 'You thought it was his money I was after?'

Daz is starting to panic now. They've gone way off the path. Kat was supposed to be negotiating for him to get work experience, not trading insults. He feels an itch on his ear lobe but resists the urge to scratch it.

It's Liz's turn to offer Kat a tight smile. Then she switches to Daz. 'I'm going to print a load of fliers, offering a couple of pounds off the door. See if we can't paper the house. I'll give you commission on every flier that gets handed in – like we usually do.' Then to Kat she says: 'Give him a chance to earn some money. Then he'll be able to buy you something.'

This should be good news. They're on to the subject they came to talk about. It should be the start of real negotiations. But Kat has been pushed into playing a different role. The change of focus has wrong-footed her. Daz can feel her tension through his linked arm. Perhaps Liz picks up on that. Or perhaps it's intuition.

'And what do you do, Katrina?' She smiles. 'For a living, I mean.'

'I work in the Jobcentre.'

'Oh, my . . .' The laugh spills out of Liz's face. 'Oh, my. That *is* a treat. Daz must be something of a special project, then.'

He's already out of the door, following after Kat.

'I hope I haven't said anything wrong,' Liz calls after them.

He catches her up at the bottom of the stairs.

'What the fuck was that all about, Daz?'

'Didn't mean—'

'She's old enough to be your mother, for Christ's sake!'

'Not—'

She stops walking and swings to face him. 'Are you telling me that there's nothing between you and that woman or what?'

'Nothing.' He swallows.

Kat puts a hand to her forehead. 'God. Why's the world so full of cows?'

He doesn't know if she's talking about herself, Liz or both. He shakes his head. 'The work thing . . .'

'I'll write in my report that she made a suggestion, but that it wasn't decided one way or the other. OK?'

'OK.'

'Now,' she says, 'I'm not on duty any more.'

She moves forward and kisses Daz on the cheek. It happens too quickly for him to respond. She pulls away and looks at him. 'And if you *had* had something with that woman – it'd be none of my business. So long as it was in the past.'

'In the past,' Daz echoes. 'Years ago.'

'Her name isn't Mrs Robinson, is it?' Kat doesn't give him

a chance to answer. She turns towards the bar. 'I need a drink.'

He follows, wondering if all this means that his present life has become Kat's business, and if that means he's now in a relationship with her, and if that means he might go home with her later.

'Vodka and orange,' she says to the barman, then she looks to Daz. 'And . . .?'

'Coke,' he says.

'You sure?'

'He's driving,' the barman says, and winks at her. 'He's always driving.'

'He can drive if he likes!' Kat snaps back.

Which Daz takes to mean that things are going well. But then Freddy and Ginger come strolling in and he starts to think that they should be leaving the Club after all.

Ginger catches Daz's hand in a low-five. 'Hey, Dazzo.'

'Hey.'

Freddy glances at Kat. 'Hello, you two,' she says, eyebrows raised.

Daz does the introductions.

There's a moment of unasked questions, then Kat says: 'Neat club.'

Freddy takes her hand and pulls her towards the doorway. 'Come on. Let me show you around.'

Kat glances at Daz. He watches the women leave for the dance hall, wondering how much more complicated life can get.

'Kept this one quiet, Dazzo.'

'What?'

Ginger prods him in the side with an elbow. 'You and her. You dark horse, you.'

'It's nothing.'

'She's a strange looker. Those freaky green eyes.'

'She looks fine,' says Daz, slightly more strongly than he'd meant to.

Ginger laughs. 'It's nothing, eh?'

The punters start to trickle in at around half-nine. By ten-thirty the bar is heaving. Freddy and Ginger are off warming up, ready for the show. Kat is pushing through the jostle, trying not to spill two drinks, towards the corner where Daz is waiting.

'That barman's trying to hit on me,' she says, handing over a plastic skiff.

'Oh.'

'I thought you should know.'

Daz takes a swallow of his Coke to fill the moment.

Kat watches him, then sips her vodka and orange.

They've stayed in the Club all evening. After Freddy and Ginger left to go through their warm-up, Daz found himself alone with Kat again. It felt strange. Attraction and awkwardness mixing together. Both ways, he thinks. Unasked questions. He's sure Freddy must have taken the opportunity to pump Kat for information while they were looking around the building together. Perhaps Freddy gave some information of her own. He wishes he could know what was said.

'He doesn't think much of your taste in drinks,' Kat says.

'Who?'

'The barman.'

'So?'

She laughs out loud. 'You're right. So nothing! That's what I like about you, Daz Croxley. You don't give a damn about what anybody else thinks.'

It's not quite true this evening, but he doesn't correct her. 'Wanna dance?'

She nods, then smiles wickedly, and a spark seems to jump from her eyes. It catches him full in the chest.

They push towards the centre of the floor, next to the stage. Freddy and Ginger are there, in the middle of their routine. They don't seem to see him, and for once he doesn't bother looking at them either.

Instead he gives himself to the music. This is Euphoric Trance. It's like being in an ocean of light and sound. Moving to it. Letting it drive him. He watches Kat close by. The waves of movement are washing her body, too, rippling across her arms, her back, her hips and legs.

There's no time here. Just beat. He's not *in* the ocean. He's part of it. Kat, too. There's a line connecting his eyes with hers, moving with them as they flow. It's the only thing he's aware of.

Track follows track. The sweat is falling from him. Her skin is a sheen of light. And somewhere in that ocean, he grips her waist, pulls her in. She presses herself close so the slick skin of her arms slips over his.

The track ends. The Doctor talks to the crowd. Daz doesn't hear anything he says.

'Going to the Ladies,' says Kat.

He lets her lead him through the crush. Hypnotized. At the toilets, she turns and grins at him, holding out a hand to stop him from following her inside.

'See you out here. OK?'

He wants to take hold of her, kiss her on the lips. Instead he nods. 'OK.'

Then he pushes through the door into the Gents. There are a couple of men at the line of urinals, so he walks into a stall instead, pisses into the bowl of the toilet. He can still hear the beat outside. It reverberates in the room. He can hear the hand drier turn on. But he's completely inside his own head and none of it really reaches him. The door slams closed. The hand drier stops.

Then he hears a sound that does break into his conscious mind. The stall door closing just behind him. The point of a knife presses into his side just below his ribs.

'Do you want to lose a kidney, Croxley?' It's a whisper in his ear. He feels the man's breath. Smells liquorice.

The hand drier roars into life again. There are people out there. Daz tries to turn but the prick of the knife becomes a screaming pain. He freezes, hands out from his sides. He's clicked the voice now. Guy, Bishop's driver.

'I don't want to have to cut anything off,' he says. 'Disappoint your girlfriend.'

Daz thinks instead of speaking. He's intensely aware of his vulnerability. But his mind is jumping up over the top of the stall, then down underneath the partition, testing all the options in a flash of wordless thought, knowing within the blink of an eye that there isn't any way to escape unless the driver pulls the knife away.

'Mr Bishop sent me to find you,' Guy whispers. 'He's been researching your story, you see. A man in a pub, wasn't it? And he knows you've been lying to him.'

The door slams outside again. Daz could shout to whoever is out there. But he can feel the knife twisting in his side, the tip of the blade digging through his skin. He looks down, sees the silver rings on Guy's fingers, the dull light of the knife.

'Mr Bishop knows that you've been telling other parties the truth – namely Paul Raglan. He wants this simple message passed to you, OK? You're going to meet Mr Bishop again. He'll arrange the time. Then you're going to tell him everything you know. Where the money came from, everything you've found out about it since. And you're not going to tell Raglan anything more. Mr Bishop will know if you do. Then he'll send me to do something bad. You understand?'

Daz nods.

'He'll leave it to my discretion what I do, see? I could put you in a wheelchair perhaps. Or on dialysis.' Daz yelps as the knifepoint digs into his side again. 'Or maybe I'll visit your girlfriend. She's a strange-looking bitch, but she might be fun, eh? Mr Bishop trusts my judgement, you see. I do what I want.'

Guy jabs the knife in harder for a moment, then pulls it away. Daz buckles at the waist. The stall door slams behind him. He's alone.

Chapter 16

Kat rests her hands on his shoulders and looks into his face as if she's trying to read a book written in some foreign language. He looks past her, first to one side, then the other.

'What's wrong?'

'Wanna go.'

'Now? I thought we were starting to—'

He cuts in: 'Now.'

He lets them out by a side door, then leads her around the back of the building, across an empty service road, between two more factories, then on to the wasteland at the back. There's a track worn through the thistles and buddleia, up the slope of the railway embankment. He leads her through a hole in the fence, across the line and down the other side.

It feels safer here. They weren't followed. And this place is an anonymous patch of wasteland. No one would look for them here. A path runs some fifty yards through the weeds to an empty road with streetlights. The place in which they are standing is quite dark.

'Where are we going?' It's the first thing she's said since they left the building.

'Home.'

'I don't live this way.'

'My place.'

She pulls a face – hammed-up surprise. 'You might like to ask. This *is* a first date, remember.'

It's the first time she's used the word 'date'. He turns to face her.

'Didn't . . . didn't mean that.'

'Didn't you?' she asks – disappointed, he thinks.

He sees her looking at him. Searching.

'Ask me a question,' she says.

'Why?'

'To help me understand you better.' Then she starts leading him across the rough ground towards the road.

He thinks as they walk, wondering why she turns everything around the way he least expects it. And wondering why he likes it like that.

'I'm still waiting for my question.'

'OK,' he says. 'How come you work for the Jobcentre?'

'What's wrong with that?' She fires the words back at him, then puts a hand over her mouth. 'God,' she says, 'that came out all wrong.'

'So what's the answer?'

She takes a deep breath. 'It's a job.'

Daz gives her a sceptical look.

'I'm on this accelerated promotion scheme. It means they put me through a range of different jobs, giving me a taste of this side of the Social Security operation. I've already done a stint in the finance office. Now it's front-desk stuff. After a couple of years they'll start me up through management.'

'You'll be the Cow Queen's boss?'

Kat nods. 'And she's making my life hell. I think that's why I'm a bit prickly about it right now.'

Daz kicks an empty can away to the side.

'My dad's a retired financial manager,' Kat says, breaking in on Daz's thoughts. 'Did I tell you that? And my mum's a hospital administrator. Jim – he's my brother – is a doctor and Tara, my sister, is a publicity officer for the Police Authority.'

'The police?' He pulls a face. 'No way!'

'It's true. We've all got white-collar DNA.'

'You, too?'

She shakes her head. 'I thought I was different. I was going to travel – to get one of those round-the-world tickets, see India and China and places like that. I could have taken a couple of years off before university. But my parents were so anti . . .' The sentence fades.

Daz wants to say the obvious – that she shouldn't pay any attention to the pressure of others, except perhaps to resist it. Especially parents. But she's revealing herself to him in a way that's quite new. He doesn't want to break the spell.

'The thing is,' Kat says. 'They offered to fund me through university. That way I wouldn't have to get a part-time job to tide me through my studies. And I'd come out of it without a huge debt. And if I went against them . . . They were being kind, really.'

Daz and Kat are halfway to the road now, but they've slowed in their walk. The ground on either side of the path is knee-deep in thistles.

Daz says: 'You could still go.'

'There's the mortgage. Dad helped me with the deposit, you know. It's hard to just up and leave . . .'

'You are what you are,' he says. 'None of that changes it.'

She reaches out and takes his hand. Her skin is smooth. They walk on for several paces in silence.

'The job's OK?' he asks. 'Other than the Cow Queen?'

She shrugs. 'It was a choice of being on one side of the counter or the other.'

'You hate it, then?'

'It's not simple like that. Maybe I'd have been something else if there'd been a choice.'

'Like what?'

'Oh, I don't know. One of those people who starts off with a welding torch and a pile of junk and turns it into an exhibition at Tate Modern – the kind of thing that people write to the *Telegraph* to complain about. That'd be good. Or some other kind of artist. It doesn't matter what – but I'd need a studio. Definitely. Lots of light and space and paint stains and a smell of turps.'

'Turps?'

'I just like it. I guess that sounds stupid.'

It doesn't sound stupid to Daz. But he doesn't say anything.

'What about you?' she says. 'If you could have any job?'

'Bungee jumper.'

She laughs. 'That's cheating.' The relaxation is easing back into her voice now. 'I want a real answer.'

Daz cranes his neck to look up at the stars. 'Never had a job,' he says. 'Not a real one. Don't know what I'd like. Working with animals, maybe.'

She nods. 'I can see that. You could be a zookeeper. Feeding the elephants.' Then, out of nowhere, she says: 'Why Coke? Everyone else was on shorts or mixers. And pills. But you – not even an E. You're not a secret Mormon or something?'

He takes his time before answering this one. 'My dad was a boozer,' he says. She isn't speaking, but he can feel all her attention directed towards his confession. 'Worked for the council. Same kind of job your family do. They don't sack no one from the council. Could booze all he liked. Haven't seen him for years.'

'What about your mum?'

'Couldn't hack it. Said she was going to find herself, whatever that means. Got a ticket to India. Not a round-the-world one, though. One-way.'

'I'm sorry,' she says.

He shakes his head. 'All happened when I was small. Don't remember much.'

'Is she still there? India, I mean?'

Daz shakes his head. 'Died.'

'Shit. Don't you have any family at all – brothers or sisters, grandparents?'

'It's just me.'

She looks as if she wants to ask more questions. But he doesn't want to give any more answers. Not tonight. He doesn't want to tell her about being taken into care, going from foster home to foster home. He doesn't want to make himself any more of a Social Security case in her eyes.

So he lets go of her hand and turns to look back the way they've come. He hears her moving towards him. His skin prickles with her closeness.

'My parents want me to marry a bank manager,' she whispers. 'Or a doctor.'

He can feel her breath on the back of his neck. Then her arms are slipping under his shirt and around his chest. Her lips brush his ear. He presses his body back into hers. 'Then why this?'

She tightens her grip. 'Like you said – I am what I am.'

He turns, finds her lips.

It's Kat who breaks the kiss, but only after a long time. She blinks rapidly, as if trying to clear her head. '*Something's* working.'

He covers her mouth with his. Again she breaks away.

'Not here.' There's an impish grin on her face now.

He kisses her a third time. She responds, gripping his back, her fingers dragging furrows in his skin. Her hands run down his sides.

Daz flinches and pulls his head away from hers. He puts his hand just below his ribcage and feels the soreness.

'What's wrong?'

'It's nothing.'

'Let me see.'

She lifts his shirt. Even in this light, she can see the cut. It's not deep, but there's a bloodstain on his skin.

'How did you get that?'

'Knife,' he says.

'Shit, Daz.'

And because he's got no will to hold anything back from Kat now, he starts to tell her about Guy. She stands half a pace back from him, watching his face, wincing when he describes the knife being pushed into his skin.

'Raglan's gunna beat me up if I don't tell him about Patty. And Bishop's gunna kill me if I do tell.'

She puts her hands on his hips, pulls him closer. 'Is that really what he said?'

Daz looks at her mouth, then her eyes. 'Something like that. And maybe that he'd hurt my friends.'

'You asked to take me home so you could protect me?'

Daz guesses that there isn't a right way to answer this question.

Kat tilts her head to one side, still looking at him. 'Don't worry,' she says. 'I'm coming with you.'

'For real?'

'But this *is* a first date.'

*

They walk back towards the bedsit. Talking about Bishop's driver has chilled Daz's mood and at first they walk in silence. He leads them along a tortuous route, keeping to the unlit and quiet places where he feels safest.

She squeezes his hand. 'How do you find your way so well in the dark?'

'Easy.'

'Without seeing the landmarks I couldn't do it.'

'Can feel the spaces up here.' He taps the side of his head.

He's relaxing now that they've come further from the Club. He pulls her closer to him. She lets her smile shine for a moment, then pulls herself away again. He knows that she knows the game they're playing.

They're cutting along a walkway under the shadow of the tower blocks now. It's deserted at this time of night – with only the distant horn-bursts of a car alarm to break up the silence. They emerge from the hidden route at the end of Guthlaxton Street. Though there are no cars moving, Daz is wary. He takes a few seconds to look up and down St Peter's Road before he leads them across. Saxby Street is still. And Severn Street. Daz exhales with relief from a tension he hadn't been aware of.

'Hey,' Kat says. 'Lighten up there.' She slaps him smartly on the thigh then walks away from him backwards, wrinkling her nose in his direction.

He tries to give her a return slap, but she jumps out of his reach, a playful light in her eyes. They're almost level with Daz's front door now. He lunges again. But this time she stands her ground. He has his arms around her, pulling her close. The full length of her body is pressed against his. He backs her towards the doorway.

There is a double clunk from the road. Two men are getting out of a parked car. Suits.

'David Croxley,' says the one from the passenger seat. 'I'm arresting you on suspicion of handling stolen property. You do not have to say anything, but it may harm your defence if you do not mention when questioned something which you may later rely on in court. Anything you do say may be given in evidence.'

Charles Street Police Station. The custody sergeant first. Daz has been through this before. He's used to the humiliating formalities. Forms and signatures. Emptying his pockets into a tray for everyone to see. Small change and a crumpled bus ticket. He welcomes the prejudice he feels from them. It defines the person he is.

He knows about the law. Once they've arrested you, they can keep you only for so long. Then it's charge or release. And while they've got you in the cells, they have to make sure you get what you need by way of food and medicine. And they have to leave you enough time for sleep. Eight hours in every twenty-four – that's what the law says. So the smart criminals wait till they're just about to be questioned, then announce that they're sleepy and need to get their regulation shuteye. Eight hours later the arresting officers have gone off shift. There's no one around who knows all the details. The hours click forward. The cell is needed for some other suspect. They let you go.

Daz knows the tricks the professionals use but he can't do it for himself. From the moment they lock the door, his only thought is to get out as quickly as possible. The cell is his nightmare.

Four walls. A high window. A metal door with a spyhole. He paces the floor. Then he measures it with his feet. Heel to toe up the length of the long wall, across in front of the doorway. There's no clock, of course. No way to track time.

And no knowledge of the building he's in. He doesn't know what's above, below or to three of the sides. More cells, perhaps.

The window is too high to see out through. So he stands next to the door, with his forehead on the metal, trying to feel through it with his mind. But there's nothing out there except an empty corridor, so his mind turns in on itself. He drops to his knees, then crawls to a corner and curls up on the floor.

That's where he is when they eventually come to get him an unmeasurable stretch of time later.

There are two of them and a tape recorder against Daz and the duty solicitor. The one officer that Daz knows is Detective Sergeant Leech. The boneless bloodsucker. The other is new to him. He's forgotten the name already.

The solicitor is a stick-like woman with disturbingly thin wrists who doesn't seem to blink at all. Daz's eyes water just looking at her. The first thing she said to him when they were alone together was not to tell her the truth. At least, that's Daz's take on it. Her actual words were: 'Tell me only the story you want to tell them.'

Now in the interview room, she keeps leaning forward in her chair. Daz hears the click of her jacket buttons on the edge of the table. 'My client would like to make a statement for the record.'

Leech looks tired – which is reasonable, because it is the small hours of the morning. 'Very well,' he says.

The solicitor nods towards Daz. He swallows.

'Used to go round to see Patty.'

'For the record,' says Leech, 'are you referring to Agnes Wattling?'

'Guess. Yeah.'

'Why?'

The solicitor tuts. 'Please don't interrupt my client in his statement. It's overbearing and intimidating.'

Daz doesn't feel intimidated, but he's enjoying Leech's discomfort so he nods. 'Intimidating,' he says. 'Used to go round, see Patty. Just being friends. Never handled nothing hot. That's it.'

'Mr Croxley has made his statement. Now, unless there is any evidence against him that you haven't already told us . . .?'

'Did he ever handle any boxed consumer electronics at Agnes Wattling's house?'

She looks to Daz. He shakes his head.

'Mr Croxley indicates in the negative.'

'So we're left with the question,' says Leech, 'of how your fingerprints got on to just such a box. One that had been stolen a couple of days before from an electronics shop in Waterfields.'

The solicitor looks at Daz. He clenches his fists under the table.

'Perhaps I might have a minute with my client alone?'

'Interview suspended at—' Leech checks his watch '—five twenty-eight in the morning.' He clicks the tape recorder off and leans towards the solicitor so that his face is surely too close for her comfort. 'Lady, I'm tired. Believe me. The sooner we can get this finished, the happier I'll be. Just give me a few minutes on my own with Daz. No tape recorders. Just an off-the-record chat.'

'No,' she says, not leaning back, not looking away from Leech, and certainly not blinking. 'My client does not wish to have a meeting without legal representation. He—'

'It's OK,' Daz says, cutting in. 'I'll do it.'

*

The door closes. Leech sighs deeply and rubs his hands over the dough-like skin of his face. 'Lawyers,' he says. 'Single-minded like sharks. It's all so simple for them, isn't it? You get charged. They get you off. Or they don't. But for you and me it's different. There are lots of things going on in our lives, eh?'

Daz looks up from the tabletop.

'I'm not saying we're always on the same side exactly – but we understand that nothing's so cut and dried as guilty or innocent. Personally, I think she'll have a hard time getting you off this one – if I recommend that we push on with investigating the case. You just lied on tape. There are the fingerprints. You know what magistrates are like when it comes to that kind of thing.'

Daz stands up, steps over to the corner of the interview room and leans his back against the wall. Leech watches him but doesn't move.

'You're unlucky more than bad. The criminal damage spree ended after you left school. You've only got one previous for handling stolen property. I've seen criminal records that make *War and Peace* look like a light read. Yours is nothing, believe me. And all those psychology assessments you had done when you were a kid – I've read the reports.'

'So?'

'So it isn't fair that a word like *arson* in your record would be so prejudicial to a magistrate.'

Daz knocks the back of his head against the wall. 'It was just a bike shed!'

Leech nods. 'And you were just a very unlucky twelve-year-old. And now, handling stolen property. In the context of a riot – where no one has been punished for all that happened—'

'What?'

'Prison.'

'For that?'

'Look at it from our side. We've found a house stuffed with stolen property – and I mean floor to ceiling – with your fingerprints all over it.'

Daz steps forward. 'Only the computer!' Then it hits him that he's fallen into a trap, and he remembers what the solicitor said.

'A computer? I don't remember mentioning that.' For a moment Leech looks serious, then he sits back and laughs. 'Don't worry, the tape recorder isn't on. I'm not taking notes.'

Daz's shoulders drop. 'Wanna see my solicitor.'

'Whatever,' says Leech. 'But all I've told you so far is that I can get you in prison. We could start with a few months on remand.'

'Could get bail.'

'Perhaps. But our assessment of it would be that you'd be likely to run. I've seen those psychology reports, remember. You have a phobia of authority, regulations, confinement. I'm not using all the right jargon, of course . . .'

'They'd let me walk!'

'Perhaps. But is it worth the risk? I know what prison would do to you.'

Daz knows this isn't true. No one could understand what prison would do to him. He'd die inside, one way or another. He pulls out his chair and sits. Then he puts his forehead on the table. The surface smells of coffee.

'Did you ever hear of Lyall-Griffiths Investments Ltd?' Leech doesn't wait for an answer. 'It's a few years back. A big Public–Private Partnership to build more social housing in the East Midlands. There was government money and a load of EU grants. On top of that they drew in some hundred and fifty million of private capital. Everyone was going to be happy. First they decontaminate a load of brown-field sites, then the buildings start going up, including a couple in Leicester – the Grassmead Tower development. Everything looks solid. The largest tranche of money gets drawn in. Then one day the managing director and his finance chief don't turn up for work. It turns out this is the same day that a line of anxious creditors start appearing at the door. Everything collapses like a house of cards.'

Daz lifts his head, looks at Leech. 'Collapses?'

'Metaphorically speaking. The buildings stayed up, more or less. But the company had been cutting corners all along. Substandard materials. Decontamination not done properly. Bits of buildings had to be pulled down. Terrible job. In the end the project cost four times the original estimates. The government paid, of course. An unfinished building looks a lot more embarrassing than a hole in a budget.'

Up till now, Daz has felt himself to be in the middle of a waking nightmare. But he's got a whiff of opportunity here. Real information. He sits back in his chair, arms crossed.

'Where'd they go – the two bosses?'

Leech shakes his head slowly. 'They managed to disappear, along with ten million pounds in cash that had somehow been accumulated in the company's safes. Pounds sterling and Euros. Up till last week we'd been thinking that they'd slipped across to east Asia somewhere. Indonesia, perhaps.' Leech stops speaking and folds his arms, matching Daz's position, only less slumped in his chair.

'And?' prompts Daz.

'And now I need to know if you're going to help me.'

'Sure.'

Leech shakes his head. 'That was too easy.'

'Want me to bang my head on the table couple of times first, then say yes?'

'Perhaps. You see, there's pain either way in this. You don't help me and you'll end up scratching your nails down the inside wall of a prison cell . . .'

'Can't say that!'

'This is off the record, remember. That works both ways. You accuse me of entering into a conspiracy to pervert the course of justice, and I'll deny it – just like you'd deny your little slip of the tongue from a moment ago. I want you to understand that if you do help me, you'll be annoying two very nasty people.'

'Who?'

Leech sucks in a long breath through his pursed lips, like a smoker dreaming of a cigarette. He seems to come to a decision. 'The men who ran off with the money are Dicks – he was the managing director – and Feildman, head of finance. At least one of them could be back in the country, perhaps both. The stolen money has started to circulate. Some of it was marked when they emptied the safe. We've had a rash of stained notes handed in with serial numbers matching the cash we're looking for. Dicks and Feildman have the money. If we can find *them*, we'll be halfway to finding *it*. And that's where you come in.'

'Don't know 'em,' Daz says.

'But you know someone who does.'

Daz shakes his head, nonplussed.

'There was a third man. He didn't work for the company and we never proved his involvement – not in a way that would have satisfied the courts. But if Dicks and Feildman are back in the country, he's going to know. He's in prison right now, serving eighteen months for another fraud.'

'Bishop?'

Leech nods. 'Smart boy.'

The solicitor is directing her unblinking eyes on Leech. 'You're letting my client go?'

'For the time being.'

'Then why couldn't this have waited until a more civilized hour?'

'Your client,' says Leech, 'is a hard man to get hold of.'

She looks at Daz next, leaning forward from the waist. 'Well?'

He explores an upper wisdom tooth with the tip of his tongue.

'Very well,' she says at last. She leaves the door open behind her. Daz starts to follow, then turns.

'What?' says Leech.

'You know Paul Raglan?'

'All too well.'

'He a police informer, or what?'

Leech looks puzzled for a moment, then he laughs. 'You know we can't comment on who is or isn't a police informant.'

'Seeing as how I'm gunna be informing for you . . .'

'It's one-way traffic.' Then he shakes his head. 'Paul Raglan,' he says to himself. 'An informant.' Then he laughs till a tear forms in the corner of one eye and he has to wipe it away – which is the sincerest denial that Daz could have hoped for.

Someone told Daz once that for every arrest it takes four to eight man-hours of work in the police station. He's glad. He doesn't see why he should lose a night's rest on his own. Dawn is coming up as he walks back down the length of Severn Street. The birds are in full chorus, and he doesn't know if he's going to be able to sleep at all.

The bedsit looks worse every day. The hole in the door has got bigger – someone must have pulled the loose wood out. Strangely, Daz doesn't mind. It's not that he likes the decay. It's just that it doesn't seem to touch him.

He slams the door behind him and closes his eyes, wondering why he's been resisting Raglan's pressure to get him out of the house. Partly because resisting pressure is what he has always done – pressure from his father, from his teachers, from the Jobcentre. But he's got friends here. And responsibilities. He steps across to his box of things, takes out yesterday's can of Tesco Economy Dog Food and the spoon. Then he climbs out on to the fire escape and sits on the windowsill.

There's a red blush in the sky over the slate roofs and brick chimneystacks. A bird on the end of a TV aerial opposite is singing the edge of its territory. Daz hasn't been so late in feeding the fox before. He doesn't know if it will turn up at this time of day. He scoops a spoonful of jellied meat and flicks it down to the back yard. Then another. And he listens for a sound.

The sound he hears is his door opening and Freddy padding barefoot across the room.

'I heard you come in,' she says. 'Are you all right?'

'Checking up on me?' he asks. 'Wanna know if I got lucky with Kat?'

'Daz!' She folds her arms, looks insulted.

But he can see the curiosity under the mask. 'Didn't,' he says.

'Aw. I'm sorry.'

But she sounds more relieved than anything. He turns his back on her, stares out into the pale sky. There's an angled brushstroke of cloud just above the roofs. Golden. She puts her arms around him, kisses him on the back of the neck. He pulls free.

'No way,' he says, standing up. 'Don't want it like that.' And the words feel like ropes being cut.

'Just a hug . . .'

'No such thing.'

'Daz . . .?'

'No!'

She's still standing, but he can see her crumpling from the inside. He holds himself back. 'I really, really like you, Freddy,' he says. 'But that's it.'

Before she can answer, he hears a whimpering bark behind him. He turns and looks into the yard. Then he runs down the stairs, across the slabs, jumping the splat of dog food. The fox is lying in the corner, twitching, its back arched in some kind of convulsive fit. There's a pool of vomit near its head. Daz touches the animal's side. The muscles are jumping, taut one moment, slack the next. He looks up to where Freddy is standing at his window.

'Get your mobile,' he shouts. 'Run!'

Chapter 17

Jim has something of Kat's face. But his eyes are blue, and they don't offer the same challenge as hers. He hasn't made any move to find out what his sister is doing with someone like Daz. But Daz can feel the unasked question every time the man looks at him.

'Poison,' he says at last. 'But that's only a guess.'

The fox lies on a bed of soiled newspaper. It's not vomiting any more, though that's probably because there's nothing left inside it to throw up.

'A vet might know . . .'

'You're supposed to be a doctor,' says Kat.

'Of people.'

'How would you treat it if it was a person?'

'That's different.'

Daz places his hand on the animal's side. He can feel the heartbeat through the ribcage, rapid and faint. 'Test people-drugs on animals, don't they?' It's the first thing he's said since laying the fox down on Jim's kitchen floor. 'Should work the other way round.'

Jim tries again. 'You could take it to a vet . . .'

'Tried already,' says Daz. 'Was gunna kill it.'

'He said it would be kinder,' Kat explains. 'Putting it down.'

'That's probably right, you know,' says Jim.

'Kill a person, would you?'

Jim looks from Daz to Kat. She doesn't offer any support. He shakes his head. 'I don't know about this kind of thing.'

'Then guess,' says his sister.

Jim puts his hand on the fox's underbelly, probes with his fingers. 'If it's been poisoned deliberately, why isn't it dead? Probably the poisoner doesn't know what he's doing. He's got hold of a bottle that says "poison" on the side, dosed some meat, then left it out where the animal could find it. Something like benzene hexachloride. Easy to get hold of. Causes vomiting and convulsions. Or a different one maybe.'

'I've never heard of it,' says Kat.

'It's an insecticide. I think they call it Lindane. But there are a load of nasties that you can buy over the counter.'

'Can you cure it?'

Jim shrugs. 'All anyone could do is treat the symptoms. Relax the muscles. Valium, perhaps – for the convulsions. Though I've no idea what dose to give it. And rehydration – it should be on an IV. I just don't know who you could find to give it a try.'

'I do,' says Kat. And she gives her brother a hopeful smile.

Daz's panic has cooled now. He's thinking that perhaps he should be anxious, but he's never been good at anxiety. The feeling that's been solidifying inside him for the last half-hour is anger. That's an emotion he's had far more practice with.

They've ridden back to Kat's place in a taxi. He hasn't spoken through the journey. Instead he's been holding the injustice in his mind, feeling its shape. And each time he runs over its outline, the more tangible it becomes.

It's eight-thirty according to the digital clock on the dashboard. Kat pays the driver and they climb out.

'Daz?' She's holding his forearm.

He's looking up the road, unfocused.

'Let's eat breakfast,' she says.

'Gotta go.' He pulls himself free.

'Are you all right?'

He does hear her words, but somehow the answer gets lost before it reaches his mouth. He's striding away up the street.

'Daz?'

There are cars on the streets now. But he doesn't bother looking as he crosses the road. One screeches to a halt with its bumper a few inches from his legs. The driver blares on the horn. Daz wills the man to get out and try to take a swing at him. It doesn't happen.

Daz is striding down the street. But in his mind he's already at his destination, on the other side of the city. He's rehearsing the violence inside his head. Kicking down a door. Throwing a brick. He feels the destruction, experiencing the sound of splintering wood and bending metal. None of this makes the anger go away. But resolving the feeling into physical action makes it somehow more bearable.

It's the car that he sees first. The maroon Jaguar, parked in the middle of the U-shaped drive, next to the mock-Georgian front door. Daz stands for a moment, in the shadow of a poplar tree, looking at it. Then he casts around, taking in the tightly clipped lawns and the hedge of rhododendron bushes that screens the garden from the road. There's a long-handled gardening fork standing upright in the soil of a rose bed. He steps across to it, picks it up and feels the weight of it in his hands.

Now he's here, he knows that this is what he's been

building up to ever since he met the man. Raglan the corrupt. Raglan the bully. Raglan the fox poisoner.

'Croxley!'

Daz jolts his eyes to the side of the house. His landlord is standing there, car keys in hand.

'I've been waiting for that name, boy. Any longer and I was going to come looking for you.'

Daz steps forward, dragging the gardening tool so that one prong bumps across the hard lawn surface, droning like some kind of giant tuning fork. He lifts it on to his shoulder as he reaches the gravel drive. Raglan is walking towards him. The car is the last barrier between them.

They stand looking at each other, Raglan wearing a smile that's only a muscle twitch away from being a bare-teeth snarl. Daz stares back, focusing his loathing. The moment stretches. Raglan's eyes widen slightly. The balance shifts between them. Daz grips the fork handle.

'Back away from here, Croxley.' The pretence has gone from Raglan's face now.

Daz raises the fork.

Raglan points a warning finger. 'Don't . . .'

But the fork is swinging already, cutting the air in a beautiful arc. It hits the windscreen just above the near wiper blade. There isn't the tinkling crash of normal glass breaking. This is a dull thud. A white spider's web of reflective cracks radiates from the impact point.

It looks as if Raglan is trying to swear, but the words must be trapped inside him by a clot of rage. Every muscle of his reddening face is set hard. A dog starts barking inside the house. Lady. Locked in a room somewhere.

Daz swings the fork again. This time it goes clean through the glass, flinging a snowstorm of white over the grey-leather upholstery. Raglan is circling the car, arms taut, eyes betraying the violence inside him. He's almost within lunging range. Daz slices the air between them with a sweep of the fork. The prongs bounce off the car's wing, leaving bare metal at the centre of a plate-sized dent.

Part of his mind can see that Raglan is continuing to circle, threatening to come at his back. But Daz is berserk now, his anger in full vent. Uncontrollable. He kicks sideways at the door. And again. Two more dents. Then he swings the fork behind him, keeping Raglan at a distance and taking out a side window in one movement.

'Going to kill you, Croxley, you little shit!'

Daz vaults on to the bonnet, stamping craters with his boots, then he steps on to the roof. Thunk! The fork prongs go down into the metal, indenting four dimples in the maroon paintwork. Thunk! This time he rams it down harder, leaving puncture marks, like a line of bullet holes from a machine gun.

'Let that dog out!' Raglan shouts into the house.

Thunk. Another line of holes.

Raglan picks up a display of geraniums, complete with flowerpot, and launches it into the air. But Daz watches it coming. He swings the fork like a baseball bat. Sharp fragments of broken terracotta fly. Earth and smashed vegetation shower down on to Raglan's grey suit.

There's blood dripping from a horizontal gash on Raglan's cheek.

'Call the fucking police!'

Thunk! Thunk!

The top of the car has become a cratered moonscape. Daz's hands are feeling numb with the repeated jolts of impact. Thunk! The fork goes in deeper this time. The prongs jam in the metal. He struggles to retrieve it. Raglan darts a hand forward, catching him behind one ankle. He falls on his back. The man has Daz's foot in two hands. He's twisting. There's a sharp pain in Daz's knee. He kicks out with the other foot. Three times before he makes contact and Raglan lets go.

Daz is on his feet again. He wrestles the fork free and jumps to the ground on the side of the car furthest from Raglan.

'You will die. You know that. If you're lucky.'

Daz takes a step back towards the road. 'Poisoner!'

Up to this point, Raglan must have thought Daz's attack came from some other motivation. Now he knows the real reason.

'You retard!' There's contempt in his voice. 'Simple-minded cretin!'

Daz makes two forward lunges, putting out both headlights. Then he turns and limps away, listening for the gravel crunch of following feet. Instead he hears the car door and the engine firing with a throaty roar. That's when he starts to run. The Jaguar sprays gravel as it wheel-spins through first and second.

Daz jumps sideways off the drive, glancing back to see the car turning, the front wheels leaping over the kerb on to the lawn, Raglan's face leering through the teeth of the broken windscreen. Daz flings the garden fork. It flies, spikes first, through the air and embeds itself in the radiator grille. Rust-coloured water spurts out.

The car is still going. It accelerates towards him. He jumps to the side again and runs towards the rhododendron hedge, forces himself between the clinging branches out on to the road and away.

PART 3

*T*here was a time before the education system gave up on Daz. He did the run of LEA psychologists. Each one put him through a set of tests. Some were impossibly hard – like remembering lists of numbers and trying to repeat them in reverse order. But when they asked him to flip shapes around in his head, that was trivial. Not even a challenge. He could succeed or fail at will, depending on what mood he was in at the time. He usually decided to get the answers wrong.

But there was one psychologist who so clearly wanted him to fail that Daz summoned up all his concentration to focus on the task of winning. The more questions he got right, the more annoyed the man seemed to be. Which was great feedback as far as Daz was concerned.

He'd long before worked out that his brain must be wired up differently from everyone else's. But it was clearly wired up in the wrong kind of wrong way, according to this psychologist.

'We're going to play a little game,' the man said. 'I'll say a word, and you say the first word that pops into your head. Here we go then . . . Blue.'

'Movie.'

The psychologist nodded as if that was what he'd expected Daz to say. He made some notes, then offered another word: 'Hate.'

Daz responded with 'Book'.

'Very good, David.' More notes, hastily scribbled, as if some great discovery was being made.

'Freedom.'

'Gun.'

'Ice cream.'

'Petrol.'

'Are you enjoying this game?' the psychologist asked.

Daz just smiled. He knew that they'd both been playing games all along. But he doubted whether the psychologist understood that.

Chapter 18

Thomas Cook stands on his low plinth, holding a suitcase and an umbrella. Daz likes the suitcase. It looks scratched and battered. He isn't sure what the man did to get a bronze statue made of him. Something to do with holidays. Perhaps that's why they've put him outside the railway station.

Daz ambles inside. He can hear the voice of the announcer echoing around the concourse, but he can't make out any of the words. A train must have come in because there's a press of people hurrying past him, out towards the taxi rank.

'Croxley.'

He turns and sees Patty sitting at the café, a Styrofoam cup on the table in front of her. She's wearing a white cardigan over her dress in spite of the heat.

'You're late, boy.'

'But—'

'Ten-thirty, we said.'

He glances at the numbers on the station clock.

'I've been waiting half an hour. They won't even let me smoke!'

She looks greyer than before. The skin of her face seems to have fewer wrinkles, as if it has been pulled tighter over her cheekbones.

'You all right?' he asks.

'Of course I'm bloody all right. I'm not an invalid, you know!' She prods him in the midriff with one finger. 'And you should take a look at yourself, boy. You look as if you haven't slept in days.'

They may have missed the train that Patty says she wanted them to take, but the service to Nottingham runs so frequently that the next one is pulling in as they reach the platform. There's a strange urgency about Patty's movement as she heads for the carriage door – as if she's had too much coffee. He puts a hand on her arm, trying to help her into the carriage, but she shrugs him off.

'Will you stop fussing, boy!'

The train is almost empty. She chooses a table and he sits opposite her. She adjusts the cardigan across her chest then pulls out a cigarette. He puts a hand on the back of his neck to wipe away the sweat.

A man sitting on the other side of the walkway coughs loudly and points to the no-smoking sign on the window. He's wearing grey-tinted glasses and a worried frown. Patty lights up anyway.

'Excuse me,' he says.

Patty ignores him.

'Excuse me.'

She takes a long drag and then holds the remains of the cigarette for him to see. 'They're good for your health. That's what they used to say when I started.'

The man looks at the no-smoking sign again, as if checking that he's not made some kind of horrible mistake. 'It's just that I . . . I suffer from asthma.'

'It might help if you tried it yourself,' she suggests. 'Kill or cure.'

The man is squirming in his seat.

Daz reaches out and takes the cigarette from Patty's hand. Then he grinds it out on the table and turns to look through the window. Patty kicks him on the shin.

He watches the trees pass the window, smeared with speed. There's a wide field of rapeseed beyond the track. Yellow as an advertising hoarding. He reaches out with his mind, brushes the surface of flowers, feeling their texture, tracing the contours of the slope with giant fingers. The clock is catching up with him now. Patty was right in what she said earlier. He hasn't slept since the night before last, and the rocking of the train is working on him already. He rests his forehead on the glass, feeling the vibration on his skull.

He thinks about the fox. He's pretty sure it's going to die – though Kat's brother will do his best. And he's wondering if the first vet was right – if death might be a release for the animal. 'Put it to sleep,' he'd said. Daz hates that phrase. If you're going to kill an animal, you should have the guts to face the fact full on.

Patty taps the table to attract his attention. The receipts are resting in front of her, held in a bundle with a paperclip. She gets out an A to Z and opens it.

'He's somewhere on this page,' she says. 'That's my bet.'

Daz drags himself back from his half-sleep. He forces his eyes open and pretends to look at the map.

'I've marked the positions of all the shops Salt has been using. There are some like this—' She taps a black Biro cross on the printed page '—a Tesco supermarket. It's got a big car park. He could have driven miles to get there. It doesn't tell us anything. But the ones I've marked in red are all small shops without car parks. Newsagent. Chip shop. Stationer. See how they're all clumped together?'

'Chip shop?'

'Are you listening, boy? I've spent good money on phone cards to work this out.'

'Never got a receipt from a chip shop,' Daz murmurs.

She shakes her head. 'I'm taking all these expenses before we divide the money, you know that, boy?'

Daz forces his eyes back open again. Patty is circling the red crosses with her finger. 'We can ask people around here. There can't be many electrical shops in that area.'

The man with the tinted glasses coughs into his hand.

'What now?' Patty barks.

He's leaning across the walkway so he can look at the map. 'It's just that I . . . I live in Nottingham. And there isn't . . . not as far as I know . . . there isn't an electrical shop in that area.'

'A second-hand shop, then?'

He shakes his head.

'It might be a small place,' Patty says.

'I think I'd know if there was.'

'Hell!'

'But you could try here.' He puts his finger on the map two inches to one side of Patty's circle. 'It's new.'

'What's new?'

Daz sees the man recoil.

'Spit it out, man!'

'An . . . that is, it's an electrical shop.'

'How do you know all this?'

'I bought a computer there last week. Excellent price.'

'What make?'

'Dell. It was shopsoiled, so he . . . he knocked off another twenty per cent for me.'

Patty nods and closes the A to Z. 'And what is the name of the shop?'

*

It's the kind of street that must have been a busy commercial area once. Before it got isolated from its customers by the widening of the main road. And before the out-of-town shopping centres started to open, with their convenient parking. There is a row of seven shops here. Three of them are boarded up. There is a kebab takeaway, a fishing tackle shop and a newsagent, which seems to specialize in top-shelf magazines.

Then there's the Discount Electrical and Telephone Store. It doesn't look as if the owner has gone out of his way to promote the place. The shop sign, badly painted, is a board leaning against the inside of the unwashed plate glass. The rest of the window display seems to be used as an overspill of the storage area.

But for all that, everyone seems to know the place. The taxi driver has told them about a nephew of his who managed to pick up a second-hand mobile phone there at a price that was more than reasonable.

'Idiot,' Patty mutters as the cab drives away.

'Who?'

'Salt. He's going to get himself put away. And me if he keeps this up.'

Daz has woken up a bit since getting out of the airless train. So he decides not to point out that she's already on the police wanted list. The old woman looks more agitated than he's seen her before. She pulls out a cigarette and lights up. After the first inhalation she coughs. Daz holds her forearm to steady her. She shakes him off and walks up to the shop door.

'There's no use hiding now,' she says. 'We've got to find him. It's time to face him and get things straight.'

But the door is locked.

'Damn and blast the man.'

Daz steps level with her. There's a handwritten sign on the inside of the glass. Three words and a number. Patty exhales her disgust towards it, together with a lungful of smoke.

'Tsch. Back in 5 minutes. He's lazy as well as stupid.'

'Sure it's him?'

'You see those boxes?' She points to the clutter behind the window. 'Two Daewoo microwave combi ovens and a cyclone vacuum cleaner by Hoover. That was the last batch he took off my hands. I worked out a healthy price in my head and then doubled it specially for him. He paid without a squeak.'

'What now?'

'We wait for him to get back from wherever he's gone.'

Daz looks down. There is a heap of mail on the vinyl just inside the door. More than a day's worth, by the look of it. He shuffles his feet, trying to draw her attention to what he's seen, but she's glaring up and down the road.

A large articulated truck rumbles past.

Patty starts coughing again. It's worse this time, and she doesn't resist when he steadies her, a hand on each of her hunched shoulders. He's shocked by how thin she feels. It's as if her clothes are hanging directly on the bone.

'Stop fussing, boy,' she says at last. 'It's a good thing you've got me here. Look.' She points to the pile of mail. 'You'd have been waiting all day.'

Daz nods. 'Yeah. So what now? Got your lock pick?'

She shakes her head, then gives him her arm to hold. 'Now we try the other side of the building. There must be a back door or something.'

There is, but it's got heavy-duty plywood stuck over it. The rear window, too.

Daz looks around the yard. Three high brick walls. A fringe of grass and dandelions outlining each paving slab. A pile of black bin-bags, knotted at the top. A heap of brown cardboard from flattened boxes. A broom with no bristles. There's a smell of frying in the air, probably from one of the houses at the back.

He turns his attention to the window. The heads of the screws that hold the board in place have all been burred beyond use. It's as if someone has taken an angle grinder to them. Daz tries pulling at the plywood, but his fingers can't get any purchase.

Patty is standing in the shade, supporting herself against one of the walls. She drops her cigarette, only half-smoked. She doesn't grind it out.

'You OK?' he asks.

She nods. 'A bit tired.' Then she points a finger at the bin-bags. There is a tremor in her hand. 'Just search those, then bring a taxi.'

He'd definitely complain, but he is too worried about her health. So he gets down on his knees and starts unpicking the first knot. The bag opens and flies swarm from the hot interior. Black, fat insects darting for the light. He gags on the stench, throws himself back and rolls over the ground to get some more distance.

'What's the matter, boy – found a body?'

Daz picks himself up. He takes the broom, holds his breath and steps towards the stench again. Then, using the handle, he prods the plastic bag, tipping it over so the contents spill out on the hot slabs. Maggots. More flies. Aluminium foil cartons. An uneaten Indian takeaway meal. A tin of mould with a picture of baked beans on the outside. A bunch of black bananas, being crushed under their own weight. A milk bottle three-quarters full of what looks like blue and green cauliflower. A spreading pool of oily liquid.

'No,' he says. 'No body.'

Patty fumbles for another cigarette. She lights up then shuffles closer to the mess. She shakes her head, as if there is some mystery just beyond her reach.

'What are you waiting for? Open the others.'

He meets Kat at Humberstone Gate, as they arranged, just outside Brucciani's. She kisses him on the lips, then takes a quick glance around the pedestrianized street. 'I've got three-quarters of an hour.'

It seems unequal that her time with him is rationed, but so much of his is available. He takes the offered hand and lets her lead him inside. It's dark in here after the glare on the street. A place of ground coffee smells and cigarette smoke. He'd like a mug of chocolate, but that reminds him of Raglan, so he goes for tea instead.

Kat orders espresso and gets a fiver out of her purse. 'My treat.'

'No way.'

'Come on, Daz. Let me pay this time.'

But this is something he can't afford to accept from her. He's had a lifetime of people offering him help. Patronizing help. And this he knows from long experience: that each time a hand was held out to give him a lift, it turned out to be sign language for his own inadequacy. He slides his pound coin across the counter.

Kat chooses a table for them. She sits opposite him, her knee touching his. He watches her sip her coffee. There's a thin line of foam on her upper lip. She licks it off with the tip of her tongue. Then she looks up and for a moment he feels exposed.

'Penny for your thoughts?' she says.

When he doesn't answer, she grins and licks her lips again, playfully this time. 'Is that what you were thinking?'

He shakes his head. 'How's foxy?'

She gives him a sceptical look. 'She's holding on.'

'She?'

'Don't you know the difference?'

They both laugh now. He strokes her knee under the table.

'Nice.'

He strokes higher.

She stops his hand with hers. 'We've not got a lot of time.'

'Something better to do?'

'Yes.' She leans her head closer to his. 'We've got to talk. You remember that banknote you showed me? Well, I found a Home Office database on the Internet for checking things like that – to see if the serial numbers match any that are listed as—'

'On the computer?' Daz feels a panicky constriction inside his ribs. 'Didn't use it, did you?'

'It was anonymous. Don't worry.'

'They'll trace it!'

She's shaking her head. 'There's no way. I did it on one of the machines at work. They couldn't know who it was. And we were right – the money *is* stolen.'

He takes his hand off her knee. 'Not right, you doing this. Too risky.'

'What? I'm too fragile – is that it? It's too dangerous for a woman?'

'It's not that.'

'Then what?'

He wishes he had the words to explain. It's not just that Bishop and his men might kill or wound or cause pain. It's that they'd do it without a trace of a qualm.

'Me – I've got no way out of this,' he says. 'But you've got a choice, right?'

'Exactly. And I've chosen. You know what it's like working where I do? Every day I see people who treat me as if I was some kind of tyrant. As if my pleasure is in keeping money back from them. Fuck that! And then you turn up and – do you realize this? – you're the first one to look across that desk and see a human being.'

'Can't know that for sure.'

'I do! And then you started telling me about your life and suddenly I'm remembering that there is a world out there beyond accelerated promotion and assessment interviews. Don't try to push me back behind the counter. I'll turn into another Cow Queen if I have to live like that much longer.'

'Wanted a round-the-world air ticket, right?'

Kat nods. 'Once.'

'Can still go do it. Rent the flat out. Take a couple of years off. But my trip's one-way. Can't come back from where I'm going.'

'Who wants to come back?'

'Wouldn't say that if you knew.'

'Then tell me! Tell me everything so I can understand. Tell me about this morning – where did you go after we left the fox?'

He'd like to tell her. Trashing Raglan's car is one of the few things he feels any sense of pride about. But he's made himself homeless by what he's done, and he doesn't want to talk about Housing Benefit and emergency payments with Kat. It would take them right back to where they started – claims adviser and Social Security hard case, sitting on opposite sides of the counter.

Instead he fills her in about Salt and his supposed stash of stolen money. How he is helping Patty to find out what the man is doing with it and where it came from. He tells her about his biggest worry – that they'll actually locate the money. Then he'd face his real problem, because Bishop and Raglan and the police are all after it as well – and all seem to think that he's the key. If he helps Raglan, Bishop will kill him. If he helps Bishop, the police will lock him up. If he helps the police, then he's a dead man from any one of a number of possible assassins.

'So why are you helping the old woman?' Kat asks.

'Haven't a clue.'

She reaches across the table and touches his face. 'Patty's like a mother to you, isn't she?'

Daz shakes his head. 'Don't want a mother.'

'I'm sorry.' There's a look of sadness on Kat's face. Daz can't understand quite where it's coming from, and that makes him uneasy.

'Went to Nottingham,' he says, speaking to fill the silence. 'Found the shop Salt was selling things from. Looks like he's done a runner.'

'A dead end?' Kat asks.

He nods. 'Found papers in the rubbish at the back, that's all.'

'Printed, handwritten – what?'

'Newspapers. Receipts. Nothing.'

Kat sits back. 'Nothing to *you*, perhaps.'

For a moment Daz feels stung, but there's no condemnation in her voice. 'Maybe Patty will know what they mean.'

Kat glances at her watch. 'Hell.'

'Time already?'

'The Cow Queen calls.'

Daz makes his way back towards Severn Street. He knows he's got to move out after what he's done to the landlord. But he needs to sneak back in so he can pick up any of his stuff that hasn't been trashed already. He has no idea what will come after that. One step at a time.

As he walks he thinks about Patty. It's not just that she's frail that's worrying him. She's had her ups and downs for as long as he can remember. But since she lost Kodak it seems as if the life has drained out of her. She perks up when there's the smell of money in the air. And she can still get around in pursuit of Salt's supposed hoard. But each time it feels as if she is being stretched thinner by the effort. Dyson is another puzzle. Threatening one day, then hardly able to bare his teeth at him the next. Daz wonders if dogs can pine over the loss of their friends, if they can fear death.

He walks up London Road then down Conduit Street next to the station. He can feel the heat radiating from the red-brick walls. He can feel it blowing against his arms and face in the gusty wind. He makes his way past the big domed mosque and turns right up Sparkenhoe Street. He's on Saxby Street now, turning the last corner. And he's longing for a drink of water from the tap.

He looks up Severn Street towards the house. It takes him a moment to resolve the image in front of him. A poster that he recognizes is tumbling end over end along the pavement – a grainy image, the silhouette of a man holding the neck of an electric guitar, bending low as he smashes it down on to the ground. Daz has a poster just like this on his wall. The Clash. London Calling. Then he sees a heap of clothes and boxes on the pavement up ahead. Raglan has done his work already.

Daz runs the last thirty paces. His bicycle is in the road, lying on its side. He stoops and pulls a pair of red vinyl trousers from the bottom of the heap of ruined possessions. Then he drops them and picks up his lime-green shirt. There's a shoe print where someone has walked over it.

There are cassette tapes and CDs mixed in with everything else, all of them cracked, as if someone has stamped on them individually. He picks his penknife from the ground, pockets it.

The remains of his banana box is wedged behind a wheelie bin. He pulls it free, looks for something to put in it. The shirt. A pair of socks. His tin-opener. When the box is full, he hauls it over to the front door so he can carry it up to Freddy and Ginger's place.

He slots in his key, but it won't turn. The lock has been changed.

Chapter 19

Daz waits till it's dark before trying to break in. He carries the box of salvaged possessions via the walkway at the back of the building to the fire escape. His bedsit window has been sealed with a sheet of plywood. For a moment that catches him – the similarity to Salt's shop. He runs a finger over one of the screw heads. Milled flat. Unremovable. He stands back as far as he can and looks at the other windows on this side of the building. More than half of them are boarded up in the same way. There's been quite an exodus in the last couple of weeks. He hasn't noticed it happening. Raglan's bullying must be driving the tenants away.

At the top of the fire escape he finds Freddy and Ginger's window closed. There's no answer when he raps a knuckle on the wooden frame, so he takes his penknife and works the blade into the crack, bringing it up behind the latch. The window opens and he climbs inside.

He doesn't turn the light on, though it is very dark. There's no point in attracting attention. He puts his box in a corner of the room then goes to the kitchenette and drinks from the cold tap with cupped hands. He's more tired than he can remember being. Even splashing his face doesn't help. He drags himself back into the main room and lies down on the floor, one arm under his head.

*

He dreams he's sitting on the stone floor in a doorway, a blanket over his knees, an empty wooden bowl in his hands. A large man – perhaps it's Bishop – drops a handful of copper change into it, then walks on down the street.

When he wakes next, there's a sheet over him and a pillow under his head. It smells the same as Freddy and Ginger's clothes. Some kind of fabric conditioner. He doesn't open his eyes. And before he can start to think about what must have happened, he slips back into his dreams.

It's the sound of hammering that wakes him, reverberating through the floor from somewhere downstairs. It feels late – perhaps midnight or one in the morning. There's a dim glow from the light in the boxroom. Daz rolls over and finds a mug on the floor next to him. He props himself on an elbow and picks it up. Cold tea. He gulps it down. There's no sign of life in the flat, so he guesses Freddy and Ginger must have dropped in on their way to the club and found him there.

The hammering noise stops.

He looks around the room. Some of Freddy's dress-up gear is now draped over a rattan chair next to the wall. Silky garments in black, green and turquoise. A lilac feather boa.

He gets up and finds that he's slept in his clothes, though somehow not in his boots. He doesn't remember taking them off. He stumbles over to the banana box in the corner of the room. He searches through it and finds some clean underwear but nothing much else of use. His toothbrush must be out on the pavement still, together with the rest of his trashed belongings.

There's toothpaste by the basin in the kitchenette. Reasoning that Freddy and Ginger won't mind, he smears some around his mouth with a finger. Then he hears footsteps approaching up the stairs, so he swills his mouth, dries his hands on his shirt and goes out to greet them.

But the voice he hears through the door is Raglan's.

'Wakey-wakey.'

There's a pounding on the door panel. A panicky feeling of *déjà vu* grips Daz. It must be less than ten days ago that it happened, though it feels as if he's lived a year in that time. The door handle rattles. Daz is caught, mid-step, muscles frozen. He's trying to figure how the landlord has tracked him here.

'Come on, boy. It's time for our business meeting.'

Calling it business must be Raglan's attempt at humour. The only business left to be settled is the degree of pain. Beating with an iron bar. Throwing from a tall building. He opens his mouth to answer and then changes his mind. He backs away, twists the window catch and opens it. His bike should still be leaning against the wall under the fire escape, unless someone has nicked it already.

More hammering. Lady barks.

'I know you're there, Ginger.'

Daz stops. He's suddenly uncertain about what is happening. But he now knows that Raglan is unaware of his presence. And it suddenly feels important that it stays that way and no one finds out that Freddy and Ginger have been helping him. He steps as lightly as he can, back to the middle of the room. He rolls up his sheet and pillow, carries them across to the corner and lays them over the top of the banana box.

'Come on, Ginger! You know the way this works. The loan repayment is due. Either you have the cash or I take goods to that same value.'

Without warning, an elbow breaks through the door panel nearest the handle. Daz dives to the floor and rolls himself under the double bed. Wood splinters and cracks outside. The door latch clicks and feet step into the room. Daz tries to slow his breath, opening his mouth wide so the passage of air doesn't make any noise. The room light comes on and he sees a pair of Nike trainers and brushed-cotton chinos lead the way across the room to the window. Polished black shoes and pressed, grey trouser legs follow. And four brown paws, dancing with excitement.

Smith speaks first: 'They've done a bunk, Mr Raglan.'

'I wouldn't have thought that was their style.'

Lady gives a series of short barks. She's straining on the lead, pulling towards Daz's covered banana box on the other side of the room. It must be Raglan holding the lead, because it's the polished leather shoes that are dragged behind the dog.

Daz watches the feet. Raglan still hasn't seen what's under the sheet. But Lady knows the smell and the treat it brought her once before. She's barking again. Daz eases himself further into the dark. There are tumbleweeds of dust here. A white sports sock. A pair of green, silky panties. His mock Docs are neatly arranged near the foot of the bed.

'Do you want me to wreck the place?' Smith asks.

There's a pause, then Raglan says 'No' as if trying the word out in an unfamiliar context. Then more definitely: 'No. Not with these two. We'll keep ourselves on the leash this time. Just take goods enough to cover the loan repayment. I'll write out a receipt. Let them take us to court if they feel that way.'

'The stereo?'

'That'll do it – for now. But he's never going to make the next payment. We'll be back for the rest next week.'

Daz watches the Nike trainers go across to the far wall. Smith kneels, unplugs some wires, then gets up and carries the first speaker from the room. Raglan follows him to the door, dragging the protesting boxer dog behind him.

Daz lifts his boots and pulls them deeper under the bed. There's not enough room for him to move freely without dragging against the carpet. Any noise will give him away – at least to Lady. He feels doubly vulnerable with only socks on his feet. He slides a hand into his pocket and touches his folded penknife.

Lady is dragging Raglan back towards the pile of sheets again. She grabs a corner of the material and worries it. The heap overbalances.

'Well . . .' Raglan bends down and touches the edge of the box. 'The little shit's been here.' He speaks the words under his breath. Daz can only just make them out over Lady's snuffling investigation of his things.

'Helping each other out, are you? Or perhaps . . .' He clutches some of the sheet material in his hand, as if feeling for body warmth. Then he looks at the open window. 'Yes . . . yes.'

Smith jogs up the stairs and back into the room. He's not rushing, but all his movements are focused on the job in hand. A professional.

'It's Croxley's,' Raglan says. 'He's been here. He's the one who ran.'

'You want me to go look?'

'Load the van first. One job at a time, eh?'

Daz watches Smith leaving with the second speaker. Staying put isn't an option any more. If he could make it to the boxroom, there's a low entranceway that would lead on to the undecorated section of the attic. It would be a crawl. No light, no floorboards. Impossible if he was being chased. But from there he could walk on the wooden joists and beams, right through into the next house, and beyond that down the row. There are five houses all connected under the roof. And if he can't slip into the boxroom unseen, he could run for it down the fire escape. But going barefoot is out of the question. And even if he could evade Smith, Lady would outpace him easily.

The hammering starts again, somewhere below him in the building. Perhaps another window is being boarded up. He quickly passes his boots down towards his feet and slips them on, the scraping of fabric not so loud against that background. The hammering stops. Daz tries to steady his breathing.

Raglan is at the door again, looking down the stairs. Lady is now straining towards the place where Daz lies hidden. Smith comes back into the room, picks up the amplifier and carries it out. Daz knows there are thirty-five steps between this flat and the ground floor. He's counted them before. He counts them off now, feeling Smith getting further away. Sixteen. Seventeen. Eighteen. When Smith leaves the building, Daz is going to roll out from his hiding place and make a run for it. Across the room, through the window and down the fire escape. And if Lady catches him, he just hopes she'll not attack. It's not as if she'll be on her home territory. He goes through the movements of the escape in his mind, counting all the time. Twenty-six. Twenty-seven.

He pulls the knife from his pocket, very slowly. The metal is warm. He unfolds the blade. Only a few steps to go and Smith will be out of the front door. Raglan, standing next to the rattan chair, is doing his best to ignore Lady's frantic attempts to get to the bed. He runs his free hand through Freddy's dresses, then picks up the end of the feather boa and lets it slip through his fingers.

Thirty-three, thirty-four, thirty-five. Smith must be out of the building.

But Raglan is allowing Lady to drag him towards the bed. He sits. Daz sees the springs depress above him. Lady drops flat, looks directly at Daz. Her tail stub is wagging double-speed. She barks.

'What is it, girl?' Raglan asks.

She barks again.

Daz grabs the silky underwear from the floor and thrusts them towards the dog. She sniffs twice, then picks them up in her mouth and pulls her head back out from under the bed so she can worry them properly.

'What's my clever girl found, then?' Raglan is speaking in his gaga voice.

Lady shakes the panties back and forth. Then she loses her grip and they fly across the room. Raglan gets up, steps to where they lie on the floor.

Daz grips the penknife handle. Smith will be coming back into the building by now, starting up the first staircase. But there might not be another chance. So Daz takes a final, deep breath and rolls out into the open. Raglan is spinning on his heel before Daz is up on his feet.

'Croxley!'

Lady seems confused. She looks up at her master, then at Daz. Only then does she lunge forward. Daz wouldn't have it in him to hurt a dog, but Raglan clearly doesn't know that because he doesn't let go of the lead.

Daz is sweeping the penknife left and right to fill the space between them. He scrambles backwards to the window, feels one leg out, then the other. He can hear Smith charging up the stairs. He turns and flings himself down the fire escape, into the dark, laces undone and whipping.

He makes two turns before Smith bursts out of the window above him. But Daz's brain is at the bottom already, picking up the bike, trying to manoeuvre it out of the yard, down the back alley. He tries it two times before he reaches the bottom, but it just won't work. Too slow, his feet getting tangled in the pedals. The rear walkway too narrow and junk filled to ride down.

So when his feet slam down on the paving stones, he grabs the bicycle frame and lifts it over the junk in the back yard to the walkway. Then he hefts it over the low wall into the small garden behind the neighbouring house.

Smith's feet make the fire-escape steps ring as he lands at the first turn. Then he jumps the flight below. Daz pushes the bike to the back door of the house. He doesn't bother to try the handle. He just kicks. The lock rips through the wood. He's into a tiled corridor, wheeling the bike ahead of him. There's a shout behind him. Raglan calling to Smith.

Daz's fingers slip once on the front door catch. Then the door is open and he's away, out on to Severn Street. He's on his bike, and his feet have found the pedals. Smith's footfalls recede behind him as he shoots down the road. A banking right turn on to Saxby Street then a left on to St Peter's Road. No braking. No looking. A taxi draws level with him. The horn blares and the driver shakes his fist through the window.

Daz allows his bike to freewheel, accelerating down the hill. It can't be as late as he'd thought before because there's still traffic on the road. He breathes deeply, trying to oxygenate his tired muscles. He checks back over his shoulder and sees a white Transit van lurching out from the Saxby Street junction. There are two men in the front seats. Smith, looking relaxed on the passenger side. And Raglan bent forward over the steering wheel.

The van accelerates. Two cars separate it from him. Daz pulls out from the kerb, riding high so no one can overtake. Then he drops his head to the handlebars and starts pumping the pedals. Feeling the wind ripping at his shirt as he powers down the hill and over the railway bridge. Ahead, he can see cars queuing at the T-junction, waiting for the lights to change so they can drive on to the inner ring road. That's when he remembers that he's cycling without lights.

But he couldn't stop in that distance and at this speed, even if he wanted to. He slips back in, tight to the kerb. He's whistling past the first of the standing cars. The lights turn amber. He passes the lead car and shoots the junction. He can hear the traffic moving behind him again. But he's got a hundred-yard start on them, and he must be breaking the thirty-mile-an-hour speed limit.

He leans left, taking his bike across two empty lanes to the outside edge of the road. He's skimming perilously close to potholes and kerbstones here. A wobble would be enough to catapult him over the front wheel, slamming him down on the road in the path of the cars that follow behind.

He risks another glance over his shoulder. There's a slow-moving Citroën in the middle lane just behind. The white van is one lane further out, moving fast to overtake. If he can just keep the Citroën between them, he'll be safe from ramming. His thighs are burning with the effort. He could dump the bike and try to run for it down a side-alley, but his legs feel like putty. They'd catch him easily.

Ahead he can see the Humberstone roundabout, a large traffic circle with a mini-woodland of close-packed trees and bushes growing in the centre, flanked on all sides by short-mown grass. He has to choose an exit – and fast. The lights ahead change from green to amber. The white van is level with him now. Only the Citroën on his right stops it swerving across the lanes and flattening him. Daz forces his legs to work. The lights turn red. The Citroën slows. Daz accelerates out into the traffic circle in front of an oncoming truck. The white van follows him, slotting in just behind the truck. Daz leans over hard and speeds across the lanes from left to right so he's skimming the innermost rim of the circle. He gives his legs one last push and moves further ahead of the rumbling wheels. He looks back. The white van is out of view, hidden by the thicket of trees at the centre of the circle. He jams on his brakes and leaps on to the grass at the middle of the roundabout, throws himself to the ground.

He lies as still and low as he can, but his chest is heaving. The low shrubs and trees are to one side. The angular outline of his bicycle is silhouetted against the headlights on the other. It lies very close to the road, front wheel pointing to the sky, rear wheel still spinning. The white van comes into view. Raglan is still leaning forward over the steering wheel, peering at the road ahead. He passes. Daz scrambles over to the bicycle, grabs it by the crossbar and hauls it back into the cover of the bushes. He's on hands and knees when the white van passes on a second circuit of the roundabout. This time Raglan is casting glances in his direction, but stillness and shadow are hiding Daz.

He lowers his body flat and feels the soft, unexpected kiss of dew on his cheek. He tenses, then submits to its touch. Somewhere behind him in the thicket of trees, a startled bird calls. He turns his head, looking towards the sound. It seems out of place next to the unsleeping ring road. The interior of the circle is a dark tangle of branches and leaves; the trees and bushes crowd thickly.

He crawls under the bushes, wriggling forward on his stomach. Within moments the road is out of view. Even the rumble of traffic sounds muffled here. The bird calls again. He lies still. Listening. Waiting for his pursuers. Hearing nothing.

At last he crawls forward again. The undergrowth is thinner in the middle of the circle. Trees blot out most of the streetlight. He gropes forward with hands outstretched. His hand touches a tree trunk. Smooth and dry. As thick as a lamppost but not as cold as metal or concrete. He sits on the ground, his back against the tree. Then he closes his eyes.

Chapter 20

Daz emerges into wakefulness so slowly that he's not sure if he's been properly asleep at all. He is cold. One arm feels numb, and when he tries to straighten himself out of the foetal position in which he's been lying his thigh and back muscles pull tight and painful. There's a rumble of traffic in the distance. There are bushes all around and a canopy of leaves above. He pulls himself up, using the trunk of a tree.

Now it's light he can see that he's not the first person to have been here. Old McDonald's wrappers. A few crushed Special Brew cans. He catches the glint of a hypodermic needle in the undergrowth.

He rubs his chin against the grain of the stubble. Then he scratches his scalp with the fingers of both hands. He's got fifty pence in his pocket, and a penknife and nothing else. He can't go back to Severn Street and he wants a chance to clean up before going off to meet Kat, so he hides his bike in the undergrowth and walks off in the direction of Waterfields.

Vicky lets him in at the front door. She's not dressed for the street today. Regular jeans and an Oasis T-shirt. She smiles at him, into him, through him.

'Vicky.'

She hesitates, as if she can't quite remember something. 'Daz?'

'The old woman in?'

'I guess so. She must be in the bedroom.'

He steps into the house, smelling its mixture of perfume and stale tobacco. It feels somehow comforting today. Dyson is stretched out on the floor, unmoving.

Daz says: 'I'll go see her, then.'

'Take the tea, will you?' Vicky points to a mug on the top of the gas fire. 'I'd be very grateful.'

Daz detours for the mug. It's cold. Stewed. With a teabag floating and an oily film on the surface. 'Better I make fresh.'

Vicky follows him to the kitchen and sits herself on the work surface, watching him getting out two clean mugs, clicking the kettle on.

He searches the cupboards and finds a packet of chocolate biscuits. 'Dyson's quiet,' he says.

She smiles sleepily. 'That's good, yeah?'

'Like dogs?'

'I suppose. But they hate me.' She picks an invisible hair off the knee of her jeans.

Daz is munching a biscuit as he stirs the mugs with a fork.

'Does she pay you?' Vicky asks.

'Who?'

'The old bag. Aunt Patty. Is that why you come round?'

He laughs. 'Pay? Her?'

'Then why do you come?'

He sniffs the milk, then pours. 'Business.'

Vicky slips off the worktop and comes up behind him. She puts her arms around his chest, her fingers working at his skin through his shirt. 'Tell me the real reason.'

Daz feels a wave of revulsion as if her attention were profoundly unnatural, incestuous. He pulls himself free. 'Forget it, will you!'

He carries the tea and biscuits to the stairs.

'Suit yourself,' Vicky says behind him.

Patty is lying on her back, asleep. The curtains are closed. Yellow curtains letting in a thin yellow light. He can see the strap of a handbag protruding from under her pillow. He puts the mug down on the bedside cabinet next to a packet of Marlboros and a lighter. Her eyes flicker open. For a moment there's alarm on her face. Then it softens into recognition. Her muscles relax. She closes her eyes again.

'I wondered when you'd get round to turning up, David.'

'Got you tea.'

She fumbles for a cigarette, props herself on the pillow, coughs into her fist. He waits, looking around the room. There is a pile of papers on the floor in the corner. It looks like the things he rescued from the third stinking bin-bag at the back of Salt's shop.

She lights up and sighs a plume of smoke into the yellow air. 'This isn't a game, you know,' she says. 'He's spending that money. Every day there's less for us.'

A sip of tea. Another drag on the cigarette.

Daz takes a biscuit and a swallow of tea. 'Really believe it?' he says. 'The money.'

'Of course I bloody do!'

'If there was none—'

'There is! Tens of thousands, boy. Stolen cash. You see that?' She points to the pile of papers. 'Bring it all over here.'

He lays the papers on the bed next to her, then kneels on the floor. She picks a bundle of handwritten receipts from the top of the pile. The same scrawl of smudgy blue letters over each one.

'Carbon copies,' she says. 'These should be in his accounts. Look.' She taps the first one with a yellow-stained finger. 'Dated last week. Received with thanks. One hundred pounds for a Samsung DVD player. It's all here. Make, model number, date, amount. I've cross-referenced this with my own accounts. He's selling on for the same prices I charged him for the goods in the first place. And for a couple of these he asked less than he paid for them! You know what that means?'

Daz shakes his head.

'It means he's got so much cash that losing twenty, thirty per cent along the way is no problem to him.'

'Could just be stupid,' Daz offers.

'Stupid?' She holds him with her eyes for a moment.

'Simple, you know. Like he's not all there.'

'No one is that stupid, boy. Not when it comes to money.'

She pulls out a newspaper from the bottom of the pile and opens it on a page full of columns of words and numbers. One line has been circled in blue pen.

'*Racing Times*,' she says. 'All the betting odds for all the races around the country. Hundreds of possible bets. He's marked the one with the shortest odds. A four-to-five-on favourite.' She pulls out another paper from the pile. 'That was from five days ago. This is four days old.' She opens the paper at a page with another Biro mark. 'Same thing. The shortest odds from all the races in the country.'

'Needs money for a gambling habit?'

'Idiot boy! People with a gambling problem bet on races where they think they can make a fortune – long odds. He's doing the opposite. He's using bookies to launder the money – getting back more or less what he put in. He's closed the electrical shop because he doesn't know where to buy his goods – now I'm not in the market any more. But this—' She pats the paper '—this seems easy to him. You always lose overall if you're a gambler. That's how bookies get to live in mansions. But following short odds, Salt isn't going to lose very often. He hands over the bent cash. And he gets back clean winnings.'

'*Seems* easy?'

She nods. 'But it puts a lot of bent cash in circulation. The wrong kind of circles. If he keeps it up, people are going to find out what's happening. And if they do, we're going to have competition in trying to get the money from Mr Salt.'

Daz explores one of his molars with the tip of his tongue. Patty always seems to judge people by the standard of her own rules. And she has a certainty that usually makes him think she's right. But he's not so sure about her understanding of Salt.

'Why you reckon I come here?' he asks.

'What kind of stupid question is that, Croxley?'

He looks at the floor.

'For the money,' she says. 'Of course.'

Kat meets him where they arranged, on a bench in a pedestrian precinct. It's shady here, a concrete canyon between the back wall of the Jobcentre and a ten-storey office building. A dry wind blows through the gap. Daz gets up as she approaches. She kisses him, her lips pressed tightly on his.

'God, but I needed that,' she says.

'Me, too.'

'Did you have a rough night?'

He tilts his head, unsure what to say.

She puts a finger to her own chin. 'You didn't shave.'

'Oh. That.'

Withholding the information that he'd had a violent bust-up with his landlord felt like a small omission when they last met. Not at all like lying. But he's more than homeless now. He's become a rough sleeper, the lowest of the low. And things he didn't tell her before have become a serious betrayal.

They sit. She puts a small package on the bench between them. Crinkled aluminium foil. He watches her unwrap it, revealing two rounds of sandwiches. Salad and something. He imagines her making them. Getting food from her fridge. A clean knife from the drawer to cut and spread. Foil-wrapped sandwiches could never be part of his own life.

'Do you want one?' she offers.

'It's all right.' He feels his empty stomach protesting.

She looks hurt. 'They're smoked ham and mustard. Really good.'

He shakes his head and watches her start to eat her way through the first one. He wishes he knew how she'd react if she discovered his secret. 'Had a dream,' he says at last.

She wipes her mouth on a tissue. 'A sexy dream?'

'No. Was begging spare change in a doorway.' He watches her face as he says this, searching for some reaction.

'A bad dream, then,' she says.

'A strange dream.'

'Did you have a hat for the money?'

He shakes his head. 'Had a weird dish made of wood.'

Her eyebrows arch. 'A begging bowl?'

He pulls his ear. 'Dunno.'

'It sounds like the story *The King of the Beggars*. Have you heard it? The man who wanted to be completely free. Detached from everything. So he gave up his job, his house. And he sat by the road begging for food. And that's how he lived.'

'Did he have a dog on a string?'

'You're not taking this seriously. The only thing he had was a begging bowl – like the one in your dream.'

Daz watches a crisp packet blow past, dragging on the pavement. When they last met it seemed so easy to be with Kat. Perhaps it's because he's now holding stuff back that he can't figure out what's going on behind her green eyes.

'What happened next?'

'The beggar goes to find the king of the beggars. But the king of the beggars isn't living in a box on the street. He's got a silk tent, held up by silver wires and gold tent pegs.'

'Couldn't use gold for a tent peg.'

'Shut up and listen. The beggar wanted to be detached, remember? That's why he gave everything up. Now he finds this rich guy is the king of his people – which he doesn't understand because the king of the beggars is supposed to be the most detached of all. The beggar sits and talks to the king – and he finds he really likes him. So when the king says "Let's go for a walk and explore these lands together", he agrees. They leave the tent and walk down the road. But the beggar's still wondering how come the king of the beggars can claim to be so detached from the world if he has all that rich stuff.

'And then, when they've gone a few miles, he remembers that he's forgotten his begging bowl. So he runs all the way back to the tent to get it.'

She takes another bite of her sandwich, her eyes still on his.

'And?'

'And that's the end.'

Daz thinks about this. 'How's the fox?' he asks.

'I spoke to Jim last night, before he went on shift. It's still alive. That's about all he'd tell me. He . . . he wanted to know about you, though.'

'What about me?'

'Like where I met you. What you do. You know.'

'And?'

'He's my brother – what do you expect?'

She starts on the second sandwich. They sit like that in silence. Daz looks ahead of him. Out of the periphery of his vision he can see her doing the same. Then her gaze drops to the pavement.

'That woman,' Kat says. 'At the Club . . .'

'Liz?'

'The other one. The dancer.'

'Freddy.'

'You and her . . . There's nothing going on there?'

'Why?'

'It's just the things she said. There isn't . . . is there?'

'No,' he says, looking away from her to the swirling litter. Then more definitely: 'No.'

She puts her hand on top of his. 'I must sound paranoid. But you're a hard man to read. Sometimes I feel like you're keeping stuff back from me.'

She stands and brushes crumbs from her skirt. 'Don't worry about the dream, Daz. It's just anxiety. Lots of my clients find they get . . .' Her sentence fades.

'Clients?'

'You know . . .'

'Am I a client?' Daz's words come out sounding too sharp.

Kat frowns. 'It's just natural. That's all I meant. Anyone would in . . . in your situation. Look – I've got to get back.'

'Another client?'

She frowns at him. Her mouth thins to a line. 'Jim was right. We shouldn't be seeing each other like this. I could lose my job.'

Daz feels his chest constrict with the pain of what she's about to say.

'Gunna leave me?'

'I *should* leave you. That would be the sensible thing to do.' Then she steps close and kisses him again. Lips open this time. And when at last she pulls back, she says: 'But Jim's the one with all the common sense in my family, so I guess you're stuck with me. For now.'

He waits until it's properly dark before starting back towards the house on Severn Street. And he takes his time. A long wait in the churchyard on the other side of St Peter's Road. Looking over the wall, searching each direction for a movement in a parked car or a shadow where there should be none.

There's a prostitute next to the phone box on the corner. She follows each passing car with the angle of her body. Bending at the knee to look in through the windows. Further down the street there's a burger van parked on a wide stretch of pavement. A group of men pass it, joking with each other.

Daz slips over the wall and crosses the road. Then he steps into the phone box and pretends to make a call, pressing the receiver to his ear, looking along the next section of his journey. Highfield Street. Again he sees nothing. Again his tension grows. He hangs up the receiver, and out of habit does a quick check of the coin return slot. A fifty-pence piece. Perhaps it is a sign that his luck is about to change.

He walks to the junction with Severn Street. This is the final stretch. The greatest danger. He stands in the shadow, looking through the windows of the cars, checking them off as his eyes search down the row. He snags on a white van. Similar to Salt's. Similar to the one that chased him less than twenty-four hours ago. He's never seen one parked there before – directly outside Raglan's property.

Daz eases himself down the pavement towards it. It's facing away from him. The only way of seeing who is in the cab would be to pass it and look back. But he's sure now that this is the ambush.

He's five houses short and unable to go any further without being seen from the van's driver seat – if it is occupied. He swings the gate of the house he's in front of. The front yard is only two paces deep, but it's overgrown with enough tall buddleia to give him some cover. There is a panel of twelve buttons next to the door. One for each flat. He presses number eleven. After a moment a voice crackles through the speaker.

'Yes?'

'Pizza delivery for flat three. Couldn't buzz the door for me?'

'This is eleven.'

'Bell doesn't work on number three.'

The lock clicks open and Daz pushes inside. He presses a wall switch and a light clicks on somewhere upstairs. This is a journey Daz has done only once before. And that was the other way round. But he's confident. He slips the fifty pence into his back pocket, then climbs three flights of stairs, trailing one hand on the wooden banister. There's a table on the top landing. He moves into the middle of the corridor, then climbs on to it. He's directly under a trapdoor in the ceiling. He pushes up with his hands and the board above him lifts. Then he hoists himself through the black rectangle into the loft space.

At first he can't see anything. There's just blackness and the smell of brick dust. Then forms start to emerge. Lines on the periphery of his vision materialize into sloping roof beams and the edges of slates.

These things he knows: Freddy and Ginger's flat is five

houses away through the roof space, beyond the first chimney it is going to be completely dark, and if he accidentally steps off a wooden joist at any stage he's going to fall straight through the plaster and down on to someone's floor below.

Daz hates walls. But he isn't claustrophobic. In this cramped, black loft space he can reach out with his mind, feeling the sky above the slates, the rooms underneath. He is blind, though he knows where he is. He has passed the boundary of three houses, marked by breaks in the pattern of joists, a change in the texture or thickness of insulation laid between them. He walks on all fours, using two parallel joists to take his weight, his hands feeling the splintery wood ahead of him. Below him somewhere must be a television. He can hear the signature tune of the ten o'clock news, muffled by layers of plaster and glass wool.

His fingers touch a thick crossbeam. He gropes on the other side of it with his fingers. No insulation, just plaster and loose fragments of concrete. He's about to cross into the last house before Raglan's. The television noise is behind him now. Ahead is another sound. Trickling water. A storage tank somewhere close. It could be inches from his face and he'd not be able to see it.

He sits himself on the crossbeam. Balanced. And as he rests he thinks about Ginger. The man's dancing. His clothes. The way he lives and spends. Always at ease with other people. A constant friend. A man without blemish. This is how Daz has always seen him before today. But now there is a new understanding.

Daz can feel the partition wall in his mind as he approaches it. It's as solid to him as if he could see it with his eyes. More solid, perhaps, because vision is so much more fickle than touch. He reaches a hand out into the blackness and makes contact with it for real. It wasn't exactly where he remembered it. A few inches further away than he'd thought. But that's no surprise. He's only been here once before.

He moves sideways until his fingers find the outline of a small door. He pushes and it clicks open. His first impression is pain as the light pokes into his eyes. Then stiffness as he stands up among the racks of clothes that fill Freddy and Ginger's boxroom.

'What the fuck!' It's Ginger, standing in the doorway, eyes wide.

'Had some trouble,' Daz says.

'You had a fight with a barrel of tar, more like. Your skin's as dark as mine, man!' Ginger laughs then, and adds: 'But not as beautiful.'

Daz looks at his hands. They're covered in black dust. 'Use your sink?'

Ginger reaches in an arm and holds back a row of leather jackets so Daz can pass without touching them. 'Hell, yes.'

Daz strips off his shirt and jeans and washes at the sink in the kitchenette. The soap turns grey and the water gurgles away black. He dries as best he can on a tea towel then walks across the main room to his box of things, which is back in the corner. The clothes inside are folded. Clean underwear, his tastefully ripped 501 copies and a bootleg Prodigy T-shirt with an image of devil-haired Keith Flint on the front and the word 'Firestarter' printed on the back.

As he gets changed, he says: 'Raglan's got someone outside waiting for me.' Then, in answer to Ginger's unspoken question: 'He poisoned the fox. I trashed his Jag.'

'Fuck, Daz. But you know how to make a point.'

Daz tightens his belt. 'Freddy out somewhere?'

'We . . . we kinda had an argument.'

'Shit. You all right?'

'We're cool. It's just normal stuff.' Ginger turns and walks across to the kitchenette. 'You want coffee or something?'

'Sure.'

Daz listens to mugs clinking. Water splashes. 'Your sound system?'

'I sent it back to the factory.'

He looks at the empty space, the paler rectangles of wallpaper where the speakers stood until this morning. Some untruths aren't important. This is a different kind. The longer Daz looks at the missing stereo, the worse the feeling at the base of his stomach.

He tries to keep his voice casual. 'Broke, is it? Or what?'

'Nah,' Ginger says. 'It's just like a car. You need to get it serviced every six thousand miles. You know how it is.'

Daz looks at the door. The smashed panel is back in place, but he can see the cracks where the wood has been glued. He could ask about that as well. But one lie is enough. He thinks of Freddy and Ginger coming home and finding the damage. No surprise that they had an argument after that. He pulls on his boots and starts lacing them up.

Ginger carries two steaming mugs back into the room. He puts one on the floor near Daz.

'Cheers.'

'Where are you going to stay?' Ginger asks.

Daz shakes his head. 'Dunno.'

'You could . . .' Ginger gestures to the floor.

'Not a good idea.' Daz takes a sip of coffee. 'Was here last night when Raggy broke the door in.'

'Shit.' Ginger runs a hand over the top of his head. 'We . . . we thought you'd moved on – found somewhere else to crash.'

'I saw it all.'

Ginger's face goes slack. 'I'm . . . God, I'm sorry.'

'How much you owe him?'

'I didn't want to lie to you. It's just—'

'How much?'

'It wasn't him I borrowed from. It was this loan company. They've got an office in town. I just needed to clear the credit cards.'

'And?'

'And Raglan did a deal with them. Bought out my debt. Now . . .'

Daz gets a sudden rush of understanding. Fragments of memory start to recombine. He feels sick. 'What else Raggy get you to do?'

'I'm so sorry Daz . . . I didn't know it was gunna be important . . . He let me hold off the repayment for another week . . .'

Daz closes his eyes. 'It was you! I told you, didn't I? And you fucking told him.'

It's like remembering a dream. At first there's nothing. Neither memory nor any awareness of a lack of it. Then comes the trigger – an idea that he's not wanted to think about before. A thought forced into his logical mind by Ginger's lie. And though he's kept this idea away till now, it does have a familiar feeling. Suddenly he knows there's something missing from his past, and he searches his mind, trying to fill in the void. Then the memory comes back to him – all in a rush. It's like hot wind whooshing into an underground station just ahead of a train.

He's in hospital, lying on a trolley. He's been unconscious and he's not really back from it yet. He tries to sit up. 'Did you give the money to Raggy?'

Ginger is looking down on him. 'Told you already, Dazzo. Chill it. You're sorted.' Then he exhales through his mouth in what Daz might have taken for a laugh if there'd been any humour in his friend's eyes.

The radiologist is laying something heavy and grey over the lower part of Daz's body. He gestures for Ginger to leave. 'You'll have to step outside,' he says.

Ginger nods. 'No probs.' Then he looks down at Daz again. 'You never told me where the money came from.'

He is backing towards the door. And Daz feels suddenly guilty. His friend will have lost an evening's work because of this. It doesn't feel right to hold out.

'Patty the Fence,' he calls. 'Got the money from her.'

Chapter 21

Raglan never walks anywhere if he can help it. So Daz feels pretty safe in the pedestrianized centre of town. He ambles, letting the sun warm his muscles. Working off the stiffness of a second night sleeping rough between the trees in the centre of the Humberstone roundabout.

He's got a devil of a thirst, so he cuts across to the public toilets and drinks some metallic-tasting water from a cold tap, sucking it from his cupped hands over the sink. On his way back to the clock tower he passes the covered market. The fifty pence in his pocket could get him half a bowl of overripe bananas. He wouldn't need to go hungry all day. But he keeps walking. Back to the clock tower, then on up Humberstone Gate.

There's a kiosk here selling sweets and cigarettes. He goes up to it, looks at the Mars bars, feeling the saliva start to flood his mouth. He could really do with the sugar kick. He dips in his pocket, feels the coin. He pulls himself back from the edge, then sets off towards Vicky's house.

It's a slow walk under the sun. He watches police cars prowl past. There have been plenty of those out since the riot, and they aren't doing anything to lighten his mood. Vicky's street is empty but for parked cars and wheelie bins. There is more litter on the ground today than usual.

He hammers on the door, then waits. No one comes, so

he skirts the block and clambers over the rear wall from the waste ground at the back. Nothing. Not even a dog bark. He puts his head close to the kitchen window and cups his hands around his eyes. Dyson's bowl is on the floor, piled high with dry dog food. Perhaps the animal is still sick, like before. It should have wolfed down its food – if it is in the house at all.

He looks in the outhouses next. There is a bike frame in the first, lots of oil but no wheels. The second has a pile of stacked flowerpots, wedged so firmly together that the top one cracks when he tries to separate it from the stack. There is also a pile of sodden cardboard fruit boxes with a tribe of woodlice living underneath. But no spare key.

Next he shields his eyes and peers through the back room window. There's an open packet of Marlboro cigarettes on the table, with three unused filter tips poking out of it. There's no way that Patty would leave them if she was going somewhere. That decides it for him. He goes to the back door, steadies himself and lashes out a kick at the lowest wooden panel. It cracks down the middle. Two more kicks and he's crawling through the splintery hole.

Inside is the familiar smell of stale tobacco smoke, dog and cheap perfume. Daz steps through to the front room and puts the door on the chain. The place is empty, so he climbs the stairs. Up here the perfume smell is stronger, fresher. There's a dead spider plant in the bathroom. One toothpaste tube, squeezed flat. Five bottles of shampoo and conditioner. Lipstick, mascara, an eyeliner pencil and other things he doesn't recognize. All hot pinks, deep reds and black. There's nothing of Patty here. He's pretty sure the old woman doesn't wear make-up, but even so he would expect some trace of her. There's only one toothbrush in the glass, and that has a handle in the shape of a naked man.

He steps up the landing to the back bedroom. Just a single bed, no carpet. There's rose-patterned wallpaper here, with patches of bare plaster, as if someone had once tried to strip it and given up after half an hour of random scraping. The bed is unmade. There is a full ashtray on the floor near the pillow end.

The front bedroom smells strongly of Vicky. It's got a pink carpet – badly stained – a dressing table without a mirror and a wardrobe that looks as if it could be the twin of the one in Daz's own bedsit.

In his search of the house he can find no hint of violence or any indication that Patty was forced out. Yet the only sign that she planned to go is the lack of her toothbrush in the bathroom. He goes back there and searches a second time with the same result.

With nothing else to do, he strips and washes, cleaning his mouth as best he can with some toothpaste and a finger. There is a pink, disposable razor in the cabinet, but no foam or gel. He shaves with it anyway, working the soap up into a functional lather. But all the time he is thinking about Patty's disappearance.

His face is still wet and stinging when the front door opens, ramming against the chain. Daz holds his breath, listens to the rattle, to the door closing again. His first irrational thought is Raglan. But his ex-landlord can't know about this house. It seems far more likely that it is Patty returning from wherever she has been. So he pulls his clothes back on and springs down the stairs, light-footed, making only one board creak as he passes. He's coming down the short passage to the front room when the door opens again. A hand feels through the narrow gap. Thin fingers push the chain towards the end of its run and free. The door swings full open.

'Where did you learn that?' Daz asks.

Vicky closes the door behind her. 'I've got slim wrists.' She holds them up for him to see. 'It's a gift.' She doesn't seem surprised to see him in her house.

He looks at her. She's certainly thin. More so than he's noticed before. But there's an aura of contentment about her today. She drops herself into a chair, a half-smile on her face. He's waiting for her to question him, but she just gazes at the ceiling directly above her.

So he says: 'Where's Patty?'

'Gone.'

'Dyson?'

She tilts her head down to look at him. 'Disgusting animal. Always jumping up. The smell . . .' Then her eyes soften. 'Forget it. It's just . . .'

He waits, but she doesn't say more.

'Gone where?' he asks.

'Gone to heaven,' Vicky says. 'She's dying, the old bag. Would you believe it, hey? Her?' Then she giggles.

Daz is kneeling in front of Vicky's chair. He grabs her arms. 'Where?'

'You're hurting me!'

'Where?'

She crumples, starting to weep. He lets go and stands.

'The Royal,' Vicky says. 'She's in the Royal.'

Patty is lying with her head and upper back propped up on the pillows. She's looking aggrieved with the world in general and with Daz in particular. There's a doctor at one of the other beds, talking to a woman with no hair.

'Why didn't you come sooner?' Patty hisses.

He can see a small plaster over the vein in her left arm. But her skin seems to have a little more colour than it did when he last saw her. The flesh around her eyes doesn't look quite so sunken.

'What you got wrong with you?' he asks.

Her scowl sharpens. 'Tests, boy. I get a little peaky and that girl has to go and call out a doctor!'

'Vicky?'

Patty puffs air over thin lips at the mention of her great-niece's name. 'We had a deal. Me and you. Sixty–forty. Are you in or out?'

Daz shrugs. 'Guess I'm—'

'The police,' she cuts in. 'They'll find me here for sure. We've got a day. Two, maybe. No time for you to go swanning around.'

'Was worried about you.'

She starts coughing then, bending forward with each wheezing exhalation. Daz glances towards the doctor, but the man doesn't seem to be paying any attention. He can hear the rattle of phlegm in her chest. Patty waves towards a glass of water next to the bed. Daz picks it up and hands it to her. She takes a sip and makes a face.

'Was worried,' he says again. 'The cough.'

'Then you should have come sooner!' she snaps. 'I've had this cough off and on for ten years. Did you know that? They used to give me penicillin for it. So many pills that I'd rattle if you shook me. So I stopped taking them and it didn't get any worse. They don't like it, doctors, when you think for yourself.'

'What's wrong?'

'It's the air, boy. It wasn't like this when I was a girl in Lincolnshire. The pollution does it.'

'Why they keeping you here, then?'

'And they've put me in this ridiculous thing so I can't escape.' She brushes the backs of her hands over her hospital gown. 'You've got to go back to the house. Get Vicky to pack me some clothes. And my cigarettes. I can't think straight without them.'

'Can't smoke in here.'

'And most important is this: I've had an idea about that man Salt. We need to be able to listen in on him, you understand?'

Daz understands the words, but that isn't enough for him to make sense of what she's saying. 'I guess.'

'How do we do that, you're asking.'

She doesn't wait for Daz to deny this. She's pushing herself further up the pillows now, levering with her elbows against the bed. And when she speaks, her voice comes out as a breathy whisper.

'There's a man I know – he owes me a big favour. James Maddison is the name. Of James Maddison Electronics. The address is in the telephone book. Get one of your friends to read it for you. Go to him. Don't be put off by anything he says. Just get him to give you something.'

Daz runs a finger over his chin where he cut himself on Vicky's razor. 'Don't get it.'

'A bug, Croxley. That's what we need. And if he complains, just remind him about the solicitor's secretary. That'll do it. And bring it all here. Clothes, bug, everything.'

Daz shifts his weight from one foot to the other. Patty seems so frail. But when she talks, the intensity of her ridiculous plan seems to pump life back into her dry flesh. He doesn't want to be responsible for deflating all her hopes. But if he goes along with what she's asking, it's like helping her to live in denial.

'Well?' she says.

'OK.'

He turns and starts walking away towards the door.

'Dyson,' she calls out after him. 'Make sure that girl's feeding him. And he needs plenty of water in this heat.'

The office of James Maddison Electronics isn't easy to find. It's north of the clock tower but within the inner ring road. There's a lap-dancing club here, closed up during the hours of day. A taxi company. A fish-and-chip takeaway. Daz sniffs the hot vinegar tang as he walks back into a side-street of old factories and the backs of retail outlets.

Even counting down the numbers, he still manages to overshoot. On his way back he sees an entrance he hadn't noticed on his first pass. Anonymous. A black wooden door sandwiched between two large properties, but with no frontage of its own.

There is an intercom panel on the wall. Words he can't read. Numbers from 2 to 5. He presses number 2 and waits.

The speaker crackles and a voice says something.

'James Maddison,' Daz says.

Another crackle. He can't make out any words, so he presses the button again. 'Agnes Wattling sent me.'

There's a pause, then: 'It's the green door.'

The lock buzzes. Inside there is a badly lit staircase, very narrow. James Maddison is waiting on the first landing.

He's a twig of a man, looking half-starved in an oversized Hawaiian T-shirt and shorts. There's a pair of headphones around his neck, the jack-plug dangling from a short length of cable. He has hollowed cheeks, spindly arms and an indignant expression.

'What's your name?' The voice is breathy, aggressive.

'Daz.'

'And Agnes Wattling sent you?'

'Patty. Yeah.'

The man nods, swinging the jack-plug on its cable. 'She's alive, then.' He flashes some teeth and steel-grey fillings. 'So, what are you – her family?'

'A friend,' says Daz.

'I didn't think she had any. But I guess you'd better come in.'

The office is no more encouraging than the front door was. Small, low, not dark exactly – but managing to feel dingy. Stale tobacco smoke and body odour in the air. There's a glass ashtray on the desk, half-full of cigarette stubs, matches, scraps of paper, ash, chewing gum wrappers.

James Maddison closes and locks the door through which they've just walked. He licks his lips. 'How's she doing?'

'Not so good.'

'Shit.'

Daz nods.

'The old bitch must be a hundred,' James Maddison says.

'Said you'd help me.'

'We'll see.' He pulls a packet of gum from his back pocket and parks himself on a corner of the desk.

'Bugs,' says Daz.

'That's what I do.' Maddison posts the gum into his mouth. 'Sound? Pictures? Both?'

'Sound.'

'Indoors, outside? Your own premises, someone else's?'

'His place. A van, maybe, or a house.'

James Maddison turns and drops the gum wrapper into the ashtray with the others. It tumbles off the pile and lands on the desk.

'What kind of target are we talking about here – suspicious, innocent?'

Daz tilts his head. 'You what?'

'I check this place for bugs – every day. That's my business. Mr Azza – the accountant on the next floor – he pays me to sweep his place once a week. His clients like it better that way. We're the suspicious kind, him and me. Then there's a model in the studio flat. She doesn't think about this sort of thing. She's innocent.' He smirks, showing his bad teeth again.

Daz guesses this is a joke he shares with most of his new customers. 'Dunno,' he says.

Maddison chews on in silence, nodding to himself. 'Can you get in and out of his place easy? Or rent the room next door?'

Daz shakes his head.

'Then I've got just the piece of kit you need.' He hops off the desk and leads the way through a door to a second room. There's a fitted workbench on one wall, complete with a fixed row of soldering iron holders. There are printed circuit boards scattered around the place. Computer chips. A colour printer.

'Long range, virtually undetectable, state of the art.' Maddison pulls a long, flat briefcase from the shelf and places it carefully on the desk. 'Laser technology,' he explains. 'So long as you have line of sight it can detect the vibrations caused by speech.'

He springs the fastenings and opens the case. There's a black metallic object inside, looking like a gun from a sci-fi movie.

'It's legal?'

Maddison chuckles. 'It's not illegal to *own* any bugging or surveillance equipment.' He picks the thing up, raises it to his eye and aims at the door.

Daz digests the carefully worded answer.

'Sometimes the recording needs a bit of cleaning up. But it's digital so that's no real problem. You've got a computer? I'll burn you a CD of the sound-filtering software. At no extra charge.'

There's something that might be an instruction manual in the bottom of the case. Daz picks it up, runs a thumb over the edge of the pages.

'Don't worry,' Maddison says. 'Half an hour and you'll be an expert.'

Daz doubts this. 'How much?'

'To buy? Don't even think about it. But I can rent it you for say – since you're a friend of Patty's – a thousand a day – in advance. Plus ten thousand for security – which you get back, of course, on the safe return of the equipment.'

Daz manages not to laugh. 'Got something cheaper?'

Maddison looks up. His chewing rate doubles. He frowns as if personally offended by the question. 'This is quality, man!'

'Got a cash-flow problem.'

'Cheaper?' Maddison closes the case, snapping the fasteners. 'And you say Patty sent you?'

'Said to remind you—'

'Remind me?'

'Yeah. The solicitor's secretary.' It sounds so stupid that Daz instantly regrets mentioning it.

'The solicitor's secretary?' The chewing slows. 'Patty told you to say that?'

Daz looks at the floor.

The chewing stops. Maddison shakes his head. 'What the heck. One good turn, eh?'

He pulls open a drawer from under the bench and extracts a small black disc that dangles from a black wire. It looks little more than a button on the end of a thread.

'Standard high-quality bugging microphone,' he says. 'You'll need to find a way of accessing the room, the van, whatever. That's the downside.'

Then he produces a silvery object the size of a cigarette box. 'Mini-disc recorder. No transmitter, so it's almost impossible to detect. The microphone is pretty low-gain, though, so you need to keep the cable as short as possible.'

He opens another drawer and pulls out a supermarket carrier bag, into which he places the equipment, together with an earpiece. Then he hands it to Daz. 'Tell Patty the favour's paid. OK?'

Daz stands in the corridor, looking into the room where Patty was on his last visit. There's a curtain drawn all the way around her bed now. It sways with the movement of someone inside. More than one person, perhaps.

He waits. The bed where the hairless woman had been lying is empty and freshly made. The sheets tight. The air smells slightly of disinfectant.

Then a short nurse steps out from Patty's bed and starts drawing the curtain. A tall doctor follows her out. Patty is lying very still, her arms laid on top of the covers, her eyes closed. Her skin almost matches the sheet. And then it hits him that he can't see any rise or fall of her chest.

He steps into the room, over-aware of the bag of clothes hanging from his hand. The nurse bustles out past him. He sleepwalks to the bedside and looks down at her.

'Patty?' He calls her name in a whisper.

She lifts the lids of her eyes, just a crack, and whispers: 'Are they gone yet?'

He glances over his shoulder.

'Pull the curtains, will you.'

He does as he's told, enclosing them. He's expecting someone to come and tell him off, but it doesn't happen.

Patty is propping herself up on her pillows. 'You'd think I was senile, the way they talk about me! No wonder people look so sick in this place.'

'You OK?' he asks.

'Not you, too, Croxley! That's the most unkindest cut.'

'But—'

'Did you speak to Maddison?'

Daz nods. He reaches into the bag and pulls out the bug and recorder.

'That's it?'

'Said to tell you the favour's paid.'

She shakes her head. 'You should have pressed him for more. You don't bargain hard enough, boy. People won't trust you if you don't bargain. That's rule number—'

'Number two. I know'

She clears her throat and Daz thinks she's going to start coughing again, but it doesn't happen. She's peering at the bag of clothes in Daz's hand.

'Did you put out water for Dyson?'

He nods.

'And food?'

'Yes,' he lies.

In truth, he tried his best for the dog – first searching and finding it lying in the weeds next to Kodak's grave. Then trying unsuccessfully to wake it. It hadn't seemed ill as such, just extremely tired. That's how he'd expected to find Patty, but she seems full of energy.

'Right,' she says. 'We're going to bug Mr Eric Salt.'

'Dunno where he lives.'

'His house in Martin's Hill. While you've been poodling around out there, I've been doing some research on the telephone. Calling in more favours. That's another reason why I get the bigger cut. Now leave the clothes and let me get changed.'

Daz stands outside the curtain, waiting for someone to tell him they can't do what they're doing. The short nurse walks into the room and past him, checks the IV drip on one of the other patients, then leaves. He can hear Patty. Her breath is more wheezy than before, but there seems to be plenty of zip in her movements.

'You OK?' he whispers.

Patty emerges, Crimplene-clad, eyes narrow.

'Where's the bug?'

Daz hands it over and watches her slip it into her handbag. Then he reaches to pull the curtains open, but she brushes his hand aside.

'Don't be a fool, Croxley. They'd know I've escaped.'

He leads her out of the ward with the reassuring thought that someone is bound to stop them before they get to the stairs. But no one does. She props herself against his arm on one side and the handrail on the other. And with each step he gets more uneasy, half-fearing that an alarm will start wailing behind them. Half-hoping for it.

In the main foyer she collars a porter and gets him to order a taxi for her. It doesn't look as if it's the kind of thing he's paid to do, but he does it anyway, and there's a satisfied look on his face when he eventually holds the door for her to leave the building. A job well done. He even smiles as he nods towards Daz.

The taxi driver shows a similar level of concern. He doesn't seem to mind that Patty's voice is so weak and breathy. He has to ask her to repeat the address of Salt's house, but the look of gentle patience doesn't leave his face.

'Martin's Hill,' he says. 'Are you sure, now?'

She nods and subsides back into the seat. Her shoulders drop and she closes her eyes. Through the rear-view mirror, Daz catches the concerned lines on the driver's face.

'I used to live in Martin's Hill myself,' he says. 'Of course, that was years ago. It's all a bit different now. A lady your age has to be careful.'

Daz also used to live in Martin's Hill, but he keeps that fact locked away. It was just after he left home properly for the first time. His dad's drinking had got so bad that even Social Services could see they had to do something. So they put him into care, fostered by a family on the Martin's Hill estate. It was while playing truant from his new school that Daz had first come across Vince the Prince and his gang. He didn't feel comfortable with the place then, and he doesn't feel comfortable with it now.

He remembers Vince at the start of the riot. There was a manic gleam in the man's eyes that night. But Daz wouldn't have thought any more of it if it hadn't been for Superintendent Shakespeare's questioning. Daz is trying to figure out why a policeman should want to protect such an obvious crook. There are only two possibilities that he can see – Vince could be doing some work for the police or Shakespeare could be doing some work for Vince. And since Daz also saw Shakespeare talking to Raglan, the possibility of a bent policeman is starting to look more likely.

The taxi turns off the main road and into the estate. Daz looks from the window and sees rows of lock-up garages giving way to streets of brick-built council houses, each with a small fenced garden at the front. The driver slows to cross a speed bump in the road. He's peering at the street names as they pass each side-road. Then he sees what he's looking for and turns off.

'You sure this is where you want to go?'

Daz looks across at Patty. Her eyes are open again, and brighter than before.

'Here,' she says.

The driver gets out and opens the door for her.

She rocks herself to a standing position. 'Wait here.'

Daz watches her hobble up the short path and ring the doorbell.

'Shouldn't we do something to help her?' the driver asks.

'Wouldn't let us,' Daz says.

Salt appears at the door. His mouth drops open, an expression so cartoon-like that it might almost be funny. He steps back and Patty hobbles inside. The door closes.

'Is it a friend's house?' asks the driver.

'No.'

Daz looks around the street, trying to map it out in his head.

'Is she your grandmother?'

'No.'

'Only you look like her. Too old to be your mother.'

'Not got a mother.'

The driver seems to take the hint at this point because he doesn't come back with a third question. He switches on the radio and tunes it to Five Live. It's the middle of a phone-in inspired by the Waterfields riots. Racism and national identity. The multiculturalism conference is less than a week away. Daz watches the front window of Salt's house, but he can't see anything through the net curtain. He tells himself he's just going to wait another few minutes. Then he gets out of the car.

'Be back,' he says.

But the front door is already opening. Patty steps out into the sun. He hurries up the path and takes her hand. Salt is watching him from inside. His eyes are wide. Spooked rather than frightened.

Patty looks much worse than before. The transformation is startling. It's as if all her energy has been used up inside the house. He lets her lean her weight on his arm. Neither of them speaks. Salt is still standing in his doorway as the engine fires.

'Where now?' the driver asks.

'Home,' Patty whispers.

'Hospital,' Daz says.

Chapter 22

The doctor is up at the other end of the corridor. He is a small-framed man with tightly curled ginger hair. A nurse is talking to him now. She points in Daz's direction. The doctor's mouth moves, then he goes back to his clipboard, working down it with a pen. The nurse nods and walks back towards Daz.

She presses her lips together as she approaches, thinning them.

'Well?' Daz asks.

'You can hang around here if you want,' she says. 'He'll see you if he gets time. But no guarantees.'

Daz waits and watches. After a few minutes the doctor glances towards him again, but looks away quickly. Then he's off through a door. Daz rests himself against a cold radiator and folds his arms. He tries to let his mind drift. He's had plenty of practice at this, but today it doesn't work. He keeps returning to Patty. To the tubes in her arms. The bag of liquid emptying and then being replaced. They're dripping fluids into her, but the vitality seems to be draining away.

Time slows around him.

The sound of a polite cough brings him back. The splash of light from the window has shifted around and lengthened, so it now angles on to the far wall. He looks up.

'Mr Croxley?' The doctor is standing two paces away, arms folded. 'I am Dr Høeg.' His voice is softly Scandinavian. 'I'm sorry to have kept you waiting.'

'Sure.'

Dr Høeg indicates a door off the corridor. 'You can come through here.'

It's a small office. There are shelves of hardback books, metal cabinets, a sink, a desk and two chairs. The doctor shuts the door and stands with his back to it.

'Mrs Wattling is your relative?'

Daz looks at his feet.

'You know she has a serious chest illness, but you take her out of the hospital. Why is this?' Though the man's voice is low, it has a tremor that suggests strong emotion under the surface.

'Told me she wanted to go.'

'And if she told you she wanted to kill herself – would you have helped with that also?'

Daz chews on the inside of his cheek.

'Leaving this building – she becomes tired. Exhausted. It speeds her illness. You know why I left you waiting? I am sorry for this, but I had no choice. I was too angry to speak with you. I use my skill to make people well. To heal them. This I cannot do if you do what you have done.'

'What's she got?' Daz asks.

'Her illness? If she hasn't told you . . .'

'Bad?'

'You've seen for herself. The external fatigue is a good indication of what's happening on the inside.'

'Told me she's had that cough for years.'

'The cough itself is not the problem. Though it doesn't help.'

'Lung cancer?'

The doctor shakes his head. 'It's not the lungs – surprisingly.'

'But it *is* cancer?'

Daz looks in the doctor's face for a denial. He finds none. 'Can't make her well, then?'

Dr Høeg sighs. 'All of us die eventually. But we can live longer or shorter.'

'And her?'

'Three months? A couple of days? I cannot tell. In the end it will come down to the management of pain. Quality of life. And what you've done has not helped.'

Daz walks into the ward, feeling heavy. Patty is lying flat, her left arm connected up to the intravenous drip. There are gas cylinders next to the bed, a clear plastic mask over her mouth and nose. He steps closer. Her eyes are closed. Her skin white. He can see the blue lines of veins. She looks like a marble statue on a grave.

Dr Høeg is standing there in the doorway, watching. He nods once, then leaves. Daz turns back to Patty. She opens her eyes, shifts her head to look at the room, then raises a hand to lift the mask away from her mouth.

'Croxley,' her voice is a whisper, no louder than the hiss of escaping gas.

Daz moves lower, bringing his head next to hers.

'Keep it down,' she whispers, 'or you'll bring them back.'

'You OK?'

'Will you stop fussing!'

'Just thought . . .'

'Well, don't. I do the thinking. That's why I get the sixty cut.'

Daz feels a prickle in the corner of his eye.

'Don't stand there blinking, boy. We've got to get the bug back.'

'Only put it in yesterday.'

'A whole day!'

'But—'

'Don't *but* me. You're not getting out of our deal now.'

'Doc said he wouldn't let you go.'

'He can't stop me.'

'He's got people watching,' Daz lies.

She sighs. 'Then you'll have to get it back for me, I suppose. Break in. And if you find the cash, just take it.'

'Steal it?'

'This won't be stealing.'

'But—'

'It doesn't count. It's stolen already.'

Kat's voice hisses through the tinny speaker. 'Wait in the hall. I'll be right down.'

The door buzzes open. The carpet feels thick under his feet. There are light-switches on the wall, but Daz chooses to stand in the semi-dark. She trots down from the upstairs flat. He can make out a skirt, a handbag over one shoulder. Not clubby. Dressed for a meal, perhaps. She places a kiss on his mouth. He feels it work on him, melting some of his tension.

'Mm-mm. Your skin smells so good,' she says. 'If we could bottle you, we'd make a fortune.'

'You, too,' he whispers. The after-glow from the kiss is fading slowly.

'Are you ready?' she asks.

'It's difficult tonight.'

'But we are going out . . .'

'Gotta do something.'

'No, Daz,' she says. 'You need one night off. We'll go somewhere different, my treat.'

Her face is hidden in shadow. He reaches out and touches her on the cheek. She puts her own hand over his, holding it there. Her skin is warm.

She says: 'Will you? Come out, I mean?'

He tries to pull his hand back, but she doesn't let go.

'Gotta go to Salt's place,' he says.

'There are more worlds out there than this, Daz. You're in the middle of something . . . I don't know what. But it's stopping you seeing straight. You need to get away. Get things in perspective.'

'Almost got it sorted now.'

'You should see yourself! You're getting deeper in every day.'

'Just need to find where Salt keeps the money.'

'And then?'

'Then . . .'

Then Raglan, Bishop, the police and Patty all expect to be told – and all require that he won't tell anyone else. He hasn't yet figured that part of the puzzle. Bishop is the most dangerous. The police have the longest reach. But he's still hoping that there can be some way for him to hand the cash to Patty.

'You need rest, Daz.'

He nods. 'Maybe.' He doesn't add that the only rest he's likely to get before this is all over is the permanent kind. A shallow grave.

'And I need you,' she says.

Then she takes his hand from her face and leads him up the stairs. He knows he should leave, but he can't pull away. He follows into her flat, through a connecting passage and into a room with a double bed and a TV on the dressing table. There's a smell of camomile in the air and a hint of wax – as if a scented candle has just been extinguished.

She turns to him. He moves forward, presses himself against her, feeling the contact between their bodies. They are kissing. Hungrily. Lips, eyes, necks, hands. His fingers follow the muscle lines down to the small of her back, then they circle around her waist and move up her body again. He cups her breast and feels a small circlet of metal through the fabric. She turns him, pushes him back on to the bed. He looks up at her as she undresses in the half-light. He can just make out the ring hanging from one nipple.

It feels as if the world has slowed. Then she lowers her body on to his and he stops thinking. But somewhere in the centre of it, as he climbs towards the peak, he gets a glimpse of himself and Kat shining in the darkness of the room. And after that his conscious mind is far away and his senses are exploding. And all the glass in the world is shattering. He watches each fragment as it falls.

'Why?' he asks her, much later.

She presses herself closer into his side. 'Because I wanted it.'

He's looking up at the splash of streetlight on the ceiling. His sweat has dried now, though his skin is still glowing. 'But why me?'

'I could ask you the same thing.'

Daz doesn't see why his desire for her should be any kind of puzzle. 'You've got everything,' he says. 'I've got nothing.'

'So you're after me for my money?' She runs a finger across his chest. 'It didn't feel like that.'

'Didn't mean it like that.'

'Then what? You don't think other women have the hots for you?'

He thinks of Freddy and Liz, each with their own reason for flirting with him.

'You like the way I look?' he asks.

'You could dress smarter,' she says. 'You could do something with your hair, perhaps. But that's not the point. You're just you. You do and say whatever you want, whenever you want. Not like me – a slave to convention. You're the one who's got everything, Croxley. Not me.'

'I'm nothing.'

'You really think that?'

'Got no job. No cash. Nothing.'

She sighs. 'I guess they must've been rubbing your nose in it all your life – saying you're a useless waster. That's why you've got such a massive chip on your shoulder. Half of your mind resents the injustice of it. But the other half despairs because you figure that they might be right. And I'm always struggling to know which half I'm talking to.'

He looks back to the ceiling. 'It's just the way I am.'

'I've met doctors who aren't as bright and clear-sighted as you! You could do so much with your life.'

'I'm the thicko in the remedial class, remember? The one who can't even read.'

'You could learn.'

'Don't go there!'

'I've got to say what I think. That's just the way *I* am.'

'Wouldn't say it if you understood!'

'Then tell me! Make me understand.'

'I'm different, that's all.'

'How so?'

'Up here.' He presses his fingers into his brow. 'Used to try to read – when I was a kid. Figured if I could just concentrate a bit more it'd all come clear. The words would light up on the page and I'd understand them. But the more I tried, the more it felt like my head was being crushed in a vice. The other kids could do it, even the stupid ones.'

'It doesn't matter if you don't get to be good at it. Just to be able to read a few lines – that would be a huge help to you. And there are specialists these days.'

'So I can pretend to be "normal"?'

'So you can be happy.'

He shakes his head. 'So everyone else can be happy. That's it. They're the ones want me to read. They want it so I can pretend to be like them. Like them – but not as good.'

Salt's house is quiet. No van outside. Just the hall light left on. A precaution that only emphasizes the house's vulnerability, the owner's desire to keep his property safe.

Daz cycles on past, keeping the same speed. He turns left at the corner, working his way around the block, mapping the layout of the gardens in his head. Three more left turns and a hundred yards of uneven concrete road brings him back to the front of Salt's place. There are no rear walkways here. He chooses a house three doors further down. It has metal grilles over the windows and a cluster of estate agents' signs in the front garden.

He reverses his bike into the side passage and leaves it leaning against the wall. He doesn't lock it. Crossing the rear gardens is easy. The fences are low. There's plenty of junk lying around to clamber over. And no dogs close enough to worry about. He's glad of that.

He's never broken into a council house before. The rear door looks too solid to kick through easily. There are no outhouses where Salt might have left a spare set of keys. Daz switches his attention to the windows. UPVC double-glazed units. Everything locked.

He wants to go. But he knows Patty won't let up until this last job is done. The electronic bug isn't going to reveal anything – he's sure of that. Salt feels like a loner. He won't be speaking to anyone. But if Daz can just find something else to bring her, she might feel satisfied enough to stop worrying. Then she might let herself get some rest. So he hunts around in the garden for something heavy. There are three painted, concrete gnomes here. Fat little men, each a foot high, their thumbs hooked in their braces. They might be heavy enough, but then he finds something even better. It's lying in the long grass next to the rear fence. A length of old scaffolding. Heavy tubular steel, covered in rust and so grown over that it takes all his strength to rip it free of the trailing weeds.

He balances it on his shoulder, pointing towards the house.

He whispers: 'This is for you, Patty.' Then he charges. At the last moment before impact, he digs in with his feet and launches the steel forward with his hands. It hits the left side of a double-glazed unit. The window implodes. The steel tube carries on into the back room, jolted out of its original course only slightly. There's a sudden, intense rain of razor-edged fragments and a crash of furniture breaking inside.

It's louder than he'd thought it would be, and more exquisitely beautiful than he could have imagined. He stands, tensed, ready to run. There's a dog barking a few doors away. It doesn't sound like a big animal.

Salt's back room is a mess. And not only from what Daz has just done. Aside from the ruined window and a smashed chair, there are piles of old newspapers everywhere. Grey twine securing them in bundles. Red-topped papers, faded with the months and years. Perhaps half a ton. The air smells stale – even with Daz's contribution to the room's ventilation.

There's a fitted cupboard next to the gas fire – just like Patty said there would be. He opens it, reaches to the back corner and retrieves the bug. He's got the earpiece that James Maddison gave him. He plugs it in and presses the button to play back the recording. He knows the thing only switches itself on when the microphone picks up something, so he's not expecting a long silence. It's still a shock to hear Patty's voice, tired and wheezy, in his ear.

'. . . just need to go,' she says.

'What about . . . about the tea?' That's Salt, speaking at some distance.

'I've changed my mind.'

'And the . . . the . . .'

Then there's a shuffle of movement. Getting fainter. A door opening. Then a crisp click and a cut to Salt's voice, much closer than before.

'. . . at do you . . . what do you think?'

A pause.

'She can't take it.'

Another pause.

'If she . . . I just don't know.'

Daz swallows. It's Salt's voice all the way through – talking to himself.

'We'll do it now,' Salt says. 'Do all of it.'

There's another double click. Another cut in the recording.

'. . . to place a bet . . . Leicester. The three-thirty . . . Number five. Branston Tiger to win . . . It's . . . It's sixty-two thousand . . . pounds, yes.'

There's a longer silence this time.

'Yes . . . I . . . I know . . . Cash. I'll bring it.'

Then the rattle of a phone receiver being put down.

After that there are brief snatches of movement between clicks. Footsteps. Household noises. A door slamming.

And then the real action. An explosion of breaking glass and smashing furniture. So sudden, it takes a beat before Daz understands that it is the sound of his own violent entry. He clicks the machine off and puts it into his pocket.

There are three concrete gnomes on the table in the front room, together with brushes and pots of paint. Patty hadn't mentioned this. He searches the cupboards and finds three latex gnome moulds – apparently identical. Bags of cement. Several large plastic bowls.

Daz has seen lots of films where precious objects have been concealed inside small statues. But even as he's thinking of breaking open a couple of gnomes to check, he gets a powerful feeling that this strange hobby is a natural projection of Salt's character. The man has a house, a van, a small business. But there doesn't seem to be any family or friends. He's a socially inept loner, obsessive in the things he does. Daz gets an unexpected pang of sadness.

He closes the cupboards and climbs up to the first floor. There are two more gnomes in the bathroom. The same design as the others. One more in the corner of the main bedroom. The door to the second bedroom is locked. Daz forces it with his shoulder. The frame cracks and he stumbles through. It takes him a moment to work out what he's seeing. Without thinking of the danger, he reaches out and turns on the light.

There's no furniture here. No carpets. The floor is crowded with gnomes. All from the same mould. Thirty. Forty, perhaps. Individually painted faces, crude but each different from the next. Arranged in rows and columns, perhaps waiting for delivery to some tacky retail outlet.

Then he hears the key in the front door and his hand darts out for the light-switch. He's not physically afraid of Salt. But for some reason he doesn't want to be discovered in the gnome room. So he backs out, closes up, creeps into the main bedroom and stands against the wall in the dark.

He can hear movement downstairs. The front door closing. Someone, Salt presumably, whistling the *Titanic* theme tune. Badly. Sounds of movement in the corridor. The door to the back room opening. Then it goes quiet. Daz can hear the breath moving in and out of his own mouth.

Then: 'Oh, hell.' Definitely Salt's voice. 'Who the hell?'

Hurried movements now. Glass cracking under Salt's feet. A rush through to the kitchen, then out and up the stairs. Daz can feel the cold of the wall against his back. He's sweating.

A key rattles in the lock of the other bedroom door. Very close. But Daz has broken the frame.

'No. Oh, no!' Panic in Salt's voice. The click of the light-switch in the other bedroom. Silence.

Daz closes his eyes. He can feel the pumping of his own heart. The fractional movement it causes in his chest and arms. He waits, listening to the man's footsteps leaving the bare floorboards of the other room. Daz opens his eyes. He sees the shadow of Salt's head on the carpet in the doorway. He reaches in his pocket and touches his penknife.

Then a knock on the front door. Salt's shadow stops.
Another knock. Not a request for attention. A demand.

'Who's there?' Salt calls. Then he's walking away. Down
the stairs.

Daz lets out the breath that he's been holding. He goes to
the window, parts a crack between the net curtain and the
wall, and looks out to see who it is that has saved him. Salt's
white Transit is parked on the road outside. And behind it,
conspicuously out of place in this neighbourhood, is a four-
door BMW. Daz can't tell its colour under the sodium
streetlamps. Then the owner steps away from the house and
comes into view below the window. Even from this angle,
Daz can recognize Raglan.

The front door hasn't opened. Daz's ex-landlord is
walking back down the short path towards the car. It's
almost a swagger. Everything about the scene is wrong.
Raglan never comes calling without hired muscle. And he
never leaves without making the point he came to make.

Daz watches him climb into the driver's seat. And
suddenly he knows that Raglan isn't alone and that he will
make his point. The BMW is easing away now. It purrs down
the concrete road and around the corner.

He can hear Salt scrambling around downstairs.
Panicking. A rattle of keys. The door opening and slamming.
Daz is down the stairs in three long bounds. He scrunches
broken glass, scrambles through the rear window. He's
clambering the fence, trying to remember which way the
Transit was pointing. By the time he reaches his bike,
leaning in the side passage where he left it, he's figured that
Salt has to have driven off in this direction. But when he
wheels out on to the road, he sees that the van is still parked.

Salt travelling on foot could have gone off in either
direction. Within fifty yards either way, the number of

routes doubles. Daz scans the road. A car drives past slowly – something ordinary with a small dent in the front wing. It's seeing the driver that sets Daz's heart beating harder again.

Smith.

Daz gets on his bike and sets off in pursuit.

Chapter 23

Daz is following Smith, who in turn is following Salt. They're moving towards the city centre. At first, Smith keeps back, pulling over every few minutes to let Salt increase the range. Then Raglan's BMW moves in and the two cars proceed in convoy, closing the distance.

Daz is trying to work out why they didn't just break down the door and beat up Salt in his own home. Perhaps they'd been there already and hadn't found whatever it was that they were looking for. But if they're hoping to spook the man into leading them to one of his other properties, they're doing it the wrong way. They're too close. He must know they're following. Perhaps Raglan's cruelty is stronger than Smith's logic.

Salt's flight speeds up. He runs fifty yards, then walks, catching his breath. Then runs again, looking back over his shoulder. He tries skipping off the wrong way up a one-way street. Raglan and Smith park their cars and start following on foot. It's a stroll for them. Daz holds well back now.

Salt is out of condition and out of breath. He cuts along a deserted road behind the multi-storey car park. There's a vicious inevitability about the pursuit. Raglan and Smith are relaxed, not seeming to hurry, but keeping the same distance. Salt scrambles, taking jittery backward glances, unable to move fast enough to get away. He clambers up on some bins, then on to a low wall and across a flat roof, arms out on either side like an overweight tightrope walker. Then he's out of sight behind the corner of a derelict building.

Daz is watching from the top end of the road, sitting astride his bike, keeping one foot on the pavement for balance. The pursuers are on the roof. Then they, too, are gone.

He hides his bike behind the bins and clambers up, following the others. He can see now that the flat roof abuts against the side of the multi-storey. There are bars above the parapet at this level of the car park, tightly spaced enough to keep people out – except that a couple are missing. Daz clambers through the gap and jumps down on to the concrete floor.

The place is locked up at this time of night. Empty of cars. The only light is that which leaks in from the open sides of the building. Daz listens. He can hear footfalls somewhere in the gloom ahead. He knows this is the moment of greatest danger. So he starts walking towards the deepest dark – the place where he will be able to see the most and be seen the least. A door swings closed on a creaking spring somewhere to his left. He looks in that direction and sees the slight movement of an upright shadow. It's about fifty yards away. Forty maybe. It's hard to tell. It's a man, standing with one hand held to the side of his head. Then a voice. Quiet but clear.

'It's me.'

Pause.

'Yeah, we've found him. Remember that multi-storey you used to use?'

Pause.

'Will do.'

Then the shadow lowers its hand and moves off across the empty car park. Daz's eyes are adjusting now, and he manages to track the figure all the way to the up-ramp, leading to the next level.

Following would be far too dangerous. He wouldn't know if the person had stopped until it was too late. So he turns in the other direction and runs across to the stairwell.

It's even darker in here, but the handrail by the side of the stairs makes the climb easy. He passes the doors to the second, third and fourth floors and carries on up to the roof level. Salt isn't going to stop until there's nowhere left to run.

Daz releases the stairwell door to swing back on its spring and flattens himself within a shallow recess in the wall. In front he sees the flat expanse of the car park roof with Salt emerging from the down-ramp. Gasping for breath. There's no illumination on the scene, just a dull gloom of back-scattered streetlight under which the man's white shirt is the only clear thing.

The door clunks closed next to Daz's shoulder. Salt reacts to the sound, staggering as if shoved in the chest. He turns, begins to stumble back the way he came. But Raglan is coming up the ramp from the lower level. In no hurry. Smith catches up with him after a few seconds.

Salt retreats. In truth, he must know there isn't an escape. But he doesn't stop until he's backed up against the concrete parapet.

'No need to be panicky about this,' Raglan calls. 'We just want to talk, eh?'

They're a couple of paces from Salt now. He's half-turned towards the edge, looking down. Five storeys. Too high to have any chance of survival if he were to jump. Raglan stops. Smith carries on closing the distance, one step at a time.

Daz misses the moment when Smith's hand strikes. He just sees Salt's white shirt move as the man is pulled clear of the edge. Dragged back by the elbow. When Salt tries to struggle free, Smith grabs his wrist and twists it round. Salt cries out.

'We don't want this to get unpleasant,' Raglan says. He puts an arm over Salt's shoulder, walks him in Daz's direction, leaving Smith guarding the ramp. 'I know most of the story anyway. You're just filling in for my curiosity's sake.'

Raglan's voice is quieter now. But he's closer as well and Daz can still make out the words.

'How did you get caught up in this?' Raglan asks.

'The . . . the money?'

'Where did it come from, eh?'

'My business . . .' Salt snivels into the back of his sleeve. 'I deal, you know . . . scrap metal. Aluminium, mostly. I . . . I do copper sometimes . . . but . . .'

Raglan is shaking his head. 'It's a simple question!'

He must be digging his fingers into the other man's shoulder, because Salt flinches and starts to snivel again. They've stopped walking now. Perhaps fifteen paces from where Daz stands. He can hear the blood rushing in his own ears. He can hear the breath moving in and out of his nose – loud enough to alert them, surely. If either man were to really peer into the darkness, they'd be able to see him.

'The money,' Raglan prompts.

'I found it. Please . . . please don't hurt me. I—'

'Found it where?'

'Concrete . . . in the load of concrete . . .'

'You said you deal in scrap metal, not bloody concrete!'

'Y . . . yes. It was in a skip. Demolition rubble. I was looking . . . I'm so sorry . . .' He puts his hands to his face, then drops them again. 'I was looking for copper piping. And I saw the edge of a packet . . . wrapped in polythene sheet . . . I didn't know it was yours! I swear it.'

'How was it hidden?'

'In the concrete. I had to . . . to break it free. A hammer . . .'

'How much in the packet?'

Salt looks down. 'A hundred and seventy thousand.'

'A hundred and seventy thousand,' Raglan echoes. 'And how many packets did you find?'

'One.' Salt jolts his head up, sudden realization slackening his jaw. 'There were . . . were more?'

Raglan turns, his arm still over Salt's shoulder, and starts walking the man back towards Smith. Daz relaxes where he stands, allows himself to breath more deeply again.

'And where did the concrete come from?' Raglan asks, his voice only just audible. 'Demolition rubble from what building?'

Salt bows lower as he walks. He's shaking his head, mumbling some answer that Daz can't make out.

'That wasn't so difficult,' says Raglan. 'Was it now?'

They walk on for a few more paces before Raglan asks his next question. 'Where is my hundred and seventy thousand now, Eric, eh?'

Daz can't make out Salt's answer. Raglan lets go of the man's shoulder. Salt starts to back away. Raglan swings a fist into the other man's stomach.

'It was *my* money!'

Raglan tries to follow up the punch with a kick, but Salt rolls out of range with surprising agility, scrambling to his feet. He's got one hand on the parapet. The other is up to shield against the blow he's expecting from Raglan. Or from Smith, who has closed the distance between them in five long strides.

Raglan swings. Again Salt dodges. Smith is hanging back, but he's close enough to grab either man should he need to.

'You lost my money!'

Salt has got one leg up on the parapet, though where he expects to go Daz can't make out. Smith is bent forward slightly from the waist, with one hand in front and one behind, like a runner on the starting line. Even if Salt tries to throw himself off the edge, Smith should be able to stop it happening.

Daz holds his breath. Salt puts his leg right over the edge, so he is straddling the concrete. Raglan bellows something without words. Then a mobile phone rings. The *William Tell Overture*. There's a second during which everyone stops moving.

Then Raglan whirls on his heel. 'Blast!' He pulls the phone from his pocket, looks at it, makes a move as if to hurl it across the car park and then reins himself back. He puts it to his ear and barks: 'Yes!'

Daz waits. Salt waits. Smith hasn't moved or changed his focus. Raglan puts the phone back in his pocket.

'Get him off the edge.'

It's done before Daz can blink. Salt is on the floor, Smith pinning him down with a knee across the chest. Raglan is still pacing.

'What now?' Smith asks.

'We wait here. Bishop has sent someone. Fuck! And we're not to touch Salt. I want to know,' he says, turning suddenly, 'how it is that Mr Bishop knows what's going on here. How does he know we're in this miserable car park when I didn't even know we were going to be here until *you*—' He pauses to kick Salt in the thigh '—until you ran in here? Who's the Judas?' Raglan shouts. 'Or is someone spying on me?'

Salt is clutching his leg. 'Not supposed to touch me!' he screams.

'No? Well, pardon me for my little mistake.' He kicks again, throwing more of his body into the attack this time. 'And what about your little mistake, eh? Chucking a hundred and seventy fucking thousand on some old nag!'

Daz is watching. Angled forward slightly from the hip. Trying to figure out if they're going to kill the man. If there might be a way to bring help in time. He could go back into the stairwell, perhaps find some way of triggering the fire alarm.

Then it happens. A pinprick in his neck. The shock of a sudden change in focus. Salt, Raglan and Smith are still there at the other end of the car park roof. But Daz's own senses have slammed back to his own imminent danger. To the point of a knife depressing the soft skin just to one side of his windpipe. To the presence of a man directly behind him. Silent. Powerful. The point has penetrated Daz's skin only to the depth of a tattoo artist's needle. But an inch to the side and life will be over for Daz.

He's being eased forwards, out of his hiding place. It's Smith who sees him first. Raglan turns to look, and his simmering anger seems to freeze over.

'Croxley. Why is this not a surprise?'

Daz doesn't speak. Even swallowing makes the steel dig deeper into him.

'Mr Bishop called you?' asks the man with the knife.

As soon as he hears the voice, Daz knows it's Bishop's driver, Guy, who's standing behind him.

'Yes,' says Raglan.

'And that's the man, Salt?' Guy asks.

Again: 'Yes.'

He pulls away the knife and thrusts Daz forward. Then he

gestures for Smith to stand back. Salt scrambles to his feet. It must be the man's nightmare scenario. Get rid of the unarmed thugs and replace them with a knife-wielding one. A hunting knife, Daz sees. A broad blade for most of its length, curving to a point in the last inch of steel.

Salt edges along next to the parapet away from Smith and Raglan, slowing as the threat of Guy increases.

This is how it seems to Daz. Everyone thinks Salt knows the whereabouts of the money. He's told Raglan something of it already; now Bishop wants a bite. They're not going to kill the man who has that kind of information. But the same safeguard doesn't go for Daz himself. The thing that's been keeping him alive has disappeared now Salt is in their hands.

So he takes a half-step backwards. Then a full step. Increasing the distance between himself and the parapet. Getting further out of their line of vision. The ramp is behind him. And he figures there must be a load of hiding places in a car park like this.

He bolts.

Smith must have been waiting for his move, because he's off at a sprint a fraction of a second later, heading to cut off Daz's way to the lower levels. Guy's feet are pounding behind. But Daz is pumped up by fear. He reaches the ramp first, flings himself down it, overbalances, ankles jarring as they hit the concrete in the dark.

If he can just get enough distance between himself and them, he'll be able to vanish. He aims for a cluster of pillars and the deepest shadow.

Two things happen then, superimposed so that at first they seem to be part of the same event. Daz's foot catches on something and he trips forward, throwing himself into a roll in time to save his face from slamming into the ground. He lands on his back with a thump that knocks the breath out of him.

And at the same moment he hears the scream.

Smith shoves Daz up the ramp. Guy walks in front. When they get to the top, Daz sees that Raglan is standing by the parapet. Alone.

'He must have been trying to escape,' says Raglan. 'Though where he thought he'd get to ... It's a damned shame.'

Guy, Smith and Daz walk to the edge and look down to the place where Salt lies on the waste ground below. There doesn't seem to be any blood. Not from this distance. But Salt's legs lie splayed underneath the torso, as if he's been folded ready for ironing. And Daz knows without thinking that the man is dead.

PART 4

*T*hree years ago Daz and a claims adviser were sitting opposite
each other, a desk of forms between them. He was eighteen,
she perhaps forty. He'd scrawled his mark on the dotted line. The
interview should have been over.

'David, I've been looking through your paperwork and—'

'It's Daz.'

She nodded. 'Daz. I hope you don't mind me asking this but
your forms have always been filled in by other people.'

'Couldn't read my writing, could they.'

'Have you ever heard of dyslexia?'

'No such thing.'

'Who told you that?'

'This psychologist bloke.'

She looked into his eyes, as if searching for clues. 'Not many
people would agree these days. And if you were dyslexic we could
find a special class for you to help you learn.'

He folded his arms. 'I'm not dyslexic.'

'Dyslexics can be very bright,' she said. 'People like John
Lennon, Richard Branson, Guy Ritchie. They can be gifted
thinkers, especially in their spatial awareness. And dyslexia is
hereditary. You might find you have a brother or an uncle with
the same condition.'

'Not got any family.'

'I'm sorry.'

'I'm not.'

'You know that dyslexics have trouble reading,' she said, *'but did you know they have problems following the time, remembering names and remembering lists of numbers.'*

'So?'

'So I just thought it sounded like you.'

Daz looked back at her, churning the new information, plotting possible futures.

'Will you let me help you?' she asked.

'No,' he said. *'None of that's me. I'm not dyslexic.'*

Chapter 24

It's morning when they step into the solicitor's office. It's in a row of small shops, sandwiched between a bookmaker and a snack bar with a smeared window. Guy prods Daz in the back, pushing him past the receptionist and down a narrow corridor. They stop outside a grey door.

Guy reaches into a jacket pocket and pulls out a small paper bag, from which he takes a black sweet. He throws it in his mouth and starts to chew. 'Don't speak unless someone asks you a question,' he says. 'Understand?'

Daz doesn't answer. He can smell the liquorice. It reminds him that he hasn't eaten in a long time. A smile creeps across Guy's face. Daz can't guess what thought or emotion lies behind the expression. Then it's gone and the man is shoving him through the door.

Raglan is in the room, sitting behind a scratched table next to Smith. Neither of them gets up. The driver seats himself on the other side. Daz remains standing. There aren't any more chairs. He looks around him. It's not what he expected to see. There are no piles of papers or legal books. Just three grey filing cabinets and a large metal safe along one wall. There's some kind of speaker-phone on the table, wired up to a cheap-looking mobile. Through the wall he can hear the faint sound of a race commentary.

'About time,' says Raglan. He seems sulky, a mood Daz hasn't seen in him before.

Guy shrugs, then keys in a number on the mobile. A ringing tone sounds through the speaker, followed by a click.

'Yes?' It's Bishop's voice, telephone distortion making it sound thinner than in life.

'I've got Paul Raglan here, sir, with his man Smith. And the boy, Croxley.'

Raglan clears his throat. 'Hello, Mr Bishop.'

'Is Salt with you?'

Raglan looks at Guy. 'Is this line . . .?'

'It's safe,' says Bishop through the phone. 'We've seen to that. Now, where's the man Salt?'

'In the car,' says Raglan.

'Then get him.'

'He's in the boot.' There's a pause, then Raglan adds: 'It was an accident. He fell.'

'Did you question him before it happened?'

'Yes,' says Raglan.

'And?'

'He found a hundred and seventy grand—'

'Of my money.'

'—which he then lost on the horses.'

Another pause.

'Which bookmaker was he using? Anyone we know?'

Guy dips his head closer to the speaker-phone. 'It doesn't look like it, sir. I think we've lost the money.'

Raglan clears his throat again. 'Mr Bishop, I hope we can come to an arrangement. My organization is here to help with the recovery of your investments. And I have . . . certain knowledge.'

'What knowledge?'

'All I ask is a small percentage—' Raglan is looking directly at Daz as he speaks '—and a free hand to settle my own private affairs.'

'What knowledge?' An edge of irritation now.

'The location of your money, Mr Bishop. It's in a certain building. Buried in the concrete.'

Raglan looks at Guy, then at the speaker-phone. Daz is aware of the race commentary in the next building, speeding up towards the finishing line.

'Ten per cent,' Bishop says at last. 'Out of which you pay your staff and your own expenses.'

'Ten?' The word explodes from Raglan's mouth. 'I'm the one on the outside! I'll be taking the risks.'

'Ten per cent. And perhaps I'll forget about your little "accident" with Salt.'

Daz can see Raglan's fist tensing under the table. But when he speaks his voice has returned to a mild, reasonable tone.

'Let's call it fifteen.'

'Ten per cent is more than a million pounds.'

Raglan wets his lips. Daz watches him digesting the information.

'What about my private affairs?'

'They're your own business.'

Daz feels the skin of his scalp tighten.

'Ten per cent and you cover the expenses?'

'Done,' says Bishop. 'I'll get things rolling. You'll hear from me.'

'Wait!'

Everyone turns to look at Daz.

'I'm hanging up,' Raglan says.

'Doesn't know where the money is!' Daz shouts the words quickly, before Raglan's finger can get to the END CALL button.

'Who?' says Bishop.

'Raggy,' says Daz. 'Knows the building, not the place in the building.'

'What does the boy mean?'

'Don't worry,' Raglan says. 'I'll make sure he doesn't bother you again.' Then his finger smothers the button and Bishop is gone.

Daz has already slid one foot back towards the door. Now he starts to move the other. Slowly. Raglan and Smith stand. Guy looks from the phone to Raglan. His hand slips inside his jacket to the place where Daz knows he keeps his knife. But it comes out again empty. Daz edges back another few inches. Smith is around the side of the table, watching.

'You heard the man,' Raglan says. 'The boy's mine.'

Guy rubs his thumb across the fingertips of his knife hand. He's the only one still sitting. 'I guess . . .'

Daz jumps back, grabs the door handle. He hears the rush of feet in the room but he's through to the corridor. He dodges past the receptionist's desk. There's an exhalation of effort just behind him and his feet are being pulled back. He's falling with someone's hand caught around his ankle. The ground smacks into his chest and a fraction of a second later Smith lands on top of his legs. Daz opens his mouth, trying to get air into his chest. His arms are being forced around behind his back. He feels an edge of hard plastic cutting into his wrists as they are pulled hard together.

'Get him out of here!' It's a woman's voice. The receptionist. She finishes lowering the window blinds. 'How many times . . .? You can't bring this business here!' She's haranguing Guy, jabbing her finger towards his chest.

'Keep your knickers on,' he says. Then he glares at Raglan. 'Better take him out the back.'

Smith hauls Daz to his feet, shoves him down the corridor.

'I *don't* want to know about this!' The receptionist spits her words out.

'He was never here,' says Raglan. 'You'll never have to see him again.' Then addressing Smith: 'Go and bring the car round.'

They've put Daz on his knees facing the safe, hands tight behind him. A cable tie, he guesses. He can feel the corner of the mini-disc recorder in his pocket. It's pressing into his leg. No one has thought to search him up to this point.

He can't hear where the driver is in the room, but Raglan is pacing like a caged hyena. Smith is taking his time getting the car. Daz tries to focus his thoughts – as if he might escape through force of concentration. But his mind keeps returning to useless observations. A cigarette burn on the carpet next to his knee. A long, curving scratch in the surface of the safe. He hadn't noticed any of this before. Somehow it seems important now. Detail is all he's got left.

Last night was the same. Hands tied like now, trying to sleep on the back seat of the car, parked in some lock-up garage, knowing that Salt's body was just a few inches away, lying on a sheet of plastic in the boot. There might have been a way of escaping, if he'd only been able to focus. But all he'd been able to think about was the smell in the stifling air, hoping it wasn't the first sign of decomposition.

Daz is brought back to the present by the trill of the phone. Raglan stops pacing. It rings two more times before someone picks up.

'Hello?' Guy's voice.

'It's me.'

Bishop. Daz twists his neck around to look. Raglan is standing, tense, one shoulder higher than the other, eyes drilling into the speaker-phone.

'We didn't finish our conversation,' says the voice through the phone.

'Yes, sir,' says Guy. He seems relieved.

'The boy, Croxley – is he still there? I want to talk to him.'

'He's here.'

Daz manages to get to his feet.

'What does he know?' Bishop asks.

'Money's hid in concrete, right?' Daz says. 'Raggy don't know which bit of the building.' He's speaking fast, afraid of the call being cut again. But without Smith in the room, Raglan doesn't seem quite so powerful.

'Is this true?' Bishop asks.

'And it's a big building, yeah?'

Raglan unfreezes himself, moves to the table. 'It won't be a problem. We can work it out from what we know already.' He's bending forward, confiding in the speaker-phone. 'If it hadn't been for Croxley, the man Salt wouldn't have fallen. The boy's caused us enough trouble—'

'You're telling me it's not a big building?'

'We can manage. Believe me. But the boy has to go.'

Daz steps towards the table. 'It's not true! The place is big. Got pillars to hold the roof up. The money's wrapped in—'

Raglan swings an elbow into his stomach. Daz folds, collapsing on to his knees.

'He knows nothing!' Raglan shouts. 'This is just what he's heard from me.'

'You didn't say anything about pillars.'

'I know lots of things. We haven't had a chance to discuss them yet. I'm the one who questioned Salt.'

Daz tries to speak but he's winded and can't get enough breath into him.

'I'm hanging up now, Mr Bishop. You won't be troubled by this again.'

'Know where . . .' Daz gasps for a breath. '. . . where the money's . . . hidden.'

'You heard this from Mr Raglan?'

'No.' Daz fills his lungs. He feels dizzy.

'He's a liar!' Raglan bellows.

'Then who did tell you?'

'Worked . . . worked it out.'

'I think, then, you'd better start from the beginning. Tell me everything you know. And Paul?'

'Yes?' says Raglan.

'Don't touch him till he's finished.'

The door opens and Smith comes back into the room. Daz sees him looking around, taking in the new situation. He doesn't seem phased.

Daz's hands are still tied, but he's in a chair now, speaking his story to the phone on the table. This is what he should have been working out while he was facing the safe. But he didn't, so now he has to make it up as he goes along. He tells Bishop how he tracked Salt to the Environ recycling shed, though he doesn't mention Patty. She's dead in this version of events. He tells how he stole a lift in the van, all the way back to Salt's workshop. And he tells about the concrete blocks, how he did the three-dimensional jigsaw, constructing the pillar in his head.

'Just reinforcing rods inside it?' Bishop asks.

'Yeah.'

'Strange.'

Daz presses on with the description, aware of how fidgety Raglan is getting. Daz watches his ex-landlord on the edge of his vision. The man keeps adjusting his suit, buttoning it, then unbuttoning it again. From time to time he shakes his head. But he doesn't speak until the story is over. Daz still hasn't got it straight in his head about Bishop and Raglan – the way the two spark off each other. It feels important.

'Is that it?' Bishop asks.

'Everything,' says Daz.

'If you could really do a puzzle like that,' says Bishop, 'you'd be professor of maths at some university.'

'Exactly,' says Raglan.

Daz doesn't answer.

'But still . . .' Bishop leaves his sentence hanging.

'You promised I'd be left to get on with my private business,' Raglan says.

'And the boy is what you meant? But it isn't quite so private . . . now we know more of the story.'

'He's a parasite.'

'Perhaps—' Bishop's voice pauses; everyone in the room seems to be focused on the same patch of silence '—but Croxley says he can identify the place in the building where the money was found? Is this correct?'

Daz swallows. 'Yes.'

He knows it's the only answer he could give. Time enough to worry about whether it's really true when he hasn't got Raglan standing over him.

'I think,' says Bishop, 'that Mr Croxley should be part of the team. And since you don't have all the information you claimed, Paul, we'll pay him out of your cut. I'm sure you won't mind. And you can be responsible for his safety.'

Daz expects Raglan to look away from him, to avoid facing

a defeat. But he does the opposite. The darkness in his eyes is unchanged. Revenge has been postponed, not cancelled.

'Croxley?'

Daz looks to the speaker-phone. 'Here.'

'The knowledge you have – don't speak it to anyone. Understand? Not any of the gentlemen with you now. Not your girlfriend. Not even your mother. It's safest for them that way – you understand?'

'Sure.' He tries to make the word sound light but it catches in his throat. The mini-disc recorder is still pressing into his thigh. He is becoming too aware of it – sure his feelings of guilt will betray him. It would be hard to explain if they found it now. They'd probably kill him and be done with the doubt.

'When the time comes,' Bishop says, 'I'll ask you and you'll tell.'

Daz's ear lobe is itching but his hands are tied. Bishop is giving instructions to Guy. Then the phone clicks to silence.

Raglan walks from the room, followed by Smith.

Guy gets out his knife and moves around behind Daz. Daz feels a line of pain as the plastic strip tightens around his wrists.

'You're one of us now. There's no going back. Remember that.'

Then there's a quiet snip and Daz's hands are free. He watches Guy leave the room. Then, heart pounding too hard, he pulls the mini-disc and microphone from his pocket and stuffs them into the crack behind the safe.

'Are you coming, Croxley?' calls Guy.

'Be right there.'

The man is introduced as 'the accountant', but he looks more like a retired rugby player. Forty-five years old, Daz guesses. Perhaps fifty. A prop-forward's body in a grey suit.

It's Raglan who's doing the introductions. 'Smith. Guy. Croxley.' He points to each of them in turn. There's no flicker when he reaches Daz. The signs of his fuming anger have gone. The accountant nods around the group, shakes hands. Daz feels engulfed by the grip.

'Call me Colin.'

'Daz,' says Daz.

'I'm project manager,' Raglan tells him.

'I thought Mr Bishop—'

Raglan smiles. 'I'm his representative on the outside.'

Colin dips his great head. 'But it was he who called me this morning. He okayed all this, true?'

Daz catches the momentary thinning of his ex-landlord's smile. He's impressed by the speed with which Colin has located Raglan's sore spot – the point of ambiguity. Raglan is the chairman of this meeting – and looking especially smart this afternoon, a clean shirt, perfectly ironed. He's changed into a fresh suit as well. The corner of a handkerchief protrudes from the breast pocket. He is going out of his way to display the mannerisms of authority. But they are still in the solicitor's office – which is clearly Bishop's territory. And it's Bishop choosing the team. That's why Daz is sitting in a chair now, not kneeling with his hands tied behind his back. Raglan has to pretend not to hate him.

The danger is hidden.

Colin lays his briefcase on the table, unlocks it and takes out a notebook computer. 'Bear with me, please,' he says.

There's a warm chiming sound as the computer starts up. Each of the accountant's blunt fingers seems to cover more than one key. But they tap away so fast that Daz can't pick out the individual movements.

'There,' he says, looking around the table. 'Time for the details. You have a sum of money, yes?'

Raglan clears his throat. 'That's the idea.'

'Or you haven't got it?'

'We will have it.'

More tapping of keys. 'You know the amount?'

Daz sees Raglan's eyes flick across the table towards him for a fraction of a second. It feels strange to see the man discomforted in this way.

'Ten million,' says Raglan.

'In what form?'

'Twenties and fifties, sterling. Some high-denomination dollar bills, some Euros.'

'Used notes?'

'New.'

Colin sits back in his chair and nods. 'This *is* the Lyall-Griffiths money, then. Yes?'

'Bishop told you?'

'He doesn't have to. Ten million is an unusual amount of cash. Though you do see it, of course.'

'Of course.'

Daz is pretty sure that Raglan hasn't seen that kind of money in cash and that the accountant knows it.

'But if Bishop didn't tell you—'

The accountant holds up a finger to stop Raglan. He says: 'The notes are new, yes? So we're not talking about the proceeds of street-level drug sales. It can only be the Lyall-Griffiths money. The job was unique. I've been wondering when the money would surface.'

Raglan's hands come together on the table, fingers interlocking.

Colin smiles over the top of his computer. 'I take my hat off to the accountant who set it up. I really do.'

'Fraud is fraud is fraud,' Raglan says.

'No,' Colin lays a hand on his computer. 'Everything's virtual these days. A property development might cost a hundred million. But there's never a room with all that cash inside. It's just numbers on a database somewhere. All the best brains work on ones and noughts.' He sighs and shakes his head.

Raglan makes a show of checking his watch.

Colin doesn't seem to notice. 'The Lyall-Griffiths job – that was old school. A cash fraud. They found some method of accumulating large quantities of notes in the company safes.' The gleam is back in his eye now. 'It was completely unorthodox. What did they tell the banks when they asked for so much cash? It must have been done over a period of years. And that begs another question. I'm assuming the auditors were in their pocket. But how did they hide it all from the Inland Revenue? And the timing was so beautifully managed. The largest tranche of money coming in to pay off the largest outstanding bills. And—' He spreads his hands, like a conjuror revealing an illusion.

'And?'

'And the safes were empty. A couple of the managers missing. Bishop – he wasn't involved, was he? Ah, yes, I see it now.'

'The history isn't important,' Raglan says. 'We just need somewhere to put it.'

'Very well,' says Colin. 'But history is our heritage, yes? Forget it and we're lost.'

Raglan glances towards Smith, then folds his arms across his chest. Again, Daz has to resist the urge to smile openly. Colin gives a small shake of the head and turns his attention back to the computer screen. He starts typing.

'We'll need to set up some companies. One in the

Caymans. Another in the Bahamas. And one more in, say—'
His fingers rattle over the keyboard '—Indonesia.' He looks up
and flashes a grin at Daz. 'That should throw them.'

'How much does all this cost?' Raglan asks.

'It's not cheap. But you do want it secure, yes? You don't
want difficult questions about unexplained deposits into
your account. Trust me. This is how it's done. The
companies make loans to each other; they charge each
other consultancy fees. It all looks fine on paper. We shoot
the accounting trail around the world a few times and no
one will be sure where the revenue really came from in the
beginning. This is how the Colombians do it. Only the
best.'

Colin starts to type again. Daz is wondering what will
happen if they do recover the money – if Bishop will be
comfortable with all these potential witnesses walking
around the streets. Daz knows he is safe only as long as he
is useful.

And he's now worrying about the place he concealed the
bug. It was certainly a good idea to get it off his person. For
one thing the recording proves that he was lying about Patty
being dead. But now he's had time to consider, he sees that
anywhere would have been a better hiding place than here.
The things being talked about in this room are too secret.
The chance of the bug being found might be small, but the
repercussions would be terminal.

Colin finishes typing and sits back from the computer.
'There's also the matter of transport.'

Raglan's face is getting greyer as the meeting progresses.
'More expenses?'

'Think about it – five hundred new twenty-pound notes
make a pile, let's say—' He spreads a finger and thumb and
looks at the gap '—five centimetres deep. Ten million

pounds' worth of twenties would make a fifty-metre pile, yes? We bale it up, of course. But you're still talking about several tea chests full. All of which has to be sent overseas – unless you want to try taking it down to the HSBC on Gallowtree Gate and handing it over the counter.

'If a twenty-pound note weighs one gramme, five hundred thousand of them will weigh half a metric tonne. All that has to be hidden. We'll need a container-load of legitimate goods to bury the money in. And all that has to be shipped out to Indonesia – with some kind of plausible cover story.'

'Is that it?' Raglan says.

'Unless you've got anything more to tell me?'

Raglan stares at the far wall.

It doesn't look like he's going to say anything, so Daz chips in. 'Stained, isn't it?'

'The money?'

Daz nods. 'Some. Yeah.'

'Well, now,' says Colin, 'there we have another issue altogether.'

It's night. They pull up next to a chain-link gate in a chain-link fence. Ten feet high with a barbed-wire top. Raglan and Guy are in the front of the car. Daz is in the back with Smith.

There is lighting here, even though they're deep in the East Midlands countryside. Security lighting. It shines on the fence and on the huge box-like buildings inside it. There are no windows in the complex, so far as Daz can see. Four silvery chimneys of different heights rise out of different buildings. He breathes in through his nose and pulls a face.

'Piss-awful smell.'

Guy shakes his head, unimpressed. 'Wait here.'

He gets out, followed by Raglan. The two men scrunch along the fence-line and away around the corner. Daz looks at the signs, wired to the gate. One shows a silhouette of a dog. Another is just writing. The biggest looks like it might be a company logo.

Daz looks at the factory building, trying to put the late Mr Salt out of his mind. He takes a breath through his nose. The air here reminds him of something. It's got that disgusting overcooked meat smell, like the pie factory on the industrial estate. But there's a hint of something even worse. Like wheelie bins left out in the heat for too long. He looks at the chimneys. A plume of steam rises from one, lit up by the factory's lights. Vivid against the black sky.

Daz isn't sure if the law would count Salt's death as murder, manslaughter or an accident. Only two people saw what really happened, and one of them was the victim. Nor is he sure about his own part in the death. If he hadn't run, perhaps Salt would be alive. And if he keeps quiet about it, perhaps that makes him an accomplice.

Guy appears across the compound, on the other side of the fence. He strides back towards the car, swinging a bunch of keys in his hand. He springs a padlock and opens the gate.

'I hope you've got a strong stomach,' he says, climbing into the driver's seat.

Daz doesn't answer.

Guy drives them in and around the edge of the complex to a wide entranceway in the side of one of the buildings. Then he eases the car through into the brightly lit interior. Raglan is standing waiting for them, holding a handkerchief over his nose and mouth. It is pale lilac, matching his tie.

Heavy industrial plant takes up most of the centre of the cavernous room. Two storeys of machinery, with a loading

area in front of it. Gantries and staircases bolted to the sides.
The place looks like it's been shut down for the night, but
there's a low vibration from the ventilator units in the wall,
and a buzz from the strip lights. A giant breathing in its
sleep.

Daz gets out. The rotting meat smell is stronger here.

'This is where you get dirty,' Guy tells him.

They open the boot. When they heaved Salt's limp body
in, they'd left it lying on its side. He must have rolled over
during the journey. The unseeing face is looking up, directly
at them. Daz takes the feet. Guy has the hands. It's like
lifting a couple of sacks of potatoes in a hammock.

'Supposed to be stiff, isn't he?'

Guy shakes his head. 'It's been hot. The rigor mortis has
loosened up. And the fat ones never go that hard anyway.'

They haul him on to the dusty concrete of the factory
floor.

'No dragging,' Guy says. 'Don't want to leave marks.'

So they lift the body and swing it forward. Lift and
swing again until they are at the base of the machine.
There's a loading hopper here. One more lift and Salt's
corpse is over the shining metal side. It tumbles down on
to a conveyor belt at the bottom. Once again it has come to
rest face up.

Daz remembers Salt's house. The man's naive attempts to
launder the money. If a hundred and seventy thousand had
been all there was, he might still be alive. Salt was so alone
that there'd been no one to warn him he was getting out of
his depth.

Raglan looks over the edge into the loading hopper, then
glances at Daz. 'It could have been you,' he says, quietly
enough so that the others don't hear. Then he adds: 'It still
could, you know.'

Guy shouts to them from a little way down the machine. 'You two go up there.' He points to the top-level gantry. 'Make sure everything works.' Then he searches through the bunch of keys, selects one and inserts it into a wall-mounted control panel.

For Daz there's no way to back out at this stage. He's still trying to work out if helping to hide or dispose of the body will make him an accessory to the killing. He's seen that happening in movies. But perhaps they were American movies. The law may be different over here.

He could go to Detective Sergeant Leech and tell him everything. But the truth seems so unlikely that he doubts he'd be believed. There are forensic tests, of course. He's not sure what they would prove – his innocence or his complicity.

He climbs the steps up to the top level – some kind of observation gantry surrounded by metal safety railings. Below is another hopper, far bigger than in the loading area below. At its centre is something that looks like a huge corkscrew.

Raglan puts an arm over his shoulder. 'Are you looking forward to this, Croxley?'

There's a sudden hum. A surge of noise. The sound of electric motors getting up to speed. He can feel the thrum of them through the metal of the gantry. He imagines the screw turning in the bottom of the hopper. A giant auger. And he knows what it is he's seeing. This is like an old-style mincing machine. A giant-sized version of what they used in Victorian kitchens, big enough to take whole cows, not just cubes of stewing steak.

He looks around, scanning with his eyes, and sees a feed on the left of the hopper. Steel scoops arranged in vertical procession. They rattle into life as he watches – juddering after one another towards the top, spilling over, then descending in line. A continuous loop.

He knows what's going to happen. Without stopping to figure out what he can do, he wrests himself free of Raglan's grip and flings himself down the metal stairs, taking them three and four at a time, swinging the corners.

Almost at ground level. He can see Guy working the controls and Smith watching. He can see Salt's body, still in the loading hopper, on its back like before. One arm across the chest, as if he was swearing an oath of allegiance. Daz's foot hits the concrete. At the same moment the conveyor belt starts.

Salt's arm is jolted out of position. It flops to the side. Not formal any more. Drunk, perhaps. Then the body is moving along the belt, climbing into a covered chute and out of view, swallowed by machinery.

Daz turns and throws himself back up the stairway, trying to find a place where he might push the corpse off the belt. He reaches the observation deck, knowing it's impossible. He grips the rail next to where Raglan stands, casting about for some way to stop the machine from destroying the only evidence of accidental death. An iron bar to throw into the works.

Then the screw begins to turn in the bottom of the hopper. The noise is sudden, intense. A shrill, fingernails-on-blackboard sound. The base roar of the motor. The high-pitched screech of something in the grinder scraping across the metal housing. And the smell. Daz staggers back as a waft of putrefaction hits him. He grabs a handful of his T-shirt and stuffs it over his nose and mouth.

'What a machine!' Raglan says through his handkerchief.

Daz isn't looking up at the feed mechanism now, so he doesn't see the moment when Salt's corpse disgorges as the metal scoop that's carrying it over-ends. He does see it bounce off the steel panels of the hopper and slide down the incline towards the mincer. Head first. The blade of the screw slices across Salt's jaw line. The screeching noise stops now, as if the machine is suddenly lubricated.

Daz turns. From the smell. From the sight. And most horrifying of all, from the sound of cracking, splintering bone. He runs, gagging. Crashing the side railings. Stumbling down the stairway. He's standing on the concrete, doubled over, head near his knees. Hyperventilating. There's sweat clinging to his skin. He feels dizzy from lack of blood to his head.

The big motor stops first. Then the others. Switched off like lights. Out of the silence come Guy's approaching footsteps.

'Don't throw up, for Christ's sake.'

Daz straightens himself. Raglan has sauntered off to talk to Smith by the control panel. Guy smiles.

'You want to know what happens next?' Guy asks.

'Pigging hell!'

'You need to understand this.' His thumb strokes the tips of his fingers as he speaks. 'All the animal carcasses thrown in here get boiled up. Fat separated from meat. Rendering, they call it. The bone, fur, cloth – all that stuff ends up in the incinerator. The meat gets sold. In a couple of weeks, bits of our friend will be in cans of dog food all over Europe.'

'Cans?'

'And in cattle feed. We've just added the seasoning.'

Guy is laughing now, through his nose. He pulls a bag out of his pocket, holds it out to Daz. 'Want one?'

The liquorice smell brings back the nausea. Daz pulls his head away. 'Why you telling me?'

'Because—' Guy's face is suddenly serious '—because you need to see how easy it is to get rid of people. You don't have to fall off a building first. You don't even have to be dead. This thing—' He gestures to the machine with his bag of sweets '—it'll grind up ropes and gags just as easily as it will bodies and clothes. Mr Bishop wanted to make sure you knew that.'

Chapter 25

Going for a drive with Smith would have sounded like a death sentence a week ago. But Bishop's involvement and Daz's perceived usefulness have changed all that. Not that anyone has started to be open about the plans. All Daz knows is that the journey will take more than an hour and that they're going to see someone called Bill Jagger. A 'freelancer' is what Bishop called him.

Smith takes the A50 out of Leicester, through Glenfield and then joins the M1, heading north.

'Where we going?'

Instead of answering, Smith clicks on the stereo. The Human League. Daz stares out of the side window and tries not to let the blandness of the music get to him. He can't read the signs, but he recognizes the Nottingham and Derby junctions as they pass. There are four more hits from the 1980s to endure after that before they exit the motorway and the scenery gives him something else to focus on. They begin to climb into the mountains. The A-road leads to a B-road, then to a wide but deeply rutted track with trees thick on either side. Then they reach the end of the road. Smith clicks the CD player, cutting off Cindy Lauper mid-phrase.

'Here,' he says. 'This is where we're going.'

Ahead of them is an expanse of mud and broken rock at the base of a mountain, the entire site is as long as a football field, though not as wide. Smith opens a gate and makes for a Portakabin near the side fence. Daz follows.

The ground is hard underfoot. There's no grass here, or weeds or anything growing. They skirt around a puddle of clay-yellow water that looks large enough to drown someone in, then up over a small heap of angular rocks. In the distance are three walls of an industrial building that might once have had four. The back wall is half-buried in the rising slope of the mountain. Above that is the edge of the site, and further back still the unspoiled slope. Rough fields and dry-stone walls all the way to the summit.

Now that he's had time to listen, Daz notices the sound of a two-stroke engine away in the distance. A compressor, perhaps, or a pump. Other than that there's just birdsong and the breath of the hot breeze. In the distance the air ripples over the baked ground.

Smith knocks on the cabin door. There's no answer. He tries again.

'Jagger?'

'Over here!' A man is hailing them from the tumbled-down building.

Bill Jagger is a man of indeterminate middle age. A wiry figure with a heavily freckled face and arms. He shakes Smith's hand, nods towards Daz.

'I thought you were coming tomorrow.'

Daz can't place his accent.

'Change of plan,' says Smith. 'We're going to move quick.'

Bill jerks his thumb into the derelict building. 'Well, I haven't got all the stuff together yet. Can't give you a demonstration or anything. But you can see some of it *in situ* if you want.'

Smith rubs a hand over his hair. 'You think that's—'

'We'd better get you kitted out though.'

The old building has no roof and no internal walls. Daz can see what looks like a narrow railway track leading straight back to a large wooden door in the rear wall. But it's mostly buried in hard-packed mud, so he can't be completely sure. Bill directs him to a line of crates by the side wall. In them he finds rubber boots, waterproofs and hard hats with lights and belt-batteries. On the opposite side of the room there is a long trestle table, laid out with electronic equipment – rolls of black cable and serious-looking boxes of switches.

Daz pulls on the protective gear. He can feel the weight of the steel toecaps as he swings his feet. The waterproof coat is trapping his body heat. He's suddenly aware of the sweat on his arms and neck where the slick fabric presses against his skin. Smith is taking a long time to get changed. He tries several pairs of boots, but still seems uncomfortable in the ones he's chosen.

Bill Jagger inspects Smith first. Then he turns to Daz, tugs on the belt-battery. It's secure.

'You'll do.'

He leads them to the back of the building and pulls open the large door. Inside is a tunnel that vanishes into blackness after a few feet. Daz feels a touch of cold on his face – a river of chill air flowing out from under the mountain. The sweat starts to cool on his forehead.

The tunnel would be wide enough for all three men to stand abreast, but they walk in line with Daz bringing up the rear. The rails are easier to see here. He can even make out a few sleepers through the broken rock and mud that cover the floor. Smith must have turned his light on before stepping inside. Daz follows Bill's lead, turning his on only after they've gone a few paces into the gloom.

He looks up at the roof. The circle of his torchlight shows up bare rock. Unsupported. He can see a texture that looks as if it might have come from hammer or chisel blows.

'It dates back to the 1790s, this,' Bill Jagger says. 'In 1903 they drove a new adit from the other side of the hill. A fair haul longer, but they could drain the mine a hundred and fifty feet deeper. Lost twenty men digging it, mind. But it saved the company a heap of cash in the end. That's what counts, eh?'

Daz isn't sure if Jagger means it, or if he's testing them out with what he's just said.

'Is it far?' Smith asks.

Bill turns his shoulder. 'Are you in a hurry?'

Smith doesn't answer.

Bill resumes his walk, his stride the same length and speed as before. 'I didn't know you were in a hurry.'

'How d'they die?' Daz asks, from his place at the back of the line.

'A couple got fried in a firing accident. A mix-up with the fuses. The others were killed in a roof fall. They say some of them lived for hours under all that rock. Had enough air to breathe but the weight of it just crushed the life out of them. Not how I'd want to go.'

Daz glances back over his shoulder. It feels as if they've been walking slightly uphill all this way. The entrance looks like a distant light bulb now.

'We turn off down here.' Bill has stopped by an entrance in the side wall. It has a lower roof and is only wide enough for one person at a time. Smith is shifting his weight from one leg to the other.

'You need to take a piss?' Bill asks him.

'I . . . Maybe.'

Bill laughs and walks into the side passage. Smith looks

back towards the entrance. Daz pushes past him, following their guide.

'Wait,' Smith calls.

Daz doesn't. He hears swearing behind him. He lengthens his stride, moving up closer to Bill's light. It's wet here. A constant trickle down the walls. Drips falling from the low roof. He bumps his hard hat once, then stoops deeper.

'Still with me?' Bill calls.

'Slow down, will you!' Smith's voice from far behind. It seems like he's started to follow them now.

Bill laughs again. 'You wanted me to speed up a moment ago.'

Daz stumbles out into a small room.

Bill is leaning against the wall, waiting for him. 'Have you been under ground before?' he asks.

Daz shakes his head. 'What do they mine?'

'Lead and copper – but that was a long time ago. In the end it cost them more to dig out the ore than they got for selling it. It's been closed eighty years. The people who own the place now – they want to find out if there's anything lurking under the surface that they've missed. The mother lode.'

'Is there?'

Jagger laughs. 'Only in their dreams.'

Smith catches them up now. He is panting, as if out of breath.

'Last stretch,' Bill says. He points to a hole in the wall next to him. 'This one's a bit of a crawl.'

Smith shakes his head. 'I can't.'

But Bill is down on his hands and knees already. Daz waits till the man's boots are out of view before getting down to follow.

'No,' Smith says. 'Stay here, Croxley.'

Daz ignores him.

'That's a fucking order!'

Smith's words reach him, but he's already gone. He's crawling over wet gravel. A drop of water falls on his exposed neck and runs inside his shirt. He stops. Bill is out of sight up ahead. Smith is out of reach behind. Daz turns the switch on his hard hat and his light goes out. Blackness. He holds a hand in front of his face but sees nothing. The air cools the skin around his nostrils as he inhales. He feels the hairs on his arms standing. He gets a sudden, vertiginous awareness of himself within the mountain – the ground surface, the tunnels, his own place within it all. It's as if the rock has been turned into glass. Then the moment of ecstasy has passed. His skin relaxes. He turns the light back on and starts to crawl forward again.

The final chamber is wider than the one where they left Smith. Daz stands up, rubs his hands on the outside of his waterproofs. Bill is on one knee, coiling a length of yellow cable. There's electrical equipment here. Wires connected to metal pegs, a portable generator and something that looks like a small computer. To the right there is the opening to yet another passage – larger than the crawl they've just come through.

'Is he coming?' Bill asks.

Daz shakes his head. 'Tricked him, didn't you?'

Bill stands. 'What's it to you?'

Daz points to the generator, then back to the low crawl. 'Wouldn't fit,' he says. 'Must be an easier way through.'

Bill grips the cable. For a moment it looks as if he's going to take a swing at Daz. Then he grins. His teeth gleam white in the torchlight. 'The man's got an idiot attitude,' he says. 'Too proud to say he's scared. I could have brought him through the main drive, I suppose. Here.'

He passes the coil to Daz. 'You do the inspection.'

'What's it do?'

'They didn't tell you?'

Daz shakes his head.

'Then why are you here at all?'

It's a good question. Daz doesn't have any answers.

Bill tilts his head for a moment. 'Hell. Bishop sent you. What's it to do with me anyway?'

'You met him?' Daz asks. 'Bishop, I mean?'

'Sure – out in the Orange Free State, back in 1983. It was an alluvial gold prospect. He was stringing some potential investors along. It never came to anything, though. Do you know what he's going after this time?'

'Sort of.'

'But you don't know what all this is for?' He prods the generator with the toe of his boot.

Daz shakes his head.

'It's geophysics equipment. We use it for mapping out the position of ore bodies. But you can use it for anything. Water resources. Archaeology. Buried corpses. You name it . . . We get a high-voltage current and shoot it through these wires to metal pegs driven into the rock. Then we take hundreds of readings of electrical resistance over different distances. All that gets fed into the computer and out comes a cross-section.'

'Of what?'

'Of whatever's under the surface.'

Daz meets Kat outside her brother's place. She's wearing work clothes. A blue blouse and skirt combination. Dark tights. Sensible shoes. She'd pass for conventional if it weren't for the eyes and short-cropped hair. He moves up to kiss her but she backs away.

'What's the matter?'

'You ronk, Croxley!'

He sniffs at his wrist, then his armpit.

'When did you last have a shower?'

'Not got one.'

'Bath?'

'Zilch.'

'You do have rights you know. If your landlord is getting Housing Benefit paid to him . . .' She peters out, as if realizing that she was slipping back into work mode. He watches as she bites on the nail of her little finger.

'You OK?'

She nods. 'Sure. It's just . . .'

He thinks she's about to ask something important or make an announcement, but the moment passes.

She shakes her head. 'We'd better get on. I've got an appointment at five.'

Then she turns and unlocks the front door. 'Just don't touch anything. OK. Not until you get cleaned up.'

He follows her backside into the house, wondering exactly what it was she just meant.

The fox is in the shed at the end of the garden. Daz looks through the cobwebbed window and sees it lying curled in a back corner. There's water in a bowl on the floor.

'Jim said there's nothing more he can do. Just have to wait now.'

'It eating yet?'

She shakes her head. 'He put something in the water to give it a little salt and sugar. But other than that . . .'

There's a question that's been floating around in Daz's mind for a couple of days. It surfaces now and he asks it out loud, even though he doesn't expect Kat to know the answer. 'You give an animal medicine, yeah, an' it's meant for people, does it do the same thing?'

She tilts her head. 'Like what?'

'Anything. Aspirin, Prozac, penicillin.'

'I guess it's like you said before – they test human drugs on animals, so why not the other way around.'

'Yeah,' he says. 'I guess.'

Then he opens the shed door as quietly as he can manage. Vomit-smelling air wafts over him. He turns his head away to take a deep breath, then steps inside. The bundle of red-brown fur doesn't shift. For a moment he thinks it must be dead, then he sees a fractional movement of its flank. He squats down to study it more closely, arms folded over his knees. Now he knows what he's looking for he can see that the animal is breathing. He gets up and backs from the shed.

Kat closes the door. 'Are you OK?'

He nods. 'Foxy smells worse than me, eh?'

She laughs, glances at her watch. 'Well, we've just got time to do something about that.'

She takes his clothes and carries them at arm's length from the bathroom. When the door is closed he lets the towel slip to the floor and steps into the shower.

Jets of hot water pressing into the skin of his face. Water dripping from his chin. Streams snaking down his chest and legs. He feels the sensation so vividly that he finds himself involuntarily drawing in breath. It's been a long time since he's experienced anything like this. He looks down and sees his dirty footprints being washed from the floor of the cubicle. Days of grime spiralling down the drain.

Daz hears the bathroom door open and close. He wipes a hole in the condensation and sees Kat grinning in at him.

'Don't forget hair,' she says. 'If your jeans are anything to go by, you'll have to use a gallon of shampoo.' She moves her head close to the glass. She's pressing her teeth into her lower lip. Her green eyes move down over his body.

He feels a rush of sexual arousal. Suddenly self-conscious, he angles his body away and looks back at her over his shoulder. The screen is steaming up again. The last thing he can see is her smile. Then it recedes into the fog.

'Keep washing,' she calls.

He takes a bottle of shampoo from the soap shelf. 'Won't mind, will he – me using his stuff like this?'

'Jim? What the eye doesn't see, the heart won't grieve over.'

Daz lathers up, less than certain that Kat has answered the real question. He's leaning forward against the wall now, hands resting on the tiles, enjoying the luxury. Hot water beating on the crown of his head, shampoo suds sliding down his chest. He feels a touch of cooler air as the cubicle door swings open, then the shock of firm skin pressed against the full length of his body.

He tries to turn to face her, but her arms are around him and she's not letting go. Her chin is on his shoulder.

'I'm just washing your back,' she whispers. 'Don't mind, do you?' There's gentle laughter in her voice.

'Tell you later.'

Then he slips around in her grip, his wet skin moving over hers. They hold each other. He kisses her but she squirms free.

'Teeth!' she says. 'Ugh. You can't blame your landlord for not brushing!'

He steps back, slightly stung. But she's still grinning at him. When they made love before it had been in the half-light.

Now he sees her breasts properly for the first time. Her nipples are very pale, hardly darker than the rest of her skin. He reaches out and traces the curve of her silver nipple-ring with one finger.

'I shouldn't be doing this,' she says. 'The Cow Queen wouldn't approve.'

'Showering with a client?' He voices the words without any driving emotion, but they come out sounding harsh in his own ears.

'I meant,' she says, 'showering with a man I hardly know.' She turns away from him. 'You can wash my back if you like.'

He takes a deep breath. Exhales slowly, trying to relax, to regain the feeling he had a moment before. He places his hands across her lower back, thumbs almost meeting at the base of her spine, and works them up towards the top. He's kneading her shoulders, his fingers probing her deltoid muscles, finding a tension there that he hadn't noticed in her face.

'How much do I know about you, Daz?'

He doesn't answer.

'I don't need to know everything. But I want to think that you trust me.'

'Course I do.'

'I mean, really trust. So you wouldn't keep something from me?'

Her shoulder muscles have hardened further. He can feel the presence of whatever it is that she isn't saying. It presses into his ears like silence.

He swallows. 'What you want to know?'

'Your secrets.'

'Got loads.'

She turns to face him again. He looks down at her body,

at the lines of light reflected in the sheen of water on her perfect skin. Then he looks to one side.

'I had that policeman call me this morning,' she says, 'the one who took you in for questioning.'

'Leech.'

Daz turns off the shower. The droplets start to cool on his skin.

'He needed to know where you were. That's what he said. He told me there was no sign of life in your flat. You are still staying there, aren't you?'

Daz steps out on to the mat and wraps a towel around his waist. 'Why you asking now?'

She follows him out. 'Look at me.'

He looks.

She raises her arms above her head and turns a complete circle. 'This is what I am, Daz. Not a uniform or a job or anything else. Just me. And I don't want to ask this now. I don't want to have to. But what better time is there?'

'What did you tell him?'

'That I'd keep a lookout for you. That's all. And pass his message on if I did find you. He wants to see you, Daz.'

'Don't want to see him.'

'He said you're in trouble, that he could help.'

'That's what they always say.'

'You're not going to see him?'

'Can't.'

'If you don't tell me what's going on, how can I help you? Don't you see, Daz? It's eating me up.'

He does see. And he does want to tell her. It would be a relief, like washing the dirt from his body. But he can't.

He remembers what she said when they were last together – that he's a man torn between resentment and despair. She was exactly right. He resents the way people look down at him and at the same time he despairs because he thinks their opinions might be true. The two emotions have always battled with each other inside his head, but he's never understood it so clearly before.

That's why he'll never allow himself to try to learn to read – for fear that the self-loathing side of him will be proved right after all and will finally win over. And that's why he can't tell Kat that he's sleeping rough – for fear that she'll see a truth that he only half-faces – that he is and always will be a failure.

She's still looking at him, waiting for an answer. 'Tell me. Please.'

'I can't.'

Then she picks up her clothes and a towel and walks from the room.

There are two empty beds in the ward now. Just Patty and another old woman in residence, both apparently asleep. There's a TV set up so it can be seen from both beds. A soap opera is droning at low volume. Bronzed bodies cavorting in the antipodean sunshine.

Daz steps closer to Patty. There's no oxygen mask today, and no IV drip. He brings his head low and tilts it so he can look into her face. She looks better than before, but he notices tension lines across her brow. A thought starts to form in his mind – that this is some kind of rigor mortis, that she might have died in the middle of *Home and Away*. Then her eyes open.

'Croxley!'

'Hi.'

She flicks a withered finger towards the television. 'If you don't turn that damned machine off, I'm going to kill myself.'

He does as he's told.

'Just because I'm getting on a bit, they think I'm braindead.'

'Could have told them to turn it off.'

'They treat me like a child, boy. Won't listen. "Take some more pills, Mrs Wattling. Time for your wash, Mrs Wattling. This looks like a nice programme, Mrs Wattling." Nice programme, my arse!'

She lies panting after the exertion of her outburst, but looks vaguely satisfied. A nurse marches into the ward and comes directly to Patty's bedside.

'Time for your medication, Mrs Wattling.' She hands over a small plastic beaker containing two pills.

'You see what I mean?' Patty grumbles as she puts them into her mouth.

The nurse passes her a glass of water from the bedside cabinet. 'You should be getting some rest now. Your visitor will have to go.'

Daz shifts his weight from one foot to the other.

'A little longer,' pleads Patty. 'He's only just got here.'

'Ten minutes, then,' says the nurse. She checks her watch, makes a note on the chart and leaves.

'You OK?' Daz asks.

'What does it look like?'

'Looks fine,' Daz says

In fact, it looks like cancer. Now Dr Høeg has told him, it's hard to look into her sunken eyes and see anything else. Patty must know the diagnosis, but she can't know that he knows. He wonders if she's trying to protect herself by keeping it secret, or perhaps to protect him.

'Did you get that bug and recorder back from Salt's house?' she asks.

'Yes.'

'And?'

'Betting on the horses – just like you said.'

Patty wipes her hand across her dry lips. 'Do you know how much he's got?'

'Hundred and seventy grand.'

Her eyes widen. Then she smiles. 'Good boy! I knew we'd get there if we kept trying. Now all we have to do is get it from him.'

Daz nods his head and manages to smile back. Everything about Patty seems different now he knows she's lying about her health. For one thing he understands that it was never the money she was after. She couldn't spend it in the little time she has left. But this adventure is her last throw of the dice. Her last chance to trick some poor mark out of his cash. And Daz doesn't have the heart to let her know that they've failed.

'I'll do it,' he says. 'Break into Salt's place again. Steal the cash. Bring it here.'

She nods approval. 'You're a good boy, Daz Croxley. And don't forget to feed Dyson.' Then she sighs. 'I get so tired these days. It's the pills. They're drugging me so I don't try to escape again.'

Daz sits himself in the chair next to the bed. He watches the hands on the wall clock. He should be sad, but he can't find any emotions inside himself. Just an empty space.

'Did you ever have children?' he asks.

She shifts her head on the pillow. 'One. She was no good.'

'Was?'

Patty looks at him strangely. 'She died a long way from home.'

And then Daz sees something he's never seen before. A tear starts to pool in the corner of her eye. 'Didn't mean to make you sad.'

'I'm not sad for me.' She shakes her head. 'I'm just sorry. So sorry.'

He's never heard her speak like this before. 'Why?'

'If things had been . . .' She closes her eyes.

'What?'

'I'm going to sleep now.'

'If things had been what?'

'Different . . . I would have told you.'

He wants to say that he knows about the cancer – that the doctor told him already. But he thinks that would hurt her more.

'Your mother—' Patty begins.

'What about her?'

'—should've been more proud of you.'

'You didn't know my mother,' he says. But Patty is already asleep.

Daz pushes past Vicky into the house. She doesn't resist. Then through into the back room, a glance into the kitchen, the garden. Weeds. Kodak's grave. Dyson lying next to it. Not moving. He steps between the thistles, crouches, touches the animal's paw, searching for warmth or movement. Finding neither.

'What was it?' he asks.

Vicky is standing behind him. 'Stupid dog. He was too greedy.'

'What was it?'

'I couldn't have known . . . Just wanted him to stop whining and barking all the time.'

'Prozac?'

She walks up closer. 'Some downers. Diazepam, codeine, I don't know. I put them in his food. Is he . . .?'

'You killed him.'

'Shit.' Her shoulders slump. 'Stupid dog ate it all in one go. I didn't know.'

'That's what dogs do. They can't stop themselves.'

He gets up, starts walking back through the house. Vicky tags along, dragging her feet. 'Haven't got a few quid you could lend me? I'd be really grateful.'

Chapter 26

They're standing outside a small factory unit in the dark. Smith is at the door, doing his bouncer thing, ushering them in one at a time. Colin the expansive accountant goes in first, then freckle-faced Jagger, and Guy, who is keeping one thumb looped in his belt.

Apparently the other meeting venue isn't available tonight. The solicitor is working late. Daz thinks again about the mini-disc recorder. He can't leave it hidden there indefinitely. It will be discovered at some stage.

'What's up with you?' Smith asks.

Daz steps through into the factory unit. 'Nothing,' he says.

There's a hydraulic car ramp inside, welding torches, a paint spray gun linked to a small air compressor. There are a couple of cars parked up at the end, one with a crumpled wing, the other with a concertinaed bonnet. There's a third alongside them, covered with a cloth. The concrete floor is mottled with old oil spills.

Daz sees a table set up with five chairs at the back of the room. Raglan is already seated. The others file across and take their places. Smith points Daz to a sixth chair, set back behind Guy and Colin, not too close to the speaker-phone in the centre of the table.

This is Raglan's venue. Raglan's show. Daz doesn't complain. The arrangement suits him well enough. Raglan shines a smile around the table. Then he starts to speak, doing the introductions. 'Mr Smith here has worked for me for three years now. Mr Efficiency, I call him. Then we have Bill Jagger . . .'

Daz is only half-listening. He knows the names already. Instead he watches the people: Raglan holding the lapel of his jacket, Smith sitting arms folded, Jagger tipping his chair back, one leg crossed on the other knee. Guy seems relaxed, except for one foot, jiggling away under the table.

The introductions pass clockwise around the group. When he gets to Daz, Raglan just says. 'That's Croxley at the back.' Then he's moved on and smiling again.

'And here's our excellent accountant. No need to say anything about him. We all know his work. Good to have you on board, Colin.'

Guy has reached out to the phone and he's keying in a number. Raglan, who hasn't given any instructions in that direction, frowns. The ringing tone sounds three times before the click.

'Bishop,' says Bishop's voice through the speaker.

'We're here, sir,' Guy says.

'Good.'

'Mr Bishop—' says Raglan.

'We'll have to make this brief,' Bishop cuts in.

'Yes,' Raglan nods. 'Indeed.'

'Jagger and Croxley?'

'Both here,' says Jagger.

'Between you, you'll be able to locate the money.'

It isn't really a question, but Jagger answers anyway. 'Given the building and enough time. There'll be a way.'

'And we'll need roof supports for when we start breaking concrete.'

'That's arranged already.'

Raglan clears his throat. 'We're going to have to have some kind of cover for all the noise,' he says. 'When we start. Otherwise—'

'Not needed,' says Bishop. 'There won't be anyone around in that part of town when we go in. Especially not the police.'

Colin coughs into his hand. 'If I may . . .' he says. 'Supposing we get into the building at nightfall. We work quickly and efficiently to extract the money. Perhaps we get out before dawn. That means we'll have a couple of hours at most before our work is discovered.'

'Enough time to get away,' says Raglan.

'But the police aren't fools,' Colin says. 'It won't take them long to work out what happened. A day. Two, perhaps. We'll still have to ship the money overseas. If they're looking for us . . .'

There's a pause. Then Bishop speaks: 'Colin. Colin. Don't worry about this. Mr Jagger is an all-round mining man. He has a special area of expertise, which is going to help us in that respect. It'll take the police months to find out what's happened. Perhaps they never will. The way we're going to work it, they'll be looking for Muslim terrorists rather than British entrepreneurs like ourselves.'

Raglan shifts in his chair. 'We'll have everything ready to go in a couple of weeks.'

'The timing is fixed already,' Bishop says. 'We're moving in three days. Starting at 2200 and working through till 0500 at the latest.'

Raglan's eyes widen. Guy smiles.

Jagger whistles. 'Three days!'

Colin is smiling. 'Very clever. All the police will be over at the football ground.'

'Not the season,' Daz says.

'Not for a football match,' says Colin. 'If I remember rightly, there's going to be a big immigration conference that day – in the stadium. There should be enough protesters to keep the police fully occupied.'

Daz counts the days forward. The raid is to be on Saturday. Breakbeat Night.

It seems to be true – the solicitor was working late. It is close to eleven and the light is still on. The blinds are down over the windows, but through the door Daz can see the receptionist locking up. He tries the handle. She jumps, puts her hand to her chest. Then her face hardens and she mouths through the glass: '*We're closed.*'

He sees her scanning the road behind him.

'I came alone,' he says.

She unlocks the door and opens it a few inches. 'He's not here.'

'Who?'

'Whoever it is you want to see.'

'Need to check something,' he says.

'The last bus leaves in fifteen minutes. I've got no time for this.'

'Lost something.' Daz points to the corridor behind her. '*Before.* You know.'

'What?'

'A watch.'

She shakes her head. 'You'll have to come back tomorrow.' Then she lets go of the door and steps towards her handbag on the desk.

Daz takes his opportunity and slips inside. This office is Bishop's territory. That's why Raglan was so uneasy here. But where that puts the receptionist, he can't tell. He starts walking towards the back, ignoring her steely anger.

'Gunna look see. Then I'm out of here.'

He gets into the room, knowing that she's following. He's got about a second to act. So he darts out his hand, pulls the mini-disc recorder from its hiding place and pockets it.

'Out!'

He turns to see her standing in the doorway. 'OK. OK.'

She escorts him to the street. Holds the door while he steps out.

'You find a watch, you tell me. Right?'

He hears the lock turn behind him.

Daz walks through the streets, back towards his own side of town. But he doesn't know where he's going. He certainly can't face Freddy and Ginger after everything that has happened. It feels as if that part of his life ended with the mutual betrayal of three friends – his own clinch with Freddy and Ginger's lies to him.

Vicky's house is in the same direction. But that thought is equally uncomfortable, reminding him of his duty to go back and report progress to Patty in her hospital bed. But he has no cash to show her. And there is no way that she could hear the truth. It would probably kill her.

The person he really wants to be with is Kat. This is the hardest feeling to put a label on. She would give him a place to sleep. But their encounter earlier in the day was so painful that he's not even sure they still have a relationship. Would she tell him to doss down on the couch, or invite him into her own bed? The thought taunts him. Desire and fear of rejection evenly balanced. But if he goes back now, admitting to her that he's homeless, that he's been deceiving her – their relationship would be over for sure.

Only when he's walking out along Humberstone Gate does he consciously understand where it is that he's going.

He skips between the cars as he crosses the road to the island at the centre of Humberstone roundabout. The place he's been sleeping since being thrown out of his bedsit. He pushes his way between the bushes and under the trees. He sweeps away some of the litter with his foot, sits down on the ground, his head on his knees, and closes his eyes. But the mini-disc recorder is digging into his thigh and he can't get comfortable.

He reaches into his pocket and pulls it out, then rests against a tree. He might get a few pounds for it – a couple of days' worth of food, or even a night in a cheap bed and breakfast. But he'd have to wipe the disc first to get rid of the incriminating recording of Salt and Patty's voices. He plugs in the earpiece so he can listen one more time.

He hears the sounds of the recorder turning itself on and off in response to background noises. A door slamming. Click. Click. Footsteps. Click. Click. A door opening. It's not how he remembers it before. Then, close and totally unexpected, a woman's voice: 'How long are you going to be?' It's the receptionist from the solicitor's office.

Daz sits up straight.

'Ten minutes, *love*.' It's Guy's sarcastic voice answering her.

The woman makes a hissing noise. Exasperation, perhaps. Or disgust. The door closes.

Daz clicks the machine off. He's trying to figure what's happened. The machine was only set to record on one occasion that he knows of. That was in Salt's house. It was definitely off when he pushed it into its hiding place. He weighs it in his hand, mimes the act of sliding it between the wall and the safe. A tight fit. And now he sees how the RECORD button stands slightly proud of the side. It might have been pushed down for the entire time it was there.

He clicks the PLAY button again.

'Well?' Guy's voice.

'Well what?' It's a man who answers this time. He must be standing on the other side of the room, or speaking into his hand, because Daz can only just make out the words. The tone of the voice is familiar, though.

'News?' prompts Guy.

'Mr Bishop was right,' says the other man.

'Shit.'

'What should I do?' The voice is getting closer now. Clearer.

'He said for you to do like you are,' says Guy. 'Don't let it show.'

'OK.' Very close. Standing right next to the hidden microphone. And now Daz knows the owner of the voice is Smith.

'What about Croxley?' Guy asks.

'He won't be a problem. And Bishop will get rid of him anyway – once it's over.'

The last sounds are the door opening and closing, then the click of the recording ending and a faint hiss of white noise.

Chapter 27

Daz leans his shoulder against the wall of an empty office block and looks up. He can't count the floors. It's a crazy height. Wisps of cloud are passing above, making it seem as if the building is tipping over towards him. After a few moments of enjoying the sensation, he looks down at the traffic snarled up on the inner ring road. The morning rush hour – three lanes in each direction, no one going anywhere fast. Then beyond them is the real target of his interest. The police station.

He's not sure where the cells are exactly, though he's been in them. It's a large building. And on each unwilling visit he's had other things on his mind as they marched him down the corridors. But once inside there's been plenty of time to absorb.

The cells are a few feet across. Big enough to lie down, to take a couple of paces before turning. That makes them a palace compared with Jagger's tunnels. The final chamber in the mine was so narrow that from a position crouched in the middle he could touch all the walls without fully extending his arms. But in the cells he always felt as if the walls were crushing him, whereas under the mountain he'd experienced a kind of elation.

He thinks of the geophysics machines – how they can see through the surface of the rock. It's easy for him to imagine them doing that. It's exactly how he experiences things – reaching through walls and rock with his mind. But only so long as he knows what's on the other side. It's when he doesn't know that the problems come. Or when he can't get out.

The traffic on the ring road is unsnarling itself now. There's a roar of engine noise as the vehicles accelerate away. One of them, a truck, is belting out a blue-grey smoke from its exhaust pipe. Daz watches the following cars driving into the cloud. He gets a momentary image of them all circling the ring road and coming round to this point again. Trapped without knowing it, always thinking that they were moving on to somewhere better. Travelling in hope.

Bishop, on the other hand, is in a different kind of trap. Walls, locks and guards. Though the man seems somehow to be able to reach out of the prison in other ways. And that poses the problem now.

Bishop has control. Daz is beginning to understand how the man keeps his control even when he can't physically touch anyone on the outside. There's a pattern to the way he arranges things. It's always done in such a way that none of the people working for him gets too much power. Daz has been asked to the party in order to get in Raglan's way. To be an irritant to the others. Smith and Guy are there to neutralize each other. Everyone is kept slightly off-balance. And part of Jagger's job is to make Daz expendable. An alternative means of locating the money inside the concrete. The reason Daz was sent to meet Jagger was so he could see his expendability for himself.

And then there is the recording of Guy and Smith in conversation. Two men who should be loyal to rival bosses, but who seem to have some secret understanding that Daz is going to be got rid of once the show is over.

The understanding has been growing slowly for Daz. And now that it's crystallized in his mind, he knows how brittle his safety is. The sensible thing would be to walk away – leave Leicester and never return, tell no one where he was going. It's that last part that is holding him back. There are still things for him to do here in Leicester. Unfinished business.

The decision to stay and fight has brought him here, to the police station. He's going to throw Detective Sergeant Leech into the mix, hoping to unbalance Bishop. And in the chaos that follows there just might be a way for him to survive.

He takes one more look up at the sky, sees the building toppling again, and then walks up the road, heading away from the police station. He'd be a fool to walk in through the front door. So he goes to a phone box instead. He drops his last fifty-pence piece into the slot. Directory Enquiries gives him the number he needs to call, but he's never been able to hold numbers in his head and it's gone before he can finish keying it in. He goes back to Directory Enquiries four times, eventually memorizing it as a pattern of finger movements on the keypad.

'Leicestershire Police. Can I help you, please?' It's a woman's voice.

'Want Leech.'

'Could you repeat that, please?'

'Leech. He works there. Need to talk to him.'

'Do you have an extension number?'

'Dunno. He's a detective sergeant.'

'What is it concerning?'

'Can't say.'

'Do you know the incident number?'

Daz feels a pressure building up across his forehead. 'Just wanna talk to him, OK?'

'Please hold, sir.'

The line goes dead. Daz knocks the receiver against the side of his head. He tries to steady his breathing. There's a click on the line.

'Can I help you, please?' A man's voice this time.

'Need Leech.'

'He's not available at this moment. Can I be of assistance?'

'When's he back?'

'I'm sorry, caller. What is your name, please?'

'Tell him Daz called. I'll meet him lunchtime – in Sparrow Park.'

Daz hangs up. The money drops. He puts a finger into the coin return slot. It's empty. He swears at the machine but feels only a little better.

A tall horse chestnut tree stands on the side nearest Humberstone Road. Then there's a beech, a small oak, a crab apple. In the middle there's a bark-mulch play-pit with a broken seesaw, a metal bench and a climbing frame covered in tags and other graffiti. There's not much room for anything else within the iron railings of Sparrow Park.

Daz walks around the path, trying to avoid all the dog mess and broken glass. The good thing about this place is that it's surrounded by bushes. Hard to see in from the road – unless you're really looking. The location is important, too. Just behind it is a maze of small terraced streets cut across by a bricked-in stream. It's a perfect landscape to lose yourself in – if you know the run of it.

He chooses the bench in the play-pit. Then he sits, watching three boys trying to get conkers down from the tree. They've got a long stick and something that looks as if it might be a bicycle pump, and they're taking turns to throw them up into the lower branches. But it's too early in the season and the conkers aren't ready to fall.

There's an anxious thought hovering at the back of Daz's mind – that he might have got the timing wrong. Leech might have come and gone before he got there. Or that he's horribly early and the policeman is destined to be late.

He waits.

The boys seem to be getting bored with their game. They toss the stick and the bicycle pump away into the bushes. Then they race each other through the far gate, past an elderly man and a dog, who are on their way in. The dog runs over the grass, sniffing and searching. The owner turns the other way and waits for his animal to finish.

'Croxley.'

Daz jumps involuntarily, his heart suddenly pounding. The word, spoken as a half-whisper, came from just behind. He doesn't need to turn to know who it is.

Raglan jumps down into the play-pit. He's got his hands together in front of him and he's twisting the signet ring on his little finger. He places himself on the bench next to Daz.

'Waiting for someone?'

Daz locks his jaw muscles. The man with the dog is strolling closer, doing a circuit of the path. He nods as he passes in front of the bench. Raglan nods back.

Daz's eyes are on the street beyond the far gate, searching for a sign of Leech. He's calculating the repercussions of discovery. He could bolt now, through the back-streets, perhaps borrow some cash from Liz, skip to another city. He's got no possessions to pack. Nothing to hold him. For a second he gets a thrilling feeling of relief from the idea that he could just abandon all his troubles.

Raglan leans closer, puts an arm over the back of the

bench behind Daz's shoulders. 'Of course, you might be just sitting waiting to score some drugs.'

Daz manages to swallow. 'Bishop said you're not to touch me.'

'Bishop. Ah, yes. He doesn't approve of drugs, you know? Not for his own people. You know that one of his men was using smack? Bishop shot him. Only in the knee, mind. It wasn't as if the man was deliberately going against him.'

Daz can feel the weight of Raglan's arm across his shoulders. He can smell the mouthwash on his breath. There's a car parking on the road outside. He tenses, ready to run.

'Have you any idea how many people Bishop's killed?' Raglan asks.

Daz shakes his head. 'No.'

'And then there's the killings he's ordered. People who've double-crossed him. Sometimes their wives or girlfriends. You know?'

A woman gets out of the car and walks away towards Humberstone Road. Daz wants to look back at the other entrance to the park – which is directly behind him, but he knows that would give away too much.

'Who is it you're meeting here, Croxley?'

'You.'

Raglan brings his hand around and slaps Daz on the side of the face. Hard. 'The trouble with you, Croxley – you're too stupid to be scared.' He gets up. 'But you will be educated, I believe. Before this is all over.'

Daz watches his ex-landlord walk away. His face is tingling on one side, feeling hot and cold at the same time. He hears a car door slam in the distance behind him. The engine fires. He turns and sees Raglan's BMW doing a three-point turn to get out of the cul-de-sac where it was parked.

And it strikes him then – more forcefully than Raglan's hand had done – that there was no way for the man to have seen him in passing.

Daz is sitting on the broken seesaw when Leech finally walks into the park. Daz scans the perimeter, but there's no one else around. The policeman zeroes in on him.

'You're a bit old for this, aren't you?'

'Maybe.'

Leech jumps down into the bark-mulch pit and takes up a position facing Daz, standing with his hands in his trouser pockets. 'Well?' he says, after a few seconds of silence. 'Have you got anything to say for yourself?'

Daz shakes his head.

'When we talked before, you were going to tell us everything that Mr Bishop was up to. Then you go and fall off the face of the earth.'

'Had some trouble.'

'I could still arrest you for handling stolen property.'

'OK.'

Leech purses his lips. 'That's not what I want, though.'

'Want me to grass up Bishop, yeah?'

'I just want to find Dicks and Feildman.'

'He'd kill me.'

'If the information's good we'll find them. There'll be no need to call you as a witness. They won't know. No one will.'

'*You* will.'

'Me, yes. You have to trust me.'

'Who else?'

Leech steps closer, drops his voice, though there isn't anyone in hearing range. 'If you become an official informant there'll be only four people who know. Two handlers – me and another sergeant. And two high-rankers. Detective superintendent or above. It's a watertight procedure – based on ethics and integrity.'

Daz thinks on this. 'Integrity? Like you threatening me down at the nick?'

'Forget that.'

'What about meeting me here – who else did you tell?'

'No one. Why?'

Daz shrugs. 'The other cop told you, right – the one I spoke to on the phone?'

Leech runs a hand over his soft face. 'I found a message on top of the papers on my desk. You were lucky I saw it.' There's a pause, then he says: 'Look, there's no point in us messing around pretending if you're not going to trust me. I'm just trying to help, Daz. I don't know how you got caught up in this, but it isn't your kind of game. These are dangerous men. I'm offering you a way out.'

Daz knows it is true. This *is* the only way for him to get out alive.

'Lyall-Griffiths,' he says. 'That big fraud – Bishop knows where the money is.'

Leech takes his hands out of his pockets and steps closer again. Uncomfortably close. Daz gets off the seesaw and climbs out of the play-pit, scanning the perimeter fence again as he does so.

Leech follows him along the path. 'Well?'

'It's hidden in the concrete. They're gunna get it out. Bishop and Raglan. Guy and Smith.'

'Where?'

'Some building. Don't know which.'

Leech has quickened his step to draw slightly ahead. He's turned side-on so he's almost walking crab-wise. 'What about Dicks,' he says, speaking quickly. 'And Feildman?'

Daz shrugs. 'No sign.'

Leech swears under his breath. His shoulders drop and he falls back into step next to Daz. 'Any others?'

Daz thinks of naming Jagger and Colin, but he holds back. 'No.'

Leech purses his flabby lips. He looks as if he's about to say something, then he continues his walk.

The path leads them between the spiralled trunk of the horse chestnut tree and a city-council-issue bird table. There's food piled here. Chapattis, rice, bread. Heaped on the table. Emptied out on the floor. Too much for the few sparrows that inhabit the park. It smells of mould and decay. Food for rats.

'Anything else that I should know about?'

Daz shrugs.

'We need a date. Once we've got the "when" of it, we'll have them. Catch them with the money and it's all over.'

'And me?'

'We won't prosecute you.'

'Then they'll know.'

'So we'll arrange it that you're not caught.' Leech gestures with an arm, as if this is the easiest thing in the world to sort out. 'Look – you'll get away. As soon as we know the details, we'll work something out.'

Daz thinks on this. The police swooping as soon as the money is out of the concrete. Him being the only one who manages to escape. Bishop sitting in his cell, listening to news of the disaster coming in.

'Trust me,' says Leech.

They're walking towards the park gate. Daz knows he can't get out of it now, so he says: 'Saturday night – that's when they're going to do it.'

Chapter 28

Kat's place bathed in harsh sunlight. Daz doesn't approach the door. Instead he sits in the small front garden, staring at the front wall. It's a semi. White pebbledash. Her flat is the upstairs part. He looks at the windows but can see only the reflection of the sky.

By becoming an informant for Leech, Daz knows he's set things in motion that he isn't going to be able to stop. If things go wrong, he'll have to leave the city. No chance to say any goodbyes. No chance to get his head straight about his relationship with Kat.

Their last meeting was a disaster. They'd been like two magnets pulling each other in. He could feel the force of the attraction. Couldn't fight it. Then something turned. Suddenly they were moving away – the same force animating them, but pushing in the opposite direction.

A curtain twitches in the upstairs of the house next door. He gets a glimpse of a woman's face looking down on him. Sour. Then it's gone. Daz lies back on the lawn with his hands cupped behind his head. There are still no clouds in the sky. Monotonous blue from roofscape to roofscape. He wishes it would rain.

Kat's front door opens. She's standing just inside, in the shadow, her head tilted to one side, a hand tucked in the crook of her neck.

'Are you going to come in, then?'

'Want me in?'

He thinks she's about to answer, but then she steps away up the stairs, back to her flat. And now he understands that this is the reason he came here – to force a decision one way or the other. He looks at the open door for a long time before deciding that walking away would be even more painful than following her inside.

He finds her in the kitchen, boiling the kettle. She gets out a second mug from the cupboard. 'I had that woman from next door phoning,' she says. 'She told me there was a strange man in the front garden. She wanted to know if I'd already called the police or if she should do it.'

'And?'

'And it's embarrassing, that's all.'

'Want me to go?'

She throws a teaspoon into a mug. 'I don't know what I want any more!'

He feels angry with himself for holding out on her and angry with her for making everything so difficult. As she stirs he notices that her hand is shaking.

'Is there anything you want to tell me?' she asks.

'No.'

'Nothing at all?'

When he doesn't answer, Kat elbows her way past him. He follows her into the living room. She's standing with her back to the window. He can't see her face because of the light streaming into the room from behind her.

'We get letters,' she says, 'at work – if a client has moved on or something. Return to sender.'

He knows what's coming next, but he can't say anything to stop it happening.

'You're not living in the old house, Daz. And there isn't

a new address for you. That means you're on someone's
floor or something. It's like you don't tell me—'

'Knew I didn't get the giro,' he cuts in. 'Knew it already.
So why did you ask like that? Trying to trap me?'

'Why didn't you tell me?'

'That I'm a useless waster – that what you want to hear?
That I'm sleeping rough? This is just me, OK? If you don't
want me like I am, then—'

'It's about being honest!'

They're both shouting now. She puts her finger to her
mouth and bites at the nail. Daz feels short of breath.

'I've not lied!'

'I want to know what's happening to you!'

'Don't need help!'

She stands rigid for a moment, as if stunned by a slap in
the face. She blinks twice then shouts back at him: 'Go fuck
yourself, then! See if I care!'

There's a moment when he just stands there blinking.
Absorbing the new reality of his life. That he's alone again.
With nothing. Then he turns and walks. Down the stairs,
out of the house and away.

Daz walks in through the door of the body shop and sees
three blue Transit vans parked side by side. Smith is
tightening the screws on the numberplate of the nearest
one. Raglan, wearing a grey boiler suit, is standing at the
back watching Jagger load plastic stacking boxes. He points
to a pile of similar suits on the floor.

'Put one of those on. Then get to work.'

Daz does as he's told. He doesn't answer back. He doesn't
ask why all this is happening when it's still Thursday – forty-
eight hours before Breakbeat Night. The plastic stacking
boxes are, he sees, full of cables and connectors. Jagger's

geophysics equipment, he guesses. He picks one up and carries it to the nearest van.

The main door opens and Guy steps inside. Behind him come three men of about Daz's age. They're already suited up, though their overalls are blue, rather than grey.

'Bishop thought we could do with some more help,' Guy says.

For a moment Raglan seems to be thrown by the unexpected arrival of these newcomers. Caught between options. He looks at Smith, who hasn't reacted. Then he checks his watch and barks an announcement to the room.

'We'll be out of here thirty minutes from now. Make sure you're all done.'

Daz gets back to work hefting boxes of equipment. He manoeuvres himself into position next to Jagger's shoulder.

'Wassup?'

Jagger glances at him. 'Don't they tell you anything?'

'Thought it was– '

'Just a planning meeting? Someone wants to keep you on your toes.' He drops his voice and flicks his head in the direction of the three newcomers. 'You know anything about those blokes?'

Daz looks. The men are loading steel tubing into the back of the next van along. 'Bishop's keeping on top,' he says. 'Keeping *you* on your toes.'

Jagger chuckles. 'He's always a step ahead of the game. Always knows what everyone else is planning. You'll see.'

Raglan is stepping towards them. 'Less of the chat. It's work time.'

One of Bishop's men takes up position in the passenger seat of each van. Raglan orders Daz into the back of number three. There are no seats, so he wedges himself into a gap between the boxes and waits.

The vans leave at five-minute intervals. Daz's is the last to go. There are no windows for him to look out of, so he takes the chance to examine the steel tubing that he saw being loaded earlier. Each section, he decides, must be one of the roof supports that were mentioned in the last meeting. He counts thirty of them on the floor of the van. They clink and roll with each turn.

He tries to follow the road in his mind, but gets lost even before they've left the industrial estate. So he gives that up and concentrates on trying to think of a way of getting a message out to Leech. He told the police officer that the raid was going to be on Saturday. Happening now means that he's in serious trouble.

When the van stops it's Raglan who opens the doors to release him. There's a sardonic smile on his ex-landlord's face.

'Plans going wrong, eh, Croxley?'

Raglan's words catch him off-balance – the suggestion that the man knows. Daz climbs out of the van, half-expecting to feel a gun pressing into the side of his head, a grave already dug. His mind is blurring with the speed of these thoughts. He feels sick.

But there's no firing squad. He finds himself in a small car park with office buildings on two sides. It's quiet here, the rumble of traffic fairly distant. And it's dark. He cranes his neck to look up at the building next to him. Twenty-something floors. The blue vans are parked in a line next to the wall. There's an open door at the front of the line. Jagger is carrying a box inside. Daz sees a CCTV camera fixed to the wall.

'Well, Croxley,' Raglan says, the smile still on his face, 'it's time for work.'

So Daz follows Jagger's lead, picking up a box and hurrying after the geophysicist. There is a concrete stairwell inside. Bare walls. It feels like a service entrance. He climbs, counting the flights of stairs. Three storeys up he finds an open door leading into a large open-plan office where other members of the team are laying their boxes of equipment. The only light here spills into the room from the stairwell. There are computers and telephones on desks. Low partitions dividing the room into a honeycomb of individual work spaces. Pillars supporting the roof.

Daz puts his box on the floor beside the others. The questions are coming so fast to his mind that he can't focus on any of them properly. They smear out, blending with each other at the edges.

Telephones. That's the first thought. He has to find a way of phoning Leech. Then he registers the pillars in the room. He's struck by their similarity to the one in Salt's workshop. But a moment later he's worked out that these are different. The shape is wrong. Close, but not the same. The same architect, perhaps. Then he thinks of Bishop and the meat-rendering plant. He's thinking that if he were to dive into one of the partitioned areas in this office, keeping his head low, he might be able to use one of the phones without being seen.

'Get a move on!'

He turns and sees Guy eyeing him from the doorway.

Daz pulls one of the steel roof supports from the van and hoists it on to his shoulder. He's stepping across towards the doorway again, but Raglan puts an arm out to bar his way.

'Not in there.'

He points to the neighbouring building, separated by a narrow walkway from the tower block they have just been in. This second building is much smaller, only three storeys, though built in a similar style. Concrete and glass.

The others are moving in that direction already, each carrying one of the roof supports. Daz follows the line. 'What about that?' he says, pointing to another CCTV camera on the wall above the door.

'Disconnected,' says the man in front. 'We've got the keys to the security room.'

'Security guard?' Daz asks.

'Don't worry about him. He's doing all right out of this.'

They're inside, walking through a corridor, and out into another open-plan office. More computers and telephones. But this time there are no partitions. Nowhere to hide. The steel clanks as he lays it on the pile. He looks around. The three men who came with Guy are lowering blinds over the windows. The lights flicker on and Daz sees that there are pillars in this room as well. He feels the pulse pumping in his neck.

'Back over here!' Guy shouts.

This time Daz ignores the command. He's circling the first pillar, feeling its surface with both hands. It has an irregular hexagonal section, almost the same as the one in Salt's workshop – but different because this is a mirror image of that one. In his mind he flips Salt's pillar upside down. The match is perfect now. But it is upside down. There was lettering stencilled on one surface of the pillar in the workshop. Daz couldn't read it, but he knows which way up the letters were.

'Don't you hear me?'

Guy's voice seems unimportant now. Daz waves it away with one hand and moves across to the second pillar. In this one the irregularity of the sides gives the column a different shape. Daz moves on without pausing. The third is a mirror image of the second. Daz is running across the room now, pillar to pillar. Like a dog sniffing each tree in a forest. He finds it on the seventh try. A perfect match. He turns and sees that the others are all watching. Jagger gives a quick nod and crosses the room towards him.

But Daz is already moving away, towards the open doors.

'Where are you going?'

'Up.'

Jagger follows him up the stairs to the first floor. This time there isn't a single open-plan room. It's a series of smaller offices, but Daz can see the pillar in his mind already, coming up through the floor. He runs through the dark corridors, straight to the room he wants. The door is locked, but he can just make it out through the window panel.

Jagger catches up a moment later.

'Raglan's got a master key,' he says. 'I'll—'

But Daz shakes his head. He's running for the stairs again. This time the pillar comes up in a small open area with comfortable chairs around the walls. There's only just enough light to see. Daz lays both palms against its surfaces, connecting it in his mind to the ground floor.

'This is it.'

Jagger circles it, moving a trolley of coffee cups away, giving access to the full length, ceiling to floor. Daz traces the surface. There's no plaster over it. Just a coat of paint. He can't make out the colour in this light. Grey or cream, perhaps.

'What's inside the pillar,' Jagger asks, 'a girder?'

'Metal rods. A square of them through the middle.'

'But space around the outside?'

Daz nods, running a finger down the line of the sharpest angle. 'Here. Just concrete on this side. All the way in to—'

He moves his hand a couple of feet along the surface '—to here.'

Jagger blows air in disgust. 'Modern architects. Cruddy, useless building. All form and no function.'

Daz gets down on his knees, feeling with his fingertips. He finds an uneven line in the surface, follows it around the base of the pillar. Jagger watches. Then he's down next to Daz.

'You say Salt had a section of broken pillar?'

'That's right.'

'Made of bad concrete. So the top section had to be pulled down.' Jagger is tapping his own forehead as he speaks. Following the reasoning through. 'Some of the building was demolished then rebuilt. Too much sand in the mix. Something like that. They were cutting corners, right? Skimming money wherever they could.'

'Salt's into scrap metal,' Daz offers. 'Comes searching for copper pipe. Finds money in the rubble.'

Jagger is nodding. 'OK,' he says. 'So somewhere down the line of this pillar they re-poured the concrete. It's a swine of a job, you know – pulling down this kind of thing and re-pouring. The question is: will we find the rest of the money further down here—' He pats the column '—or is it in one of the other blocks they poured at the same time?'

'You can tell us, right?' Daz asks. 'Like in the mine – find out what's under the surface.' There are footsteps approaching from down the corridor. Two people, by the sound of it. Daz looks at Jagger.

'It's not that simple.' Jagger drops his voice. 'If there are steel reinforcing rods inside, then I can't use electrical or magnetic methods.'

'What?'

Jagger shakes his head. 'It might be a bit tricky.'

'Shit! Then why did you take the job?'

'You're the one who said you knew where the money was! And besides, I do have another bit of kit we could try.'

'Try?'

Raglan comes striding into view, with Guy just behind him. 'Is this the place?'

Jagger shakes his head. 'We just need a bit of time.'

Half an hour later. Daz and Jagger have worked their way down to the ground floor, moving from pillar to pillar with something that Jagger calls an ultrasound generator. It looks like two metal cylinders, linked via short cables to a box with a tiny green screen. Daz holds a cylinder against one side of each column while Jagger holds the other cylinder on the opposite side. Each time the geophysicist examines the display and shakes his head.

They're standing at the base of the first pillar now – the one that matches the rubble in Salt's workshop. Daz is remembering the assurance he gave to Bishop – that he would be able to find the place where the money was stored. In fact, the top of this pillar is the one place in the whole building where they know the money can't be hidden. That's obvious now he thinks about it. The bit he can identify is the bit that was removed and replaced with fresh concrete.

He turns, catches Raglan staring at him from the other side of the room, and turns away again, quickly. He reaches up and presses the ultrasound cylinder to the concrete in the way Jagger showed him. He waits.

Jagger is swearing under his breath. 'It's still not working,' he hisses.

'Fuck!'

'Well?' Raglan calls. 'Where's the money?'

'Here,' Jagger calls back, patting the column. 'This is the one.' Then adds in a whisper: 'It's got to be a good bet, right?'

Daz gets a sudden premonition, a moment in which he is vividly aware of a future, not under his control, rushing to meet him. In a few minutes Guy and Raglan will start breaking concrete. If there is nothing inside the column, Daz will be killed.

He feels Jagger's hand on his arm. The touch makes him jump.

'Come on,' the geophysicist says. 'We'd better get moving.'

Daz finds himself being led out into the night and across the car park. He's thinking that perhaps Jagger is going to make a run for it. Any failure to find the money would have repercussions for both of them. But instead of continuing away from the complex, Jagger heads for the other building.

Daz tries to keep his voice level: 'What now?'

'More work for you and me.'

Jagger seems calmer away from the others. That has to be a good sign, Daz reasons. But he still can't relax. There is too much he doesn't know. He follows the other man up to the third floor.

'This place,' Daz says, 'it's the same as the other one, or what?'

'Different building,' Jagger tells him. 'But they're both within the Grassmead Tower development.'

'Then what we doing here?' Daz asks.

'Just watch and learn.' Jagger walks to where they piled the equipment earlier. He pats a large roll of cable. 'We'll see how good you are at laying out fuse wire. Take this, do a loop around the pillar and then run the rest of it out and down the stairwell, then across to the far side of the car park.'

Daz does as he's told, letting the reel unwind as he walks. 'Don't tread on it on the stairs,' Jagger calls.

It's heavy at first, but by the time he's down at the entrance it's lost half its weight and he finds he can move faster. And the ominous mention of fuse wire is making him think that perhaps he should choose this moment to skip the city even if Jagger is intending to stay. All he has to do is carry on running when he reaches the end of the car park. This might be his best chance. He knows he'd never be able to come back to Leicester in safety. And there would be no time to say goodbye. It wouldn't just be Bishop out for him. Leech and the police would be trying to hunt him down as well.

He reaches the boundary fence and puts the reel down. There are half a dozen turns of the thin black cable still on it. Either someone measured it very carefully beforehand, or it's a lucky break. He turns and looks back at the tower block. If the money is hidden in the low building, he doesn't see why he's laying fuse wire out from the tall one. There are too many questions he still hasn't answered.

Then the door of the lower building opens and Raglan strides out. Behind him come Bishop's three new workers, each with a steel roof support over his shoulder. Raglan comes across towards Daz.

'Time to reel it back in,' he says, prodding the fuse wire with his toe.

Daz is watching the men reload the vans. 'Don't understand,' he says.

Raglan laughs. 'This is only a dry run, Croxley.'

'Fuck!'

Raglan wets his lips. 'What's the matter? Been worrying about something, eh?'

'Should have told me!'

'Ah, but there are lots of things we're not telling each other, right? I bet you haven't told Mr Bishop either, have you, about your little chats with Detective Sergeant Leech?'

Daz's muscles lock. As if any movement might make his situation even worse than it's just become. He forces his fists to unclench. There's a prickle on the skin of his arms and shoulders and a sweat starts to break through.

'Don't worry,' Raglan says. 'Your secret's safe with me. For now, anyway.'

Chapter 29

It is Saturday morning. Daz spent Friday alone, paralysed by indecision. When he finally gathered up enough resolve to go to the hospital, he was told that Patty was asleep. He's back now, after another night sleeping rough.

'You can go through if you like.'

Daz starts walking towards the door.

'Though I don't know if she'll be conscious,' the nurse says after him. 'Just so you know. But she *is* comfortable.'

Patty has her eyes closed when he sees her. A clear plastic mask over her nose and mouth. Her breath sounds wheezy. Grey hair. Grey lips. Grey-white skin hanging from the bones of her face.

'Hi,' he says.

Her eyes open slowly. 'David?'

'Yeah.'

She lifts one of her hands and pulls the mask off her mouth. 'How's Dyson?'

'Barks as loud as ever.'

She seems to sink into herself for a few seconds before summoning the energy to speak again. 'The money?'

He crouches down next to the bed, his face close to hers. He swallows. 'We got it.'

'Tell me.'

'A hundred and seventy thousand quid.'

'Oh . . .' She puts one of her hands on his. 'A hundred and—'

'Twenties and fifties.'

She closes her eyes and lets out a breath. 'Sixty–forty, remember.'

He watches her face. The same lines, but deeper than before. He thinks of putting the oxygen mask back in place.

'Was thinking,' he says. 'Seeing as how I done most of the work. Could make it fifty–fifty.'

Her eyes open, more slowly this time, and they stay open for only a few seconds. 'Nice try, Croxley. But we agreed.' And then she smiles.

'Can't blame me for asking.'

'Good boy.'

Her eyes have closed but she's mumbling, still.

'. . . would have told you . . . should have told you . . .'

'It's all right.'

'He wouldn't let me . . . made me promise . . .'

'Who?'

But there are no more words. He lifts the mask and places it back over her mouth and nose. When he's sure she's properly asleep, he leaves.

He sits outside in the corridor for a long time after that. Nurses and doctors keep on with their work. No one bothers to move him on. He watches dusk forming through the window. The branches of the trees lose their colour, fading to silhouettes. The streetlights flickering on red, brightening to orange.

It's dark outside when Dr Høeg finally comes to speak to him.

'It's over,' he says. 'She's gone.'

Daz nods.

'Do you want to go in?'

He doesn't know how to answer so he just gets up and walks towards the ward.

They've drawn the curtains around her. He takes a breath before stepping inside, fearing that she will be changed in some way. But she looks just as she did before. Better even, because they've taken out the IV and the monitoring equipment and the mask has gone from her face. He takes her hand, expecting it to be cold and stiff, shocked that it isn't.

'Patty?' he whispers.

But she isn't there.

'Excuse me?'

Daz turns. He must have been sitting by the bed for some time. A nurse he doesn't recognize is looking in through the curtain.

'We're going to be moving her now. If you're ready . . .'

He gets to his feet, follows her out.

'Are you all right?'

He nods.

'You're David Croxley, right?'

Another nod.

'I'm sorry to bother you now. But I'm filling in the paperwork and I need you to sign for her things.' She smiles encouragingly at him. 'If you're ready for that.'

'Why me?'

'You're the next of kin.'

He shakes his head. 'That's Vicky. Patty was her great-aunt. I'm just—'

'According to the admission papers, you're Mrs Wattling's grandson.'

'Then someone wrote it wrong.'

'I don't think so. Mrs Wattling filled that part in herself.'

There's no need to question what the nurse said. Daz recognized the truth as soon as he heard the words from her mouth. It had been what Patty was trying to tell him towards the end. *Your mother should have been proud of you.* And there were clues before which he only now sees the significance of – the family resemblance, which made it so easy for everyone to believe that Patty and he were related. He replays her words in his head. *Half the men in my family never learned to read – my brother and my father and Vicky's dad.* And now Daz himself, Patty's own grandson, all possessed of the same family trait.

He thinks about his mother as he walks down the street. He can't remember what she looked like, only what she did – leaving him, dying in India. Patty spoke about her no-good daughter who died a long way from home.

He wouldn't let me . . . made me promise . . .

Daz now recognizes his father in Patty's mumbling words – the man who didn't want him to have any contact with the disreputable Patty. Daz wonders how she must have felt when he walked unknowing into her house all those years ago. Her own grandson. All she had to do was encourage him and he kept coming back.

And now she's gone.

He can feel the bundle of twenty-pound notes in his pocket. Two hundred and sixty quid. It had been in Patty's bag – given to him by the hospital. There was nothing else of value – just the keys to Vicky's place and a set of lock-picks that he doesn't know how to use. He's wondering where the rest of Patty's stash has gone. As next of kin, it should be his by rights. But Vicky has probably found it already. She'll blow it on smack in a couple of weeks. She might not even survive a legacy like that. Strange how money can save one person's life and kill another just as surely.

Patty is gone.

There's a kind of numbness inside him. Shock, grief, rage, reunion and loss, all viewed from a distance, as if they are happening to someone else rather than him. He finds himself wondering where the next train out of the station will be heading.

The house on Severn Street seems even more run down than it did a few days ago. There's a fresh scrawl of paint-spray graffiti on the new plywood covering one window. It looks as if someone has had a go at kicking in the front door.

Daz tries his key without thinking. It doesn't work, of course. He looks at the bell push. This is going to be painful, but he doesn't see any way out of it now. So he lifts his hand and presses the button for Freddy and Ginger's flat. There's a long pause. He can feel his heart beat in his chest. Then the intercom hisses.

'Who . . . who is it?' Freddy's voice, strangely taut.

'I'm going away,' he says to the speaker. 'Leaving Leicester. Come to say goodbye.'

'Oh, God . . . Daz.'

The lock clicks open and Daz steps inside – thinking about the hysteria in her voice, knowing it was there before he told her his reason for coming. He walks up the stairs, dreading whatever it is that he's about to find. She meets him on the last landing. The skin under her eyes is puffy. She steps forward, wraps her arms around his shoulders and presses her face into his shirt. He can feel her sobs. He eases her back into the flat.

This is the second shock, because the place has been turned over. Books and spider plants spilled. Black compost on the carpet. A litter of papers, odd clothes, wall posters, trampled. Everything else gone. Furniture stripped.

'Raglan did it?'

A nod of the head.

'When?'

He can't make out her answer.

'Where's Ginger?'

'I'm scared he's . . . he's going to . . . don't want him to die . . .'

'Ginger? He'd never!'

'But . . . all this . . .' she lets go of him, sweeps her hand around the room without looking. 'We couldn't . . . couldn't make the payment.'

'Not Ginger's style to kill himself,' Daz tells her. 'This is just stuff. It's you he loves.'

'You don't understand.'

Her voice is higher now. Tighter. She clings to him again, her face in his neck this time. His first reaction is to pull away. But this time things are different. He no longer wants her in that way. There's no reason to be afraid. So he puts his hand on the back of her head and draws her closer.

'I shouted . . . at Ginger. Screamed. I've messed . . . messed everything up. And then . . .'

'We'll find him, OK?'

'You don't understand! We fought. And then . . .' She draws a sobbing breath. 'Oh, my God. It's all such a mess.'

'Then what?'

'That man of Raglan's . . . he came back. He . . . he took Ginger.'

*

Raglan's house. The lawn cut in stripes. Immaculate. The BMW on the drive, looking as though it's just been waxed and polished. Daz stands tensed, staring at it, putting off the moment that he'll have to walk past it without kicking in the headlights or dragging something abrasive across the bonnet.

There's a movement of a curtain in an upstairs window. A face. Raglan's wife, Daz thinks. He squats for a moment to pick up a handful of gravel. Then he works his hand, squeezing and releasing, feeling it digging into his skin.

The front door opens. Raglan saunters out, Lady pulling in front of him.

'To what do I owe this pleasure?' he asks.

He's uncomfortably close to Daz before he stops. The dog is sniffing at Daz's mock Docs and the legs of his jeans. Raglan turns and takes a meaningful look at the gleaming car.

Daz gets the message but ignores it. 'What you done to him?'

Raglan raises an eyebrow.

'Ginger. What you done with him?'

Raglan nods slowly, the light dawning. 'Him? Just a warning.'

'Warning about what?'

'It's business, Croxley. That's all.'

'Trashing the place is business?'

'It's progress. The only business. Urban regeneration, they call it. Two years from now, that whole section of town is going to be developed. There's SRB money coming in. The riots achieved something, after all, eh?'

Daz doesn't want to give anything to Raglan. But he doesn't understand, and his ex-landlord must see that because he laughs.

'Government cash, Croxley. The Social Regeneration Budget. That means turning out wasters like you and bringing in professionals. It's going to be media studies graduates as far as the eye can see.'

He laughs again, deeper this time, his belly heaving.

'Never wanted my cash,' Daz says, knowing it's the truth only as he hears his own words.

'Smart at last,' says Raglan.

'Just wanted to sell the place.'

'Not sell. Develop. But not with you people still in there. You're worth more to me gone than you'd ever be as tenants.'

Daz wants to swear. He wants to lash out. He does it in his mind – hurling the gravel into his ex-landlord's face. Again and again. He squeezes, feeling the sharp edges bite on his skin. Letting the pain flood into his mind. Trying to submerge the feelings of rage. He couldn't win a physical fight, one to one with this man, even without the boxer dog to contend with. And any violence from him would just give Raglan the excuse he's looking for. The perfect explanation to hand to Bishop.

'You know the really funny part, eh?' Raglan steps closer still. Daz can smell his aftershave. 'You were the easiest one to get rid of – out of all my tenants. Because you always do the opposite to what you think people want.'

Daz's free hand goes up and pulls on the safety pins hanging from his ear. 'Where's Ginger?'

'What's it to you, anyway?'

Daz doesn't answer. Raglan's eyes gleam. He nods, as if digesting some new information. 'He's got a pretty girlfriend, eh?'

'Keep off her!'

Raglan smiles. 'Don't worry. He'll be back at the flat by

now. It was just a warning. Helping them on their way, so to speak. They're the last ones.'

Daz turns to go. Anger and relief are washing through him, and he doesn't trust himself not to take a swing at his ex-landlord.

'Hold your horses, Croxley. There's still the little matter of Detective Sergeant Leech.'

Daz stops but doesn't look back.

'Oh, yes! Did you think I was going to forget about your dirty little deal – that they won't prosecute so long as you provide them with the details they need.'

'Why do you think that?'

'I don't *think*. I *know*.'

Daz doesn't need to ask who told him. The answer comes flashing back into his mind. The map of connections. The meeting in Victoria Park. Raglan handing over Salt's twenty-pound note. And what would Detective Superintendent Shakespeare have done with it? Checked it against the records. Matched serial numbers. Reported back. It isn't Raglan informing for the police like he'd thought at the time. It's Shakespeare informing for the underworld. And if Shakespeare is in the pay of criminals, it explains why he put pressure on Daz not to inform on Vince the Prince and his gang.

'This time you're going to do what I tell you,' Raglan says. 'And I'm going to keep what I know secret. That's our deal. I want you to contact Leech again – tell him the timing has been changed. We're still going to get the money on Saturday night, but tell him he's got to swoop at 0300. Understand? No police anywhere near the building before that time or it'll scare us off.'

Daz opens his hand and lets the gravel drop to the ground. Lady barks. He hears her panting as she strains on the leash.

'You'll want to mess me about, of course,' Raglan says. 'I know that. Do the opposite of what I'm asking, eh? But this time it's going to be different. I know what buttons to press.'

Daz jogs back towards Severn Street. He wants to see Ginger before he leaves the city – to make sure he's back with Freddy. He turns the corner, thinking about the warning Raglan said he'd given Ginger, wondering if they hurt him or just took him for a ride. He slows as he approaches the house. Then, just like before, a car door opens. But it's not the police waiting for him this time.

Smith gets out. 'Message from Mr Raglan,' he says. 'He wants you to know that he's got that woman friend of yours. Keeping her safe – just in case you think of skipping town.'

The front door is ajar. Daz runs up the stairs, three at a time. He swings himself around the landings, passes his old bedsit. He sprints the last flight and flings the door open.

Ginger is there, one side of his face swollen, a cut on his lip. His eyes are wide with fear and anguish.

'Where's Freddy?' he cries. 'Have you got her?'

They search the house first. The bathrooms, the fire escapes, the back alleyways. There's no way she could be in any of the other flats because all the doors are boarded shut.

'She might have gone to stay with a friend,' Ginger tries.

Daz shakes his head. 'Where they take you?'

Ginger's hand goes up to his cheek. He touches the skin, flinches. 'Nowhere. Just drove around.'

'Beat you in the car?'

A nod.

'Smith and who? Who drove the car?'

'I couldn't . . . they put a sack over my head. Maybe Raglan . . . But Freddy won't . . . they wouldn't . . .' He puts his hands over the back of his head and bends forward, rocking his body. 'It's all my fault.'

'No.' Daz takes hold of his friend's arm and pulls him towards the stairs. 'Raggy just wants you out. Would've done that to you anyway. This is something different.'

'Where are we going?' Ginger asks.

'The Club. She could have gone there.'

They take a taxi from the rank at the front of the station. Daz pays with one of Patty's twenties. The driver grumbles, making a big show of searching through his pockets for a five and a ten. Daz can feel the energy building inside himself. Crackling like static. He snatches the change from the other man's hand and runs up the steps towards the front entrance, ignoring the queue, catching up with Ginger next to the door.

'Where the fuck you been?' the bouncer shouts.

Daz shoulders past him. The music is loud already – hard and pumped up. There's a press of bodies just inside, men and women dressed for clubbing. In the main room he can see some retro punks slam-dancing.

Daz squeezes through the crush. There's sweat here, mixed with perfume and aftershave and spilled drinks. He reaches the stairs to the mezzanine, dimly aware that Ginger is still following. He's elbowing people out of the way. He can see their mouths working. He can lip-read. But he doesn't respond.

There are fewer people at the top. He runs the last steps,

pushes open the door. He sees Liz standing behind the desk, done up in black. She's saying something he can't hear. He steps into the office. The door closes behind him. The music is suddenly muffled. Ginger is crossing the room. That's when Daz turns his head and sees the woman standing by the wall to his right.

It's Freddy. Ginger is wrapping her in his arms.

'We thought they'd got you . . . I thought . . .'

She's shaking her head. 'I couldn't stay in the flat. I . . . I came here.'

The sweat feels suddenly cold on Daz's skin. He swallows. 'What's the time?'

'Time I had a floorshow,' Liz fires back.

He snaps back at her. 'What's the pigging time?' His hands are in his hair. He can feel everyone looking at him.

'Quarter-past ten.' Liz says. 'Is everything all right?'

He's shaking his head, turning towards the door. 'No.'

Liz takes him in her MG. Across town, ignoring the speed cameras. He knows there's a danger the police will stop them. If that happens, he's going to have to say something about Leech and hope that's enough to get them off his back.

'This is going to cost me,' Liz says. 'In speeding tickets. I might lose my licence.'

'Time?' he demands.

'Ten thirty-three. You should get yourself a watch.'

Daz points to a junction. 'Down there.'

She brakes hard, then turns the wheel, accelerating as she comes out of the bend, tyres screeching over the tarmac.

'Here!'

He's pulling himself out of his seat before the car has fully stopped. Up the path to Kat's house. Starting to bang on the door, realizing that it's swinging free. He's bounding up the stairs towards her flat, turning on the light, seeing the chaos. The telephone and corner table overturned on the carpet, a single tone alarm sounding from the spilled receiver. And he knows he's too late.

Chapter 30

'Where the fuck have you been, Croxley?'
   It's Guy who's shouting at him, cutting through
the air between them with his hand, the silver rings flashing
as they catch the light from inside. Daz steps past him and
into the body shop. There's a film of sweat over his skin.

'Had some trouble,' he says.

Guy is right behind him. 'Then you'd better tell us what.'

Raglan puts out an arm to separate the two men. 'It's a
miracle he's here at all. You don't know him like I do. The
boy's always late – right, Croxley?'

Daz nods.

One of Bishop's people slams a van door. 'We're ready,'
he says.

Guy spits on the floor. 'No thanks to him.'

Raglan is taking up most of the passenger seat, his shoulder
pushing Daz towards the driver's side. There's no one behind
the wheel yet and no one in the back. The lights go out in the
body shop. Smith is outside, operating the roll-front doors.

Daz watches as the first of the vans moves out on to the
road and away.

Raglan checks his watch. 'I'm glad you did show up,
Croxley.' He speaks quietly, not turning his head.

'What you done with her?'

'She's my insurance policy. Safe enough – so long as you play your part.'

Daz called Leech a few minutes ago – from the phone in Kat's house. The policeman wasn't pleased with the late change of plan. But he swallowed it in the end – or said he had.

'Done it,' Daz says. 'Told him to come at three in the morning.'

Raglan takes a mobile phone from his pocket and holds it out for Daz to see. 'I already know what you've done,' he says. 'And I will know if you try anything.'

Daz clenches his fists. The second van pulls out and drives away.

Raglan checks his watch again. 'But I'm a fair man. No grudges, eh? There's ten million in used notes that's going to pass through our hands tonight. We can all be better off at the end of it. But go against me and people get hurt.'

'Smith knows?'

'About your girlfriend? Yes. He's the one who grabbed her. But I've not told him about you and Leech. Time enough for that. Don't worry though. Smith will be with us when the time comes.'

Daz shifts in the seat, feeling the safety belt gripping across his chest.

'All you need to do,' Raglan says, 'is watch for my signal. When you see it, all you have to do is drop whatever you're doing and you leave the building. If you're with someone, make an excuse. Go straight to the van with the money – whichever that is. Wait there for me.'

Daz listens, knowing for certain now that Raglan is planning on double-crossing the others, not sure how he thinks he's going to get away with it. Bishop may be in prison, but he's got a long reach.

'When you gunna let Kat go?'

'Tonight. Just as soon as we're done.'

He checks his watch again and then waves his hand. Smith comes across and climbs into the driver's seat.

They park, as before, close in under the tower block. Daz follows the others across to the smaller of the office buildings. Raglan is in his stride now. In command. He pushes open the door into the darkened office. The operation is under way already. Bishop's men are putting up blackout curtains. Clipping them in place. Then Guy flicks the switches and the strip lights flicker on. He doesn't look comfortable.

'Clear the tables,' Raglan says, pointing a finger towards the area of the concrete pillar.

Daz hurries across the room and starts dragging a desk across the carpet, trying not to spill the computer. But Guy steps in his way.

'Stop piddling about. This place is going to be rubble in a few hours.' Then he grabs the monitor and hefts it over the edge. It crashes on to the floor. 'Get moving.' Then under his breath: 'Frigging waster.'

Daz works quicker now, shifting furniture, clearing a wide circle around the pillar. Bishop's men are positioning the first of the steel roof supports. The top of it breaks through the ceiling tiles. Crumbs of polystyrene drop like snow on their heads and shoulders. Then one man turns a small handle while the others hold the steel shaft vertical. The top inches higher until it comes up hard against the solid beam above.

Within ten minutes they have eight supports in place and there's a stepladder ready. Then Guy starts work with an electric saw, touching the blade on to the concrete just below the ceiling. A teeth-jarring whine. Grey dust venting from the line of contact. Daz can see what the man is doing – slicing a vertical fissure down the side where they think there are fewest reinforcing rods. The whine of cutting concrete suddenly changes pitch. There's a spray of bright yellow sparks. Guy is swearing.

He pulls out the saw and begins another cut, at an angle to the first. He slices in until a wedge of concrete skits free and falls. He climbs down the stepladder and Smith moves in with a welding torch. A soft roar. The pencil of blue flame turning brilliant yellow where it touches the metal.

Daz stands back, waiting. Watching the digital clock on the wall. Nine minutes past eleven. Just under four hours short of the time when Leech is due to swoop. By then, what will have happened? If this is the wrong pillar, they're going to have to start searching again. They might not even have found the money by three in the morning. He notices for the first time that Jagger isn't in the room.

Guy is cutting again. Pea-sized fragments of concrete are flying out from the blade, clattering off the desks and computer monitors.

Daz shoots a glance at Raglan and sees that the man is looking directly at him. Daz's eyes flick to the wall clock again, but when they return Raglan is looking the other way.

Guy and Smith are sweating, but the job won't be hurried. Four times the saw has to be removed and the welding torch brought in. It's 11.55 before Bishop's men move in with the sledgehammers. But now things start to happen faster. Big lumps of concrete break away easily along the line of Guy's cut. It takes three hits before Daz knows that his first problem is over. A block falls, revealing a plastic-wrapped bundle, looking like a fossil in a fractured rock surface. Jagger's guess was right.

Raglan is the one who reaches up and pulls it free. He rips a hole in the cover and grins. Then he shows it around. There are cheers from some of the men. Raglan hefts the bundle through the air. Daz tries to catch it, but stumbles backwards under its weight. Guy laughs.

'Take it to van three,' Raglan orders.

Daz picks himself up, turns towards the stairs, away from the action. So he's the first one to see the two men standing just inside the doorway.

'What are you waiting for?' Guy shouts. 'Get the money to the van.' Then he, too, sees. And his face goes from anger to shock and then to the broadest grin Daz has seen him wear. 'Mr Bishop, sir . . . I thought—'

The hammering stops. Everyone turns. Bishop strides over to join them. Colin the accountant, briefcase in hand, follows after.

'It's only temporary, Guy,' Bishop says. 'I'll be back inside tomorrow. Before I'm missed. Now, what have you got for us?'

Daz holds out the bundle.

Bishop nods. Colin snaps open his briefcase and pulls out a set of digital scales, which he places on one of the desks.

'The first package?' he says.

Daz puts the bundle on the scales and watches as Colin copies the readout into a small notebook.

'Well,' says Bishop, 'what are we waiting for? In the van with it.'

Daz hurries on his way. But before he leaves the room he takes a last look back and sees Raglan, fists balled, staring daggers into Bishop's back. And he wonders, not for the first time, how Bishop always seems to be able to stay one jump ahead of the other man.

*

Even if he'd thought of running off with the money, it wouldn't be an option. The third of Bishop's men is here, standing guard in the shadow next to the wall. He steps forward when he sees Daz.

'This is it?'

Daz shows him the ripped plastic, the faces of fifty-pound notes showing through.

'How many more?'

Daz shrugs. He looks across up at the tall building, trying to detect light in the second-storey windows. But there's nothing to see.

By the time he gets back, there are four more parcels stacked on the floor and a fifth on the scales. Guy has started making a second cut in the pillar. Bishop is sitting on the corner of a desk. He's got a can of diet Coke in his hand. He turns to Daz, lifts the can. 'Cheers.'

Daz picks up one of the packages and starts hefting it towards the stairs.

'Leave it,' Bishop says. 'I've got a different job for you. Go over to the tower. See if Jagger needs help with anything. Do whatever he tells you. Understand?'

As he walks across the car park Daz stops and looks up. The tower block has nothing to do with the money. He's sure of that. Though the buildings must have been put up at the same time. They're both part of the Grassmead Tower development – which was started by Lyall-Griffiths Investments.

He thinks of the directors skimming a portion of the company's money. Using the cheapest materials. Fixing the accounts. He imagines one of the missing men taking bundles of cash from the safe, driving them on to the site, dropping them into the open shuttering, ready for concrete to be poured. It doesn't sound like the kind of thing a man would do if he intended to travel to South America or Indonesia and live off the proceeds of his crime.

And suddenly it hits Daz that one of the directors might have been hiding the money from the other. Or from Bishop. If it hadn't been for the substandard concrete, the money would have remained undiscovered. The more he thinks about it, the more the concrete pillar seems to have been a bad idea. Not a well-thought-out hiding place but the last-minute act of a desperate man.

Jagger is working alone on the third floor of the tower block, laying a wire between two of the pillars. He looks up when Daz enters the room. There's a kind of concentration on his face that Daz hasn't seen before.

'Did they send you to help?'

Daz nods. 'No one else helping?'

'This stuff makes them feel nervous.' He gestures to the room around them.

'What about you?'

'Me, too.'

Daz thinks on this for a moment. 'Bishop's here,' he says.

Jagger doesn't seem surprised. 'Has he told you what we're doing yet?'

Daz looks at the room's pillars, smaller than the ones in the other building. Less of an architectural statement, more a functional support. Each has a yard-high band of plastic wrapped around its base. Wires trail from the wrapping. He sees now that Jagger is wearing surgeons' gloves, and it strikes him for the first time that none of the people in the other building are doing anything to stop themselves from leaving fingerprints or clothing fibres around the place.

'Blowing the place up?' he offers.

Jagger nods. 'That's the other reason Bishop wanted me along. Access to mining explosives and the knowledge of how to set them.'

'Can blow through reinforced concrete?' Daz asks.

'It isn't concrete. This building has a steel frame. But yes, I've set plenty enough to cut through them.' He points to the desk nearest him. 'Put some gloves on.'

Daz follows Jagger's instructions after that. Holding ends of cable. Carrying boxes from one part of the large office to another. Waiting while the other man checks everything, then checks again. He watches Jagger's fingers splicing the end of a wire to a small cylinder.

'What's that?' he asks, pointing to the object on the end of the wire.

'It's a time delay. To make the columns on this side of the building fire a few tenths of a second before the others.'

'Why?'

'Questions. Questions.' Jagger points to a large reel of black cable. 'Remember what you did for me the other night? You're going to do it again. Lay out the wire, then go back to the other building. I'll manage from here.'

Daz glances at the digital clock on the wall. It reads 1.55. He wonders if Leech is going to arrive when he said he would or turn up early just to throw them.

He pays out the wire, making sure he doesn't tread it into the hard angles of the concrete steps. Down six flights to the car park, then across it in a straight line to the fence at the edge. It seems crazy to lay explosives on the third floor of the building instead of the ground level. He puts down the almost-empty reel and looks back. He tries to imagine it, everything above the third floor collapsing downwards. And then he tries to imagine the supports on one side of the building going a few tenths of a second before the supports on the other side. This time it happens differently, toppling like a falling tree, hundreds of thousands of tons of demolition rubble falling directly on to the roof of the smaller building.

Only then does he understand. If they blow up the tower, that's what the police will focus their forensic investigation on. Not on the smaller building, which happens to have been crushed underneath it. It might take months before anyone reaches that – and then it'll just be workmen clearing away the rubble. It's like Bishop said: the police will be searching for Islamic terrorists.

It's all action now in the open-plan office. Smith and two of Bishop's men are ferrying plastic-wrapped bundles down to the vans. The first column is a pile of rubble already. There's a ring of roof supports around the column next to it. Guy has started working with the saw. Sparks and dust.

'Half the money's still missing,' Bishop tells him. 'You don't happen to know anything about that?'

Daz shakes his head. He sees Raglan glancing at the clock on the wall.

'Well, you can have the honour of opening up the next column.'

Daz takes a sledgehammer and hefts it across towards the action. Guy turns off the saw. He is grey with a paste of sweat and dust.

Daz lifts the hammer, rests the shaft on his shoulder for a moment and then launches it on a downward curve, hitting the concrete full on. Grains fall from the crack but the block remains intact. He lifts it again. Swings. This time a chunk the size of a brick breaks free and falls. Daz can see a corner of black plastic in the fractured surface. He's aware of Raglan and Bishop coming up behind him to look. He lifts the hammer a third time and sends it forward with more force. Feeling the arc it cuts through the air. Accelerating it towards the moment of impact. Then the jarring crunch. A large block breaking free along the line of the saw cut. Falling. He sees now that this plastic bundle is much bigger than the others.

Bishop pushes Daz aside. He reaches towards the plastic but then pulls back as if unsure. He casts around and settles on a leaf-shaped fragment of concrete on the floor. With this he probes the bundle. The plastic gives way easily, ripping to the side. Revealing the hollow eye sockets of a skull staring out at them.

It's Raglan who speaks first. 'Shit!'

Then everyone's talking at once.

'What the fuck!'

'Who . . .?'

'My God. I don't want . . .'

Bishop holds up his hand. 'We carry on.' Then he puts his fingers into the eye sockets and pulls the skull free. 'But we don't leave him here.'

'Who is it?' This is Guy's question.

'Feildman,' Bishop says. There's a chilling note of authority in his voice.

'Why not the other one – Dicks?'

'Because Dicks took a trip to the meat-rendering plant a long time ago. It must have been him who dumped Feildman in here.' He tosses the skull at Daz. Daz catches it, an automatic reflex, then feels the revulsion surge in his stomach.

'Get it out of here,' Bishop says. 'Every last splinter into the van. We'll dispose of it later.'

Daz puts the skull on the nearest desk. It's dry – though he can't think where all the flesh and fluid can have gone. Soaked away, perhaps. The concrete around the skeleton is certainly discoloured. He reaches in his hand and pulls the plastic. It comes away easily, collapsing out of the hole, bones clattering against each other as they fall. What's left is somehow more disturbing than the skeleton. A man-shaped void. The same height as Daz, but fatter. A negative image of Feildman as he was in death, slightly smoothed by the shroud of black plastic that once covered his body. The hands are tied behind the back.

'It's like Pompeii,' Bishop says. He holds out the hammer to Daz. 'Smash it. Nothing but dust for the cops to find. You understand?'

Daz shakes his head. This is something he can't do. The body is too tangibly real in the space it has left. Bishop stiffens, jabs the hammer towards him again.

'Take it!'

Raglan steps in between them.

'Go outside, Croxley. Get some air.' Then he turns to Smith. 'Go with him. Make sure he doesn't do anything stupid. He's been behaving strangely all night.'

This last comment is louder than the others. Daz feels Smith's hand shoving him towards the stairs. Just before he leaves the room he glances at the clock. It's 2.40.

On the way down, they pass Jagger going up. 'The explosives are ready,' he says.

The car park is quiet. Daz looks out into the darkness but can't see any sign of the police. He wonders if they're in position already.

'What's up?' Smith says suddenly.

'Up?'

'Raglan and you. Something between you.'

'Hasn't told you yet?'

Smith glances up at the building. 'He's not trying to cross Bishop?' There's alarm in the man's voice.

'Scared?'

Smith steps closer. 'Tell me!'

It's the power and urgency in Smith's voice that catches Daz. Unexpected. But then Smith's role switches in his mind and it all makes sense.

'Raggy doesn't trust you?'

Smith steps closer again, within striking range now. But Raglan comes hurrying from the building before anything can happen.

'In the van,' he says.

Daz does as he's told, sliding into the middle passenger seat. Raglan follows. Smith is the last one in. Visibly reluctant.

'Now drive.'

It's 2.50 by the dashboard clock. They're out on the road – a narrow cut with an old factory on one side.

'Now kill the engine.'

Smith pulls in next to a white van. The engine dies. Lights out. Daz watches the clock. A minute passes. Two minutes. And then it happens. Three unmarked cars driving without lights. Daz sees them in the wing mirror. Rolling into the car park behind them. A police van follows. Men are getting out, running to the doorways of the two buildings. He hears the shouting, even from this distance. Sergeant Leech has arrived a few minutes early.

Then Raglan gives the nod. They ease out of their parking place.

'Wanna see Kat,' Daz says.

'First things first,' says Raglan.

'Like what?'

Raglan puts one hand inside his jacket, pulls out a small handgun and places the muzzle against Daz's neck. 'First we drop the play-acting.'

Chapter 31

Darkness. Face pressed into cold metal. A floor, perhaps. Arms pulled up tight behind him. No feeling in his hands. The van has just stopped after a long drive. The silence is sudden and threatening. He doesn't remember being thrown in here – he must have been unconscious. There's a pain where his teeth are pressing into the inside of his cheek, and wetness on his face. A trail of saliva or blood running from the corner of his mouth.

The van doors clunk open and he's squinting into the sudden light. There are packets of money around him. Plastic-wrapped. Then he notices a pair of feet. A woman's feet. He's seeing the soles, so she must be lying down. She's not moving.

'Kat?'

No answer. Panic.

'Kat!'

Her feet shift to one side. She groans.

There are hands gripping his legs, pulling him across the floor of the van. His ankles, he now realizes, are tied like his wrists. It's Smith who's pulling him, lifting him on to a shoulder like a side of meat. Out of the van.

His first thought is that they're in some kind of warehouse. Then he breathes in the familiar smell of the place. He's being held face down, so it takes a couple of moments for the location to click inside his head. This is when he starts to struggle, because he knows that they've brought him to the meat-rendering plant.

Smith dumps him on the floor next to the feed hopper, then walks away. It's now that Daz starts to feel the ache in the back of his head. He remembers standing by the side of the road, Raglan's gun pointing to his chest. But it must have been Smith who knocked him from behind.

He rolls on to his back. His crossed wrists are now pressed into the hard floor. He tries again to work them free, but the binding is too tight. A shadow falls over him. Raglan's face between Daz and the lights in the high ceiling.

'I've been looking forward to this, Croxley.' He wets his lips. 'You've been helpful to me. I wanted you to know that. Before it's all over, eh? Mr Bishop's going to want to know what happened to the money – from his prison cell. And you know what we're going to tell him? It was all that Croxley's fault. The police came. In the confusion, you just got behind the wheel and drove away with the money.'

'Won't believe you.'

'Perhaps.' Raglan straightens himself, looks across to the van. 'At first. Even with Smith's word to back me up. Bishop isn't a trusting man. He'll want to know who tipped off the police. And you already know what he's going to find, eh? That a certain police informant has gone missing. Leech will think you've double-crossed him, too. That's the real beauty of it.'

Raglan points at the meat-rendering machine. 'They won't find you, though. You'll be gone, spending Bishop's money. Perhaps some of it'll turn up in Spain. Who knows? We'll have to see what we can arrange.'

Smith is carrying Kat from the van now, over his

shoulder in a fireman's lift. She's struggling. Her hands are tied at the wrist like Daz's, but in front of her body instead of behind.

Raglan points to the feed hopper. 'Put her in there.'

The metal booms as her body hits it. She cries out through the gag in her mouth.

'And take Croxley to the viewing platform. I don't want him to miss the show.'

Smith leaves Daz kneeling on the metal gantry, overlooking the auger grinder. Raglan is standing over him, elbows resting on the railing. The lights dim for a moment as motors whine into life. Daz feels the vibration. The terror is like a vice pressing into the sides of his head.

'No!'

Raglan smacks his lips, as if he's about to enjoy some rare delicacy.

'Don't!'

'This is the best bit, Croxley. Why would I stop?'

'Smith's against you.'

Raglan ignores this.

'The night Salt died – how did Bishop know to call?'

Raglan glances down, sneers. 'Nice try. But no.'

'Smith phoned him. I saw it. In the car park. And at the solicitor's place—'

'What about it?'

'Smith's outside for an age, right? What's he doing? He comes back and Bishop calls. He phoned his boss.'

'I'm his boss, cretin!'

Below them, the auger grinder starts to turn. Metal screeches against metal. The smell of rotting meat wafts up from the jaws of the machine. Daz retches. He can see the metal buckets start to move, climbing on their chains, upending at the top of the run, then clattering in procession down the other side.

'Looks like your luck's over, eh?'

'And tonight,' Daz gasps. 'Bishop turns up. He knows you're crossing him.'

'*He* didn't know the police were coming, though, eh?'

That's when the first doubt touches Raglan's face. A flicker.

Daz is struggling to stand up. 'Because you didn't tell Smith! The one time Bishop messed up is when you didn't tell Smith!'

Raglan is shaking his head. Slowly.

'And I heard them. Smith and Guy. Talking about you. Orders from Bishop. I recorded it all.'

'Recorded?' Raglan snaps.

'A bug and recorder.'

'You . . .?'

Then the machine stops. There's a shout from below. Smith calling. Raglan swears under his breath. He storms down the steps. Smith shouts again. Then there's a scream. It's Kat. No gag in her mouth this time.

Daz hops to the top step and sits. He pulls with his feet, dropping himself to the one below. And again. Grazing his wrists on the metal edge with each fall. Knowing he's moving too slowly. Not feeling the pain. Only the thumping metronome of the pulse in his neck. He's round the first corner.

Smith's shout: 'She's wedged in there.'

Raglan: 'You should have tied her better!'

'I didn't know you were going to do this!'

'Just crawl up there and pull her out.'

Daz is halfway down to the bottom level now. He can see the two men leaning over the feed hopper, peering up the enclosed metal chute. He remembers Smith's claustrophobia in the mine.

'What are you waiting for?' Raglan barks.

Smith puts one leg into the hopper. Then the other. He starts moving towards the chute, then shakes his head. 'I . . . I can't.'

'Not loyal enough?' Raglan jeers.

Smith is gripping the edge of the feed hopper, trying to step back out. But Raglan slams his hand down on the other man's fingers. The metal booms. Smith is shaking his head.

'What did you tell Mr Bishop?'

'It's not like that.'

'What did you tell him?'

It's only now, with real fear in Smith's eyes, that Daz can see him as fully human. Raglan slams down on the lip of the hopper again, keeping Smith from clambering out.

'Go up the chute and get her out,' Raglan says. Then he presses the button on the control panel and the machine whines into life. Smith falls as the conveyor pulls his feet away from under him. He's being dragged.

Kat screams again. Her voice is coming from inside the machine. She must have wedged herself across the width of the chute. Smith going up will knock her back on to the belt.

Daz is at the bottom of the steps now. He works his wrists against the metal edge, trying to cut through the cable-tie that binds him. But it isn't sharp enough. He pushes himself to his feet and starts jumping towards the back of the van.

Smith is scrambling around in the hopper, trying to keep pace with the belt, to keep on his feet. He throws an arm over the edge, hooking himself by the elbow.

Daz is at the back of the van. He's searching for a tool of some kind, or a sharp edge. His eyes fix on the nearest bale of money. He turns, reverses up to it, grips it in his hands and starts shuffling back towards the hopper.

Raglan is reaching into his pocket. He pulls out the handgun, points it at Smith. 'Why?' he says.

'It's not . . . not like that.' Smith falls again and scrambles back to his feet. 'Please, Mr Raglan . . .' His hand is on the side of the hopper.

Raglan fires. Smith's shoulder jerks back and his legs fold underneath him. Daz is close now. He sees Smith scrambling against the direction of the conveyor belt. Not keeping pace.

Raglan is leaning over the edge, watching Smith being carried into the chute. He shoots again. A bullet hole appears in the side of Smith's head.

Daz's fingers are cramping, and he knows he's got only a few more seconds before he has to drop the bale of cash. He pushes himself forward. He's a pace short of Raglan's back when Kat screams again. Smith's body must have reached her. Daz twists his own body around and releases the bundle. Raglan sees him. But too late. The bale of money has tipped over the edge into the feed hopper.

Raglan shouts. Swings an arm. Daz feels the impact on his face. He's falling back to the ground. His head hits the concrete, dazing him for a moment.

Raglan jumps sideways and hits the STOP button. The machine noise dies.

'What do you think you're fucking doing, Croxley?'

He takes one last look at the START button – too high for Daz to reach with arms tied – then climbs over the edge into the hopper. Daz watches him clambering up the incline and into the mouth of the chute where the bundle of money has just gone.

Then he sees Kat, climbing out of the top, where the chute feeds into the chain of metal buckets. Somehow she's worked free of her bonds. She starts letting herself down the outside. Daz is scrambling to his feet, trying to reach the START button with his head. But even when he jumps it's out of reach.

Raglan is backing out of the chute. He throws the bundle of money clear of the hopper. Kat sees him. She lets go and drops the last ten feet to the floor. Raglan still has the gun. He raises it, points it at her. She slaps her hand on the START button. His feet are pulled away and the shot whines off the metal. Raglan is down, being dragged back up the conveyor. But he's not panicked like Smith was. He's not injured. And he's agile enough to regain his feet. He grips the edge of the chute to steady himself.

'The money,' Daz shouts.

Kat sees the bundle. Picks it up. Throws it towards Raglan's face. He raises his hands and fends off the blow. But he's lost his balance. The belt pulls his feet away. He falls sideways. His head crashes into the metal. Then he's gone.

Time has passed. The circulation has come back into Daz's feet and hands. He's almost stopped shaking. He walks to the van, lifts out two bales of money and carries them back to the feed hopper. Kat follows him with another bale.

'You could be rich,' she says.

'You, too.' Then he throws his bundles in. 'Could never spend it, though. Not for years.'

Kat drops her bundle in after his. They watch them disappear.

'How much is there?'

'Millions,' he says. 'And nothing at all. Come on, we've got work to do.'

Chapter 32

Daz is sitting on a bench at the top of Majestic Park. His cuts have mostly healed now, and the bruises have faded to the point where he can only see them because he knows where to look.

He stares out at the sweep of grass and trees below, and beyond that the slate roofs of terraces and, further away still, gardens and trees belonging to bigger houses, all the way out to the edge of the city. There are some clouds – the first he's seen in weeks – making the landscape a drifting patchwork of light and dark.

'Nice day.'

He looks around to see Leech walking towards him.

The detective lowers himself on to the bench with a slow exhalation. 'You wouldn't believe the paperwork I've had to get through.'

Daz does believe it. He's had his own brush with bureaucracy in the last couple of days. Though it was a string of claims advisers who did the form-filling on his behalf. Each one sceptical about his story. Each gratifyingly shocked by the police papers when he handed them across the desk. Somehow there was never an appropriate box to tick for his particular situation, so they ended up writing pages longhand. He got his first giro cheque a few hours ago.

Leech rubs a hand across the fat of his cheek. 'So,' he says. 'Have you heard anything?'

'Bishop sent a bloke – like you said he would.'

'And?'

'Asked me a load of questions.'

'Threats?'

'Nah. It's not me he's gunning for.'

'Did he say anything about Dicks?'

Daz shakes his head. 'But he said he'd pay me big money if I could help him find Raggy and Smith.'

'If you did – and they ended up floating in the river . . .'

'Don't sweat it. No way I'm gunna help Bishop.'

Leech sighs. 'I just hope that we get to them before Bishop's people do. The whole thing is messy enough.'

'Least you found Feildman,' Daz offers.

'As a corpse – thereby turning an unsolved fraud into an unsolved murder. No one's happy about that kind of statistical swing.'

A cloud shadow moves across the grass, up the slope and over them. Daz feels his skin start to cool. Leech is quiet, though still frowning. The moment stretches. It's Daz who breaks the silence.

'How come Raggy knew to run just when he did?' he asks. 'Right before you lot turned up?'

When Leech answers, it's with a deliberate voice. 'There is . . . an investigation. Internal. An officer whose . . . whose integrity has been compromised. I can't mention a name, but it's just possible . . .'

'Shakespeare, yeah? Saw him and Raggy meet up in Vicky Park.'

'Then why the hell didn't you tell me?'

'Tried to. You laughed.'

Leech folds his arms. 'Are you thinking of mentioning this to anyone else?'

'Want me to?'

The detective pauses before answering. 'It'd make things even more complicated.'

'Gunna catch Raggy, you reckon?'

'Perhaps.'

'And the money?'

He angles his body so he's looking directly at Daz. 'We know the serial numbers of most of the notes.'

'Saying he couldn't use them?'

Leech's eyes flicker. 'It did *all* go in the van, I suppose? A package didn't happen to fall out as they drove away, or something?'

Daz looks down to the floor, shakes his head.

'You'd have to bury it for a long time, Daz, before you could use it. It wouldn't ever be really safe. Better to hand it over and be done with.'

'I guess,' Daz says. 'But like I said, I ain't got none.'

It's a tall room. White walls. Coving on the ceiling. An old-style window looking out on a sun-filled garden.

The woman sitting opposite has steel-grey hair and steel-rimmed spectacles that make her look like a teacher Daz once had. But then she smiles, and he knows she can't be quite the same.

'What shall I call you?' she asks.

'Daz.'

'Well, Daz, I couldn't help noticing in the paperwork that you're paying for these sessions privately. Is that correct?'

'That a problem?'

'Not at all. But there *is* funding available. You'd just need to put your name down on the waiting list.'

'Wanted to get started,' he says. 'And I've got the cash.'

She smiles again. He searches her eyes but can't find any trace of condescension.

'Before we start,' she says. 'I'd like to know what you want to achieve. Why are you here?'

No teacher has asked him this before. The question has always been the other way around – him wondering why they wanted him in the back of their classrooms. Usually they didn't.

'I want—' But the words won't form.

She nods anyway, as if she understands. 'My son's dyslexic. He hated school. I used to sit by his bed as he cried himself to sleep, night after night. So I'm not here to push you to do anything. We're here for your goals, not mine. You just tell me what you want. I'll try to help.'

'Just want to learn to read,' he says.

Daz and Kat have chosen the waste ground behind the industrial estate. It's a triangle of rubble and sparse undergrowth, bounded by the railway embankment on one edge and by factory units on the other two. It might be three hundred paces across in daylight. But it's double that at night, carrying a heavy wooden crate between them.

They're far from the road. The ground is dappled with patches of impenetrable shadow. They reach a patch of smooth concrete at the centre of the triangle, the foundation of some building long gone. They lower the crate to the ground. It's the perfect place.

There's a slight breeze, just enough to shift the tallest weeds. The air smells of moist earth and buddleia flowers. Daz breathes it in as he stretches the cramp from his arms and fingers.

'Gunna rain,' he whispers.

There's a dull orange glow in the sky, a reflection of the city's streetlights. Only the brightest stars show through.

'Tonight?'

'Maybe. Or tomorrow.'

He stares into the distance, lost for a moment.

'Penny for them?' she says.

'Was just thinking – if I'd known Patty was my gran, I might have taken against her from the start.'

Kat puts a hand on his shoulder. 'You were good to her. That's all that matters.'

'Idiot boy,' Daz says, raising the pitch of his voice. 'Wasting my money on lessons!'

Kat laughs. 'She wasn't really like that, was she?'

'Worse.'

'Well, I think she'd have been proud of you for what you've done.'

'Anyway,' he says, 'she should have hid her stash in a better place if she didn't want me to find it.'

There's the drone of a distant engine high above them. They both look up, but the aeroplane is hidden in the misty air.

After a moment, Daz says: 'Let's do it.'

He slips the penknife from his pocket and steps over to the wooden crate. Then he starts working the blade into the crack where the side panel is attached, twisting it one way, then the other, easing the nails out of the wood. He puts his fingers into the new gap and pulls. The panel falls away. He steps back and crouches next to Kat. Waiting.

There's a shuffle of movement from inside, a moment of silence, then the fox emerges. It sniffs the air, turns to look at Daz and Kat, and then sets off in a loping run away from them and into the darkness.

Author's Note

Although this is a work of fiction, many of the scenes are set in specific and clearly identifiable places in Leicester. Of the remainder, most are composites in which details from several different locations have been brought together on the page: for example, the Jobcentre, the Club and the house on Severn Street. But the meat-rendering plant, the Grassmead Tower development and the prison are entirely fictional, as are the Fresh Horizons Project, Lyall-Griffiths Investments and all the characters.

Daz Croxley's curious mixture of abilities and disabilities are drawn from my own experiences as a dyslexic.

Acknowledgements

Sincere thanks to Liz, Dave, Bridget, Lesley and all other LWC members who helped so much with their comments. Heartfelt thanks to Hannah Griffiths and Kate Lyall Grant for their encouragement and advice. For information on concrete, explosions and recycling, thanks to Juliana, Ian and Darren. And finally thanks to whoever first thought of Working Families Tax Credit, without which this novel wouldn't have been started.